Raising Mary Jane

In 1970s Big Sur

Christian Van Allen

Raising Mary Jane
Copyright © 2019 by Christian Van Allen, WanderWorld Press

www.raisingmaryjane.com

All characters and events in this book, other than those clearly in the public domain, are fictitious and any resemblance to real persons, living or dead, is purely coincidental.

All rights reserved. No part of this publication may be reproduced, distributed, or transmitted in any form or by any means, including photocopying, recording, or other electronic or mechanical methods, without the prior written permission of the publisher, except in the case of brief quotations embodied in critical reviews and certain other noncommercial uses permitted by copyright law.

Ordering Information:

Quantity sales. Special discounts are available on quantity purchases by corporations, associations, and others. Orders by U.S. trade bookstores and wholesalers.

Editing by The Pro Book Editor
Interior Design by IAPS.rocks
Cover Art by Chelsea Belle Davey

ISBN: 978-0-9600925-0-5

1. Main category—Fiction/Action & Adventure
2. Other category—Fiction/Small Town & Rural

First Edition

To my mother, Adrienne,
an avid writer herself,
who once told me the hardest
part of writing is keeping
your fanny in the chair.

PROLOGUE

Two vehicles from the Monterey County Sheriff's Department sped south from Carmel along the narrow ribbon of California State Route 1. Deputy Burt Pickett pulled the steering wheel sharply to his left and accelerated his marked cruiser past a slow moving car in front of him, quickly dipping back into his lane to avoid oncoming traffic. He accelerated again and leaned hard into a left-hand curve, glancing into his mirror for Deputy Barrister.

In a white unmarked pickup truck, Doug Barrister passed the same car and caught up with Pickett.

Pickett glanced over at his partner in the passenger seat, Deputy Alan Kaiser, and noticed he was holding on tight to his armrest. Pickett and Barrister were energized by these fast drives down the coast from Carmel to the south coast of Big Sur. It was code three driving without the lights and siren, and it almost always became a race between them.

Pickett's surveillance flights the week before had opened his eyes to just how many marijuana gardens were growing along the coast in plain view from the air. With photographs and a little mapping, he was able to pinpoint where the pot gardens were in relation to the roads and landmarks. He had three gardens he was putting out of business today. First stop was the Rummsen Ranch. He had contacted the Ranch Foreman, a guy named Richard Gable, and arranged for the gates to be open. He didn't want to piss anyone off by cutting a bunch of gate locks unnecessarily. The foreman assured him they'd be open bright and early. If the gates weren't open when he got there, Pickett had already decided he'd cut the locks anyway.

Pickett keyed his mic. "S3, we're about ten miles out. Follow my lead, code two. I don't want anyone to know we're comin'."

There was a crackle from the speaker in the marked cruiser, and Barrister answered, "Copy."

In the white pickup, Barrister glanced at the deputy sitting beside him. "Should I pass him?"

"Sure, just let me out of the truck first!" Deputy Wilson said through gritted teeth, staring straight ahead.

Deputy Pickett powered through the turn below Nepenthe Restaurant south of Big Sur with Deputy Barrister in close pursuit.

Richard Gable had positioned himself on a south knoll high above Fuego Creek. Sitting behind a clump of sage brush growing at the edge of a meadow of tall yellow grass, he watched the Apple Tree House through a pair of binoculars. He figured he didn't have a dog in this fight. He felt neutral about it. If Wesley Daggert was gonna grow marijuana right out in the open, then it was his own damn fault if he got caught.

Richard had opened the two gates an hour before just like the sheriff asked. He figured the sheriff was gonna come through the gate one way or the other and he might as well save himself some repair work.

He had first noticed Wesley was growing grass while working on the road near the Julian Fuego Homestead, just above the south side of Fuego Creek. Hearing shoveling across the canyon where there shouldn't have been any, he had taken his binoculars from his truck and walked to the edge of the road to search the far side of the canyon. After a few sweeps, he saw the camouflage nets stretched below a line of oak trees. They blended in so well, he never would have seen them without the binoculars. Someone was working under the nets, and since Wesley was the only one living up Fuego Creek, it had to have been him.

Richard moved the binoculars, pointing them up the canyon to where he knew the nets were. Yep. There they were, still hanging from the trees. He moved the glasses back down to Wesley's cabin and then up to the other garden growing above it in plain sight. He froze.

It wasn't there!

"What the hell?" Richard said.

He moved the glasses around the area, but the garden was gone. It had been tall and green, like a small jungle growing proud and blatant out in the open. He could just make out where it had been, but now it was just a bare spot across the road from the cabin.

Richard laughed. "Son of a bitch!" he said under his breath. "Wesley, you dodgy bastard."

From far down in the canyon, the sounds of multiple vehicles racing up the dirt road grew closer. A cloud of dust rose up through the trees below, and he followed the rattles and squeaks up the canyon road to where it crossed the creek. The engines roared as they took the steep hill out of the canyon.

Richard had the glasses on the Apple Tree House when the door burst open and Wesley Daggert ran out naked, stopping to lock the cabin door with a padlock. Two sheriff vehicles emerged from the trees and slid to a stop on the road just above the cabin. Wesley, naked as a jaybird and carrying an armload of clothes, jumped from his deck and rolled a few times, then got up and ran right into the dense brush below the deck. Richard could just make out the paleness of his skin through the covering foliage.

Four sheriff's deputies emerged from the two vehicles. Two walked down to the cabin. The other two walked up the hill to where the garden had been. One deputy was banging on the cabin door, but even from his vantage point through the binoculars, Richard could see the door had a padlock on it. If Wesley had been inside, there was no way he could have opened it! The other deputy walked down below the cabin and stood right where Wesley had disappeared into the brush.

Richard swept the glasses back and forth but couldn't see Wesley anywhere in the foliage.

The deputy turned and rejoined his partner at the cabin, and they walked back up the driveway to the garden site above the road. After a few minutes, the four deputies returned to their vehicles. There was some discussion, and one walked back down the driveway to the cabin. He stuck something on the cabin door and then walked back to the others. That was it. They started the motors, turned around, and sped down the canyon road with rooster tails of dust behind them.

Richard listened until they passed below him and out of earshot, then looked up the canyon through the glasses. The nets were still there.

After about an hour, he watched a fully clothed Wesley emerge from the brush and look around as he walked up to the cabin, then up to the garden site and back. Wesley unlocked the cabin door and went inside. After a few minutes, he came out and sat in a chair on the deck. Kicking his feet up on the rail, he popped open a beer.

"Wesley Daggert," Richard said. "You are a wily coyote..."

CHAPTER 1

"If a person was born a thousand lifetimes, they would always recognize this place by the smell of sage and kelp in the sea breeze."

–Wesley Daggert

ALONG THE ENTIRE EIGHTY-MILE STRETCH of California Highway 1 from Cambria to Carmel, you are on the edge of a cliff cut into the Santa Lucia mountain range high above the wide Pacific Ocean. The poet Robinson Jeffers called this tumbling of mountains into the blue Pacific 'the greatest meeting of land and sea in the world.' While private roads disappear from the highway up into steep rugged canyons, there is only one valley in the entire drive that shelters the highway from the ocean. It lies twenty six miles south of Carmel and holds in its folds the small settlement called Big Sur.

It was April of 1969 when I first drove up from Cambria through the fifty miles of desolate South Coast and landed in Big Sur. It was not my destination—I had intended to make San Francisco by nightfall—but during the drive, I was overwhelmed by the steep sea cliffs and open expanse of ocean. After pausing in several roadside pullouts, I stopped at Nepenthe Restaurant, its high perch cradled by the mountains, and sat on its terrace. From there I could see fifty miles south. I ordered coffee and gazed back down the coastline I had just driven.

From my vantage point on the outskirts of the terrace, I could look back over the red cement floor to the two double doors of the wood-beamed restaurant. Every now and then the doors would open and characters would emerge in a colorful flourish, carrying baskets of food or trays of beverages to tables occupied by hungry and thirsty patrons. The restaurant employees seemed young and energetic, and even those who were obviously older had a flair of youthfulness about them.

There seemed to be a connection among the staff, as though they were all sharing a common secret and were perhaps even members of the same family. Their smiles were slightly mysterious, and their eyes held mischievous twinkles that hinted there was much more to their story than food and beverage. I watched them and wondered where they lived, where was the community where they gathered? I couldn't see it, only mountains and sea, but I knew it must be close. I began to watch the waitstaff more than I was taking in the view, and soon I was smiling at their antics.

In those days, Big Sur was a combination of two local cultures. The first was an aging breed of old-time settlers who had carved their lives out of the rugged mountains, establishing remote homesteads perched on promontories or settled deep within hidden valleys. This group was rarely seen out and about except at community gatherings or at the local post office. The second was a colorful population of locals who had come more lately, drawn by the dramatic setting and intense beauty of the area.

This latter group, most often encountered on visits to Big Sur, included artists, writers, and characters from every walk of life. Carpenters, sailors, and carneys were playing cards with actors, musicians, and architects, while the old timers with family names like Pfeiffer, Trotter, Post, and Harlan walked among them as living legends, doing the heavy work of road building, mountain carving, and wood splitting. These two groups lived shoulder to shoulder, running the businesses and sharing the stewardship of Big Sur.

A third transient group of people were growing in numbers every year and did not share in the stewardship of the Big Sur coast. They were the traveling tourists who were learning, in exponentially larger increments each year, of the spectacular drive from Carmel to Cambria. Though the tourists contributed nothing to the stewardship and, in fact, *added* work to the maintenance of the coast, they did bring the all-powerful dollar, and in so doing, were welcomed along the highway in spite of their insensitivities.

The year 1968 had seen the Monterey Pop Festival, and 1969 brought Woodstock to rural New York. Disillusioned soldiers were returning from Vietnam. They were dropping out, joining the growing psychedelic subculture that had left home and was traveling freely around the country. Students had grown their hair long, donned colorful clothes, and were openly smoking marijuana, all the while asking burning questions of anyone in authority. The temperate climate of California's central coast, coupled with its natural beauty, was a magnet for this movement, and destinations like San Francisco, Santa Cruz, and Big Sur became meccas.

Everyone who lives in Big Sur has a great story to tell you about their arrival and subsequent decision to stay and call the coast home. Mine is that I had driven out from New York after graduating high school to attend a junior college in a small beach town south of Los Angeles. The school had sucked, and I had left my schoolwork on my desk, packed my car, and blazed a trail north on Highway 1 toward points unknown. I was nineteen years old, driving a 1953 Pontiac, and had my life's savings of $300 stuffed in my pocket.

Big Sur had been my first stop on my escape from L.A., and I decided right then while sipping coffee at Nepenthe that if I left this magnificent place, this small community etched into the mountain cliffs above the Pacific, it would haunt me, and I would spend the rest of my entire life trying to get back. The realization was electric, and it freed my soul. I had found my home, and suddenly I looked at everyone differently. I saw people as those who were just passing through and those who had decided to stay. I respected both groups...I had been in one and was now in the other. I would learn later the two groups would always be juxtaposed, destined to have very different experiences along the same coast they were attracted to.

It took me three months to find a job, during which time I camped along the river at the state park. I parked my car there next to my tent and hitchhiked everywhere I went in order to meet more people. My first task at hand was to find work, and I applied at every establishment along the coast. Being it was early spring, no one was hiring, so I started over and reapplied everywhere again. I was finally hired by Bob Steadwith, manager of the Redwood Lodge in the Big Sur valley. He told me later he hired me because he was tired of seeing me in his office.

He looked up at me from his desk on my fourth visit and said, "You again? I got to hand it to you, kid, you're persistent. All right, I'll hire you, but you've got to take off that goddam bow tie!"

The job he hired me for was campground manager, and it came with a cabin by the river. The following few months were an intense introduction to life under the redwood trees of Big Sur. I met the people who were already calling the river life under the redwood trees 'home,' most being younger people like myself from distant locations. I soon fell into a raucous life of bars and mind-altering drugs, keeping in step with my close neighbors, all the while meeting people every day who would be deemed crazy anywhere else on earth.

That first summer and fall seemed to last forever, and yet the damp earth beneath the redwoods never completely dried out. My job as manager of the campground put me in a position to be threatened six times by angry men with loaded firearms. There seemed to be something that came over men when they were camping, some sort of throwback to the wild west. Your average desk jockey suddenly became Mean Mountain Dean when he stepped into the forest in his flannel shirt and put his feet up next to a campfire. At five-foot-eight and 175 pounds, I must have looked like a pushover; it seemed no one took me seriously about the simple posted campground rules. The seemingly simple job of managing the campground was, in reality, an intense daily misadventure.

I worked twelve hour days for peanuts and, except for trips to town to wash laundry, had little time to go exploring. My cabin was dark and run-down but seemed cheerful because of the babbling river running by it, the warm shafts of sunlight that found quiet places on the ground where the flying insects buzzed, and the ever-moving branches of the trees being pushed by the river wind.

That first year, deep into December, after almost drowning while attempting to cross the swollen Big Sur River, I lost my job over a warm bowl of soup. The day it happened I was out looking for a Christmas tree to cut for the cabin and, of course, the trees looked better on the other side of the river. I attempted to cross and was swept away in the rapids. I was able to pull myself out 200 feet downstream and lay on the bank to catch my breath. Cold and shivering, I walked up to the restaurant to eat something warm and found it closed. Being the campground manager, I let myself in with my master key and heated a can of soup in the kitchen. Management found out, and I was charged with eating soup on my day off. I was promptly fired and, since they were connected, I lost my humble cabin as well. Merry Christmas to all.

I talked to a new friend who studied law as a hobby. He told me about a little known rental law regarding eviction. The eviction had to be in writing. My manager wasn't aware of that finer point and was instead under the impression he could just yell "Get out!" at me and it would suffice. In the end, I was able to stay two extra months, rent free, before Redwood Lodge finally got it right. During this period, I sold my old Pontiac and bought a '56 International Travelall—a truck-like van with voluminous space behind the front seat. I gutted it in front of my cabin and converted it to a small apartment on wheels. Inside I built a couch that converted to a bed with storage underneath it. There was a small dental sink that emptied through the floor onto the street, and a hanging locker for my shirts. My refrigerator was a small ice chest. The windows had colorful paisley curtains, and the double back doors could be opened together, exposing the inside to whatever view I was backed up to.

There was an incredible feeling of freedom that came with this. I could park it anywhere I wanted for the night. Wherever my truck was parked was my home. I could drive down the coast for a few miles to watch the sun set, and after the stars had all appeared, climb into bed in the back and crash. Most mornings found me in a fresh new setting. I learned places where I could shower, how to stay neat and organized, and met other people who were also living in vehicles, often in groups parked in pullouts along the coast, perched for a spectacular sunset or moonrise.

My rent was the total of my truck expenses, and at $1.75 a gallon, gas was expensive in Big Sur. Food was also expensive, and by spring my money was running short. I desperately needed to find work. Driving by Nepenthe one March morning, I decided to stop and see if they were hiring. I parked in their lower lot and walked up to the restaurant. The restaurant hadn't officially opened for the day yet, and a shirtless, well-muscled African-American man was polishing the red terrace with an electric buffer. The sun was out bright, and I was again taken aback by the incredible view down the coastline. The man flashed me a happy smile as I walked across the terrace and through the open front doors.

Inside, a tall sandy-haired man wearing glasses stood holding a pencil to a clipboard. He was busily talking to an attractive woman in her early twenties. He looked up at me, stopped talking, and gave me a quizzical grin.

"What can I do for you?" he asked.

"I'm looking for a job," I said, glancing quickly at the woman.

He looked surprised, then smiled widely. "You're kidding! I just had somebody quit this morning!" He looked me over, then got more serious. "Are you twenty-one? It's a big deal here; you have to be twenty-one."

"Yes," I lied.

"Do you have a place to live?" he asked.

"Yes, I do," I said.

"You're hired!" he said exuberantly. "Can you start today?"

My eyes widened in surprise. "Sure!"

"What's your name?" he asked.

"Wesley. Wesley Daggert."

He shook my hand vigorously. "I'm Jack. Jack Sievers, I'm the manager. Boy! Welcome to Nepenthe, Wesley. It's a great place. You're going to love it. Come back at eleven, and I'll get you started!"

CHAPTER 2

"The restaurant is just theater, we're in the entertainment business. With this setting, we could serve shit on a shingle and still be busy."

–Kade Rudman

I STARTED WORKING AS A DISHWASHER at Nepenthe in March of 1970 and within weeks had a completely new group of friends. The energy and mood of the restaurant was light and upbeat, in stark contrast to the life I'd been living under the redwoods. Sitting at 800 feet above the ocean with a stunning world-class view of Big Sur's South Coast, the place seemed perched a little closer to heaven than anywhere else. The staff was young and colorful, supervised by an avant-garde group of older adults who had themselves gravitated to the coast to escape a myriad of intriguing past lives. These past lives, I would find, were great spice for their conversations.

The goal of most of the employees was to become a waiter because that was where the money was, and I shared that aspiration. I also wanted to be a bartender and work under the tutelage of the dashing Portaguee, George Lopes. With his tan skin, broad mustache, and white blousy boat shirts, George was as much a class act as I had ever seen. He stood at the helm of the Great Ship Nepenthe's rounded bar—his "Stern Watch," he called it—with twinkling eyes and graceful gestures, greeting people both coming and going, all the while making drinks with wry comments under his breath.

I had my aspirations, but alas, moving up the ladder at Nepenthe was a slow process. No one was leaving of their own volition, and no one was dying—we were all too busy being reborn.

Within a month I was promoted to busboy, a definite step up the ladder to success that immediately put more money in my pocket and access to the stage floor of the great bustling restaurant. Wandering around all day, in and out of the large dining cathedral, picking up plates and ferrying them to the dishwashers, enabled me to meet more people and see more sunshine.

During this time, to make even more money, I joined the early morning cleanup crew led by Mickey, the man I had first seen running the electric buffer on the terrace, and Stan, a guitar player who wore a black hat with a silver conch hatband. This meant getting up at five AM and thoroughly cleaning the entire restaurant in and out. I enjoyed this job for the sunrises and the quiet, as well as the pride of being able to transform the dirty restaurant into a shining jewel by opening time. Often, after cleaning, we would roll right into a day's work on the restaurant floor.

Not too long after I began the cleanup job, I began training to be a waiter *and* a bartender. I had finally arrived at the pinnacle of sought-after working positions at Nepenthe. Being cleared to work at night was all that remained. I was fortunate to be working the bar with a group of exceptional mixologists. Their knowledge and varied histories made my training fun as well as educational.

Waiting tables was no less exciting, although it was possible to become *so* busy as a waiter that you were actually running from table to table, your head full of frantic strategies to maintain equilibrium. This would happen at the same time the host or hostess was figuring out new ways to seat additional people at your tables, and your name was being called over and over by the fast-moving cooks to come pick up your food.

The bar didn't feel quite that rushed. There you were separated from the general public by 'The Planks,' the actual wooden bar, and were more dependent on your own speed and proficiency, something you could always improve upon. Don't get me wrong, I got buried there as well, taking care of people who were standing three deep at the bar while also trying to service seven waiters in line for cocktails. In any case, when all was said and done, we were a team, the money was great, and in spite of occasional thoughts otherwise, the end of the shift did arrive every day.

During this time, I was still living in my truck and parking in the seldom-used overflow lot below the restaurant. I was not alone. There were about five other people parked there who were likewise calling their vehicles home. We parked close together, side by side, resembling a modern-day arrangement of covered wagons on the prairie. There was a bathhouse providing toilets and showers behind the restaurant that we were able to use, and the view out to sea from the parking lot was glorious.

This was an amazing time of freedom and ease that lacked much of the stress and responsibility associated with more 'normal' everyday life someplace else. We would back our vans up to the view, open our back doors, and pull out a folding chair. Everything we needed was at hand, and no one was charging us rent. We laughed, told jokes, talked about where we grew up, and exchanged the locations of other magic places to park along the coast.

I had metal luggage racks on my van's roof and a metal ladder attached to the back door for access to the top. I bought a piece of plywood, bolted it to the luggage rack, and used it as a bed platform during the warmer clear nights. I would haul my bedding up there and sleep under the stars. What a sight it was to wake up in the middle of the night and gaze into the Milky Way.

On one such night, my friend Jack, who was parked next to me, spent the evening in his van tripping on acid; he had taken a hit of Orange Sunshine someone had left him as a tip earlier that afternoon. I'd seen him at sunset, and his pupils had turned to huge pools of black. A couple of hours after dark, I grabbed a handful of pea gravel and climbed to the roof of my van. One by one, lying there under the stars, I started throwing small pieces of gravel down, bouncing them off the roof of his van.

Every couple of minutes, the back door of his van opened and Jack stuck his head out to look around. Seeing no one, he ducked back inside and slammed his door. I waited a few minutes, then resumed bouncing gravel off the top of his van until the van door flew open again, and Jack stuck his head out to look around suspiciously. Seeing no one, he retreated back inside.

Finally, after another couple of gravel bounces, the van door flew open and Jack jumped out screaming at the top of his lungs, "What the *fuck* is going on?!"

I was laughing so hard he heard me and jerked his head up in surprise, seeing me on the roof of my truck. "You're a malevolent asshole, Wesley Daggert!" he yelled, and ducked back into his van.

Thinking back, the only thing Nepenthe ever asked of us motorized gypsies was to keep our vehicles running and not to pee in the parking lot. To my knowledge, everyone's truck ran great.

CHAPTER 3

"Fire has a way of reducing your life to the essentials of survival."

–Buddy Miles

IT WAS A HOT SEPTEMBER night with no moon, and the wind was blowing down off the mountains like a hair dryer. The stars in the black sky were the only light on the darkened coastline. After the restaurant food service had stopped and only the bar remained open, a group of us were sitting out on Nepenthe's terrace under the stars with cocktails. The night was sweltering, and the large double doors of the restaurant stood open to the outside air. Someone suddenly pointed down the coast at a glow on the south coast mountains and shouted, "Fire!"

We all sat up and leaned forward to focus on the bright spot. It was a fire for sure and was growing larger by the moment as we watched. It looked like it was past Lopez Point, maybe forty miles south.

"Looks like a big one," I said. "and getting bigger. Look at that! It's moving up the hill!"

"We should go down there and help put it out," Bob was standing and talking to all of us.

"They probably have plenty of guys on that fire," Jack threw in, "I hope so, anyway, it's getting bigger by the second!"

I was thinking that given the hot night and the wind, the Forest Service was going to need all the help they could get. I stood up and downed my drink. "I'm for going down there. What the hell, anybody else?"

"Me too," Bob volunteered. "I'm in!"

"I'm game," Jack said.

Everyone else spoke their agreement.

Buddy Miles, the maintenance man for the Big Sur Coast Gallery, was looking down the coast. "I'll give them a call."

Buddy walked into the restaurant and called down to the Forest Service Station from the restaurant phone at the host station. The woman who answered confirmed there was a fire burning fifty miles south of Big Sur in the Salmon Creek drainage. The fire was out of control and burning toward the north. Buddy said he was part of a group of guys sitting at Nepenthe willing to help out if they needed any volunteers. He hung up and filled us in. We waited.

We each ordered another drink and sat back out on the terrace, watching the distant glow grow in intensity. Thirty minutes later the restaurant phone rang through the open doors. It was the Forest Service calling for volunteers. They asked us if we could drive down to the Big Sur Station and grab some hand tools to bring to the fire. We said we would. After a brief discussion, we agreed to go home for the appropriate clothing and to meet back at the restaurant in thirty minutes.

Buddy Miles was driving the Coast Gallery Pink that night, a VW pickup painted bright pink with painted flowers decorating the sides. It was owned by the Coast Art Gallery that sat along the highway a few miles south and was used primarily for deliveries. We all piled in and drove to the Forest Service Station. We were met there by a woman who opened a shed, revealing a cache of various hand tools. We loaded several McLeods, Pulaskis, and shovels, along with two chainsaws, into the open bed of the Pink. She told us to go straight to Pacific Valley Station, some forty miles south, where we would be met by fire personnel. We headed south, three guys in the cab and seven riding in back. Those of us sitting in the bed of the truck were getting battered by the wind, and we huddled close to the cab for protection. We tried to get comfortable sitting on the tools underneath us in the bed of the Pink as Buddy drove like a maniac, careening through the turns. We were on a mission to save the coast from burning.

Apparently, the last thing the Pink had hauled was hay, and the short yellow leftover strands were whirling around our heads. Someone in the back lit a joint and took a hit. The wind blew the burning ember off the joint in a shower of sparks, and it swirled under the layer of hand tools. Within seconds the hay had ignited into a small fire that quickly grew. We were banging on the rear window trying to get Buddy's attention, but he was focused intently ahead.

I'm not sure if it was all the banging or if he saw the glow of the fire in his mirror, but Buddy suddenly swerved to a stop in a pullout with the Pink's bed on fire. Everyone piled out. We had no water, so we were pouring beer on the flames. Two guys jumped up into the bed and started pissing on it. Slowly the fire subsided. We were humbled. We had set ourselves on fire on our way to the fire! We decided no one could know about this embarrassing debacle when we got to the real fire, or they would probably send us all home. We formed a circle and swore each other to secrecy.

Once at Pacific Valley Station, we off-loaded the tools and were told to form a line for inspection. Two of us not wearing boots were rejected.

"You can't fight fire in sandals!" the fire captain declared.

Eight of us got back in the Pink and, waving to our two rejects, followed a fire truck south. Though no flames were visible, the glow was bright, towering above us and illuminating the night sky in yellow and orange. We pulled into the Salmon Creek Ranger Station and were issued hand tools, then formed a long line with professional firefighters and set off into the brush.

Our objective, we were told, was to cut a firebreak around the station. The chainsaws went first, then the Pulaskis, then us volunteers wielding the McLeods, which were a rake-hoe combination. We worked feverishly, tossing brush and moving slowly forward. Suddenly the flames broke over the top of the ridge above us and scared the shit out of everybody. The flames looked closer in the dark. We watched the flames crown over the crest and begin to burn down toward us.

We continued at a faster pace until dawn gave us some light to see by. In the smoky gray morning haze we could just see the results of our work. We had just clear-cut an enormous swath through a jungle of poison oak. I had already suffered through a nasty case of the dreaded stuff and knew we were going to be in bad shape. We'd had no clue what we were cutting in the dark, but now it was clear we were doomed.

We were then told to reassemble at an art gallery up the road a couple of miles and cut a fire break around it. We piled into the Pink and drove up the road to the small roadside structure called the Sun Gallery. By late afternoon, having completed our task, we were lying alongside the road, exhausted and itching like crazy. Firefighters in fresh uniforms drove past us on their way to the front lines.

A fire camp had been established on the marine headlands at Pacific Valley. All the arriving strike teams and water tenders were staking out a piece of ground there before receiving their orders and being dispatched out to the fire. Our boss, a grizzled old Forest Service captain, came over where we lay at the Sun Gallery and told us we were being laid off because they had hundreds of firefighters coming in. He said we could leave our names and addresses at the Fire Camp Headquarters, and we would be sent checks as compensation for our work.

We drove into the fire camp in the Pink, drawing more than a few stares from the professionals. We looked like veterans all right, covered in dirt and ragged from no sleep, but the pink VW pickup covered in painted flowers belied that first impression. We left our names and addresses at the incident command tent, then stood around watching the bustling scene. Fire trucks from all over the western states were parked and settling in, waiting for orders. Firefighters in fresh uniforms stood beside their trucks organizing their gear. Not far from us was the fire camp 'supply store,' which was two big box trucks backed up to three folding tables. The trucks had their rear doors open. Inside the trucks were assorted hand tools, rolls of fire hose, and cardboard boxes full of safety gear for the firefighters.

Buddy gathered us together by the Pink and leaned in close so no one else could hear. "Listen," he said. "No one knows we got laid off. Let's supply ourselves while we're here. Some of the local residents down here are gonna need some help, and we need tools!"

We pulled up and parked in front of the tables. Buddy announced to the guy working the store, "We're the Big Sur Volunteers."

The guy didn't bat an eye.

Once again, we loaded the Pink with shovels, Pulaskis, and McLeods.

They also had water bladders with nozzles on them, informally called 'piss pumps,' so we grabbed a couple of those too. We outfitted ourselves with fire retardant overalls, helmets, goggles, gloves, road flares, canteens, and durable jackets called brush coats. We kept looking over our shoulders, but no one seemed to notice our pink hippy rig parked in front of the supply trucks. I think we all just looked too dirty and nasty.

The guy working the supply line kept forking over the gear until we were outfitted. Climbing back into the Pink, we drove out of the fire camp in a cloud of dust and color, headed back toward the fire.

We stayed on that fire for a week. Two other guys joined along the way, making us ten strong. By sunset of day two, we all had terminal poison oak. The nasty rash was having its way with us. You could get it by physically touching the plant, touching someone or something that had been in contact with it, or from the smoke as it was burning. It formed a red rash, sometimes with oozing blisters, that itched intensely. It was spread easily by scratching, and it was impossible not to scratch it, especially when you were sleeping. It was all I could do to stay focused. We had rashes and blisters all over our bodies.

Many of the locals were torching the ground around their houses and barns to burn the fuel in front of the advancing fire. These uncontrolled backfires were moving rapidly up and down the ridges. We would hear of someone needing help and drive there, Buddy at the wheel, sliding through turns on unfamiliar dirt roads to hidden houses up remote dirt drives. We would jump out, talk to the residents about a plan, and start doing what we could. We got good at assessing risk, and sometimes we advised evacuation. By day six, we had helped save twenty-six houses.

My last day on the fire was up on Willow Creek Road, where I had been helping other volunteers prepare the Arbaum house for the approaching fire. That morning I had hitched a ride down off the mountain to find something to eat. My ride dropped me at Pacific Valley Center, a roadside gas station and restaurant complex resting east of the highway on a headland above the Pacific Ocean. The temporary Fire Camp was set up below.

I was standing in the parking lot eating a donated sandwich and talking to a woman who had just evacuated her home. I looked terrible. She said her cabin was located way up Willow Creek Road. She stood there in the parking lot, her blond hair blowing across her face, holding the hands of two small barefoot children. Her old pickup was parked behind her, loaded high with personal belongings lashed down by strands of rope. She asked me in a quiet, intent voice if I was fighting fire. I told her I was volunteering, and she then told me her story of living at the Curtis homestead. She explained her husband was away on a road trip to Oregon and knew nothing of the fire. She gave me directions to the house and asked me if I would check on it and maybe even save it if I could. I told her I would try.

Not far away there was a green out-of-state fire truck parked next to a phone booth. The driver side door was open, and a uniformed man was talking on the phone while the crew waited in the double cab. I decided to talk with them. I stood outside the phone booth and waited. When he emerged, I could see his clothes were clean like he had just arrived on scene. He took one look at me standing there all blackened in soot, oozing poison oak, and said, “Where’s the fire?”

“It’s up Willow Creek,” I said, looking over at the fire truck, “and they could really use your help.”

He motioned over to a tall semi-truck carrying a large water tank. “Can I get that up there?” he asked.

“Easy,” I said. “It’s a good road, plenty wide enough.”

“I don’t want to get stuck in some box canyon,” he warned.

“I know what I’m talking about.” I held his gaze. “I’ve been up there, you’ll be fine.”

“You have a vehicle?” he asked.

“No, I’m walking,” I said, looking up the highway.

He waved me up onto a platform behind the cab of his truck. “Saddle up, boys!” he yelled. Then, looking at me, he asked, “What’s your name?”

“Wesley.”

“Just tell us where to go, Wesley!” He climbed up into the cab and behind the wheel of the fire truck.

The drive up Willow Creek Road was slow and lumbering. Finally, after what seemed like an eternity, we drove down the driveway to the Arbaum place to a chorus of cheers from the volunteers working around the house. The water tender and the six-man fire crew pulled into a large clearing near the house, where we were immediately surrounded by the people working there.

I left them there at the Arbaum place and, following the woman's directions, continued uphill on foot to find the Curtis homestead. After about a quarter mile of walking, I saw a guy sitting in the shade of a tree just off the side of the road.

He was chewing on a piece of grass. I stopped alongside him. "Hi, I'm Wesley Daggert."

"Bill," he said, looking up. He kept chewing on the stem of grass. "Where you going to?" he asked.

I looked up the dirt road. "I heard there's a homestead up the road a ways. It's owned by the Curtis family and there's no one home. I'm going to see if it's still there. If it is, maybe it can be saved from the fire."

"I know the place," he said, getting to his feet. "I'll go up there with you."

Bill was a stocky guy with a large blond head. We talked as we walked. Bill had been working the fire solo, offering his services to whomever needed them. There was an air of calm innocence about him that was refreshing amid the chaos of all that was going on around the large wildfire.

Around a bend in the road he pointed down a driveway that disappeared into trees, and we walked down it. The Curtis homestead was cut into sloping ground high above Willow Creek. The cabin was set in a clearing with a hitching rail and a water trough in front of it. The house was built of hand-split redwood, and upon entering the house, the craftsmanship was even more apparent. The rooms were small, with the kitchen open to the living room. The bedrooms were almost afterthoughts. In the living room in front of a wall of tall multiframe windows was an ebony baby grand piano taking up most of the space. Sheet music stood above the keys. It gave the room an intimacy and grace as though the last music played was still in the air.

Outside we saw that the dried summer grass was growing up close to the house, and several oak limbs grew out over the roof. The air was hot and still, and the fire was burning aggressively in the canyon far below us.

I turned to Bill. "Nice place."

"Yeah, needs some work though. Too much grass and wood up close to it."

I was looking at the piano sitting proud behind the window above us. "There's a woman and two kids in the parking lot at Pacific Valley that live here. I think we can do this. What do you think?"

He locked eyes with me and nodded. "I think we'd better get busy!"

We knew it was going to get dicey but decided to try to save it. We found what tools we could use in an outside shed and worked for hours clearing the ground around the little house, dropping limbs, and raking duff away from the walls. During the night, we could hear the fire below us gaining ground, raging and crackling until it roared up the canyon and over the top of us, crowning treetop to treetop, sucking the oxygen off the ground and forcing us into the horse's water trough to survive. A tall redwood tree exploded as its sap boiled just thirty yards from where we lay submerged. After the fire passed over us, we ran around the house for the rest of the night putting out spot fires. Without that all-night effort, the house would surely have perished.

The next morning, in the gray smoky mist of first light, the house looked frail in the midst of the black charred ground around it, the piano visible like a sentry through the front windows. We worked the edges of the clearing for a couple more hours, dispersing hot spots to be sure it was safe, until finally hearing the sound of a distant chainsaw. Someone was clearing the driveway to the cabin of fallen trees.

Soon an older, black step-side pickup truck pulled in next to the house. The door opened and a guy I knew as Army Jack stepped out. Inside the cab sat a woman I knew from Big Sur named Tracy. They were both smiling. Army Jack stood on the running boards of the truck and snapped a crisp military salute to Bill and me, saying in a deep, rumbling voice, "You are relieved! We got this now!"

An hour later, after showing Jack and Tracy what we had done, Bill and I were walking back down the road to the Arbaum house to check on the efforts there.

"It was fortuitous to meet you, Bill, there was no way I could have saved that house by myself."

He turned to me with a grin. "Good to meet you too, Wesley. It did get a bit sketchy, didn't it?"

The Arbaum house had no shortage of volunteer help, and we worked with them through the afternoon. I was told the fire crew I had brought up had not felt safe and had driven back down to the highway. As for me, I was running out of steam and had a splitting headache. The fire could be heard deep in the canyon below us, devouring acres of vegetation. I was sure it was getting ready for another run up the hill. As it started to get dark, I walked away from the bustle around the house and into the woods to a point above the canyon where the creek ran a thousand feet below. Looking down, I could see the dense smoke column, colored by the setting sun, billowing up toward me. Underneath that, further below, I could hear the fire's roar. It sounded like jet engines. I was no longer feeling safe.

Up until that point, I hadn't been too worried, but something was changing inside me. Maybe I was just tired. I knew I wasn't the only one. I found Buddy and told him how I felt. Bill was close by and said he'd like to get off the mountain too.

Buddy drove Bill, me, and a woman named Sherry, a Nepenthe waitress volunteering at the fire and also looking to get off the mountain, down Willow Creek Road in the Pink. The fire was roaring up the sidehill below us, and at one point we stopped in front of flames burning completely across the road. We sat there idling, looking at the flames through the windshield. We were going to have to drive through them if we were to go any further. Flames were closing in directly below us on the hillside.

Buddy turned to us. "The Pink has a gas leak underneath. It's just a drip. It might catch fire. I'm going to go for it. If you want out, now's the time!"

Before either of us could say anything, Buddy popped the clutch and drove into the flames. Everything turned yellow and orange, the heat suddenly intense on my side window. After about ten feet we broke out into darkness on the other side. Buddy stopped the Pink short and jumped out. He grabbed a rag from the floorboard and crawled under the Pink. In a moment he was up and got back in the cab. "Gas leak. I thought it might catch fire."

I was wide eyed. "Did it?"

"Are you kidding?" he laughed. "Hell, yeah, it was burning pretty good!"

Bill had his arm braced against the windshield. Sherry was shaking her head. "Oh, my God!"

I just looked ahead and took in the enormity of the week we had just endured. It seemed a lifetime had flashed by since we had first seen the fire's glow from Nepenthe's terrace. So much work, so many acts of heroism—or was it foolishness? The words seemed interchangeable now as the week's memories raced by.

At the bottom of the hill, Bill hitched a ride south from Willow Creek, and I never saw him again. Sherry caught a ride to Pacific Valley with some friends with room for one more. Buddy drove the Pink back up the hill against the advice of the Forest Service, and I hitched a ride north to Nepenthe in a truck loaded with fire refugees. I learned later that Buddy had helped evacuate twelve people stuck in a swimming pool below the Arbaum house when the fire crowned back over the mountain. They all rode down the mountain in the Pink.

I was fried. Everyone in Big Sur had poison oak, either directly from the south coast fire or from touching someone who had been there. I had it so bad I didn't have to worry about spreading it. I discovered right away that if I submerged myself in a hot bath, all the itching went away. The feeling was orgasmic. One afternoon while soaking in steaming water, I had what seemed like a brilliant idea and added a few glugs of laundry bleach to the bath water to clean out my pores. Within a couple of days, the poison oak started drying up. I was ecstatic! I had found the cure!

Nepenthe had a bulletin board on the back door that served as a community message center. Many people were posting advice for treating poison oak on notes stuck to the board with pins. "Go to the beach, get naked, jump in the ocean, and then roll in the sand. Let the sun dry you off," read one. "Go to the hospital and get a Prednisone shot," read another. "Rub aloe vera all over." And so on.

I posted mine there, among the others. It read, "Draw a hot bath and pour a few glugs of laundry bleach in the water. Soak for fifteen minutes!" I signed my name, Wesley Daggert. Big mistake. Two days later, I heard Tim McCleary, the maintenance man at Nepenthe, was looking for me. He wanted to kick my ass.

My friend Bob took me aside in Nepenthe's parking lot. "Wesley, stay clear of McCleary," he said, scanning the walkway up to the restaurant. "He tried your poison oak cure and lost all the skin on his testicles!"

The thought of McCleary with a raw scrotum was too much for me. I burst out laughing. "Well then, Bob, I don't think it's a problem. I should be able to outrun him!"

CHAPTER 4

"You decide your life's course, moment to moment, with every small decision you make."

–David Stafford

IT WAS EARLY 1971, APPROACHING the end of my first year at Nepenthe, when I found my first real house to rent. I was sitting at the bar having a drink with George the bartender and a waitress in her early twenties named Susan. While we were talking, a local couple walked by us, and we overheard them saying there was a house for rent at Three Acres, a property just a mile north of Nepenthe. Both Susan and I were looking for a house, and we caught each other's eyes for a quick moment. Three Acres was a small parcel of commercial property owned by the much larger Rancho Arbolado that spread over the mountain above it. I had been up the ranch road once before on the invitation of a friend who rented a cabin at the ranch's summit. I'd met the foreman of the ranch on that visit and knew approximately where his house stood along the ranch road.

I slipped off the bar stool first and fast walked to the pay phone at the back of the restaurant to call the Rancho Arbolado foreman. It was the first house lead I'd had in a long time, and I was excited. There was someone on the phone and someone waiting to use it. There was another pay phone down near the parking lot, so I started walking toward it just as Susan from the bar got into line for the phone behind the restaurant. I could see she was very intent and avoiding my eyes.

I half walked, half ran down to the parking lot and the other pay phone. I hoped the foreman's name was in the local phone book. Approaching the booth, I saw that someone was using that pay phone as well, so I ran to my truck. I would try to find him physically. I started the truck and sped out of the parking lot, careening around corners until I came to the entrance of Three Acres. I pulled through the gate and parked, then walked until I reached a second gate that was locked. The ranch foreman lived about a half mile up the dirt road behind this gate.

I jumped the gate and began running up the dirt road. After several minutes and turns in the road, I came to a lovely two-story whitewashed house. The foreman was outside the house raking leaves. He was a kindly looking man and was smoking a pipe that hung from his mouth. I came to a stop in front of him, my chest heaving, completely out of breath. "Excuse me, sir," I wheezed.

"Why, hello," he said, taking the pipe from his mouth, "What can I do for you?"

"Sir, I heard you have a house for rent at Three Acres, and I want to rent it. Is it still for rent?"

"Why, yes, it is," he said. "Did you just run all the way up here to rent that house?"

"Yes, sir." I replied, wiping some sweat from my forehead with my sleeve. "I didn't want to miss out." I extended my hand. "My name is Wesley Daggert."

We shook hands. "Good to meet you, Wesley, I'm Don," he said evenly, giving me an appraising look.

Just then I heard a phone ringing inside the house. "Excuse me for a moment," he said, and walked inside. A minute later he walked back out and said, "Boy, word gets around fast! That was a young lady asking to the rent the same house. I told her I had already rented it." He stuck out his hand. "It's yours."

It's an interesting thing to talk to people about how they came to have their first house in Big Sur. For some it was because they knew someone, for others it was handed to them on a silver platter the first day they arrived. Some found caretaking gigs, while many others lived in houses provided by their employers. Some people tried and never found a place to live, but one thing was for sure: in 1971, houses were very hard to come by.

I was so dumbstruck to finally have a house that I walked back down the road in a hazy dream with little detail. I couldn't believe it. I had gotten there first by only a minute. I was sure the young lady on the phone was Susan, who had been sitting beside me at the bar. The house was called the Top House, being the topmost house of the three at Three Acres. It was a small cabin with a kitchen and a front porch that looked across at Mount Manuel. I looked at the mountain as I passed the cabin and saw that it was bathed in the soft reds of sunset. I walked the rest of the way elated, down the road to where my truck was parked.

I moved into the Top House a week later. The cabin was small; the bedroom and living room were separated by a short half-wall with a walk through in the middle of it. The kitchen was tiny but seemed larger because of two walls of windows that opened up to the outside, letting in the sunlight and fresh air. The front porch was simple, just boards on girders with no railing, but the view of proud Mount Manuel and the steep Big Sur River gorge, where the river spilled out of the back country, was inspiring. I moved my belongings out of the truck and scrounged around town for a couple of chairs, a bed, and a chest of drawers. It felt good to get out of the truck and into a house, however small it was. I was soon entertaining, having friends over for the sunsets, watching the golden light glide over the mountains, fully enjoying the privilege of having a house of my own.

Spring and summer went by fast and October brought the late Indian summer to Big Sur. The days were getting shorter but were still hot with the onshore afternoon winds turning and blowing warm off the mountains during the evenings. The autumn moons seemed larger, and the fallen rusted-yellow sycamore leaves lined the highway, shifting in the rush of the occasional passing car. Kids were back in school, and the tourists had returned to work. It was a time for us, the locals, to reclaim the coast, to slow down and revel in its beauty.

One such October afternoon in 1971 I was tending bar at Nepenthe. The bar described a semicircle just inside the two double doors that opened to the red concrete terrace. I was working 'B' side, which faced out the large windows overlooking the terrace and the mountains beyond.

The ‘B’ side of the bar ended in a cul-de-sac that was aptly named the ‘Dirty Corner.’ Backed by the large picture window that looked out over the terrace, it was where the locals would sit, perched in the windowsill or high on the cushioned stools, telling stories and holding court. This day was sunny with an open blue sky, and the terrace was scattered occasionally with diners enjoying lunch and the view. I served a beer to a waiter on ‘A’ side and turned to find a gentleman sitting alone in Dirty Corner.

He was a big man, with dark unruly hair and a trimmed black beard, wearing a tan flannel shirt. He was leaning forward, his large hands folded in front of him. “Hey,” he said, looking up. “Give me a vodka rocks with a squeeze of lime. Make it a Stoli,” and then he added, “hundred proof.”

I made his drink and set it in front of him. “Nice day down here,” he said stirring his drink.

I was wiping the bar top next to him with a rag. I replied, “This is a great time of year. Weather is perfect and not so many people.”

After some small talk I introduced myself. “I’m Wesley. Wesley Daggert.”

“Luca Renzo,” he said, and extended his hand. “Good to meet you. I get down here as much as I can. I live in Monterey.”

Over the next hour and a half we talked about anything that crossed our minds. I learned he was Sicilian and had grown up on the Monterey Peninsula, was working as a painter, and that he had hunted wild pigs throughout Big Sur. His stories were large with a flair of the outlaw life. He mentioned he loved Big Sur and was looking to get down the coast more. Our exchange was easy, and the time flew by. By shift change we were laughing in unison. I felt I had known him for a long time. In the coming months Luca visited frequently. I had no way to know it then, but I had made a friend that I would know for the rest of my life.

The next couple of years were a whirlwind of work, parties, and a protracted trip to Europe with three of my friends from Nepenthe, Mickey, Stan, and Jack. I sublet my house to a couple I had known in high school, who, on a cross-country adventure, just happened to show up in Big Sur. My friends and I took the winter off from work and crossed the pond to Europe.

It was an epic trip that saw Mickey and Jack get deported back home from Holland, and Stan and me studying four months in Spain and Italy with Maharishi Mahesh Yogi. It was an intensive meditation course set on the Mediterranean island of Mallorca, just off the coast of Barcelona, Spain. We were immediately immersed in fourteen hours of meditation per day, broken only by meals and lectures from Maharishi. After three months on Mallorca, Maharishi moved the course to Fuiggi, Italy, where we continued in deep silence and meditation for another month. After the four months were up, Maharishi met with us individually and gave us the final instruction we would need to go out into the world and teach transcendental meditation.

Seven months after leaving, Stan and I were back in Big Sur, looking to get our jobs back at Nepenthe and teaching transcendental meditation to anybody who wanted to learn. It wasn't long before we had our jobs back again; the coast was getting busier, and Nepenthe was beginning to hire for the coming season. I moved back into the Top House at Three Acres, and my friends who were subletting it moved on to new adventures in Hawaii.

Luca Renzo and I were becoming good friends. He would show up at my house with his truck full of lumber cutoffs from various construction jobs he was working on the Monterey Peninsula. "More firewood!" he would say. One evening while having dinner at his folks' house in Monterey, he introduced me to his brother, Raffe. The mustachioed Raffe was a bit younger than Luca, and a bit taller. The two brothers were obviously close. Raffe told me he was selling his truck, and we went outside to look at it. It was a tall forest green 'Hi Boy' Ford with four-wheel drive and posi-traction front and rear. It had a strong custom lumber rack and front bumper, and important to me, it was a four-speed manual. I fell in love with the truck immediately and made arrangements to buy it right then. Two weeks later, I took possession of the truck in a pullout overlooking Bixby Bridge. Luca drove me there to meet his brother. I gave Raffe the cash, and Luca drove his brother back to Monterey. Within weeks, after driving the truck up and down the Big Sur mountains, I was referring to it simply as the 'Bad Ford.' There was nothing it couldn't do or anywhere it couldn't go.

Luca had met a woman while I was in Europe. Her name was Joan, and they had started dating. Joan was building a large home south of Big Sur, and Luca was getting involved with the project. "I don't know, Wesley," he said to me one day sitting on my deck, "this could be the one! She wants me to move in with her." They were married a year later, and Luca moved down the coast for good.

Life on the Big Sur coast was frenetic for those of us in the hospitality business. Somehow, we were all working full time, closing bars, and still getting up with the sun. We couldn't have been sleeping more than five or six hours a day. There was always something going on—a party on the beach, a midnight dance in a large pullout somewhere along the highway…even the Esalen Baths didn't open until one AM, and they were always full. I saw the dawn break over the gray coastal surf from that vantage point several times a month.

Redwood Lodge, a classic local bar/restaurant with motel units, had been sold to a family from Cambria. It was now called Fernwood, and the locals were on a mission to break it in properly. When the other bars and restaurants closed, everyone went to Fernwood for a nightcap. I'm sure the bar scene from the movie *Star Wars* was inspired by the late night Fernwood shenanigans.

By 1975, a top-flight resort named Ventana Inn was putting the finishing touches on construction and planning its inaugural opening. The firm had purchased 160 acres that had been split off from the sprawling Post ranch. Everyone wondered how a high-end resort was going to make it in a secluded backwater place like Big Sur. For the really old timers, the essence of Big Sur had changed forever with the construction of the highway in the 1930s. There may have been an old timer somewhere on the coast who shook his fist in defiance when the new resort was being finished, it's hard to say, but for most of us, the coming changes to our secluded lives on the coast were still over the horizon and could not yet be seen.

For example, we didn't know then that the Post family, one of the larger land holders in Big Sur, was in negotiations to sell the rest of their property to developers who planned to build another exotic resort just across the highway from Ventana. Times were changing.

CHAPTER 5

"I now have absolute proof that smoking even one marijuana cigarette is equal in brain damage to being on Bikini Island during an H-bomb blast."

–Presidential candidate Ronald Reagan

Buying marijuana in Big Sur in the early seventies was as easy as finding Ed Westbrook, an older guy in his thirties with a weather-beaten face, sad eyes, and a gentle smile. It usually took only a drive through the five miles of the Big Sur valley to find him standing outside one of the restaurants or gas stations, dutifully distributing his product. He called it Big Sur Green, or Holy Weed, and was well known for his fat, one-ounce plastic bags of pot for $10. In those days, it was mostly sticks, stems, and seeds, but the portion was generous. Ed believed in getting as much Holy Weed to as many people as he could. His face would light up when he passed you the bag and wished you well.

When I first moved to Big Sur in 1969, I had been smoking grass for just two years. The funny part was, for all my trying, I had never really enjoyed it. After taking a couple of hits from a joint, I would clam up and get paranoid. My thoughts would turn sour and run rampant over reason, causing me to withdraw inside myself and want to hide. It was ridiculous. Everyone I knew smoked grass for breakfast, lunch, and dinner, and sometimes in between, but I couldn't deal with it. I was okay with psychedelics, acid or mushrooms were a breeze, but smoking grass just kicked my ass. Despite knowing this about myself, I still took the occasional hit to be social, to hang with friends, knowing full well I would more than likely regret it after a few tokes.

One summer day in 1975, while working as a waiter at Nepenthe, I served a tall, well-groomed man lunch on the terrace. He had dark, meticulously combed hair, and a modest goatee that served to extend his gaunt, clean-shaven face. He was affable, quick to laugh, and soon our conversation became lively. During one exchange, I learned his name was David Stafford. After I finished work, he was still sitting on the terrace reading a book and nursing a drink. I joined him with a drink on the furthest reach of Nepenthe's terrace, a section known as 'Siberia.'

We sat facing down the coastline exchanging stories. It turned out he was a house painter from Santa Monica and drove an immaculate '49 Chevy pickup. He had a dog named Zip that he communicated with in a made-up language that only he and his dog knew. It made the dog responsive to only him, he explained. David enjoyed taking extended road trips up and down the coast and found himself in Big Sur often.

"Where do you live?" he asked me.

"Up the highway a couple miles."

The sun was getting low in the sky, and the hills were turning the warm colors of late afternoon. I pointed to the hillside above Nepenthe. "It's the Gracelight period." I said.

He looked at me. "The what?"

"Gracelight. The hour or so before sunset. Great for photography."

"You mean Alpenlight?"

"Same thing, I think."

We were studying the soft warm light.

"You got any grass?" he asked.

"I do, down in my truck. Finish your drink, and we'll take a stroll."

We walked down to the main parking lot, and he stopped at his truck. His dog Zip was sitting at attention on the passenger seat with the window rolled all the way down.

"Wow," I said, "this truck is a showstopper! Very nice! Does your dog ever jump out the window?"

"Not unless I tell him to." David looked at his dog. "Zip, nash!"

The dog leaped from the window to the ground in a single fluid movement.

"Neesh!" David commanded.

Zip sat erect at David's leg.

"Amazing!" I said. "Very impressive! Can I use that language with women?"

"You can try," he laughed. "But don't get your hopes up."

We started walking down to the lower lot where my truck was parked.

"Leemo!" David commanded, and Zip fell into stride beside him.

At my truck, I opened the back door and pulled out my two folding chairs. The ocean view from the back of my truck was spectacular, and I motioned for him to sit down, then stepped inside, dug out my stash, and rolled a joint.

"Can I offer Zip some water?" I asked, stepping back outside.

"Sure," David said.

I handed him the joint and poured some water into a bowl, then placed the water on the ground next to Zip. David lit the joint, inhaled, and passed it to me. I took a hit.

"Nice address," he said in a tight voice. "Your digs look pretty comfy too." He exhaled and extended the joint back to me.

"No, thank you," I said, "one poke is good for me."

He motioned inside my truck. "Did you remodel it?"

"Yeah, I did. It solved a housing crisis for me for about a year before I got my cabin." I pointed to his dog. "Zip is just looking at the water."

"Oh," David turned. "Zip, bing!" And Zip dove into the water, lapping it up. "I forgot to give him permission."

David told me about his life in Santa Monica, his small apartment near the beach, taking over his father's painting business, and his sideline job of leading yoga classes on the roof of his apartment building. "Yoga is amazing," he said. "The view is great, and I stay limber!"

After that, he started asking for me when he visited Nepenthe, and we became friends. We had shared a few joints over the months; mostly it was Big Sur Holy Weed we were smoking, but one day, while walking down the road to Deetjen's Inn, he reached into his shirt pocket and pulled out a joint of his own. He told me that a buddy of his who lived in the Malibu Mountains had come up with a way of growing marijuana that made it much stronger. He explained that a marijuana patch had female and male plants in the garden, that the females excreted a sticky resin, and the males would pop pollen from little yellow flowers so it would drift over and stick to the resin, which pollinated the females to produce seeds. He went on to say that producing seeds robbed the grass of potency. His friend had found that by pulling the males from the garden before they bloomed, and thereby robbing the females of the pollen, the females would literally get horny and start oozing more resin in search of pollen. This process eventually produced fat, sticky, oversized buds that when smoked, resulted in a very powerful, potent high. He lit the joint and passed it to me. He said it was called 'sinsemilla,' which meant 'seedless.'

When I took the hit, my eyes bulged out, and I started coughing like a coal miner smoking Camels. I suddenly felt like my eyes were windows and I was standing back from them about ten feet. I thought Big Sur Holy Weed was strong, but this stuff kicked my butt like a can down the street. I was devastated. The rest of my conversation was tentative and sounded like Blah, Blah, and Blah. I felt completely exposed. I had never been that high from smoking grass in my life, and the rest of that day is just a foggy memory.

Apparently, I wasn't the only one in town experiencing sinsemilla for the first time. The potent weed started popping up in small group-smokes we called 'safety meetings' up and down the coast. It had a unique sweet fragrance and a powerful high. I heard some friends say they were trying to grow it in small hidden gardens and some whispered words about pulling males and identifying females. I was intrigued, but I felt my cabin at Three Acres was too exposed to passing ranch traffic to try growing a pot garden.

CHAPTER 6

"Some meadows in the mountains exist in a vacuum that can only be filled with a cabin."

–Richard Gable

I LOVED MY CABIN AT THREE Acres. It was my first house and wasn't connected to my job. It was, however, very small and relatively close to the highway, with the rushing sound of passing cars drifting up through the trees all day and night long, invading the tranquility of the scene. I had visited many homes higher in the mountains and longed for their quiet settings and eye-stretching views. The air smelled different up higher, spiced with manzanita, sage, and vinegar weed.

One early August night in 1975, while bathing at the Esalen Hot Springs, I struck up a conversation with my friend Bo Rummsen, who was there for a soak. I had initiated Bo and his wife Pam into transcendental meditation at the Top House in 1972, and we had remained distant friends. The conversation got around to me saying that I wanted to find a place higher up in the hills away from the highway to live. Bo understood as few could. His dad owned a 2,000-acre ranch that bordered both sides of Highway 1 for a couple of miles. Bo had built a magnificent house on the ranch at 1,200 feet, perched on a cliff above the Pacific. The ranch encompassed the watersheds of four large creeks that ran from the ridge tops to the ocean. The northern part of the ranch was a 500-acre parcel that included the Fuego Creek drainage. On it was the old Juan Fuego homestead house, an abandoned sixteen-by-twenty-foot hand-split relic that was slowly leaning over and falling down the hillside.

Vacant for almost forty years, the lizards and pack rats had claimed it as their own. It was called the Apple Tree House because of an old yet still prolific apple tree that grew beside it. There was also an ancient English walnut tree growing above it that shaded the site. Bo explained to me that his dad had always been after him to rebuild the homestead cabin, but he hadn't found the time. He said if I thought I was up to it, he would recommend me to his dad as a means of getting it rebuilt. I said I was very interested, and he arranged a meeting between me and his father, Tom Rummsen.

His father and I met at his office in Monterey one afternoon, and during the interview, we worked out a deal. I was to supply the labor and the materials for the rebuild, and in exchange, I would get occupancy with four years of free rent. Mr. Rummsen would help with support from the ranch when he could, including help from his ranch foreman, a bulldozer, a backhoe, and a wide variety of heavy ranch tools.

The move to the Rummsen ranch would add a ten-mile commute to Nepenthe every day I worked there, but the drive was spectacular, and I thought I would also enjoy the drive south from Big Sur into the wilder and more remote South Coast to get home. The ranch property was just what I had been looking for, with a wide ocean view, good elevation, and absolute quiet. Having 500 acres to myself to explore was just icing on the cake.

Juan Fuego Road branched off the main Ranch Road a quarter mile from the highway and ascended the canyon along Fuego Creek. The dirt road passed under an impressive stand of first growth redwoods, then climbed steeply through an area of fractured rock and bay laurels. It left the trees and wound past the cabin at 500 feet of elevation. The road then continued up another mile, finally coming to an end on a windswept bluff above the ocean.

The Apple Tree House was leaning steeply on a sidehill below Juan Fuego Road, in the middle of a two-acre patch of long yellow grass growing some 200 feet above the rushing Fuego Creek. To the west, the site enjoyed a wide ocean view. There was no driveway from the road to the cabin, nor were there any windows or doors, only the openings where they had once been. When I looked inside, I could see the floor was long gone and was now just huge piles of lizard and rat droppings among a carpet of weeds.

The story was that old Juan Fuego built the cabin from wood he harvested in the canyon and had lived there with his wife Estelle. Water had to be hauled up from the creek below along a steep, narrow trail, but despite this hardship, the soil was rich, and there was an abundance of stone and wood in the canyon.

After living there a few years, it became obvious to Juan the real problem with the site was rolling boulders. High above the site, about a half mile up, was a large natural rockslide, and when the second boulder rolled through the cabin, almost killing his wife, he thought it was bad luck and abandoned the claim.

The first task at hand for me was seeing if the cabin could be righted from its precarious lean toward the deep canyon below. Here I was offered help from the very capable ranch foreman, Richard Gable. Richard drove the bulldozer up, carrying a hundred feet of heavy steel cable in the bucket, and positioned it above the cabin. We wrapped the cable around the cabin and secured it to the bulldozer. Very slowly, in small increments, Richard backed the dozer up. The cable grew taut, and the cabin groaned and popped but started to move. After a tense half hour, I was holding a plumb level on the cabin wall, and Richard shut off the machine.

We left it like that, secured by the cable for the next few weeks as I used hydraulic jacks borrowed from the ranch to raise the canyon side of the cabin to level. There was no water or electricity at the cabin, so Mr. Rummsen paid to have 3,000 feet of NSF-rated black poly pipe delivered to the site, and I bought a small generator along with an assortment of power tools with money I had saved. I installed the water line up Fuego Creek to a source high above the cabin, uncoiling the pipe and rolling it over land down to the cabin site.

Fuego Creek, like all coast creeks, runs to the ocean, dumping its precious fresh water onto a beach. If you are fortunate enough to live in a creek drainage and have no one else living below you, the water is there for the using. Because the creek water was running into the ocean anyway, I felt it was okay to irrigate my property constantly, keeping the land around the cabin lush and green. There was plenty of pressure at the spigot even with the rain birds going.

After I mixed concrete and poured a new foundation, Richard came back and took the tension off the cable holding the cabin. With a couple of creaks and pops, the old homestead settled into a plumb and square position. Richard then took the bulldozer up to Juan Fuego Road and cut a driveway down past the walnut tree, pushing the dirt and creating a large turnaround just west of the cabin. It was an excellent start. I could now drive down to the cabin, which looked quite stately with its new posture.

In early 1976, Fort Ord, an army post on the outskirts of Monterey, was changing its mission statement. Long an installation for basic training, it was reverting once again to the home of the 7th Infantry, and many of its barracks that had been used for new recruits were being dismantled. The wood siding, floors, doors, and windows were being carefully salvaged and sold to the general public at very reasonable prices. They really just wanted the salvaged material carried away. I made several trips to the fort in the Bad Ford during my days off from work at Nepenthe, purchasing loads of two-by-tens and one-by-twelves. The windows were classic, made of six panes framed in wood, and I bought twelve of them. I hauled everything back to the Apple Tree House and stacked the materials in the turnaround in front of the cabin.

Over the next two months, the project progressed steadily. The cabin was slowly transforming into a home. The floor was first, as the joists and two-by-ten floor planks were laid. The original hip roof of hand-hewn redwood beams was still in place, and I covered them with the one-by-twelves, then rolled out forest green asphalt roofing on top. The multipaned windows brought charm to the building, and I made a rough paneled door for the entry. I bought a large steel boiler from the fort, and Bo used his welding skills to attach legs and a door, turning it into a fireplace for the cabin. A propane company brought a 500-gallon tank to the site and set it outside the cabin. I plumbed it to the water heater, a propane Servel refrigerator, and a cooking stove.

I built a ten-by-ten-foot bathroom extension that was accessible by climbing three stairs from inside the cabin. It boasted a toilet, a sink, and a clawfoot tub with a shower. On the shower wall was a window that looked down into the canyon. A freestanding deck was erected on the canyon side, separated from the cabin by a bed of planted roses.

In six months, the place had been transformed. Entering through the only door, there was a table on the right sitting in front of windows opening onto the deck outside. Straight ahead was the bed, flanked by two windows, and the steps leading up to the bathroom. To the left of the entry door was the kitchen and stove-range wrapped in a four-foot-high wall that set it aside from the rest of the floor plan. There was a loft over the kitchen for storage. A foldout couch facing an overstuffed chair filled out the rest of the space. The view from the kitchen window was ocean, while canyon views and the tops of redwoods filled the other windows. It was charming, cozy, and felt like home.

Upon completion, I gave notice at Three Acres that I was moving. The foreman accepted my recommendation, and I was able to pass the Top House directly to my friend Jack from Nepenthe. That settled, I made the move up to the Apple Tree House.

During my six years working at Nepenthe, I had made good money and had saved up a fair nest egg. I began work on what would soon be my shop, framing up a twelve-by-sixteen-foot building with a plywood floor and stud walls just off to the east side of the cabin. The shop cantilevered out from the sloping hill to a height of ten feet off the ground at the canyon side. It featured a work bench with a set of windows above it, not unlike a windshield above a dashboard of a car, that faced the south canyon view. It would house my tools and give me a place to work inside during inclement weather.

CHAPTER 7

"All you need to grow good grass is full sunlight, rich soil, water, and balls of steel."

–Donald Macinlay

DURING THE REBUILDING OF THE Apple Tree House, I realized I had plenty of places to start a marijuana garden. I had 500 acres of hiding places and decided to start my first pot garden using the techniques Stafford and others had passed on to me for producing the prized sinsemilla. Many were growing for their own consumption, but that wasn't my focus. The fact that I was not comfortable with the high and smoked it sparingly did not keep me from understanding the plant was definitely worth growing as a cash crop.

I cleared brush from a flat across the road above the cabin, creating a thirty-by-forty-foot space for the garden. I fenced it with chicken wire, ran water to it, and dug forty holes. The dirt that was removed was mixed with chicken manure, bone, and blood meal, and returned to the holes. I was given a small bag of marijuana seeds from a friend and started them in peat moss cups on the deck of the house. It was late March of 1976.

In those days, there were no overflights by the county sheriff searching for pot fields, so the plants were able to grow in full sun. Through conversations with friends I learned that I was not the only one trying to grow sinsemilla in quantity. In fact, at least five others I knew were growing, and one guy in particular, Larry Klein, seemed to know a lot more than the rest of us. I had many questions, starting with what do the females look like? How do you spot the males early? What is a good plant food? What is the pruning process? Just to mention a few.

Larry agreed to come up and look at my garden, but when he showed up, he kicked some dirt around, said he liked my site, then said he would give me some advice in exchange for ten percent of my garden proceeds. I said no. In fact, I think I said "fuck off." I knew there were others I could ask questions of who were not after a cut of my action.

The plants thrived and soon it was June, and I was into the declaration period. This was the time in the growing season the plants would show themselves or 'declare' themselves to be male or female. The females would show little sacs at the crotch of the stem from which two small white hairs would emerge in a 'V,' while the males would develop 'balls' that hung in the same crotch area of the plant. These 'balls' would become the yellow flowers that popped the pollen that would ruin your sinsemilla garden. I developed the courage to pull very healthy four- and five-foot plants out of the ground when they showed their little balls and learned to pinch back the leading tips of the females to create a bushier mother plant. I took a friend's advice and started feeding the plants Miracle-Gro, a liquid plant fertilizer. I would go into the garden daily to look for males, dragging a green rubber garden hose through the rows and watering constantly.

Rattlesnakes were a problem. They liked the cool moist earth around the plants and would slither down the hill to take their naps there. I had to be vigilant. The plants loved the sun and the chicken-shit-rich soil; they were growing inches every day, and I was soon walking through a green jungle. The buds were pushing out, probing, looking to be pollenated, searching, but finding no pollen. The fan leaves were so broad they could block sunlight to the plant's interior, so some had to be pruned off to allow more sunlight in.

One day I noticed a branch was hanging, apparently nibbled off by some predator. Upon further inspection, I found more branches were chewed. I thought it was deer jumping the fence, so I extended my fence poles and strung new wire in higher runs, but to no avail. The damage continued. Concerned I was going to lose my crop, I walked up to my garden late one night, crept through the pitch dark, and quickly turned on my flashlight. Suddenly I was staring into the faces of about twenty large pack rats! The rats were everywhere, perched on the fence, up in the branches of surrounding trees, and within the plants themselves. They were eating my garden. I darted around shooing them off, and they retreated, but I knew this wild discovery would require drastic action to keep them out.

I bought rat poison and placed it in several places in the garden, then went deep into the surrounding brush and found the huge twig mounds that were the rats' nests and destroyed them by pulling them apart and killing their young. The damage to the garden slowed down, but I was still having to spend every night chasing some away. I bought snake shot for my .44 Magnum pistol and shot them when I could, blasting holes through my plants in the process.

This war with the rats was maddening. They were nocturnal animals with a huge advantage over my daylight existence. Within weeks, I noticed blue jays lying dead where they crash-landed abruptly from flight and realized it was the poison I was leaving out when one day I caught a bird eating from the rat bait.

I went to the County Department of Agriculture and, without mentioning my crop, reported a rat infestation on my property. They gave me proper "pet proof" boxes to use with the rat poison, and I slowly gained the upper hand in the battle. I also noticed that as the plants matured and began dripping with resin, the rats didn't like them so much. They were perhaps getting 'too' stoned and, in a reversal of human behavior, easing up on their nightly eating frenzy.

It was right about then that I made another discouraging discovery. When stressed by the absence of males and pollen in their vicinity, certain females had the ability to generate a male flower. Called 'hermaphrodites,' the female plant could simply switch one of her buds or even one of her branches to the male sex and thereby pollinate herself along with other plants in the local area. This happened in one corner of the garden, and I caught it early, but this new wrinkle meant it was imperative that I check every branch of every plant, every day, for hermaphrodites.

I asked around about the problem and slowly began to understand the issue. Looking at a handful of seeds, I noticed there were some obvious differences between them. Some were smaller with an even tan color, and some were much larger and speckled with black spots. The larger seeds were indica, a potent, stockier strain with fat tight buds sprinkled with purple highlights. The smaller seeds were the sativa strain, a taller, leggier plant that, while also very stony, tended toward 'bolting' and thinning out. Some of my friends thought it was the sativa strain that was most likely to have the hermaphrodite characteristic, but no one was really sure. We were all learning as we went along.

The labors became increasingly more focused, and the smaller wars were fought and won with minimal casualties. Entering September, I had twenty-four seven-foot plants that were bending over with heavy resinous buds. When lightly squeezed, the buds gave off an exotic perfume that foretold of their potency and flavor. The garden smelled like a skunk had sprayed nearby, and the white hairs of the buds, crystallized with resin, glowed under a flashlight at night.

It was late September when, unannounced by any forecast, it rained. The afternoon had seen an increase of dark clouds drifting in from the south pushed by a building wind. By nightfall the air was heavy and moist, and smelled of rain. At one AM I awoke to the plops of heavy drops on my roof and immediately thought of my plants. Dressing quickly, I raced out of the cabin with a flashlight. By the time I reached the garden the rain was coming down steadily, causing the heavy buds to bend low with the extra weight of the water. The lower branches dipped into the mud and whole plants were leaning over, almost touching the ground. I rushed back to the house for some string and a knife and returned to the garden. I then began creating a support system for the plants. String was stretched from the plant trunks to the fence line in an attempt to hold the plants up from the ground. I was soaked and frantic, cursing every bud that hit the muddy ground.

By dawn, the rain had stopped, and I was surveying the damage. There were broken branches and leaning plants burdened by the muddy rain-splashed buds. I harvested the broken branches, taking them into my cabin and hanging them up to dry. I sprayed the muddy buds with hose water to clean them, and after a few days of sun, realized the resin wasn't all that water-soluble. The hot sun, in a week's time, had the plants dripping resin again, shaken but not ruined, and ready for harvest.

In retrospect, those days, while busy with rat wars and worry, were, overall, definitely the good ol' days. They were the days of wine and roses. No overflights, no paranoia, just wide open sunshine. They were days in a time that would not last long.

CHAPTER 8

"Without buyers, growing marijuana would just be a hobby."

–Larry Klein

I HARVESTED THAT FIRST GARDEN OVER a ten-day period as the sunlight thinned and the days grew shorter in late October. I hadn't really thought it out very well and hung the first cut plants whole, upside down from rafters in the cabin. They quickly wilted, their leaves drooping and clinging to the buds I wanted to expose. The large hanging plants also made it difficult to move around in the relatively small space of the cabin. In addition, I hadn't appreciated how much time it would take to remove the leaves from around the buds and what a mess of brittle dried duff the process would leave on the cabin floor.

After some experimentation I figured out that it was much easier, and made much more sense, to harvest smaller amounts of pot and trim the leaves off the buds while they were still fresh. I was delighted to learn this also yielded a potent side product. When the plant was still fresh, the resin was sticky close to the bud, and it would accumulate on your fingers as you worked. Black and thick like a coating of paste, I found that by rubbing my index finger and thumb together, it could be 'bugger-rolled' into small balls and stored. These balls of resin were essentially a high-grade hashish and became a coveted by-product of the trimming process. Another by-product was the leaves themselves. The leaves closest to the buds had a light sprinkle of resin on them and, once dried, could be smoked for a light high or sautéed in butter to be used in baked goods such as cookies and brownies.

With my technique polished I was on a roll, busily trimming buds whenever I wasn't working at Nepenthe. The trimming process continued over the course of five days, until my ceiling space in the cabin was a sea of green manicured buds hanging from the rafters. Sitting in my chair looking up at the hanging buds, it was easy to picture the whole process from garden preparation to harvest, the trials and tribulations, and all the work invested. I still had many questions about the final product. How much to dry it, how to package it so it stayed fresh, and most importantly, where to sell it...

Understandably, nobody knew what to charge for the sinsemilla. Few people had ever bought it before; it seemed it was just being passed around in smoking circles with everyone agreeing it was the best pot anyone had smoked. I talked with a couple of friends about it and finally ended up coming to an agreement with Larry Klein, of all people. I mentioned to Larry that sinsemilla was ten times better than Big Sur Holy Weed. Larry said, "Well Holy Weed sells for $10 an ounce, so sinsemilla should sell for $100!" It seemed like a nice round number, easy to work with, and definitely covered our time and expenses. Clearly, $100 was a lot of money in those days. In 1976, gasoline was selling at $.60 a gallon, postage stamps were $.13, and the average rent was $250/mo. But we were fresh from the hard labors of growing and trimming the product, and the price seemed appropriate. Not everyone had the right place to grow it, or the tenacity and steel to make it to harvest. It wasn't something just anyone could do. So it was that the $100 ounce and the $1,600 pound came into being locally. Some growers charged less and quickly ran out of product. Word got around, and other growers adopted the price. We were in business with an unofficially agreed-upon price for Big Sur Seedless.

When the pot was dry, it had to be stored in airtight containers, and I began by going out and buying a quantity of Ziploc baggies. These left a lot to be desired. The baggies were not airtight for extended periods and over time did not protect the delicate buds from damage. It was David Stafford during one of his visits up the coast who recommended I use new two-gallon paint buckets. It was mid-November, not long after the harvest, and we were up at my cabin looking at the pot I had grown and discussing the price.

"Nice stuff," he croaked, exhaling a cloud of smoke. "I'm blasted. Sure you don't want some of this?" he asked, holding out a joint.

"No, thanks. I've tried it. It fucks me up too much."

"Isn't that what it's supposed to do?" he asked, then laughed and started coughing.

"Yeah, but I've still got things I wanna do today like talk and walk and make dinner." I grinned.

David looked at the joint. "You know this stuff is going for $150 an ounce in LA?"

I was surprised. "I had no idea."

"Yeah, even more in Hollywood. You know, I think you might want to consider keeping your pot in new plastic paint buckets. They're clean, durable, and seal airtight. I keep my rice and other grains in them at home. They come in a two-gallon size, that might be perfect."

I thought it sounded like a good idea. A few days after he left I bought twenty-five from a paint supplier. I transferred the pot from gallon baggies to the paint buckets. They worked great.

Now that the pot was stored airtight in the containers, I felt good about stashing it outside. I cleared a small area in the brush not far from the cabin and built a large plywood box. I moved all the buckets into the box and covered the trail with the cut brush.

That first year's harvest, after packaging, weighed out to just over eleven pounds of seedless buds. I had purchased a triple beam scale through *High Times* magazine. Conveniently, a weighed half pound of bud fit nicely inside a two-gallon paint container. I had no idea who was going to buy it or how I was going to begin to move it. I had no desire to be a pot dealer, I just wanted it magically gone. Everyone I knew had all the pot they could smoke. Selling grass in Big Sur that fall was akin to selling snow in Alaska. I sat on that first crop for two months, trying to come up with ideas for selling it.

Once again, David Stafford entered the scene. Stafford had been thinking about my stash and was impressed with the smoke. He called me at Nepenthe one afternoon just before Christmas and said he wanted to visit. He asked me if I "still had that rock collection." I understood his code, said yes, and told him to come up. He arrived at my cabin a few days later in his pristine cream-and-brick-red pickup, the bed covered with a black vinyl tarp. Inside the cabin he pulled four stacks of bills bound by rubber bands from a leather shoulder satchel and placed it on my table. "Let's do business!"

I retrieved several buckets and the scale from the brush. It was obviously good business to reweigh the pot in front of the buyer. We checked the weight on ten buckets, emptying them out one at a time into a large stainless steel bowl, weighing the bucket empty and re-adding the pot for a final check. Five pounds in ten buckets were sitting on the table.

Stafford sat down at the table. "Sixteen, right?"

I nodded. Stafford pulled some rubber bands and started counting the money.

Five minutes later Stafford pushed the money over to me.

I counted out $8,000, mostly twenties, then slid $200 back over to him. "For your trip," I said. "How are you going to travel with it?"

Stafford stood up from the table. "I'll show you."

He grabbed some buckets and walked out to his truck, where he pulled back the tarp, showing me about fifteen white paint buckets stacked up close to the cab. "Paint," he said with a smile. He then moved the paint buckets back from the cab and started stacking the pot buckets in their place. The buckets were identical. Once he finished placing the pot buckets, he restacked the buckets containing paint around and above them, secured the buckets with netting and rope, stretched the tarp back over the bed, and secured everything with straps. "If I get stopped, it's all paint," he said.

After Stafford drove away, I sat at my table and looked at the stacks of cash, grinning ear to ear. *A guy could get used to this,* kept running through my mind.

My first dope deal was behind me, and I still had six pounds of seedless bud, manicured and in safe storage. Things were looking good. I'd never had $8,000 cash hanging around. I was feeling flush. Up until that point I had been living on $1,500 a month, depending on my tips. Sometimes a little more, sometimes a little less. I was good at saving money and always had a small reserve for emergencies, but it would have taken me three years to save $8,000, maybe more. I peeled off a thousand for my pocket and buried the rest in a three-pound Folgers coffee can under my shop, not far from the house. A cutoff piece from a bridge timber lay as a marker over the burial site.

Several friends of mine also had successful harvests, and we were comparing notes in quiet conversations around Big Sur. Most everyone agreed to the $1,600/pound price. Everyone had their version of the perfect fertilizer and pruning techniques, and were willing to share, but one thing was being guarded by everyone: who they were selling to. I wasn't the only one who didn't have a clear idea about selling the pot, but I did have an ace in the hole with David Stafford, and I kept his name out of every conversation.

It was obvious that some growers were spending their newfound money. New pickup trucks were appearing all up and down the coast; old, dusty family sedans were suddenly brand new Volvo station wagons; and some folks were talking up their good fortune to anyone who would listen, though fortunately, they were in the minority. Most growers were quiet about their exploits, and I tended to stand next to them. One of my first splurges was the purchase of three large redwood wine tanks. A friend named William had purchased twenty tanks of various sizes from a Fresno winery. The winery was converting to stainless steel storage tanks. The tanks were essentially large wooden barrels. William cut the metal bands that held them together and stacked the pieces of each barrel in individual piles.

It was said the redwood tanks could be made into creative places to live, and I bought three. The tanks were all twenty feet tall and varied in diameter. I bought a twelve-, a seventeen-, and a twenty-two-footer. My thought was that one day I would build a house with them on property I owned. A dream for sure, but something to look forward to. The tanks were delivered by semi-truck and trailer to a pullout on the highway across from the ranch road. Luca and another friend with a pickup truck helped me haul the loads up to Fuego Creek Canyon below the cabin. We stacked them there. The cool shelter of the redwood canyon would keep the redwood tanks nicely in their own natural humidor.

My money was buried in a can, and that felt right. The wad of cash in my pocket lifted me to a new place in life where financial concerns were a thing of the past. My possibilities had been expanded, and my spirit felt free.

I knew who was growing. It was, after all, a small town. Growers would catch each other's eye and have a pretty good idea what was going on with the other, but very few words, if any, were ever exchanged. Quiet discretion seemed to be the order of the day. I had friends come up to me and ask me how my crop went, and I would look them in the eye and tell them I wasn't growing. They would laugh, knowing I was lying, but I stuck to my story. Sometimes I would just stare at them, saying nothing, until it was their questions that felt completely out of place. It wasn't an ego thing for me as much as it was about opportunity and security. Silence was golden.

Stafford returned a couple of weeks later in early February 1977 and bought the rest of my pot. We put six pounds of manicured buds in plastic buckets into the back of his truck. There were ten buckets of paint already there.

He handed me $9,600 in twenties. "Any chance of a discount? I mean this is pretty convenient for you, my driving up here and all." He was smiling with his head leaning to one side.

I did some quick calculations in my head, knowing Stafford was right. This was perfect for me—low risk and very convenient. "Buy more than five pounds and I'll sell it for $1,500 a pound," I said, then counted out $600 and pushed it across the table to him. "Thanks, David!"

We shook hands.

"Good doing business with you," he said, and drove off down the hill.

CHAPTER 9

"Nobody meets someone for the first time thinking it's going to last forever..."

–Susie Reynolds

IN 1977, THE DOT ON the map that was Big Sur included four bars, eight restaurants, three campgrounds, five general stores, five gift shops, three gas stations, one delicatessen, and a post office. Spread out along seven miles of highway, it didn't seem like that much, but to the locals who clustered there it was a town with a heartbeat.

About two weeks after David Stafford bought me out, I was driving through Big Sur and decided to stop at the upscale Ventana restaurant. With its fresh cedar walls and natural parquet floor, the creative architecture of the place always intrigued me. I sat at Ventana's bar talking with Andy the bartender about the news of the day when the conversation got around to owning land. He had recently purchased a piece of land on a local ridge top and was drawing up plans to build a house on it. I was impressed. I mentioned how much I wanted to own my own place in Big Sur, and how it was an ongoing dream of mine.

"There are still some parcels of land for sale up by me," Andy offered. "You should go up and look at them."

He laid out a bar napkin and drew a map to the parcels of land for sale on Simson Ridge, the mountain separating the Big Sur valley from the ocean. After finishing my beer, I thanked Andy and set off to find the parcels.

The road began with a locked gate at the highway that he had given me the combination to and then continued up four miles of steep, rutted dirt road to the ridge summit. There the ocean was spread out 1,200 feet below in a wide vista. I drove over the crest and down a mile more of curvy road, the bar napkin folded over my steering wheel. I located some landmarks, found the parcels, and spent a couple of hours walking around on them.

One in particular appealed to me. I was amazed at the expansive ocean view and the 800-foot elevation. Eight hundred to 1,000 feet was known to be a relatively bug-free zone with few mosquitos and biting flies. Many of the original homesteaders had built at that elevation for just that reason.

The realization hit me like a bomb. The property could be mine! I could actually do this! I went back down the hill and called the Realtor, a kindly, retired Army Airborne colonel, Frank Abrams, who lived in Big Sur. He said he was free and agreed to meet me at Nepenthe. An hour later he walked in waving at people and shaking hands. I waved to him and he joined me. He spread a topo map out on one of the tables and placed his finger on the map. "So this is Parcel B right here on the turn of the road, and this road here branches off to Parcels C and D."

I pointed to Parcel B and said, "That's the one I liked the most."

"They're asking $20,000 for that one," Frank said. "It has a spectacular view. What you need to know about these parcels is that they have no water and no electricity. You'd have to figure that out for yourself."

I thought about that. The parcel was amazing. The closest neighbors had electricity and water, and I figured even if I couldn't get those essentials, I would still be able to sell it to one of my neighbors for what I paid for it. "I'll buy it!" I said.

I wrote a check for $500 and handed it to Frank as a deposit.

Frank shook my hand. "I'll contact the seller right away. Since it's a full price offer, I don't see any problems. Congratulations! You're now a Big Sur landowner!" I felt like it was a dream come true.

Later that evening I attended a party at a friend's house across the river from the River Inn Resort in the Big Sur valley. I was in a mood to celebrate, and the party seemed like a perfect venue. I parked my truck at River Inn, then walked over the bridge spanning the river and up to the house. I knew almost everyone at the party and fell right into the swing of things. After an hour and a half, I began to feel the slow creep and tingle of a psychedelic taking root in my body. Asking around, I learned from a giddy friend that the punch bowl had been laced with mescaline.

"Oh, perfect!" I laughed. "I've had two glasses!"

I stayed another fifteen minutes and then walked outside for some air. The night was cool and the colored lights from the River Inn reflected on the black water of the river running by. The lights of the restaurant looked inviting, and I decided to walk over and have some dinner. I studied the moving water and thought that instead of walking back to the bridge I would try to pick my way across it. I could see outlines of river rocks illuminated above the water's surface in the spill of the restaurant's lights. I started across.

I was doing fine until I slipped on a moss covered rock and gave a little jump to the side. Instead of landing in shallow water I landed in a deep hole and found the water around my waist. The water was ice cold. Unfazed and certainly buoyed by the mescaline, I continued to walk forward until I was walking up the riverbank on the other side toward the restaurant.

I stood outside the entry door and looked down at my legs. I was soaking wet with water puddling at my boots as I looked through a wide restaurant window placed next to the door. The dining room was a large open room built of massive logs supporting a high ceiling. There was a large stone fireplace with a fire burning at the far end. It looked warm and inviting.

I opened the door and walked in. The restaurant was half full of diners, and I got a few stares as I walked to one of the empty tables, leaving wet footprints behind me. After a few minutes of waiting, a tall, slender woman with green eyes and long brown hair walked up to me, looking with amusement at the puddle of water under my table. "You're all wet!" she said, suppressing a laugh. Then she looked at my cavernous eyes, which I'm sure lacked pupils, and said, "And that's not all!"

"Are you here for dinner?" She looked at me askance.

"Yes, and also to meet you, I think!" My words surprised me as much as her.

"Oh, boy…" She turned and I watched her walk away. Her slender body was graced with curves in all the right places. She returned shortly with a mop and pushed it around under the table.

"How did this happen?"

"I walked across the river."

"Why?" Her brow was arched, her eyes curious.

"Well, it was a straight line, the shortest distance from where I was standing. I wanted to have dinner, and I see now, to meet you." I smiled.

I couldn't stop staring at her.

"Stop it. I'll get you a menu." She turned and walked away again.

The menu was inviting, and I ordered without restraint, but when the food arrived, I could only eat a little bit here and there. I was just too stoned.

"Not so hungry?" the waitress asked in passing.

I reached out and stopped her. "I don't even know your name."

She looked down at me with the slightest smile. The top button of her blouse was open, exposing the rise of her breast. "Susie. And yours?"

"Wesley. Wesley Daggert. You know, Susie, you're incredibly lovely. You have very beautiful lines, like"—I looked around—"like that redwood tree outside."

She looked at the redwood tree growing straight and tall outside the large restaurant window. "Oh… Thanks a lot. I think."

A half hour later I stood with four to-go boxes in front of the fireplace, trying to dry off my pants. I imagined myself as a burger being flipped on a grill. Through more conversation I had learned that Susie's last name was Reynolds, that she lived up the coast with her boyfriend, and that they were building a cabin. It wasn't the best news to hear, but three times after moving to the fireplace I caught her looking at me. Once she almost smiled. It was enough to give me some hope. When I left I took a detour and paused beside her as she tallied someone's dinner bill.

"You're very beautiful, Susie. Thanks for dinner."

She looked into my eyes and nodded. "Nice to meet you, Wesley."

I awoke the next morning with a slight headache. I looked across my cabin to the kitchen where the four to-go boxes sat on the counter. I remembered walking through the river in the dark and meeting Susie.

"Oh, boy..." I said out loud. I knew I'd have to go see her again soon under more normal circumstances.

I got up, wrapped myself in a robe, and made some coffee. I took my first sip outside sitting at my picnic table on the deck. It was February 20, and the air above the canyon was brisk. I thought about my garden. March was the optimum month to start seeds. The plants needed about seven months to fully mature. You could start later, but the early bird growers were in the ground in March. I had bought promising seeds from another grower but still had all the garden prep work ahead of me. There was fertilizer to buy. Chicken manure came in thirty-pound bags and had to be hauled up to the garden. I was going to expand the site, dig more holes, and upgrade my irrigation to a drip system. It was time to start thinking about going back to war with the rats, setting the traps, and generally kicking the whole operation in the ass.

CHAPTER 10

"Opportunity knocks but once, unless you're lucky. Then it may just knock again, walk boldly in, and leave the door wide open."

–David Stafford

IT WAS FIVE DAYS LATER, and I had gotten home late from Nepenthe after a night of howling at the moon and counting stars. I was surfacing from a deep sleep, in the middle of rolling over, when my cabin door burst open and banged against the kitchen counter.

Kade Rudman stepped through the door. "Hey! Time to wake up!" he said.

I rolled out of bed. "Jesus, man, what's up?"

"I got something I want to talk to you about," he said.

"Yeah? We just talked yesterday. What's up?" I said, looking for my pants.

Kade was also working as a waiter at Nepenthe. We had worked together for about a year. He was of Moroccan descent, lean, about five foot ten, with short cropped hair and beard, and dark skin. He'd immigrated as a child with his parents from Morocco and spent his childhood in New Jersey. He was married and had a son and a daughter. He was not a close friend, and truth be known, I was not sure we could be close. The man was irritating as hell. He had this ability to stay calm and collected while being an obviously insensitive prick. We had bumped heads at work a couple of times. You could not ruffle his feathers or cause him bother. He had no conscience or awareness that your life was anything other than a comma in his compound sentence. His voice had a tight edginess to it.

"I don't know if you know, but I grew grass last year," he said.

"I never thought much about it." I was bent over, hopping on one leg while pulling on my pants. "So how did you do?" I pulled on my socks and walked over to the stove. "Coffee?"

"Sure." Kade pulled out a chair at the table. "I did good. I have a good place to grow, with some restrictions. Thing is, I want to grow more and can't do it where I'm at. I need to branch out. I need a partner. I worked my ass off last year and figure I can do a lot better with some help. You grew, right?"

"Yeah, I did pretty good. What are you thinking?" I asked.

"I'm thinking you and I could be partners in a new garden."

"Partners? I've got a patch; I'm doing fine," I said.

I joined Kade at the table while the coffee perked.

Kade looked out the window. "The two of us could do more," he said. "A lot more. We could grow a shitload."

"I don't know, man. We don't know much about each other, and I'm doing fine by myself." I walked back into the kitchen, got two cups down from the cupboard, and stared at the coffeepot.

"Well, you could do better. *We* could do better," Kade said.

"Why me?" I asked. "Why are you asking me? I'm not sure I even like you that much." I poured coffee into the two cups.

"Doesn't matter," Kade said. "I've watched you for a while, and you keep your mouth shut. That's important to me. I don't know how hard you work, I guess we'll find out, but I'm needing a partner, and I'm asking you."

I took a slug of coffee, handed Kade his, and nodded my head. "Well, I do have some potential sites around here. How would we split our money?" I asked.

"We share expenses, we split the money. We don't split the product. If you have a buyer, we split the proceeds. If I have a buyer, we split the proceeds. Everything is fifty-fifty. The only thing we split is money. The product belongs to both of us until we sell it." He was staring at me intently for an answer.

I was thinking. "I want to keep my own garden for myself," I finally said.

"Of course. I've got one too. Just no mingling, we keep our personal stuff separate." He tapped on the table.

"Okay. Let's give it a shot, Kade. When do you want to start?"

"Right now. Put your boots on and let's get going. March is around the corner. Let's go see some of these garden sites you mentioned." Even though things were happening a little faster than I wanted, I was intrigued. I finished getting dressed, and we set off.

We walked down Fuego Creek Road from my cabin and cut up the sidehill along my water line trail. Like most of the coast creek canyons, Fuego Creek Canyon was deep, cut narrow at the bottom nearer to the ocean with the water running over large boulders, and growing wider as you hiked toward the top. My water line lay right along the upper edge, snaking up the north-side canyon rim. The trail was steep when it left the road and then flattened out to a gentler rise as it traversed the side of the canyon, high above the creek. We walked about a half mile. The water line and the creek were coming closer together as we neared my water source, and finally we stepped into the creek bed itself.

The catch basin for my water system was a stainless steel kitchen sink dug into gravel beneath a small natural waterfall. The sink was covered with a stainless steel screen that served as a filter, and my water line was attached to where the drain would be in the sink bottom. Kade was looking up the creek at a large waterfall. "How far up do we still have water?" he asked.

"About a half mile farther up the canyon. It flattens out up there, and the Rummsen cattle use it for drinking and shade in summer. The Julian Fuego homestead has a water source up there too."

Kade was already walking. "Let's go," he said over his shoulder.

We climbed over the waterfall, traversing large boulders the size of cars. Here the canyon widened out into a flat, and we could see some cattle ahead, standing in the creek. There was a wide trail, large enough for a vehicle, leading away from the creek on the south side. Up ahead we saw a concrete box with pipe coming out of it. I pointed. "That's the catch basin for the Julian Fuego homestead."

Kade bent down and cupped some water, splashing it on his face, then stood back up. "We want to be higher than this; let's keep walking."

We walked past the cattle standing in the creek watching us for another hundred yards until the canyon became narrower again, finally coming to a choke of large stacked boulders, the creek gurgling out from underneath them.

I wiped some sweat from my forehead. "This is as far as I've been."

The canyon was completely canopied by redwoods, oaks and laurels growing up from the sides, and the air was damp and smelled of rotting leaves. Kade nodded his head toward the boulders. "Let's go higher."

In front of us, still under the redwood trees, the canyon formed a steep 'V' and was filled with large fallen boulders from rocky outcrops above. Thick brush grew out from the hillsides, weaving itself into a thick, seemingly impenetrable mesh. The easiest approach seemed to be straight up and over the boulders. Climbing the rocks was like climbing a ladder with the brush providing handholds. We broke through the brush as it receded up the hillsides and kept climbing, the water still murmuring below in the dark recesses of the rock. The large boulders thinned out into smaller rocks, and the canyon began to widen out again up ahead. We saw that the canyon forked into two narrow ravines, with water trickling out of both. We walked up the north side ravine for about 500 feet and stopped at a pile of rocks with a small cascade of water flowing over the top.

"This looks good for our water source. What do you think?" Kade asked.

I was catching my breath. "I think it's a pain-in-the-ass hike to get here."

Kade laughed. "Come on, man. You're just out of shape. If it's hard for us, it'll be hard for someone else to find it." He was smiling.

I looked around. We were standing on the north edge of Fuego Creek Canyon, well above the tops of the redwood trees. Above us the hillsides were covered in brush and green grass. "We have to stay on the north side of the canyon, or we're too close to the Julian homestead," I said.

From where we were standing, the ravine was narrow enough to almost touch both sides at once. We walked down a hundred feet or so to ensure some fall from the source and then started cutting up the west side. The going was rough because the hillside was overgrown with dense brush woven with poison oak growing steeply down into the canyon. Instead of making a trail, which would be visible from above, we tunneled through the brush, staying as high as we could while continuing to fall lower from our source. The tunneling process involved crawling through the brush, cutting or breaking branches, and stuffing them laterally under the brush to our sides, while at the same time being careful to leave some foliage over the top of us to hide the trail from above.

We made our way through the brush for about 200 feet until we reached a rock outcrop where we could climb out and gain some perspective.

"Shit!" I said, running my sleeve across my face, dripping with sweat. We were both bleeding from scratches on our face, hands, and arms, and it felt good to be out from under the brush. "Christ almighty. Well, at least we can see where we are."

We were high on the north edge of Fuego Canyon and could hear the water running far below us. Across from us were the tops of redwood trees growing up from the canyon. Turning back the way we'd come, we could see the narrow ravine where we planned to draw our water from. It climbed steeply with the mountain slope and lost itself about a half mile up. The south fork did the same. The skeleton stalks of last summer's yucca plants stood out like sentries on occasional ledges. Below us several hundred feet, toward the ocean, was a stand of oaks. The blue of the Pacific Ocean was visible above the trees.

"Let's head down to those oaks," Kade said, pointing.

We dropped back down into the brush and continued tunneling toward the oaks, finally breaking out just above them on an open rock-littered knoll. The stand of oaks was actually six large tan oak trees that sat on a narrow ridge. Facing south from the trees was the precipitous Fuego Creek Canyon, and behind the trees to the north was a shallow ravine that dropped down into brush. There was a pile of boulders above the trees, and we sat there surveying the site.

The brush, a combination of chamise, sage, manzanita, and poison oak, grew tight up to the tree line. The ground was clear directly beneath the oaks. The soil looked good, dark and loamy, a mulch of a hundred years of falling leaves and probable ash from past wildfires.

Kade waved his hand. "We could clear this brush back from the trees and terrace it down a ways. There's plenty of rock around to work with."

"We're wide open to the south here," I said. "The road to the Julian homestead is right up there in the trees." I pointed up to the south side of the Fuego Creek drainage. "We're sitting ducks."

We fell into silence for a few minutes sitting on the large rocks above the tan oaks. There was a warm breeze easing down the mountain rustling the leaves below us.

Then an idea came to me. There was an active military base that sprawled just east of the coast range mountains. The base was accessible by the only east-west road on the coast, Nacimiento-Fergusson Road. The base granted firewood permits to the general public, and I had been to the base several times in my truck to cut firewood.

The base was used for live fire practice for military regiments around the country. On two occasions I had passed tanks and artillery pieces set back into the trees covered in a camouflaged netting. The netting was woven with material in varying shades of flat green and made the equipment almost invisible. I turned to Kade and said, "Maybe we could get some of that camo netting they cover tanks with, stretch it up into the oak branches, and tuck it into the brush line. What do you think?"

"I've never heard of it. Where do you get it?" Kade was chewing on a stem of grass.

"Maybe army surplus stores. There're two in Monterey." I tossed a rock into the canyon abyss. "We can check 'em out."

"Let's drop down out of here along this ravine and find our way back. Maybe there's another place to grow," he said.

Kade stood, looking for a path over the boulders. We climbed down to the base of the trees and set off along the tree line. We walked for a quarter mile but didn't see anything with the same good sun exposure as where we had been sitting. It wasn't long after, beating downhill through the brush, that we came across my water line that led to the cabin.

"Civilization!" I laughed.

We followed the line back to my place and sat at the picnic table on the deck for a while drinking beer and talking about the new site we had just visited. Without the netting or some form of mitigation from prying eyes the site wouldn't work for our new garden.

Kade was looking out to sea. "I don't know anything about that netting. Maybe it's visible as hell. Maybe it won't blend in. I mean, does it really look like brush?"

"Only one way to find out," I said. "Let's go find some!"

CHAPTER 11

"Sometimes you can't see the forest because there's too many trees."

–Marisa Wilson

THE BAD FORD WAS PARKED in the driveway in front of the cabin and we jumped in, me behind the wheel, for the trip to Monterey. It was midafternoon, and the highway was mostly clear of traffic. There were two army surplus stores on the Peninsula, one in Seaside and the other on the way to Santa Cruz in Moss Landing. The one in Seaside would be our first stop. We covered the forty miles to Seaside in an hour and a half. The surplus store sat right on Del Monte Avenue where Broadway came in from upper Seaside and terminated. We parked in front.

Walking to the back of the store, we found piles of the camouflage nets lying on the floor. Random rubberized shapes in alternating shades of flat green and dark tan were woven throughout the netting.

The owner of the store walked over. "They're radar reflecting," he said with a smile.

I gave him a quick glance, thinking it was a curious remark. The bundles appeared to be different sizes and different prices, but nothing was more than seventy-five bucks. "Can we spread one out somewhere?" I asked. "I want to see how big they are."

"Sure," he said. "You can't do it in here though. Take 'em outside. There's some lawn across the street."

Kade and I carried this big ball of netting across Del Monte Boulevard in front of God and country and untangled it on the small patch of lawn opposite the surplus store. The small triangle of lawn served as a divider for two major streets and a left turn lane. We got it stretched out with Kade standing in the northbound lane of Del Monte and me in the westbound lane of Broadway, each holding a corner and pulling against the other. Cars were whizzing by with more than one driver laying heavy on the horn.

"This one's about thirty feet across," I called out.

A bit later we had the big one rolled up and the smaller one spread out.

"This one is a triangle shape. Maybe fifteen feet on a side!" Kade yelled. "It looks pretty good."

A delivery truck passed close, honking his horn.

"I like this shit. Let's buy it and get it down the coast," I shouted.

Kade agreed. We bought all the store had, both of us producing wads of cash at the register.

"We'll have to start a ledger for this stuff," he said.

I agreed.

We had three thirty-foot squares and three fifteen-foot triangles of netting rolled up in individual balls on the floor of the surplus store. We carried them out and loaded them into the pickup.

"We may as well buy the water line while we're here," Kade said. "The irrigation store is right over there." He pointed through the windshield toward a low single-story building across the intersection on a frontage street. It was surrounded by a high anchor fence with stacks of pipe behind it.

I looked across the cab at him. "You want to buy the pipe before we know if the netting works?"

"I think it works," he said writing on a piece of paper. "We can throw brush on it if it doesn't. We're going to need the pipe in any case, might as well get it."

We drove over, parked, and walked around to the back of the building where black poly pipe was stacked all across the back fence.

"How far do you think we are from the source?" I asked.

"At least 1,500 feet," Kade said.

"You want 500-foot rolls or hundreds?" I asked.

"You want to carry 500s up there or hundreds?" Kade squinted at me.

"I see your point," I was looking at the bulky 500-foot rolls. It was important to remember, and sometimes discouraging, that everything we bought for the garden would have to be carried up on our backs.

We paid cash for fifteen 100-foot rolls of three-quarter-inch poly pipe and a bag of assorted connectors, splitting the total amount down the middle. The truck was full, and we headed for home. On the way, I stopped at the gas station at Rio Road for a fill-up. We got out of the cab together. I started pumping gas, and Kade checked the load. A guy putting gas in his car asked Kade if we were landscapers.

Kade stared at the guy before answering. "Yeah, we're landscapers. Why? You need something planted?"

I was cracking up. We were dusty from head to toe with fresh scabs all over our arms and faces. We must have looked like we had just escaped from the gulag.

"No. I was just noticing all the pipe," the guy said, looking at the bed of the truck.

Kade turned his back on the man. "It's for moving water," he said over his shoulder.

Back on the highway I drove the truck south while Kade made notes on paper held in a clipboard. He looked up and turned, looking out at the ocean. "So this is our ledger. We can keep it in the truck. Today we each spent $276. We won't worry about loose change. I've got a couple of receipts at home to add to this for stuff we can use. Do you?"

I glanced over at him as a car passed me honking his horn. I honked back. "Not yet."

"Well, let's keep them together. When we get a receipt, we'll clip it to the board. This shit is going to add up."

A couple miles down the road Kade laughed. "This is a pretty good business for us. Neither one of us likes pot that much! We won't smoke the profits!"

Other than the work we were doing, I had never hung out with Kade socially. I had no idea he didn't smoke grass. I looked across at him in the truck. "You don't like it either? Probably makes things simpler."

He looked out his window at the passing scene. "Less distractions."

We both had to work the next two days at Nepenthe, but the day after that, we were back on the hill. We decided to raise the camo netting to give us some cover from the Julian Fuego homestead property above us to the south before doing anything else. I had gone back into town and purchased a few rolls of green parachute cord along with a few hand tools to use for hoisting the nets.

Kade showed up early at my cabin with two military packboards made of molded wood and laced with canvas shoulder straps. The packboards were laid flat on the ground and the load, in this case a bundle of netting, was placed and then lashed to the board. The board was then picked up by one of us and the other guy slipped under the shoulder straps. Once on, the packboards were remarkably balanced.

We decided to go up the way we had first come down because it was an easier route than walking up the creek and over the boulders. We would use this route to set up the garden and then close it off when we were done and create a more difficult path, one not so easy to follow, for watering the plants through the summer. The hike up to the garden carrying the nets was challenging. The netting caught on everything it touched, and I was clearly out of shape. In fact, I was thinking I had never been in the kind of shape required to work like a donkey carrying heavy loads up steep, unimproved trails. We arrived at the site and plopped over on our backs, red faced, leg muscles screaming, breathing hard.

I slipped my arms out of the packboard and sat up. "Shit!" I exclaimed, expelling the breath from my lungs.

Kade was already untying his load and looked over at me. "Come on. Let's go. We've got to get the rest of it!"

The man was a slave driver.

The hike back to the cabin served as our rest. Once there, we repacked the boards and set off again up the hill. The second trip up was more difficult than the first. My legs were shaking when I stood up for the return trip. We made four trips up, getting all the nets and two rolls of pipe to the garden site, stashing everything under the oaks. During the fourth trip, I had tapped into a place inside that can only be described as pure determination in order to keep placing one foot in front of the other and will my legs up the hill.

Over the next few days, when we weren't working at Nepenthe, we were hauling pipe up the hill. A 100-foot roll of three-quarter-inch poly pipe fit crossways on the torso like a bandolier, hanging from one shoulder across the body. They carried pretty well, and in three days' work we had everything on site for the water system and raising the nets.

The nets caught on everything they touched. Spreading them over the brush was not an option, as we would never unstick them from all the prickly protrusions, so we decided to clear the brush from the garden site first and then raise the nets. The challenge was not being seen from the road to the Julian Fuego homestead during the process.

We were each leaning against an oak in the shade above the garden site when Kade came up with a plan. "We'll crawl around and saw the brush off at the ground, but leave the brush standing in place," he said. "Then late in the day, at sunset, we'll throw all the brush off to the sides. Next morning, at first light, we raise the nets." He was looking at me for approval.

"Sounds good," I said, looking around. "Maybe we should set up the parachute cord, have it hanging in advance to save time."

He just shrugged and stood up. "Let's get at it."

We crawled around under the brush with limb saws cutting everything off at the base. By late afternoon, we had the site ready to clear. The parachute cord was in fifty-foot lengths, and we tied one end to a hammer and held the rest in a loose coil. Tossing the hammer over limbs on the oak trees carried the cord with it, and soon we had cords hanging from strategic limbs, ready to hoist the nets. At sunset, we started tossing brush away from the garden site on three sides. By dark, we had a clearing thirty feet wide and seventy-five feet long. We walked back to the cabin under moonlight.

The next morning, Kade arrived at my cabin at five AM. We walked up to the garden in the dim gray light of predawn, rolled out a thirty-foot net, and spread it out in the clearing. It caught on everything. It was maddening. We tied two hanging cords to two corners of the net, choosing two cords that would stretch the corners tight, and started pulling the net into the air. This comedy involved one guy pulling the cords and one guy running around freeing the net from brush stumps and sticks. After a while, and much cussing, we had the net hanging from the tree. We then each grabbed a corner and pulled the net across the clearing, attaching it with cord to the uncut brush line.

We had two nets up by a half hour after dawn, and the rest except two of the smaller triangles up by nine. It looked amazing. We tweaked it for hours, pulling it here, stretching it there, tying them together here and there, until it was tucked up under the oaks and tied down to the brush line. We had a ceiling of about ten feet in most places and more like fifteen at the tree line. In areas where we needed more headroom, we cut saplings and used them as poles to prop the netting up. We were now walking under a large camouflage tent and free to work without being seen.

The next morning, we walked up to the top of south Fuego Creek, to just below the Julian Fuego homestead road, and sat hidden in the brush, looking across the canyon at our camouflaged garden site.

"It looks good," I said. "I mean, if you look right at it, you can see it's a different texture, but it blends with the brush and the tree line pretty good!"

"We need to cover up the top part of the garden over there," Kade pointed, "and we're going to have to work quietly. I can hear birds chirping from under the nets. Sound carries."

"And shovels hitting rocks," I said absently. "Hopefully no one ever stops here and listens."

Kade had to work at the restaurant that afternoon, so I took the rest of the day off myself. I drove down to Nepenthe where I ran into Luca Renzo sitting outside on the terrace. I sat down next to him as he sipped his drink. I nudged his shoulder. "How's it goin', Luca?"

"Hey, Wesley! Good to see you on this side of the bar. I was just leavin'!"

"Where you off to?"

He downed the rest of his drink. "I thought I'd stop by the River Inn on the way back into town, see what's up there."

I thought of Susie. "I'll meet you there."

I followed Luca through the Big Sur valley, and we parked in front of the River Inn, me next to a white Volkswagen bug.

Inside the restaurant, we were walking to the bar when I saw Susie come out of the kitchen carrying a tray of food. I turned to Luca and said, "I'll be right there."

He followed my gaze. "Got it."

Susie set the food down and walked up to me.

"So we meet again," she said, and dipped her eyes.

"Hi, Susie, how's your day?" I smiled.

She turned, waving to acknowledge a table. "I've had better. Look, I'm busy now, you going to be around for a while?"

"I'm with a friend at the bar, so yeah."

"Maybe I'll have a minute later." She turned and walked over to the table.

I sat next to Luca at the bar and ordered a tequila tonic. Susie walked quickly by and flashed me a smile.

Luca put his glass down. "Woah. Who's that?"

"Her name is Susie Reynolds. I met her here a while back. I like her, but she's got a boyfriend."

"Well, judging from that last smile, he may be in trouble!"

I raised my glass in a toast and smiled. "I saw that."

A while later after Luca had left for town I was outside sitting on a rock by the river, nursing the rest of my drink.

Susie walked across the lawn and sat down next to me.

"I'm off early, I have to get home, but I've got a minute."

"What's the hurry, is your boyfriend waiting for you?

She pulled some grass from the lawn. "No. We broke up."

I snapped my head to look right at her. "Really? I'm sorry to hear that…I mean, not really, but I hope you're okay."

"I'm fine. It's been coming for a long time. It's his loss."

We sat on the lawn and talked for the next fifteen minutes. I learned about her relationship and her dissatisfaction with it. I told her about my cabin and working at Nepenthe. It was clear there was an attraction between us, and I invited her for a trip down the coast to see my cabin on one of her days off. She said she would like that and stood up to leave.

I looked up at her. "I'm looking forward to seeing you again soon, Susie."

"Me too, Wesley." She turned and walked away.

On the drive home I stopped in at the Fernwood gas station. I was filling my tank when Officer Eddie Krebs pulled in to gas his CHP cruiser. He got out of his car and said in a loud voice, "Mr. Daggert! I think you're going to jail." He walked toward me and added, "Stick out your hands, I'll have to cuff you!"

This took me by surprise, and I took a step back. "What are you talking about, Eddie?"

Officer Krebs smiled widely. "Why, you look a little nervous, Daggert. Everything okay with you?"

"Yeah, sure," I looked away, "I don't often get threatened with arrest when I'm getting gas is all."

Officer Krebs put his hands on his gun belt. "Wesley, if you're not guilty, don't worry about it. You sure you're okay? I'm starting to worry about you."

I replaced my nozzle on the pump. "Yeah, I'm all right. You just caught me off guard. Thought maybe I had an outstanding parking ticket or something."

Officer Krebs smiled wide again. "Just keeping you on your toes, Daggert. You be careful."

CHAPTER 12

"We have to stay ahead of everybody in our thoughts and in our actions."

–Kade Rudman

KADE AND I WERE BOTH at work the following day, Wednesday. Kade was waiting tables while I was bartending. He was standing in the service area, talking to me across the bar about setting up the water system.

"We're going to be visible for about fifteen feet between the garden and the brush line at the top. The black pipe coils are going stand out. Anyone seeing them will know what we're doing. Somebody spots us, we're busted. I think we should set up the line from the source to the garden before dawn or after sunset to avoid being seen."

I handed a lime wedge to another waiter and turned back to Kade. "All right by me, I don't relish crawling around in the brush in the heat of the day anyway."

"You don't have enough desert blood in you," Kade quipped. He turned and walked away.

We both worked as waiters the next day. I got off early and waited for Kade to finish his tables. At 3:30 he followed me up to my cabin, and we walked up to the garden. As the sun went behind the oaks on its journey to the sea, we each grabbed a pipe coil and headed into the brush tunnel. We crawled all the way back to the source, rolling the pipe along like a tire as much as possible, breaking off branches to make room for the coils when necessary. After several trips, we had the pipe coils staggered every hundred feet along the trail and called it quits for the evening.

While we were preparing the garden site, we had painted a five-gallon bucket flat black and attached a three-quarter-inch PVC nipple to the bottom side of the can to serve as the catch basin. The next morning, we carried the black bucket to the water source and began laying pipe. We secured one end of the pipe coil at the water source with large rocks and began unrolling it toward the garden, working carefully so as not to crimp it. It was a two-man job, bringing coiled pipe ends together inside the brush tunnel. When we reached the end of a coil, we brought the next coil into position, attached the connector with hose clamps, and continued to unroll that coil of pipe. This was continued until the water line stretched from the source to the garden. Incredibly, at the end, there were only twenty feet of pipe to spare. Kade's estimate had proved to be accurate.

We set some big rocks on the garden end of the pipe to secure it in place and crawled back to the source, where we attached the pipe to the bucket nipple and placed the bucket under the small waterfall. After weighting the bucket down with a rock and placing stones around it, we placed a piece of screen over the top of the bucket and secured it with wire. Our water source was installed! When we got back to the garden, the water was already flowing. We gave ourselves a slap on the back, then attached a faucet to the end of the pipe and shut it off.

Two days later I met Susie at the River Inn. She was with her dog, a big husky she called Thor. She followed me down the coast to my cabin. We had a nice afternoon walking and talking around the property, and I made her a late lunch that we ate sitting out on the deck. I learned she had grown up poor in a broken family and had been on her own since she was fourteen. She had moved to Big Sur with her boyfriend only to discover they had totally different values. We watched the sun go down in a fiery display while sipping wine, and hours later watched it rise again while holding each other beneath the blankets of my bed. Our being together seemed natural, and we held each other tightly. Her dog Thor just lay on the cabin floor, his eyes closed, his chin resting on his paws.

Before getting out of bed we were lying still, staring at the ceiling. I looked at her. "You know, if we got married my name would be Wesley Reynolds."

She poked me in the ribs. "You're getting *way* ahead of yourself, buckaroo!"

Over the course of the next week, Kade and I dug our holes in the garden. The area we had chosen turned out to be full of rocks, and as we uncovered them, we used the rocks to support terraces down the natural slope of the land, seven in all, each about twenty feet long and ten feet wide. All were beneath the camouflage canopy. The terraces stepped down the steep terrain like a mini Machu Picchu.

A few days later we returned to Monterey with the truck and bought fifty bags of chicken shit, other assorted fertilizers, and 100 feet of five-foot fence wire with green metal posts. On the way home, as we passed the River Inn, I saw Susie getting out of a white Volkswagen bug in front of the restaurant but couldn't stop. I continued on to my cabin where we off-loaded all the supplies. They were ready to be carried up the hill over the next several trips to the garden.

The day shift for waiters and bartenders at Nepenthe restaurant started at 9:30 AM, two hours before opening. The cooks came in earlier to start the food prep for the day. Waiters would fill the ketchup and mustards, and wipe their tables clean, while the bartenders hauled ice to the bar and cut up fruit for cocktail garnish. One morning at Nepenthe, before our shift started, Kade said he wanted to show me something. He led me out back to the lettuce cage, where the heads of lettuce were chopped in preparation for the day's salad making. Outside the cage was a stack of #10 cans that had once contained kidney and garbanzo beans used in the signature bean salad mix served at lunch and dinner.

"What am I looking at?" I asked.

"Bean cans," he said. "We cut the bottoms off and put them around our starts so the bugs can't get them."

I looked at Kade with a frown. It was true, the starts were vulnerable when they were young, easily attacked by rats, sow bugs, mealybugs, earwigs, and everything else. A couple of bites and they were dead. But I was thinking the cans made a bulky load to hike up to the garden. He must have read my mind.

"We smash them. The cans are just gonna be tossed anyway," he said. "We tell them we have a use for them and haul them away. Before we take them, we use their commercial can opener, cut off the bottoms, and then smash them flat. They'll stack great for hauling up the hill, and it won't take much to pull them back to a round shape."

It seemed like a good idea, and Nepenthe was glad to have someone removing all the cans, though there were some questions about what our purpose was. "Fireproof siding for my barn," was one answer I used. Kade's was that he was selling them as weight to a recycle company, which was plausible enough, but that encouraged others to start grabbing them too. We still managed to get enough bean cans to encircle all the marijuana starts in all our gardens.

For a week in late March we carried the bags of chicken manure up to the new garden. I called them the "chicken-shit marches." Kade seemed to relish placing two thirty-pound bags of shit on my packboard and watching me struggle up the hill.

"You're a donkey," he would say as he held the packboard for me to slip my arms through the shoulder straps. "An out-of-shape donkey at that!"

I would help him into his packboard, and we would stand there hunched over, leaning forward, shifting the weight for comfort and balance. Once underway, the bags would sometimes get punctured by branches along the trail, enabling the chicken shit to slide under my collar and to the small of my back, where it would sit in a damp clump before the jostling enabled it to slide in small increments down my pant leg.

The supply trail was fairly open, but it had a couple of sections that were steep and precariously close to the canyons edge. The sixty-pound loads were cumbersome, and we were easily thrown off balance. We would occasionally slip and fall flat on our faces against the steep hill and have to push our way back to a standing position to continue our climb. If you fell backward or off to the side, you might roll for a while. Roots and branches were used as hand holds to pull ourselves up. We were getting in phenomenal shape. My legs and arms were tighter, the loads seemed lighter, and we rested for shorter periods of time.

Looking back on those days, we were close to the ground like animals are, oblivious to ticks and ants or spiders. We were filthy all day, with splotches of poison oak here and there among the ever-present scabs of congealed cuts, nicks, and scratches. Our faces and arms were dark from the sun, and our vision and hearing were keen, attuned to the wild setting we were in. We spoke little, knew what our goals were, and got them done.

Our garden under the nets was located below a huge rockslide area that covered the mountainside above us. If you could focus in on our garden and then pan back, you would see that we were toward the bottom of a monumental natural rockfall. On the topo map it was called the 'Devil's Quarry.' The rocks and boulders running up to the crest of the mountain were a perfect environment for rattlesnakes, so we had to be watching constantly. Actually, we didn't so much watch for rattlers as we 'expected' them, and that small distinction gave us the edge we needed to avoid being bitten.

It was March 27, and we were set up. The bags of chicken shit were stacked, the garden was fenced to the brush line, the water was in, and the starts were ready to be carried up the hill. We were ready to plant.

CHAPTER 13

"Killing for survival is tolerated by the gods. Killing out of greed is not."

–Wesley Daggert

WE CARRIED THE STARTS IN their peat moss cups up the hill in groups of twenty four, wedged tightly in square plastic garden flats we held out in front of us like tribal offerings. We walked like bridesmaids, slowly and deliberately, careful not to spill our precious cargo on the steep trail. The flattened bean cans were strapped to our packboards. In my mind, I could imagine the slow rhythmic cadence of a thousand pious, chanting slaves hiking to work at the pyramids. But then, I was pretty tired, and my mind easily wandered on those walks. It took us each four trips to get all the starts and cans to the garden.

The planting was quick and easy, fun actually, as the hard work was done, and the future ladies were going into the ground! We broadcast a time-release, high-nitrogen fertilizer over the flat terraces just before planting. We dug 150 holes and mixed chicken manure, blood meal, and bonemeal into each hole, making the soil dark and stinky. Where it made sense, we planted two starts per hole, a strategy designed to maximize the female count after declaration season. Around each pair of starts, we placed a bean can, twisting it into the soft soil just below the surface. We worked wet, meaning the water was running the whole time so we could craft canals beside each set of starts, directing the water back and forth and then from one terrace to the other. We let gravity do the work until we had a slow-moving mini-river flowing through the entire garden.

Our bait traps for the rats had been set for weeks, with the poison being consumed voraciously. We loaded them up with fresh poison. The last thing we did was scatter sow bug pellets around the cans. The little munchers came out at night and seemed to love the poison more than the plants.

Aside from our own personal gardens needing a bit more work, we were planted. We were "in the ground," in our own vernacular, and it felt great. We covered up the supply route to the garden with dead brush and branches, plugging the trail for about twenty feet and removing any sign of our passage. From here on out, we would use a much more difficult and lengthy trail, also well camouflaged with brush, to reach the garden.

We watered every day at first, each of us taking an alternating day. We wanted to visit the gardens daily to check on the progress of the delicate starts and ensure the water source stayed consistent. In areas under the canopy where it was too dark, we removed some of the camo material to let in additional light.

I had been working in the evenings and early mornings on my own personal garden, finding time whenever I could to keep it coming along. The plants were a deep green and were looking vibrant. It wasn't visible from anywhere except the sky until you came right upon it. Hidden behind a large stand of ceanothus, it enjoyed a spectacular ocean view and was a pleasure to work in. I had expanded my planting to forty holes, but that was about all the protected space I had. With two starts to a hole, I was hopeful for a larger harvest than the preceding year.

As the plants grew taller and started to bush out, Kade and I changed our watering schedule to every two days for the shared garden. Nepenthe was getting seasonally busy, so we were working there more. Everything was going smoothly; the plants were thriving, and we were in a holding pattern while waiting for the declaration period.

It happened in my personal garden first. Being in full sunlight, my plants' growth was more advanced than the shared garden under the nets. I was checking the plants one afternoon, and there it was, a white V sticking out from a nodule. A female! Other plants had what looked like balls, but it was too soon to tell. The next month was spent identifying males and pulling them out. A few hermaphrodite branches were found and surgically removed. The pulled males were carried away, stacked, and covered with a tarp to prevent the errant spread of pollen. The females were pushing huge buds into the air, searching for pollination. There was no pollen to be found, and the growth continued.

The water source faltered once during this period, drying up enough that our little waterfall wouldn't fall into our catch basin. We went below the source about twenty feet and dug a hole where we found water and repositioned our catch basin. It worked, but the flow was reduced to a trickle, too little to water the garden all at once. Our solution was to set up an inflatable kiddy pool at the garden's upper edge and let the water trickle into it. We covered it with black plastic and then cut brush. When the pool filled, the excess overflow was directed into our garden canals.

One day while looking for males, I looked straight down at my boots and saw a huge rattlesnake stretched out in the moist ground under the plants. It was as big around as the business end of a baseball bat and had a slightly greenish tint to its scales. Fortunately for me, it was lethargic from the cool water, so I had a chance to step back. I dispatched him with a shovel and added his skin to my collection.

In the four years I lived at the Apple Tree House, I killed thirty-four rattlesnakes. It was just part of life there. I skinned them, leaving the rattles intact, poured salt on the moist side, and stretched them tight on a flat board, fastening them down with small brad nails. After a few days in the sun, they were dry, and I hung the skins on my walls. I made a few hatbands with them, stitching the skin around a length of leather strap, leaving the rattles hanging at the front over the seam. A few I sold through the gift store at Nepenthe, but most I just gave away to friends. I never felt bad about killing the rattlers—there were just too many of them near the cabin and gardens. They were dangerous. That being said, there was one killing near the garden I've always regretted.

The summer was hot, broken by cycles of fog, and the plants thrived. Susie and I were seeing as much of each other as we could. I would visit her at night when she worked, and many times she would follow me home. Most of my off days from work were spent in the gardens. The plants in my own garden were monsters, enjoying full sunlight, and in our common garden under the netting, they were doing almost as well. Where more sunlight was needed, material from the netting was strategically torn down. Where we needed more cover, we tossed cut brush up onto the netting. Our common garden was pretty much invisible from my cabin's deck, but if you knew where to look, you could see just a corner of it emerging from under the oaks.

One day while sitting on my deck, I looked up and saw a deer at the edge of the garden. I got my binoculars and brought him into focus. It was a young four-point buck, and he was nibbling at the pot. I immediately hiked up to the garden, finding the young buck still standing there at the fence line. I walked toward him, waving my arms and whisper-yelling at him to get away. He retreated about twenty yards up the hill, stopped, and looked back at me. I picked up a rock and threw it at him. "Get out of here!" I said as loud as I dared. "Beat it!" I tossed another rock, and he retreated a few more feet and stopped, turned, and stared at me. I looked right at him and said aloud, "If you eat any more pot, I'll come back up here and kill you!" We stared, eyes locked, for several moments, and then I left and walked back to the cabin.

Back on the deck, I picked up the binoculars and brought them to bear on the deer. He was slowly walking back toward the garden. My heart sank but I felt committed. I grabbed my .308 rifle, checked the magazine, and hiked back up to the garden. The buck was standing fifty feet from me with his head just above the garden fence. He stood there, ears focused forward, looking at me curiously as I raised the rifle, pointed it at his head, and pulled the trigger. His head jerked sharply with the report of the rifle, and his legs buckled. He fell straight down and slipped into the ravine behind the garden, gliding on fallen leaves. The shot still echoed off the mountain as I walked down to where he was lying. Many things were flashing through my mind. I couldn't just leave him. I couldn't waste the meat. I had to work at Nepenthe that night and didn't have much time. I tried dragging him down the hill, but he was too heavy. He must have weighed close to 150 pounds.

Strangely, a few days earlier at Fernwood's bar, I had sat talking with a man I didn't know about field dressing wild boar after a hunt. It was an odd conversation for me to have, as I had never been much of a hunter. The guy seemed knowledgeable and was full of very specific information about skinning animals, the proper knives to use, and the cuts to make. Somehow the conversation got around to skinning a deer, and the do's and don'ts of that procedure. I'd soaked up as much as I could of the conversation, and it was still fresh in my mind.

I removed my Buck knife from its pouch and slit his belly open, careful to avoid his bladder. His organs were steaming, and I reached in and pulled them out, cutting where I needed to. I was bloody to my shoulders. Soon he lay open and empty, and I dragged him down the hill to the road. I walked up to my cabin, got my truck, drove down, and wrestled him into the bed. At the cabin, I unloaded him in my driveway above the shop, dragging him to a point beneath an oak branch. I didn't have a pulley, so I threw a rope over the branch, tied it around his hind legs, and tried pulling him up off the ground. He was too heavy, there was too much friction on the rope, and I couldn't get him off the ground. I dragged him down to my deck and moved the table aside. I got a hacksaw and a hatchet from the shop and went to work dressing out the deer.

Finding an old sheet, I wrapped the butchered venison up and placed the bundle in the back of my truck. I would take the meat to work with me and see if I could borrow some space inside Nepenthe's walk-in freezer. What was left of the deer I dragged over to the cliff and tossed it over. Looking at my watch, I realized I was out of time. I showered and drove to Nepenthe with the venison.

I explained to the supervisor that I had killed a deer at my cabin and had run out of time to finish the packaging. She was sympathetic and let me bring the meat into the downstairs kitchen to finish the job. She said she would cover my section in the restaurant until I was finished. I washed the meat in warm vinegar water on a prep table, made some final cuts, and wrapped each piece in white butcher paper. I kept thinking this proud animal had been walking the hills above my cabin just a few hours before.

After labeling the cuts on the butcher paper, I placed the pieces into three cardboard boxes with my name on them and placed them into the large walk-in freezer behind the restaurant.

Later that night, after finishing my shift and driving home, I was outside my cabin with a flashlight, looking at the deck where I had butchered the buck. It looked like there had been a gruesome murder there. The boards were stained with blood splatter, and the saw and hatchet were still lying where I had dropped them.

I went inside and lit the oil lamps, feeling really bad, like I had done something very wrong. I felt a little spooked, like hidden eyes were watching me from the darker recesses of the cabin. I lit a joint and settled back in my big easy chair, thinking about the buck...how stately he had looked...how proud and unafraid. I closed my eyes and massaged my forehead, remembering the buck looking right back at me as I raised the rifle, looked down the sights to his head, and pulled the trigger. At that very moment, a large plant hanging from my loft in a ceramic pot broke through its macramé harness and fell three feet to the kitchen counter, exploding on the edge of the sink into a hundred pieces. The loud crash made me jump and my eyes popped open, my blood suddenly running cold. I felt like I was in the presence of a higher entity, and the entity was very pissed.

I felt judged and found guilty on all counts of a great crime, as though I had killed the prince of another species in cold blood and was in deep trouble for it. I don't know if it was the grass I had smoked. I sat there shaking in the golden lamp light. I said I was sorry out loud, and swore if I was given another chance, I would never kill another deer again. I meant it too. The coincidence of the falling plant was too strange, too timely, too violent, to ignore. I had the chills when I crawled into bed that night and was actually surprised when I woke up the next morning. I felt as though I had been granted a reprieve.

CHAPTER 14

"If you can't handle the toils of spring and the heat of summer, there'll be nothing for you to harvest in the fall and nothing to smoke in the winter."

–Donald Macinlay

BY EARLY OCTOBER WE WERE looking forward to an incredible harvest. I was standing in my personal garden watering and picking sun leaves, the large leaves with the classic marijuana shape that could block precious sunlight to the plant's interior. The day was clear and hot, and the Pacific Ocean looked like a placid lake. I was standing in a jungle of seven-foot-tall pot plants, inspecting them one by one, when I heard the sound of a plane. At first, it was just a distant hum off to the north, and then a hum with varying pitches, like the plane was turning, maybe sightseeing along the coast. The sound grew louder until a single engine Cessna emerged over the ridge to the north, heading straight toward my cabin.

I was transfixed. I watched as the plane flew low over my cabin and then increased power in a steep turn toward the ocean. It turned out to sea and then began a wide turn that brought it back toward my position. Instinctively, I ducked in close to one of my tall plants and watched as the plane approached and then banked east into a circle around my cabin. It took two turns and then flew up Juan Fuego Creek, over the common garden I had with Kade, then turned south, over the Julian Fuego homestead and out of sight.

I stood there dumbstruck, knowing I had been spotted. I could hear the plane circling farther south over some other property of interest and had an ill foreboding. I didn't know it then, but I had just seen the first flyover by the Monterey County sheriff searching for marijuana.

Through the years up until that point growing pot on the coast had progressed pretty much without consequence. I had heard from the few people I knew who grew grass that a safe place to grow and sealed lips were the main ingredients to a successful crop of marijuana. A person hid their plants from prying eyes and kept their mouth shut. Up until that day, there had been no active air searches, no airplanes sweeping over the ridge tops with spotters leaning out of the windows with binoculars or cameras trying to spot pot gardens.

In fact, in the early seventies, there was an annual Harvest Party held high on a ridge on the south coast by a legendary man named Donald Macinlay. Macinlay was well known on the south coast as a no bullshit, Katy-Bar-the-Door, can-do mountain man. Bigger than life and a legend in his own time, he was a big-time grower who, on his lofty mountain top, began having Coast Parties that celebrated the marijuana harvest. I had been to two of them, as the invitation was open, though not all were welcome.

My first was in 1970, when I drove my International panel truck up there. My truck was, at that time, also my home, and as I barreled up the hill to his cabin, I was met by a man standing in the road holding a rifle. I stopped and leaned out my window.

"What are you doing here?" he asked.

"I'm here for the Harvest Party," I said.

He waved his hand up the road. "Go ahead."

I continued on. Soon there were two other guys standing in the road. I could see a cabin through the trees above to my left, and they waved me up a steep incline like they were parking cars at a concert. About halfway up the incline, my tires spun out, and I backed down.

"Get a run at it!" one of the guys yelled.

I backed the truck up, put it in gear, and floored it up the grade, my tires spinning and throwing gravel. Suddenly, I was launching over the top, into a field packed with cars, and could hear someone cheering. I found a level place to park amid all the other cars and got out.

There was someone singing on a ramshackle stage below the parking area, playing electric guitar. I could hear a generator running in the background. Scanning the area, I could see children playing; women, some bare breasted, walking and talking; and a large fire burning with men standing in brimmed hats, holding beers and smoking. It was a colorful scene of costume dress that defined local attire in those days. Set back into a tree line was a rustic cabin, its door hooked open and people wandering in and out.

I set out to take a look and walked by a group of men passing a joint around in a circle, recognizing a guy from the north coast who gave me a smoky nod and a grin. Stepping up on the cabin's porch, I could see a long family table built of big wooden planks and a woman dressed in shades of gray and brown busily shifting pots on a large woodburning cook stove. On the table was a kerosene lantern, a large bowl of the biggest hand-rolled marijuana cigars I'd ever seen, several bowls of salad, and a gallon jug of clear liquid with a scattering of small jars.

A tall man brushed past me in the doorway, then turned to check me out. He was wearing boots, Levi's, and a purple shirt beneath a multicolored vest. His beard was bushy, streaked with gray, and his eyes shown bright blue. His hair was long and held back with a red scarf.

He extended his hand, saying, "Donald Macinlay."

"Wesley," I replied, shaking his hand.

He pointed to the table. "Welcome. Help yourself to some smoke. There'll be some pig later." He grabbed the jug off the table and poured some in a small jar. "House brew," he said, then hammered it back with a throw of his head. "Help yourself to what you want." He turned to the woman working at the stove. "Pig's ready at five, Mama. Betty Sue and Trina are comin' down to help out. I gotta bring in some wood. Some asshole is off the road down the hill, and I may have to pull him out. I got Dennis on it." He spun and walked out the door.

I poured myself two fingers of the house brew and sniffed. It would peel paint. I threw it back. It was hot and seared my throat. There was an involuntary shudder. I looked at the cigars but left them where they lay. There was no way I could have smoked that much grass. At the door, I reconsidered, turned around, and pulled a stogie from the bowl. I caught the eye of the woman at the stove and said, "Thank you," then turned and walked out the door.

A flute player and a conga drum had joined the lone guitar on the stage, and a rhythmic melody line filled the air. People were spinning and dancing in the dusty smoke beside the fire. I made my way to a spread of lawn with a small pond in the center of it. Sitting there, I could see the gathering spread out in front of me and searched the crowd for familiar faces.

There were the Luszon brothers, two dapper characters from Boston who had moved to the coast together. They had arms around the waists of two women dressed in boots and western dresses, both politely involved in smiling conversation. Rabo, an ex-carney, was standing before a group of people, leaning back with his face to the sky, balancing a huge Bowie knife on the tip of his nose. A group of young girls holding hands in ribbon-laced dresses were running and laughing barefoot through the crowd, being chased by a scattering of young boys carrying sticks and mischief. There were huddles of people blowing smoke and passing pipes, laughing in splendid stupors, and a few lone outcasts who were well overdone, lying alone in the outgrown grasses. Army Jack, who had relieved me after I saved the Curtis house from burning during the Buck Eye fire, was sitting on a tree stump. Frank LaPont and the Wilson sisters, two lovely siblings from Big Sur who were also known in Carmel, stood near the fire. Frank, himself a classic character in pleated slacks, a large mustache, and a flair for the wild, had fathered a large family and owned a storied past of whiskey, women, and disregard for fuck-all. He had his arm around Marisa, one of the sisters. Saul Smith, a dark-skinned Spaniard who lived out of his VW van and preyed on beguiled women, was holding court under a shade tree. Crazy Paul from Worcestershire, Massachusetts, who killed spiders in his cabin with a shotgun and was known to peek through windows with a leering smile, was setting up his tent beside his car.

I struck a match against the breeze, palmed it, and lit the green stogie. I inhaled deeply and then immediately tapped it out against the earth as the world began to morph into more vibrant hues. Another conga had joined the stage and a geyser of sparks rose into the sky as someone tossed more wood on the fire. I stuck the stogie into my shirt pocket and stood up just as a high pitched zaghareet heralded the twirling entrance of two barefoot belly dancers to the stage. A tabla player joined the group, as did the steady beat of a cowbell.

I walked up to my truck and turned around to survey the party scene below. The sun was low over the purple ocean, casting golds and reds that silhouetted the tree line, bathing the scene in warm Gracelight. The cabin, with soft yellow light spilling from its windows, sat serenely and apart from the large bonfire illuminating the people dancing. The stage was full of musicians and costumed dancers whirling in front of them. Off to the right, men stood around the grill watching a pig on a spit slowly turning, the pall of smoke settling over a swelling crowd and a hundred parked cars.

A group of people was standing two cars over from my van as the sun was setting. One of the men was pointing at the horizon and everyone looked transfixed. I joined them.

"We're looking for the green flash!" a topless girl said to me as I joined them.

I looked at her. "Green flash?"

The man who had been pointing spoke without looking away from the sun. "Yeah. Sometimes just after the sun sets below the ocean there's a green flash. Kind of like a green flash bulb going off. Not always, just sometimes."

I joined the group in staring directly at the orange setting sun, which was now halfway below the horizon. We followed it until it was just a burning dot of light resting on the horizon. As it blinked out the ocean seemed to turn a deeper blue, and then there was a flash of green light that lasted just a fraction of a second.

"Oh!" someone gasped.

"I saw it!" the girl said, pointing.

"That was it!" The man turned to the people gathered behind him. "We saw it! That doesn't happen very often."

I was impressed. I had seen the green flash on my first attempt! I left the excited group and returned to my van, seeing spots of light in my eyes from staring into the sun. I opened the twin rear doors and converted my day couch into my bed before the golden hour of sunset gave way to dark. I drank some water, watching the crowd grow around the grill, and at the sound of cheering from the grill area, I walked down the hill to eat.

A plethora of salads, fruits, and cheeses were laid out on wooden planks that rested on sawhorses, awaiting the arrival of the pork being sliced and pulled from the pig that was still skewered above the grill. I waited in a line that stretched for a hundred feet as the mountains above the party turned purple and gold with the setting sun. Twenty minutes later, with a plate of food in hand, I made my way back to the patch of lawn and sat down to eat.

Not far away was a ceramic crock that had a small spout at its bottom sitting on a tree stump. Occasionally someone would bend over, grab a cup, and pour from the spout. I set my plate down, walked over to the crock, and read the label, 'Rotta Organic Red Wine, Templeton.' I poured some into a cup and returned to my plate on the grass. The wine was good, rather sweet, and complemented the food nicely.

On the stage, I could see some familiar faces setting up instruments. It was a group of local musicians that called themselves "Big Sur Light and Power," a wildly popular homegrown band with a subculture all their own, featuring the steady rhythm of several sets of conga drums, a classic trap set, a complement of guitars, and a flute. Led by Colin Bishop, a tall man with red hair, dressed in white, and the more edgy Kidd Arcola, they took over the night. The slaps of a lone conga began pulsing through the air, the rhythm starting heads to nod; it was soon joined by a second pair of drums. A shrill zaghareet filled the air, and more people joined the dancing close to the fire. Musicians began moving on the stage. Someone sat behind the trap set, pulling out drumsticks, sliding into a snare to base drum roll into a steady skip beat on a large cymbal. Another set of congas joined in, and someone strummed an electric guitar, producing a loud screech of feedback that set off whoops from the crowd. Bishop crossed the stage nodding his head and began playing a silver flute as the crowd erupted in a cheer. The only light besides the full moon came from the oil lamps in the cabin, the bonfire, and a few scattered tiki torches.

I struck another match to the green stogie and watched the dancing around the fire swell to fifty people. I smelled musk, and then a woman dropped down beside me. I turned into the face of Marisa Wilson, one of the sisters. "Hey! How ya doin'," I said, surprised.

Marisa was tall and very pretty, and I had seen her around several times in different settings, always very well dressed and always with a different man.

"I've met you before, haven't I?" she asked.

I struggled but couldn't remember exactly where. "I've seen you around quite a bit," I said. "I think we met at Sly McFly's in Carmel. My name is Wesley."

"That must be it," she said. "I'm Marisa. Are you by yourself?"

"Yes. You came with Frank, didn't you? I thought I saw you two standing together."

"Well, we came together, but he left. He just said he had to go and then he left. I really like Light and Power, don't you?"

"Yeah. They're great! Would you like some wine?" I asked.

She smiled. "Yes."

"I'll be right back." I walked over to the Rotta wine crock and poured two cups, then sat back down beside her, handing her a cup. "So, Frank just left?"

"Yes," she said. "You never know with Frank. He's always up to something."

"Where's your sister?" I asked.

"She's here somewhere. I haven't seen her for a while. Is that pot in your pocket?" She was looking at my shirt where the huge green stogie pointed up at the sky. I nodded and reached into my pocket. "Wanna get high, Marisa?"

She turned her head and smiled. "Sure."

I handed her the stogie. The green monster was as large as a fat cigar and looked even larger in her pale hand. I struck a match, cupping it in my hand. She leaned over close and puffed on the stogie until the end burned like a coal. The air was filled with the scent of musk and marijuana smoke. She handed me the stogie, coughing. I took a hit and offered it back. She shook her head "no" and coughed again. I stubbed out the huge joint on the ground and put it back into my pocket. It was the gift that kept on giving. I figured I would still be smoking that thing at Christmas.

"Wow!" she exclaimed. "That's really strong!" She took another sip of her wine and coughed again. She looked back toward the bonfire. "It's so pretty here."

"Lots of stars," I said, looking up. "That's Orion..."

"Oh! There's my sister!" She was pointing at the fireside. "I have to talk with her." She stood up and walked away.

"Damn!" I said under my breath. She had seemed like she was interested in my company, and one toke of pot later she was walking away. I decided to mingle with the revelers, so I stood up and walked over to a group of people I knew.

The party raged on into the night under the full moon that hung in the sky like a huge lantern. Smoke and dust drifted in the air above the drums that had never stopped, while a steady stream of musicians entered and left the stage. Another shower of sparks rose above the fire as more wood was tossed on. I was feeling the Rotta wine and was definitely stoned from the various pulls on the great green stogie.

I made several turns around the party, leaning into conversations and greeting people I knew. It was like the Marvin Gaye song. "Hey, man!" "What's happenin', brother?" "What's goin on, man?" "Hey, dude, good to see ya. Take a hit off this shit." I was very sure that there was not one sober, straight person there. Nor should there have been. Some, however, were blithering idiots. There may have been a spiked punch bowl somewhere, but I suspected acid was making the rounds. One of my friends from the north coast was walking around in his underwear, calling for his dog. Another older woman with long gray hair was sitting cross-legged on the ground, having a conversation with a garden statue. Naked dancers were jumping through the flames of the bonfire, while others spun like dervishes with their arms held out. Somewhere a shot rang out and echoed up the canyon, but no one noticed. A guy cupped his mouth and coyote-howled to the moon.

I was feeling like I needed some quiet time and decided to pull back from the party. I walked over and plopped down on the lawn. From there I scanned the scene, moving my eyes from one cluster of people to another until out of the dusky firelight, I saw Marisa walking toward me, almost in a trance, and I waved to her. She walked up and sat down.

"How are you?" I asked.

She looked very stoned and shook her head. "I'm not sure what to do."

"Where's Frank?" I asked.

"He's gone."

"Where's your sister?"

"With some guy," she said.

"Do you want to stay with me?"

"Where are you staying?" she asked.

"I live in my van—it's parked right over there. There's room for you."

"Okay," she said. "I'm so stoned."

"Let's go, Marisa. You need to lie down." We walked up to my truck, and I opened the rear doors.

"I have to pee," she said.

I ripped off some paper towels and handed them to her. She lifted her skirt, squatted right down, and peed. I helped her into the van and lit my oil lamp. We lay down on the bed, and she began to unbutton her dress. In a moment, she was naked, and I was shedding my clothes. I leaned over to kiss her, and she put her hand behind my head. "You're very nice," she said, and pulled me down into a deep kiss.

Our lovemaking was slow and exploratory, the newness of the other filling our senses until a while later we collapsed in an embrace and quietly fell to sleep. In my dream, I was running over very rocky terrain, smoothly negotiating the rough surface. The ground dropped off on both sides of me into deep canyons as I raced along. It was a blue night sky above me with brightly shining stars; my breath was easy, and my legs felt strong. In front of me was a broad oak tree, and I ran toward it.

A loud pounding on my truck door woke me with a start. Marisa had not stirred. Someone pounded again on the door, and I sat up and opened the back door.

There stood Frank LaPont holding a bottle of 151 rum. "Morning, brother! It's five AM, and I thought you might need a shot of some rum!"

I looked at him and mumbled something like, "Jesus!"

Frank looked fresh as a daisy as he pushed the bottle toward me. "Take a shot! I had to go all the way to Monterey for it," he said.

I reached for the bottle, took a slug, and passed it back.

"It's gonna be a fine morning, brother. See ya around." Frank turned and walked off.

I closed the door and sat there for a minute, then turned and looked at Marisa. She still hadn't moved. I lay back down on the pillow, waiting for another knock on the door, but it never came.

A couple of hours later, the sun had cleared the mountain top, and the truck was getting warm inside, so I sat up and slipped on my pants, reached over, and slid a window open.

Marisa rolled over and opened her eyes. "What time is it?" she squinted.

"About seven, I think."

She sat up and reached for her bra, hooking it behind her back. "I have to pee," she said as she dropped the dress over her head.

"Frank's back," I said. "He was here this morning, knocking on the door."

"Frank's back?" Her eyes flitted to the truck's window. I opened the back door, and she stepped out and squatted on the ground, then stood and smoothed her skirt. "I better go find Frank. Thank you for taking care of me," she said, then smiled and walked down toward the cabin.

I sat on the edge of the truck bed and watched her go. There was no sign of Frank. The place was mostly deserted except for a couple of walking-wounded party veterans shuffling about with their heads down. One lone conga player was on the stage trying unsuccessfully to establish a rhythm. My head hurt, and I smelled like smoke, wine, and musk. I stood up, closed the rear door, and pissed on my tire. I got in behind the wheel and started the truck, wheeled it around, shifted into low, and rolled slowly down the steep earthen ramp to the road below.

On the way down the road, I passed a line of disheveled warriors walking back to their cars. My own head was listing slightly to the left, and I thought about looking for a shady pullout somewhere where I might pull over and crash in the back for a while. It had been a hell of a party.

I stood there in my garden listening to the drone of the airplane getting farther away and thinking about Donald Macinlay. He was the poster child of individualism, growing pot in the wide open, doing what he pleased, and celebrating it with huge Harvest Parties, and yet it was he who had accepted an invitation to be interviewed by *High Times* magazine. In the article, Donald bragged about being far ahead of the sheriff, boasted about his Harvest Parties, and said marijuana was here to stay on the coast as a cash crop.

While everyone else was crawling through the brush on their hands and knees, Macinlay was giving interviews to magazines. I heard the sheriff had read the article and passed it on to the County Board of Supervisors. They had felt the need to intervene in the lawless free-for-all purportedly going on along the Big Sur coast. As the sound of the plane disappeared to the south, I said to myself, "Thanks, Donald. Thanks a lot."

Later that afternoon Kade stopped by my cabin before going up the hill to water the garden. We were sitting on my deck drinking a beer.

I took a long pull from the beer bottle and set it down heavily on the table. "I think the sheriff flew over here today. A plane came over from the south and circled here two times."

"What did it look like? Did it have any markings?"

"Just a plain high-wing Cessna with numbers on the tail. But it was definitely interested."

Kade swallowed some beer and looked down into the canyon. "It probably was the sheriff. I heard there's been some pot busts up Palo Colorado Road and before the busts there were some overflights by a small plane." He looked back at me.

"Do you think they saw our garden?"

I looked up the mountain. "If he did, he didn't circle it, but I don't know. He definitely saw mine, circled here twice from two different approaches, and then flew up Fuego Creek. I don't think he saw it, he just headed south."

"You better harvest, even if it's early," Kade was leaning back in his chair.

He was right, it was early, but the plants looked really good, having spent their whole lives in full sun. The buds were firm and sticky, and, I was sure, very stony. Losing them now and getting arrested was not a sound option.

I looked at Kade. "So, what about our garden? Should we pull it?"

“Do you think they saw it?” he asked, staring back.

“I told you, they didn’t circle it. I don’t think so,” I said.

“It takes balls to grow grass,” he said with a grin. “This is where we earn our money. If it were easy, everyone would be doing it. You can’t pull your plants every time a plane flies by, or you’d never make it to harvest, although in your case, with your garden wide open in full sight, I would recommend pulling them. Soon!” He was laughing. “Don’t worry. If they arrest you, I’ll bring you magazines in jail.” He smiled. He was having fun.

CHAPTER 15

"Expecting the worst can shorten your reaction time."

–David Stafford

THE NEXT DAY AT NEPENTHE, I told the shift supervisor I was running a fever and felt like shit. He told me to take a couple days off. I was going to pull the plants but had no place to dry them and no time to clean them. The only possible place was my shop next to the house. It had no windows except in the front, facing the canyon, and they were ten feet off the ground. The windows were dusty, covered in sawdust, and only good for letting light in. If I moved some tools around, I might get all the plants in there, and I could hang them from the ceiling.

I went into my garden with clippers and began cutting branches off the plants, stuffing them into large black garden bags. In the shop, I had rearranged things, clearing the floor, and strung construction string tightly from wall to wall every foot or so. I pulled the plants from the bags, wrapped the stems in groups with wire ties, and hung them from the strings. I worked in a frenzy, running up and down the hill, for a day and a half, and then cut the remaining stalks that were standing, like naked sentries, down to the ground. I tossed those stalks over the cliff on the other side of my shop where I had thrown the deer carcass.

In my shop, the stems hung green from the strings, filling the entire room with buds. With the door closed and no windows to look through, there was nothing to see. I slid the bolt closed and locked it. I then went through my cabin and boxed anything that looked illegal. I grabbed my book called *Sinsemilla* and a book on *Absinthe* off the shelves. Those and any grass or paraphernalia went into the box. I bagged the box in a black plastic bag and stashed it in the brush. The cabin was clean, but I felt ridiculous having the buds hanging in the shop right next to the cabin. If the sheriff came for me, I was more than likely busted.

I returned to work the next day and worked through the weekend. It was Indian summer. The air was hot, moving slowly through the hills covered in long yellow grass. I stayed late, sitting on Nepenthe's terrace, sipping a beverage and looking down the coast. The wife of a friend of mine sat down next to me and said, "Hi," then told me she had a friend who worked in the sheriff's substation in Monterey. She had my attention. Her friend's name was Irene and she was a dispatcher, so she knew what was going on within the department. It turned out she smoked grass and was sympathetic toward growers. She said that Irene had heard there were going to be some busts in Big Sur in the coming week, and maybe I could put the word out. She patted me on the arm and walked away. There wasn't much I could do right then, but come tomorrow, I would put the word out.

The next morning was Monday, my usual day off from Nepenthe. I woke up early, drank some coffee, then stepped into the shower. I had built the shower with a south-facing window that looked down into the canyon, and I enjoyed the view while showering. From there I could see a portion of the road below, winding its way up from the highway through Fuego Creek Canyon to my place. Through the right side of the window was the ocean.

I was shampooing my hair when I heard the vehicles in the canyon. I opened my eyes and looked out the window just in time to catch a white car with a logo on the door speeding up the canyon, a rooster tail of dust curling behind it. A white truck was in close pursuit. I turned off the water, rushed out of the shower, and grabbed a pair of pants, a shirt, and my boots. I rushed out the door, closed it, and slammed the padlock shut, then jumped off my deck, stumbling into a roll on the ground.

In front of me was the old homestead path that Mrs. Fuego had used to walk to the creek for water. It was now overgrown, so I pushed my way through the brush, finally dropping down underneath the foliage, out of breath. My heart was pounding like a triphammer.

I could hear the cars arriving above the cabin and struggled to pull on my pants and shirt without being seen. I could hear talking and doors slamming as I pulled on my boots, then the sound of shoes on gravel got closer. I pulled back under the brush and froze, trying to control my breathing. I farted. It was a nasty fart. I imagined the noxious smell wafting above the brush. I heard loud knocking on my cabin door but couldn't figure out why they were knocking on a door that was locked with a padlock. I farted again. What the hell was happening? I heard footsteps not far from me and started imagining the arresting officer laughing and saying they'd found me because of my farts.

There was more knocking on the cabin door and then a voice called out. "Wesley! Monterey County Sheriff! We know you're here, come out!" Then, "Wesley, come out. I want to talk with you."

They were talking among themselves, and I couldn't quite make out the words. I heard more walking around and then footsteps walking back up my driveway. I was still frozen in place, having never heard the closest footsteps walk away. I figured he had smelled my fart and might be standing still, waiting for me to move. I stayed still, listening to footsteps coming back down the driveway and then my door lock rattling, then footsteps walking away. More voices and then a car started. Then another car started, accelerated up the hill, and turned around, and then I heard tires on gravel driving quickly back down the hill.

I thought if I were them, I would have left someone behind to catch me coming out of the brush. So, I sat there still as a statue, albeit a farting statue, wondering what had caused all the gas. I listened for an hour and didn't hear a sound; then, and only then, I slowly made my way up the trail, breaking out into open air. There was no one around. I walked to the cabin door where there was a business card shoved into a crack of the wood. I grabbed it. The front of the card was standard Monterey County Sheriff, but there was writing on the back:

Wesley, call me. We need to talk.
We can have lunch.
Burt Pickett

I slid Deputy Pickett's card into my pocket and went around to the shop where I had left the pot buds hanging. The shop door was still locked. I looked around and then walked up to my garden, finding footprints that showed they had walked up there. I returned to my cabin and stood on the deck, figuring if they were coming back, they'd be back soon, certainly before dark, and there was also a good chance they would be parked at the bottom of the hill all day.

I opened the door to the cabin, went in, and threw down a shot of tequila, then grabbed a beer. Somehow, they had missed the hanging pot in the shop. My garden was a bust now that it had been found. It was dead. I couldn't grow there again. But I was sure the common garden with Kade hadn't been touched. I sat outside drinking beer and watching the canyon until the sun went down.

CHAPTER 16

"Two-legged rats are the worst kind."

–Kade Rudman

THE NEXT DAY I WENT down to Nepenthe and used the pay phone to call the only attorney I knew, Bob Daniels. I told him what had happened at my cabin and about the business card left in the crack of my door.

Bob was quiet for a moment and then said, "I'll tell you this, Wesley, if you decide to go have lunch with this deputy, I will not be able to represent you in any case that might follow."

"So I should do nothing?"

"Exactly," he replied. "Call me if anything more comes of this, and please, avoid any further contact with the Sheriff's Department."

I hung up the phone and drove home. I had a lot of work to do to trim the pot hanging in my shop.

Fortunately, I was working nights at Nepenthe that week and had my days free. Three days later, after three marathon sessions of trimming, I had moved the manicured buds out of the shop and down to my plywood box hidden in the brush. I rehung them there to dry. I swept out the shop while thinking I had probably swept more marijuana into a trash can than most people had ever seen. I went up to the garden, dug up all the plant stumps, and threw them over the cliff. I dressed the garden area with a light rake, removing any pot leaves and putting them all into a bag, then spread the contents out on the ground away from the cabin to shrivel in the hot sun. Finally, I cut some fresh brush and threw it down the cliff until it covered any sign of the pot stalks.

One week later, I packaged all the buds in the plywood box into buckets and weighed them. I had twenty pounds of high-grade seedless pot packaged in forty sealed, two-gallon buckets. I had two other buckets of manicured seeded buds that had been victimized by a rogue hermaphrodite stem and marked those buckets as "seeded."

Kade and I were still working an alternating schedule at our common garden. We were about two weeks from harvest, but for all intents and purposes, the crop was ready. It was Kade's turn to water. I was sitting on my deck early in the afternoon when I heard his truck pull down my driveway.

Kade got out and almost ran to the deck. "We got problems, man! Somebody topped our garden!"

"What? What do you mean?" I stood up.

"Somebody walked in and topped our plants! Clipped the biggest buds at the tops of the plants! Fuck! I found their trail and followed it down to the creek. It goes up the hill, toward Julian's homestead from there. Let's go!"

We hiked up to the garden. The theft was definitely surgical. Someone had carefully clipped the largest buds from the tops of the plants but left everything else. There were still some large buds growing.

"They'll be back," Kade said. "We have to catch 'em. I'll shoot the bastards."

We followed their trail down from the garden to the creek, where the ground was freshly disturbed with scattered black dirt from under the leaves. From there we could see the fresh trail heading up the hill. I looked around the creek's edge. "I only see one set of boot prints here," I said. "The lugs are all the same coming and going."

Kade was looking up the hill. "Probably why we still have some donkey dicks up there; he couldn't carry them all. We gotta catch this guy. He's gonna come back. Let's follow this trail."

We followed the trail up the south side of the canyon where it broke out onto a pullout for cars on the Julian Fuego homestead road. We found the same lug prints from the boots there with recent tire tracks.

"Whoever it was parked here and walked over to our garden," Kade said, kicking the dirt.

"There's not too many people who would feel safe about parking their car here unless it was Alan, the guy who lives here. Or the foreman of the Rummsen Ranch." I was looking up the road. "But I agree, whoever it was will be back."

"They'll be back soon because it's harvest time." Kade looked across the canyon. "They know we'll pull the plants when we find they got topped. We gotta lay in wait for this asshole."

We hiked back to sit on my deck and formulate a plan. A weather front was blowing in from the south and rain was in the forecast. The thought of our plants getting soaked and blown around in the mud was on our minds.

Kade was talking. "He won't come alone. Too much to carry. He'll bring a friend. We have to be in the garden when they come. It's gonna rain. They'll come in the night under the cover of the storm. They won't have to be quiet, the rain will cover the sound, and they won't think we'll be there. I've got two walkie-talkies. I'll be at the highway across the road from the gate, you'll be at the garden. I'll radio you if they come up through the gate; you radio me if they come in by the trail, and I'll drive up. In any case, we'll have them trapped from top and bottom."

I didn't speak for a moment and just sat looking at him. "So, you're going to be warm and fat in your truck while I'm getting soaked in the garden? Great plan, Kade. How about you wait in the garden in the rain, and I'll fuck off in the truck at the bottom of the hill?"

"It has to be me at the bottom of the hill. Whoever it is thinks they're stealing from you. They don't know I'm involved, so they won't worry about seeing my truck at the bottom of the hill."

"Well, I'm going to get soaked," I said. "I'm going to be carrying my shotgun. It's going to get soaked too. I don't like the idea of standing out all night long dripping wet. Your plan sucks. They probably won't come anyway."

"They're comin'," Kade said, lost in thought. "We'll build you a duck blind, a lean-to with a tarp over it. You'll be high and dry. Let's go!"

Five hours later, I was above the garden at the bottom of the oak trees, lying under a green tarp covered by cut brush. It was dark and raining steadily. The moon was large above the storm clouds and shown with a dim light outside the opening of the blind. I was looking out at the garden, and I was getting wet. I had my shotgun beside me, covered by a plastic bag. I was thinking about what I was going to do if someone walked into the garden, feeling strangely helpless. I was not going to kill the thief. I would just try to scare him, but what if it was two or three guys? What if they were armed and shot at me? I might have to defend myself. Somebody could very well get killed. This was nuts. I would just fire up into the trees over their heads. They'd probably get scared and run. But what if they didn't?

I was working out my strategy when there was a crackle on my radio that made me jump. The sound was too loud in the dark confines of my hiding place.

"Big Turkey, Big Turkey, this is Ranger One. Come in!" It was Kade.

I grabbed the radio and squeezed the talk lever. "Ranger One, this is Ranger Two, go ahead."

"Big Turkey, this is Ranger One, how's everything there?"

"What's this Big Turkey shit?" I barked into the radio.

"Big Turkey, this is Ranger One. You're Big Turkey and I'm Ranger One. How's it goin' up there?"

"Fuck you, Ranger One. It's quiet here, or it *was* quiet here. Over."

"Big Turkey, this is Ranger One, say as little as possible, copy? Big Turkey, it's quiet here too. Ranger One, over and out."

I couldn't believe this guy. Ranger One and Big Turkey, my ass. Kade was having a good time, warm and dry in his truck. I went back to watching the dripping shadows and listening for footsteps in the night.

I must have dozed off because I opened my eyes with a start, like waking up while driving. I thought I heard someone talking. I eased the shotgun up into firing position and froze, scanning the garden for any movement. This might be it! But the pattering of rain and occasional wind in the branches was all I could hear. I sat still for another hour pointing the shotgun from the blind, my eyes roving back and forth, my heart beating hard. There were several leaks in the tarp, and I was soaking wet and shivering.

"Big Turkey, Big Turkey! This is Ranger One, come in!" The radio blared.

I grabbed it and clicked it on. "This is Big Turkey," I said, surprising myself. "What's up?"

"All clear here, Big Turkey. How are you up there?"

"All clear here, Ranger Dick. Over."

"Okay, Big Turkey. Ranger One out."

Another hour later I felt a shit coming on. I was over the whole wet, soggy ambush thing and extricated myself from the blind. I walked around the garden peering into the dripping night and seeing nothing, decided to head back to the cabin to relieve myself. I hiked down the hill with the shotgun at the ready and hiked up the road to my cabin. I used the toilet and took off my wet clothes, draping them over the shower rod. I got dressed again for the return trip up to the garden and sat down on my bed to lace up my boots.

CHAPTER 17

"My idea of torture would be having to sit here with you manicuring buds every day."

–Wesley Daggert

THE CABIN DOOR BURST OPEN, and my eyes flew open in surprise at the daylight and Kade standing in the doorway.

"I knew it!" he yelled. "You fucking went to sleep! I've been trying to reach you on the radio. I thought you were dead. Jesus, man!"

I felt bad. I couldn't remember falling asleep, though obviously I had. I must have lain back for a second after putting my boots on. "Sorry, man. I had to take a shit. Guess I lay down."

"What time did you come back here?" he demanded.

"About three thirty." I pushed some hair away from my eye.

"Well," he said, calming down, "nobody came. I went up there looking for you. You're not very dependable."

"Yes, I am, you asshole! Mister 'sit his ass in the pickup truck.' You and your Big Turkey bullshit and your hot thermos of coffee. You're a fuckhead, Kade, and you know it!"

"Well, if you're done sleeping," he said, "we need to start thinking about harvesting that garden. They could come back anytime and get the rest. We need to get busy."

We walked back up to the garden to check for damage from the last night's rain. The buds would need a couple of days of sun to dry out before we could harvest them.

Over the next couple of days, one of us stayed close to the garden at all times. We needed to build two drying boxes to hang the pot in, so I went to Monterey for plywood, two-by-twos, and a couple of packages of hinges. We painted a sign on a piece of wood that read "THIEVES WILL BE SHOT!!!" and posted it along the trail the thief had used when he topped our garden. We found a good place to set up the drying boxes two turns up the road above my cabin. It was a point of land that stuck out toward the ocean with a stand of tall ceanothus on it.

We made our wood cuts at the cabin, painted the plywood a dark flat green, and then hauled it to the site. We went in under the ceanothus and made a clearing, then slid the plywood sheets down the path along their edges under the trees where we stacked them. The drying boxes were simple, four full sheets for the sides, one half sheet for each end, and two-by-two-inch stock for all the interior edges.

At the site, we assembled the boxes with screws, placed them side by side, and covered them with the cut brush. Each one provided a four-by-four-by-eight-foot-long space. On the insides, baling wire was stretched back and forth, side to side at the top to be used for hanging the buds. We were ready for harvest.

Over the next several days, we hauled buds from the garden to my cabin, where we spread a sheet out on the floor and picked all the green leaves away from the buds. This trimming process was slow and tedious. Kade and I both hated it. We'd sit for hours and not say anything of any consequence, heads down, eyes focused on the buds, careful to remove the leaf right down to the bud without disturbing the bud hairs. After a trimming session, we would bundle the buds by their stems with wire ties and collect the bundles in black plastic bags. The bags would get carried up the road to the drying boxes, where the bundles would be hung from the cross wires to dry. We were getting on each other's nerves, causing this sort of inane exchange to go on for hours:

K: "You're slow."

Me: No response.

K: "I've never seen anyone so slow."

Me: "My pile is as big as your pile."

K: "Hardly."

Me: (Reaching for another leafy bud) "I don't want to hear about it."

K: "We're going to be doing this at Christmas."

Me: "Maybe you will. I'll be in the Bahamas."

K: "You're not going anywhere until we sell this pot."

Me: "Watch me."

K: "Can't you work any faster?"

Me: "Leave me alone."

K: "I can't, you're sitting right in front of me. Fuck you."

Me: "What do you mean, 'Fuck you'?"

K: "Just what I said."

Me: "Why did you say it?"

K: "I just thought it."

Me: "Well I'm just thinking 'Fuck you too!'"

K: "Why would you say that to me?"

Me: "Because you're fucked."

K: "You have a lot of hidden problems."

Me: "Like what?"

K: "You need to be understood, to have other people understand you."

Me: "That's a problem?"

K: "It is with you."

Me: "Buzz off!"

K: "See what I mean?"

Me: "You're an asshole who doesn't care about anybody."

K: "Why should I?"

Me: "Because we're all humans."

K: "Why should I care that we're all humans? Maybe we're not, have you considered that?"

Me: "You're impossible to talk to."

K: "Nobody's perfect."

This dark banter would go on back and forth without either of us looking up from our fingers busy with cleaning the buds. Thinking back, I suppose we may have been getting high from the resin soaking into our bodies through our fingers, propelling our tongues without benefit of thought.

K: "Who named your mother?"

Me: "What? Her parents."

K: "No, really, who named your mother?"

Me: "None of your business. My grandfather."

K: "Did he name you too?"

Me: "Who named you, asshole?"

K: "My name is not asshole."

Me: "Could have fooled me."

K: "I'm just wondering."

Me: "I bet you are."

K: "Who named you?"

Me: "Father Serra. When he wasn't busy at the Mission, he worked at the hospital."

K: "He should have given you an Indian name."

Me: "Like what?"

K: "Slow Picker."

And so it went. We were driving each other crazy, and the work of trimming buds was progressing way too slowly. Finally, I threw out a suggestion. "We gotta hire somebody to help with this."

Kade looked up from his hands. "Oh, right, we're going to trust somebody to know all this."

"We need some help, Kade. We train them. We bring in a couple of bags of bud and throw them on the floor. When they're done, we pay them and send them home."

"Pay them?" Kade looked up. "Maybe in buds..."

"Whatever they want. I say twenty bucks an hour cash, or the equivalent in buds."

"Twenty bucks an hour is too much!" Kade complained.

"Not if you want a good job and a closed mouth," I countered.

"Fifteen-fifty," Kade said.

"Come on, man. Fifteen-fifty...are you saving quarters now? Twenty. Paid out same day. We give them a bullshit story about the garden being down the road and the drying house being up the highway. Maybe we get this done in our lifetimes."

"Who do you know who would wanna do it?" he asked.

"My girlfriend Susie for one, I'll ask her."

"I know a woman at Esalen that might work," Kade stretched out his arms and looked out the window.

Three days later, there were four of us trimming buds on the cabin floor. Susie had agreed to help right away and had gained experience manicuring buds from helping her neighbor with his crop. Kade's friend from Esalen, Sandra, a plump stringy-haired woman with thick glasses, was a quick study, and soon we were humming along and the drying boxes were filling up.

The addition of Susie and Sandra to the trimming sessions tempered the dark banter between Kade and me. It was a more balanced group. Susie also brought scissors to use instead of her fingers. Her neighbor had demanded it. "Resin on your fingers is resin that's not on the bud," had been his observation. We bought four pair. The scissors were much more precise, enabling us to get closer to the bud with less damage. There was still a buildup of resin that had to be scraped off the scissors, and each person kept their own scrapings in small plastic boxes that Susie had brought from home.

We built another drying box, a half box, to dry some of the leaves that were in large piles after our trimming sessions. A large percentage of the leaves had resin on them, and we thought they might be worth something, perhaps as the magic ingredient for some baker, "Alice B. Toklas" style.

The first buds we'd hung in the drying boxes five days ago were now dry enough to package. We left Susie and Sandra fresh bags of bud to trim while Kade and I walked up to the drying boxes and packaged the dry buds in the two-gallon paint buckets we had stashed there under a tarp weeks earlier.

CHAPTER 18

"Never put all your eggs in one basket."

–The Easter Bunny

THE ENDS OF THE DRYING boxes were hinged at the bottom and when open, provided a clean floor that was four feet square. Kade and I would sit on inverted plastic buckets, facing each other, each with three buckets in front of us and several bundles of dried buds beside us on the floor. We used diagonal wire cutters we called "dikes" to clip the buds into the buckets.

It was important to include as little stem as possible when clipping the bud. Buyers wanted just the buds, and they wanted the buds tight and firm, without air, or space, inside them. They wanted the buds to be covered in crystallized resin, free of extraneous leaf, and dried just right to be squeezable and not too brittle. It was a challenging task to accomplish all this. We were working outside in the brush, with large quantities, in uncontrollable conditions. The foggy nights and blazing hot days could easily influence the dryness of the buds.

As we clipped, we were evaluating each bud with all these criteria in mind, sorting them into buckets that were either top quality, lacking top quality, or seeded. When a bucket was filled, we weighed it to a half pound, and if it was too dry, we would drop a fresh orange peel into the bucket and then seal it. The bucket lids were difficult to seal, requiring maximum pressure to close. Opening them was no picnic either, and many a fingernail was bent or broken in the process. Once sealed, the buckets were airtight and marked with a plus or minus sign denoting the grade of the buds each held. The finished product was stacked in the back of the drying boxes.

For some reason, unlike the trimming sessions, the packaging process brought out the best in Kade and me, and our banter was more conversationally civil. I figured it was because this was the final phase in the process and every clip of the dikes was a dollar sign. We worked fast, in unison, sitting perched on our seats, filling our buckets with sinsemilla. There had been no more visits from our thief, and we were all but done with our harvest.

We were pushing November, and the rainy season was upon us. We added portable propane heaters to our drying boxes to compensate for the cool dampness of the late autumn nights. We had fifty-nine pounds of finished product packaged and stacked in our boxes, with another little bit hanging, waiting to dry. My own private stash of twenty pounds, make it twenty-one with the seeded pot, was in my drying box in the brush near the cabin.

One evening after our shift, Kade and I sat on Nepenthe's terrace in a couple of director chairs, drinking a beer and looking down the coast. His forehead was furrowed with concern. "I don't think it's smart to have all our pot in one place. Right now it's all at your place. I think we should move half of it over to my place."

It was true that we had all our eggs in one basket, and I knew one thing to be true: if shit could happen, it would happen. My concern was that I hadn't spent much time at Kade's place and didn't know much about his scene.

"Do you have a safe place to store it?" I asked.

Kade set his beer down. "Yeah. I've got six boxes over there stashed deep. Two are empty. I'll show you. I'll keep my stuff separate, and you'll have access to ours."

"It's getting complicated," I said. "Maybe we should just split the product now."

We sat there awhile and didn't speak. Kade looked around and took a swallow of beer. "Let's finish the harvest first and then figure it out," he said. "Right now, we need to spread the shit out a bit. It's all at your place, and that's not smart."

It made some sense, so the next day we loaded up his truck with fifty-six buckets and drove them over to his place. Kade was in a lease/purchase agreement with old man Rummsen on seventy-five acres of land between Plumas Creek and Deer Creek.

We could drive to Kade's place from my cabin without leaving the Rummsen Ranch, and after turning left from Fuego Creek Road and driving a mile, we pulled off the road, into a steep driveway that wound down into the tree-covered drainage of Plumas Creek. We crossed the creek and followed the road up and out of the canyon, around two more turns and into the sunlight. The road opened up from the trees onto a large flat of ground that had been bulldozed out of the hillside. There were a couple of cars parked there in front of a cabin tucked in close to the road with a lush vegetable garden growing beside it. The vast Pacific took up the view to the west. Kade's two kids ran out from the cabin in front of his wife, Serene. The kids were about five or six years old, close in age, and had the same auburn hair as their mother.

"Daddy!" they called, running up to Kade and hugging his legs.

Serene walked up to Kade and said something in his ear.

"No!" Kade said a little too loud. He turned to me. "Come on, I'll show you the spot."

I followed him down a path to an outhouse set back in the chamise.

Kade removed a chunk of brush from beside the outhouse that exposed the opening of a trail going back for another twenty feet. He removed another plug of brush and another trail was revealed. We walked another forty feet to a stand of ceanothus, where Kade dropped down and crawled under a low branch. Under the cover of the trees were six plywood boxes, each four-by-eight foot, like the ones we were using at my place. They were painted flat black and flat forest green in a camouflage pattern.

He pointed to the two boxes on the right. "Those are empty. We can stash the buckets in them. My stuff is in these four over here." He turned to face me. "Look, man, here's the deal. I can't have you just coming and going here. Serene doesn't like all this shit, and I've got a sticky situation with Tom Rummsen. If I get caught growing here, I lose my place. It's in the lease-purchase contract. So no coming in and out without me, understood?" And then, as if to underline his point he turned to me and said, "I'm serious, man."

I didn't like this. The idea that I was stashing pot that belonged to me in a place I wasn't free to visit seemed wrong, and I said so. "Kade, this doesn't work for me. Maybe temporarily, until we're completely harvested, but then we should just split the buckets up and I'll take mine home."

"Whatever," Kade said, "I'm okay with that, but I feel better not having everything over at your place. Come on, let's haul those buckets down here."

"Do the kids come down here?" I asked.

"No. They're not allowed down here."

"Even to use the outhouse?"

"It's not a real outhouse. It's just a prop. It gives a reason for the initial trail from the house," Kade said.

The buckets all had metal handles on them, and we carried four in each hand, down the trail to the hiding place, until all were stashed. At some point in the process, Serene put the kids into a car and called to Kade. He walked over, and they started to argue. Kade waved his hand and yelled, "I don't care! What do you want me to do? I'm too busy for this shit!" It made me feel bad, and I felt embarrassed for Serene. It seemed all was not well in Camelot.

After she drove off in a cloud of dust, I asked Kade if everything was okay.

He waved his hand down the driveway. "She's crazy! She doesn't like that I'm growing, and she bitches to me about it all the time."

"Should I be worried?" I spoke the obvious question. "Is she gonna do something nuts and fuck all this up?"

"Don't worry about it," he said, and kicked a rock out of the driveway. "She's not *that* crazy."

By the end of the next week, we had harvested and trimmed the last of the garden. The buds were hanging in the drying boxes at my place, Susie and Sandra were happy to call it quits, and I was ecstatic. No more trimming! When the hanging pot was dry, there'd be one more push to finish packaging, and we'd be done for the year.

CHAPTER 19

"Investing in a stranger requires intuition and a leap of faith. Study their eyes and listen for intention."

–Luca Renzo

THE NEXT DAY, THE FIRST of November, it was raining with a vengeance, and Big Sur was hunkering down for the winter. The Big Sur River was running full through the valley and the highway, with its falling rocks and occasional road closures, was mostly deserted. We still had pot drying in the boxes and even with the heaters, the rain was slowing the drying process down. Susie was spending a lot of time at my place, and one night over dinner she told me she had met a guy a couple of times at her neighbor's house when she was there trimming buds. He'd been there to buy pot. She said he had wanted to buy more than her neighbor had to sell. She told the buyer that her boyfriend had pot to sell. He had slipped her a phone number.

She got up from the table and walked to her purse. "I saw him yesterday in town. He said he'll be around for a couple of days." She found the piece of paper and gave it to me. I looked at the number. It had a pound sign and the number seventeen after it.

"Is seventeen the room number?"

"I don't know what it is."

I called it from the Nepenthe phone booth the next day.

A man answered, "Holiday Inn. How may I help you?"

"Number seventeen," I said, taking a guess.

"Room seventeen. One moment, please."

There was a click and then another ring. A different male voice answered, "Hello?"

"Hey," I said. "I got your number from my girlfriend, Susie. You gave her your number."

"So I did," he replied. "Are you in Big Sur?"

"Yeah. I'm at Nepenthe."

"Will you still be there in an hour?"

"I could be," I said.

"How will I know you?" he asked.

I looked down at myself. "I'm wearing a black ball cap and a green corduroy shirt."

"I'll see you in an hour," he said, and hung up the phone.

I walked into Nepenthe's bar, bought a beer, and took a seat outside on the terrace to wait.

About an hour later, after I'd watched every new arrival from the parking lot, a medium-sized man wearing glasses and dressed in khaki slacks, a blue shirt, and a plaid fedora walked onto the terrace from the parking lot. He looked every bit the tourist. He paused for a moment and looked around. His eyes fell on me, and he walked over and sat down. "My name is Jimmy," he said.

"My name is Wesley." I shook his hand.

He looked at me. "You have pot to sell?" he asked.

"Are you a cop?" I asked.

He gave a laugh. "No. Are you?"

"No," I said. "Yeah, I've got some pot to sell."

"Is it clean sinsemilla?" he asked.

"Very."

"I'd like to see it."

"You'll have to follow me to my place." I said.

He was driving an older model Oldsmobile that took up every inch of the parking space—I used to call them "land yachts"—and he followed me out of the parking lot and down the coast. Once we were through my gate and it was locked behind us, I led him up to my cabin. I couldn't grab my personal stash without his seeing where it was hidden, so I decided I would show him pot that Kade and I owned in common. I told him to sit tight inside and went up the road to the drying boxes where I was out of sight of the cabin. I grabbed two buckets of bud and the scale, then walked back down and opened the buckets on the table.

"Paint buckets. Interesting," Jimmy said. He took a bud and looked at it. He reached into his pocket and pulled out a jeweler's eyepiece and leaned into the bud like he was examining a diamond. "Good," he said squinting. "Not the tightest I've ever seen, but good. Do you grow in shade?"

"Yeah."

"I can tell. Can I smoke some?"

"Of course." I walked to the kitchen, grabbed a plate from the shelf, and placed it on the table in front of Jimmy.

Jimmy produced a small pair of scissors from his shirt pocket and carefully cut a pipe load from the bud. It dropped neatly on the clean white plate. He reached into his trouser pocket and produced a small stainless-steel pipe and loaded it. I struck a match, let the sulfur burn off, and lit the load. He inhaled deeply, leaning his head back. He coughed slightly and smiled. "That's nice," he said. "Good flavor." He put the pipe down on the plate.

"Is it all like this?" he asked.

"Yeah. Very potent."

"What's your price?"

"Sixteen," I said.

Jimmy removed his glasses and began to clean them with his shirt. "Any chance of a discount?" he blinked.

"No." I looked at him straight.

"Pity." He slid the glasses back on his head. "I'll take seven."

"Buckets?" I asked.

"Pounds," he said, and walked out to his car.

An hour later, I had fourteen buckets open on the floor of the cabin, and Jimmy was inspecting all of them. Several times he reached for his jeweler's eyepiece and held it to a bud for scrutiny. Occasionally he would sample a random bud in his pipe. He didn't seem to get stoned but rather acted like a sommelier tasting wine for quality.

"My clients are very discerning," he said at one point. "They trust me to spend their money wisely."

When the buckets were all resealed, he placed a briefcase flat on the table and opened it. He removed a manila envelope and opened it. It was full of cash. I watched as he counted out three piles of cash and handed them to me. I sat down and recounted it.

"Eleven thousand, two hundred. All twenties," he said. "Do you have more?"

"Yes. A lot more," I said.

He smiled and extended his hand. "Well, in that case, I'll be seeing you again."

I shook his hand. "You can leave a message for me at Nepenthe Restaurant," I told him.

The fourteen buckets fit easily into the cavernous trunk of the large Olds, and I drove in front of Jimmy back to my gate where I unlocked it and wished him well.

"You took a risk coming up here," I said.

He smiled. "Actually, you did. Mine was minimal. Your girlfriend has honest eyes."

Back home, I dug up my coffee can under the shop and stuffed $5,600 into it. The can was full, so I was going to need another one or maybe a safety deposit box. I replaced the plastic lid on the can and reburied it, placing the chunk of bridge timber over the top. Tomorrow was a workday for me at Nepenthe, and I'd give Kade his cut there.

The sun was setting low in the sky between two towering thunderheads, bathing the Apple Tree House in a golden light. Thinking of Jimmy and how unlikely he looked to be a major buyer, I walked back up to the drying boxes and did a better job of covering my trail.

CHAPTER 20

"In a given situation, your first impulse is often gifted with the most clarity."

–Wesley Daggert

On November third, Big Sur and business at Nepenthe were slow. Kade and I were working as waiters, and some of the staff were being sent home. I had a popular indoor section, so I knew I was going to be there all day.

Kade walked up to me as I was returning glasses to the bartender. "They just cut me loose." He set his tray down on the bar.

"Let's take a walk," I said under my breath.

We walked up the ramp to the back parking lot and strolled over to a bench that sat under an old oak tree. I reached into my pocket and pulled out the wad of cash. "Fifty-six hundred dollars," I said.

He glanced around, then took the money and quickly stuffed it into his front pocket. "You sold some pot?"

I told him the story about meeting Jimmy and the subsequent pot deal, explaining why I had chosen not to sell my own personal weed.

"Pretty risky," he said to the ground. "Don't get me wrong, I like the money, but you didn't even know that guy."

"He had some history with Susie, so I felt okay with it."

"Just the same, don't get greedy, it'll cloud your thinking, you'll make mistakes," he said, then turned and walked down the driveway to the parking lot. I returned to the restaurant.

The afternoon progressed with the slow cadence only a winter day could have at Nepenthe. New guests arrived just as others casually finished their meals and stood to leave. There was no waiting list and no hustle-bustle. The temperature pushed hard to reach seventy degrees, as the warm mountain air and the breeze off the ocean wafted over us.

Around three PM, just after the peak lunchtime hours, I was standing with my back to the bar, looking out at the terrace. A tall balding man wearing white linen and sandals, wrapped in a beige shawl, came walking up from the lower lot. His gait was long and graceful, his head dipping up and down as he walked, and his eyes were focused straight ahead. I knew this man! The last time I had seen him was in Italy, where we had met in a teacher training course taught by Maharishi Mahesh Yogi. We had spent four months with Maharishi, meditating long hours, eating in silence, or discussing the ramifications of a stress-free, rested nervous system. His long, slow stride bespoke a mellow confidence, and I remembered how I could easily pick him out of a crowd at the course, walking with a blanket draped over his shoulders, taking long easy strides, mellowed by long meditations.

As he approached the glass door to the restaurant, I opened it with a flair. "Solomon!"

Without breaking stride, as though he expected me, he walked up and embraced me. "Wesley! My man! How are you?" He pushed me back at arms' length and looked me over. "Let's get a look at you!"

"Good to see you, Solomon! Watching you stroll across the terrace brought me back to Spain and Italy." I laughed.

"Five years ago! Those were good days," he said, spreading his arms. "And they continue. What a magnificent day we have today!"

I sat my friend in my section and brought him some tea to pass the next hour until I was off work. Later, we sat at an unused table and caught up on the last few years.

Solomon had been flipping houses in the northwest, buying cheap and then remodeling, and had an antique business on the side. He seemed very busy, working hard, in contrast to the very laid-back, slow-paced man I had known in the meditation course.

It was nearing evening when he nudged my arm. "Come down to the parking lot, and I'll show you what I'm up to."

I followed him down the stairs to a large box-style step-van taking up two spaces in the parking lot. He unlocked the large rear door and rolled it up, then flicked on a light switch that illuminated the interior. It was stacked from floor to ceiling with wicker furniture. Chairs, dining tables, end tables, and coffee tables—some with glass inserts, most in a warm straw color, and some in a mix with a darker shaded reed. I was impressed.

"Wow! You're in the wicker business!" I said.

"I'm helping a friend furnish his new coffeehouse in Bellingham. I run across odd stuff in my antique business, and my friend thought he could use this furniture. I picked it up in LA, and I'm on my way back to Washington. Do you have room for me and my van to spend the night?"

"Of course," I grinned. "I'm meeting my girlfriend here for dinner soon. Join us, and we'll head up to my cabin afterward."

Susie arrived about six and after introductions, we sat down to eat. Dinner was filled with stories of Europe and Maharishi, all of us enjoying a salad, Lolly's roast chicken, and a bottle of wine. After dinner, we left Susie's car at Nepenthe, and Solomon followed my truck down the coast to my cabin. His large van struggled up the two-mile dirt road, and I had to stop several times to allow Solomon to catch up. I led him to a turnout above the Apple Tree House and got him turned around in a parking place. We all walked down the road to the cabin.

It was a cold night, with a clear view of the stars, and we paused on the porch as I unlocked the cabin door. I pushed the door open, waved Susie and Solomon inside, then walked in past them and one by one lit my oil lamps. The cabin was cold, uninsulated, and drafty.

"Brrrr!" Susie said.

The warm light from the lamps slowly spread into the recesses of the cabin.

"Nice digs, Wesley!" Solomon threw his bag on the couch.

I rubbed Susie's shoulders. "I'll start a fire," I said into her ear.

She walked to the kitchen. "I'll make some tea."

I opened the door to the old boiler that served as my fireplace, loaded it with wood and paper, and tossed in a match. The fire caught and started to build. I walked to the sink and turned on the faucet to wash some soot from my hands. No water came out of the faucet. "Damn! There's no water!"

It was a recurring problem I had living there. My water system was simple, just black poly pipe stretched from the source high up in the canyon, over a half mile of open ground, to my cabin. The fall in elevation was about 300 feet, giving me an overabundance of water pressure at the house. I had Rain Birds going twenty-four-seven to minimize the pressure, but even then, the line would come apart occasionally.

There was one place in particular where this was a fairly common occurrence, a small dip in the trail about a quarter-mile from the house. All the connections were double-hose clamped and cinched tight, but one would still come apart occasionally. I had walked up there many times to reconnect the line, but the trail involved skirting a steep area of rockfall on a narrow ledge that was sketchy to traverse in daylight, let alone in the dark. It was late, and I wasn't looking forward to the hike. I turned to Susie and Solomon.

"I have to walk up the canyon and fix the water line," I said.

"It's too cold out to walk up the canyon, Wes," Susie said. "It can wait until morning."

"I won't be needing water," Solomon said.

I was feeling swayed. Susie and Solomon seemed okay without water. I had two gallons of water in the cupboard, after all, and I could walk up in the morning to fix the water line for showers. Deciding not to go up for the repair, I headed toward the pantry instead, asking, "Brandy, anyone?"

"Now we're talking!" Solomon smiled.

"I'll have one," Susie said.

I reached for the bottle of Metaxa Grande Fine and poured it into three snifters. I sat in the big easy chair, Solomon was across from me on the couch, and Susie arranged some pillows and leaned back on the bed. The cabin was filled with the soft yellow light of the oil lamps, and the fire peeked through a small opening in the boiler door, warming the room to a comfortable temperature. We sat telling more stories and enjoying a second snifter of brandy until about midnight when we called it a night. I unfolded the couch for Solomon and loaded a few more chunks of wood into the fire box.

Solomon had slid under the covers. “Feels, good, man,” he yawned. “I’m glad we hooked up.”

“It’s really good to see you again, Solomon.” I looked around the room. Susie had crawled into our bed.

“Goodnight, Solomon,” she said across the room. We were all cozy. I blew out the oil lamps, got undressed, and joined Susie in bed.

CHAPTER 21

"All you ever really have is an exact moment in time. The rest is past or future."

–David Stafford

After sleeping a few hours, I found myself in a desperate nightmare. I was ankle-deep in sand, fighting with six Arabs whose faces were hidden beneath red-checkered veils. Dressed in white robes, they had long curved knives and were attacking me from every side. I was fighting frantically when I was suddenly awakened from my dream by Susie shaking me and shouting, "Wesley! Wake up! Wake up! The house is on fire! The house is on fire!"

I struggled to open my eyes and be present, finding Susie pointing at the wall and Solomon sitting up in bed. I could see a dull orange glow up on the ceiling, pervading the room, and then noticed a small lick of flame emanating from between the boards on the wall. I jumped up from my bed, naked, and raced outside to get the water hose, remembering only then that the water line was broken.

"Fuck! No water!" I yelled.

"Oh, no!" Susie screamed.

Solomon was scrambling from his bed and grabbing for his clothes.

"My God. What do we do?"

I ran back inside, looked to the wall behind the fire box, and saw the flames licking through between the boards. There were more now, in different places along the wall, and smoke was starting to accumulate at the ceiling. I ran back outside, and as I passed the kitchen counter, my elbow caught a hurricane lamp, knocking it to the floor, the glass breaking in shards in front of the door.

Once outside, I ran to the deck and pulled the picnic table closer to the outside wall of the cabin, opposite the fireplace. Inside the cabin I heard Susie scream, "What should we do?"

I heard Solomon say, "Get dressed!"

I climbed on top of the table and began to punch a hole with my fist through the old wooden shakes in a location where I believed the fire to be. The shakes were thin and brittle, curled from fifty years of sun and rain, so I was able to break through. I got my fingers inside the hole and began pulling the wooden shingles off and throwing them down to the deck below me. When I had a hole large enough, I stuck my head in and could see the fire burning the asphalt building paper that wrapped the house inside the wall. The wall's interior was fully involved with fire, and I knew at that moment, if I had been holding a water hose, I would have been able to extinguish the fire easily. However, lacking water, I had only a single fire extinguisher in the house to fight the fire with.

I jumped off the table and tangled my feet, tripped, and fell backward down to the deck. I put my arms out behind me to catch my fall and as luck would have it, I impaled my left hand with three nails sticking up from one of the wooden shakes lying on the deck. I felt the pain and, raising my hand to look at it, saw that the shake was still attached to my hand, nailed through in three places. With my right hand, I pulled the shake free, got up, and ran back into the house to retrieve the fire extinguisher. As I did so, I ran through the broken glass of the hurricane lantern in my bare feet, slicing a huge gash in the bottom of my right foot. Despite the pain, the adrenalin spurned me forward to the fire extinguisher.

"There's broken glass here!" I shouted as Solomon, now dressed, began kicking the glass clear of the doorway. Susie had gotten dressed and was running out the door with an armload of clothes. "Grab what you can!" I yelled. "I'm going to try the fire extinguisher!"

"I can't believe this!" Susie screamed.

I grabbed the extinguisher and ran back outside, jumping up on the table. Susie and Solomon were yelling and running in and out of the cabin. I pulled the pin on the fire extinguisher, inserted the nozzle into the hole in the wall, and squeezed the handle. Moving the nozzle up and down and side to side, I was able to extinguish all but just a little flicker of flame before the fire extinguisher ran out of propellent.

"Fuck!" I screamed in a complete panic.

I put my eye up to the hole and looked inside the wall to see if I had gotten all the fire. There it was, a flame the size of a match-head burning in the lower corner of the stud bay, growing brighter by the second. So small, almost faltering as it fought to stay alive. It flickered, and I thought it might go out, but then right before my eyes, the flame burst to the size of an orange. It was too far away for me to reach it. Out of options, I realized I was going to lose the house.

I began shouting at Susie and Solomon to start evacuating the house of all its belongings. I had a fairly extensive library of books and pictures on the walls, and of course, my clothes that I wanted to save. I could hear Susie and Solomon's voices reaching the higher notes of panic as I rushed around to help. We grabbed anything we could carry and ran from the house to my pickup truck parked in the driveway outside the cabin, dumping armloads into the bed and running back inside for more.

The fire had progressed from the wall and was now licking along the high ceiling, beginning to crackle and puff. The entire inside of the cabin was glowing orange and the heat was beginning to sear, getting hard to take.

In and out we ran, armload after armload, calling to each other until from the outside, looking toward the house, it looked completely engulfed in flames. Susie and Solomon stopped and yelled at me to not go back into the house, that it was too dangerous, but I ran in through the door once more to grab whatever I could. Running to my closet, I grabbed a handful of clothes, throwing them from the bathroom window across to the driveway alongside the house. I looked into the cabin from the bathroom area and saw the place was gone, completely engulfed in flame. The fire was roaring now, puffing, pulling air in and out of the cabin like a huge bellows. Flame was up one wall and into the curved peak of the ceiling, forming a tunnel beneath. Susie and Solomon were outside screaming. I took one more look around, ducked my head, and ran through the burning inferno to the front door and out into the night. I ran out to the driveway where Solomon was holding Susie because she was crying. I turned around and stared at the burning cabin being engulfed by the angry, roiling flames.

Only then, standing there beside Susie and Solomon, did I realize I was still naked and began shivering from the cold. I walked up the driveway to where I had tossed some clothes and found a pair of pants and a shirt lying on the ground. I got dressed while watching the embers from the blaze shooting a hundred feet in the air and falling in the surrounding brush. Small spot fires were burning in several locations around the cabin, and the shop had started burning on the wall closest to the main blaze.

My impaled left hand was stiff and hard to open. I still had no shoes on and my cut foot was killing me. The fire in the brush below the cabin was burning slowly to the west, directly toward my drying box, where the twenty one pounds of packaged sinsemilla and a scale were hidden and stacked.

The house was gone. I ran toward the drying box, yelling for Susie and Solomon to follow me. "We have to save the pot! There're twenty pounds in the brush! It's going to burn!"

The open hillside between the burning cabin and the trail to the pot was heavily overgrown with Russian thistle, a waist-high menacing plant with inch-long stinging thorns all over it. We ran through the thistle and down the trail to the box. I opened the door. "Grab some buckets!"

"Where are we going to take it?" Solomon asked.

I looked up the hill and saw his box van dimly illuminated by the fire. "Can we put it in your van?" I asked frantically. The fire was now only twenty feet away and steadily moving toward us.

"Let's do it!" he yelled.

We all grabbed as many buckets as we could carry and began running up the hill toward his van, the thistle tearing at our clothes. Our arms and legs were massacred by the ripping plants, and my feet became pin cushions for the stinging thorns. At his van, Solomon opened the back door and climbed inside, and Susie and I handed him buckets that he stacked among the wicker furniture. I looked back toward the drying box and in the canyon below and saw the headlights of trucks coming up the road. It was the Big Sur Fire Brigade. Someone had seen the flames and called 911. I knew some of the members of the fire brigade were also members of law enforcement. If we were caught with the buckets of pot, all three of us were going to be arrested.

"Let's get the rest!" I yelled.

The three of us ran back down through the thistle, screaming obscenities, grabbed the remaining buckets and ran back up the hill.

Susie screamed at the top of her lungs. I heard it echo back from the dark canyon. "What is happening? Why is this happening? Wesley! What is wrong with your life?" She was still crying.

We were passing buckets into the van when the first trucks arrived at the cabin. I told Solomon to lock the van and stay there with Susie, then ran back down the hill to the drying box. I was looking at the last two buckets of pot and the triple beam scale when I saw the fire brigade chief, who was also one of the resident California Highway Patrol officers, walking toward me across the field in his yellow helmet and fire coat. The other firefighters were running down the driveway, dragging a hose and carrying tools.

Someone yelled, "Water!" and water started spraying from a hose.

I looked down at the scale and the remaining two buckets of pot in the plywood box and decided to leave them there, afraid the CHP officer would be curious about the scale and buckets. The advancing brush fire was so close that it was surely going to burn the box and destroy the evidence. I left the box and walked out into the field toward the chief. The burning cabin was now encircled by firefighters.

Just then my cache of .308 rifle ammunition caught fire in the loft, and a rapid staccato of gunshots began echoing through the canyon.

Someone yelled, "Bullets! Bullets are going off!" and everyone hit the ground.

The chief and I were about ten feet apart, lying flat in the thistle, when he hollered in my direction, "You got any more surprises for me?"

Bullets continued to explode from inside the burning cabin like popcorn in a kettle for about thirty seconds and then subsided. Someone shouted, "Jesus Christ!" I stood up slowly and walked up to the chief. "What happened?" he asked.

"Fire started in the wall," I said. "I've got no water. My water line broke up the hill. I couldn't put the fire out."

He looked at me and shook his head. "Goddamn it! Are you all right?"

"Cuts and burns, but yeah," I answered.

"The cabin's gone. I'm going to try and put this brush fire out," he said, and then turned and walked briskly back toward the cabin.

I was in no shape to help the fire brigade; my foot was hurting so badly at this point, I could barely walk. I limped over to my pickup parked in the driveway to look for shoes. A couple of firefighters I knew walked over and said how sorry they were. I climbed into the bed of the truck and found a pair of shoes. I sat on the edge of the truck's bed in the glow of the fire and took a minute to pull thorns from my feet before putting the shoes on.

The adrenalin started wearing off and a deep chill settled into my bones. It was getting hard to move. I rummaged through some clothes, found a sport coat, and put it on. Suddenly the last standing portion of the house collapsed in a rush of embers and sparks that reached high into the night sky.

Someone yelled, "Jesus Christ!" while someone else yelled, "Shit!"

More headlights raced up the hill. A group of firefighters had gotten below the fire and were cutting a line. The chief was directing hose lays, focusing the water into the brush line. I limped over to a firefighter who was manning a hose, pointed down the hill toward where my shop used to stand, and said, "Can you direct some water down there? My life's savings are buried right down there."

He redirected the stream of water. "Right around there?"

"Yeah, thanks," I said. "Just cool it off a little."

"Okay, man. Hey, I'm sure sorry about this. Looks like it was a nice place."

"It was. It was a very nice place."

CHAPTER 22

"Sometimes there's nothing left to do but get over it."

–Bo Rummsen

THE ENORMITY OF THE LOSS was beginning to dawn on me. My home, my home base, was gone. So much work had gone up in smoke. I wasn't sure what had been saved, but I knew I had lost a lot of valuable things. My tools were all gone, now just bent steel glowing red on the hillside, and the cabin was reduced to a large pile of burning embers with a few large beams protruding proud and black above the glow.

My friend Dan, who lived across the highway from the Rummsen Ranch, walked down the driveway toward me as more trucks reached the fire. "Are you all right?" he asked me. "I saw the flames and called 911."

"Well, you saved the coast a major brush fire if they can stop it here. I'm okay," I looked down at my foot. "I need to get this road open, so I can get my buddy's truck out of here. Can you help? My foot is cut pretty bad, and I can't walk very well."

"I'll see what I can do," he said, and jogged back up the driveway.

The fire chief walked over to me carrying a McLeod. "So no clue how this happened, Wes?"

I shook my head. "I don't know, Chief. From the fireplace, I guess. We woke up in the middle of the night with the inside of the wall on fire and no water at the spigot. We were fucked. I couldn't put it out."

He looked around. "I think we got the brush fire knocked down. Too bad about this, Wesley. Nice place."

I nodded. "Chief, is it possible to move some equipment? My friend has to get his truck out of here."

He looked up the hill. "Sure, we'll move some shit around. Let me know if you need anything else."

"Thanks, Chief," I said.

He walked up the driveway, and I limped the other way and then up the hill to the box van. Solomon and Susie were standing alongside it, wrapped in blankets and talking to Dan. We all gave each other hugs.

"They're going to move some trucks around to open the road," Dan said.

"Thank you, Dan. I asked the chief too. My fucking foot is killing me!" I said.

"Let's take a look at it." Solomon knelt down. "Which foot?"

"Right." I sat down on the step of the van and stuck out my foot.

Dan produced a flashlight he directed to the bottom of my foot as Solomon removed my shoe. Solomon's eyes got wide. "Oh, man…this is bad. You have to get to a hospital, buddy. You've got a huge gash in your foot!"

"Shit, Wes…" Susie said, looking over his shoulder.

"How bad is it?" I asked.

"It's bad," Solomon said. "It's a J-shaped cut from the middle of your big toe, across the joint, to the middle of the ball of your foot. It's about an inch wide and packed with dirt. It's not bleeding, but you have to have this looked at right now! You've also got splinters or something all over your foot."

"Fucking thistles," I said, putting my shoe back on.

"I've got them in my legs!" Susie complained.

"I'll drive you to the hospital, Wes," Dan offered.

"That works good, Dan. I can't drive, and the box van is a lousy ambulance." I winked at Solomon.

Dan walked down the road to get his car. I was thinking of my friend Luca Renzo and his wife Joan, who lived not far away on the west side of the highway. They owned a flat parcel of land hidden by pine trees a mile north of my place. I turned to Susie. "Ride with Solomon down to

Luca Renzo's house. It's a good place to stash the box truck for tonight. If that doesn't work, I'll look for you at Nepenthe when I get back from the hospital." I gave her a hug. "So sorry about this shitty night," I whispered.

I looked at Solomon. "My friend Luca will park you off the highway. We'll sort the rest out tomorrow."

"It's already tomorrow," he said, looking at his watch. "It's three AM."

I limped back down the road looking for Dan. The road was clear enough to move a vehicle through, and Solomon's big box truck rolled slowly past with a wave from Susie. I was glad to see the pot slowly escaping the scene. I looked from the road down the hill to where the drying box would be. It was still there. They had stopped the fire right at the box. It was more bad news. If they found the buckets of pot with the scale, I might be charged with possession with intent to sell. I saw Dan, and he waved to me. I limped to his car, and we drove down the hill for the trip to the hospital. On the way north, we passed Solomon's truck parked on the highway at the Renzo gate.

At the hospital, I was treated for the cut on my foot and minor burns. I was sitting on an emergency room table with my shoes and shirt off, while a nurse held my left hand and administered strategic shots of lidocaine to the holes in my palm. I felt dirty under the bright lights of the clean room. Another nurse walked in, smiled at me, and asked loudly, "What happened to you?"

"My house burned down," I said.

She locked eyes with me and said, "That's terrible." She rested her clipboard behind me and looked at my face. "Raise your arms." I could feel her finger trace my arms and back. She took my foot and raised it, placing it on a stainless steel extension from the table I was sitting on and pulled up a stool. "Let's have a look at your foot," she said to me, then turned to a male nurse. "I'll need a debridement kit." Then she turned back to me. "Okay. You have a nasty cut here. We'll have to clean this out and see how it looks. Your burns aren't bad. Level one, second degree. You might lose some skin, but no scarring. Are you allergic to any medications?"

"Not that I know of," I answered, my voice sounding far away to me.

She tore open a package and produced a syringe. "We have to numb this area so we can treat it. This might sting." She began injecting my foot.

I flinched. The nurse holding my hand was pushing a cotton-tipped tool dipped in Betadine into the three holes in my hand. I watched her for a couple of minutes. I felt pressure on the bottom of my foot and looked down to see the nurse scrubbing the wound with a small brush dipped in soapy water. She used tweezers to pull some of the thorns. "You're lucky," the nurse said. "There's no ligament or tendon damage to your toe. It's going to be sore, but you should heal just fine. Can you handle Vicodin?"

"I prefer Percocet."

"I can do that. I'll give you both. You're going to need them. Follow the directions for the meds and try to stay off your feet for a while. Raise your foot if it starts to throb. Any questions?"

"Who killed President Kennedy?" I asked.

She looked up at me. "Lee Harvey Oswald."

A half hour later, they were still stitching the bottom of my foot. By six AM, I was bandaged, hand and foot, and, after thanking the nurses, being pushed in a wheelchair out the door to Dan's car waiting at the curb.

A male nurse handed me my new rented crutches. "Do you know how to use these?" he asked me. "They're adjustable."

"I guess I'll figure it out," I said. "There're going to be a lot of adjustments."

CHAPTER 23

"Don't look down, something might be falling on your head."

–Luca Renzo

WE LEFT THE HOSPITAL PARKING lot and turned south on Highway 1. The trip down the coast was surrealistic—dawn colors, crisp air, me smelling of smoke and consumed by the loss and uncertainty of what the next few days would bring. We got down to Nepenthe, where through the trees I saw the now-familiar shape of Solomon's van parked in the lot. There must have been some problem at Luca's. Dan pulled off the highway and parked next to the van. I limped over with my crutches and knocked on the van door, finding Solomon and Susie sleeping in the front seats of the van.

Susie told me her horrible experience after finding the Renzo gate locked. She had climbed over and walked down the driveway a short distance, only to come face to face with Luca's crazy pit bull, Gonzo. Luca and Joan were apparently not home, and Gonzo was on patrol. Gonzo had attacked her, bit her, and tried several times to jump up and grab her by the neck. She had fended him off, screaming his name, and retreated back up the driveway. Gonzo had miraculously given up the attack. Had she tripped and fallen, there was no doubt what the outcome would have been.

She had washed her bite wound in the bathroom behind Nepenthe and said she felt all right. I told her I would ask Luca about Gonzo's rabies vaccination. I thanked Dan for his great favor of taking me to the hospital and said goodbye.

I turned to Solomon and said, “I need you to follow us back to the cabin site so we can off-load the pot from your truck.”

“Okay. Just give me fifteen minutes to make some tea and wake up. It’s been a long night.”

I borrowed a pen from Solomon and wrote down the gate combo on a piece of paper and handed it to him.

“Remember how to get there?”

“Yeah, no problem. I’ll be there in a few minutes.”

Susie and I climbed into her VW and headed down the coast. We drove without talking at first. The local anesthetic was starting to wear off, my foot was starting to throb, and I took a Vicodin.

She looked over at me. “What are you going to do?”

“About what?”

“About everything!”

“I don’t know. Maybe buy a trailer and put it on the site, maybe move onto my land on Simson Ridge. I can’t grow along Fuego Creek anymore, that’s for sure, but I like it there. I don’t know. How’s your leg?”

“It hurts. That dog is vicious. I hurt all over. I have thistles in my legs. I can’t believe any of this. Your life is fucking crazy.”

“You were lucky with Gonzo. He’s *really* crazy. Luca always has him tied up. I never thought he’d be loose. I’m sorry.”

“I survived. I was lucky I knew his name.”

Turning off the highway onto the Ranch Road, we found yellow caution tape draped in the brush, and the gate was open. We drove up the hill to the cabin site and pulled into the driveway behind a green US Forest Service truck. We got out, and I stuck a crutch under my arm. I could barely put any weight on my foot. I noticed that there were about ten firefighters with shovels digging in the area of my buried cash. One guy was close. I guessed the word had gotten out regarding my life savings. I leaned over and whispered to Susie. “Go down and borrow that guy’s shovel. Dig into that pile of white ash. The money is there in a can.”

I leaned on my crutch watching as Susie made her way down the slope and took the shovel from the firefighter. I heard her say, "Thank you. I'll take it from here."

All the men stopped digging and looked at her. Two shovels full of dirt later, she pried up the coffee can. She handed back the shovel, bent down, and picked up the can. She removed the plastic top, which was partially melted, and looked inside. A smile broke out on her face, and she looked up at me and gave me the thumbs-up. The firefighters shook their heads and drifted away. Susie brought the can up the hill.

"It's fried at the top, but I think it's okay," she said under her breath.

I looked inside and replaced the melted lid on the can. "Thank you, Lord!" I said to the sky.

Word got around right away to all of the volunteer firemen that we were back and the money had been found. Susie and I were standing in the driveway just above the smoldering ruins, beneath the blackened English walnut tree, me on a crutch, Susie holding the money, when a uniformed officer of the United States Forest Service walked up to us and introduced himself.

"Jim Handley, US Forest Service. Are you Wesley Daggert?"

"I am." I shook his hand.

"I'm sorry for your loss. I'm here investigating the cause of this fire."

"What's to investigate?" I asked. "I think the stove got too hot. I was here, and *I'm* not sure what happened."

"Look, Wesley, I probably shouldn't tell you this, but I found marijuana and a scale in a wooden box in the brush just down from the burn site. That makes this a crime scene. I can't turn my back on this. Being an officer of the United States government, I had to call the Monterey County Sheriff's Department. They're on their way now. Other than that, I'm sincerely sorry for your loss."

I was incredulous. I had just lost everything, could barely stand up on crutches, and this man had just called the police to come and arrest me. He stared at the money can, and I wondered if there was going to be a fight over it when, at that very moment, down in the canyon, I heard the steady grind of Solomon's truck coming up the dirt road below. Thinking of the twenty pounds of manicured marijuana headed toward my crime scene with the sheriff on his way, I turned to Susie and said, "Let's go!"

We turned away from Officer Handley and hurried back to Susie's Volkswagen, me working the crutch as fast as I could. No one tried to stop us as we got into her car.

"We have to go down and stop him from coming up here! Shit!" I said, picturing the sheriff blazing down the coast with his lights and siren.

Susie backed the VW up, turned it around, and spun gravel down the hill to intercept Solomon. I was in a panic. There was no way of telling how close the sheriff was. We slid to a stop in front of his van, causing Solomon to stop short. Susie pulled up to his window and rolled hers down. I leaned across her and shouted across to him.

"Turn your truck around and follow us! The sheriff is coming!"

"What?" His face sagged, and he leaned out his window looking behind his truck. "Jesus Christ!" he barked, turning his wheels and slamming his truck in reverse.

Susie took off down the hill with Solomon in hot pursuit. When we got to the main ranch road, instead of turning right toward the highway and possibly into the path of the sheriff's department, we turned left and drove toward Kade's place. Solomon was right behind us in a huge cloud of dust. We reached Kade's driveway and turned in, driving down into the shelter of the trees at the bottom of the canyon.

"Stop here," I said to Susie.

I got out and hobbled back to Solomon's window.

"What the fuck is going on?" His voice was tight and hoarse.

"Forest Service found some pot in the brush and called the sheriff. They're on their way."

"Jesus Christ, man, this is too much! I'm pretty much over this shit!" Solomon said, holding his forehead.

"I want to wait here and see if we're being followed. I don't want to lead them into Kade's. We'll give it a minute, and then follow us in," I said.

I limped back and slid into the VW. My foot was killing me, so I took a Percocet. After a few minutes and nobody behind us, we started up out of the canyon and pulled in front of Kade's house. I got out and yelled, "Kade!"

He came running out, and we filled him in about the fire. All he said was, “What? Holy shit! At least you saved the pot!”

He pulled his truck up to the van, and he and Solomon urgently began transferring the pot buckets. We threw a tarp over the bed of Kade’s truck, covering the pot, and made arrangements to meet in a couple of days.

“Don’t get this mixed up with your stuff or our stuff,” I said to Kade.

“Don’t worry about it. How’s the pot we have hanging in the drying box?”

“It’s okay, nobody found it. Look, I have to hide out for a while,” I said. “There’s probably going to be a warrant out for me. I can’t work anyway; my foot is too sore. The other drying boxes are okay for now, but don’t go up there for a while. The place is hot. Bad pun, I know. I’ll be in touch.”

Kade stared at me. “So, no more cabin, huh? Bummer. You couldn’t grow there anymore anyway.” The guy seemed devoid of emotion.

“I’ll be in touch,” I said again.

Susie and I left the ranch with Solomon following in his van, driving north on the highway. It wasn’t long before we passed the sheriff’s deputy driving south, lights flashing.

“There they go!” I said.

Susie was grim, focused on the road ahead. “Where’re we going?” she asked.

“They’re going to be looking for me,” I said. “Let’s check into the Big Sur Lodge. I can hole up there for a week or so, and you can go home and catch up on your stuff.”

The Big Sur Lodge was set well off the highway, inside Pfeiffer State Park. Solomon followed us in and parked the big truck in the parking lot. Susie checked us in using some very crispy bills. I stayed in the car to avoid being seen.

When Susie came out, Solomon grabbed his bag and rode up with us to the room. The rooms were large and private, nestled in close to the mountain where no highway noise could be heard. Once inside, we all took turns bathing to wash off the grime and soot. I opted for a bath so I could keep my bandages dry. Susie and I had to put our dirty clothes back on while Solomon, who had saved his travel bag, looked spotless with a fresh change of clothes. We sat and talked for a while until our voices grew tired and there was mostly silence. There were plenty of beds, so we each picked one and faded away.

The next morning, after a sound sleep, Solomon left for Washington. We hugged and slapped each other's backs. He and Susie shared a long embrace. I grabbed my crutch and walked him outside.

"This has been fucking nuts, Wesley. I feel like I need another four months with Maharishi. I don't know what to say. It might be a long time before I visit you again."

I thought he was joking, but there was too much gravity in his voice. He looked fried as he gave me a smile. "Good luck to you, man. Do some meditation." He threw his bag over his shoulder and set off with long strides toward his van in the parking lot.

Susie and I carefully dissected the crispy contents of the #10 coffee can. For all it had been through, the $19,000 stuffed in the can, buried in the ground six inches beneath a piece of bridge timber, then scorched by a blazing inferno raging over the top of it, was amazingly intact. The bills at the top of the can were blackened and crumbled to the touch, but after carefully extracting the currency from the can, we were able to save all but just a couple hundred dollars.

Susie drove up to Nepenthe and told them I was off my feet and would be for about a month. Then, later that week, we drove to the bank and told a wide-eyed teller our tale of woe, spreading the blackened cash out in front of her. Any fragments without both serial numbers had to be forfeited. In the end, after much hoopla, we walked out of the bank with fresh money in neat stacks of twenties and hundreds.

Back at our "hideaway" at the state park, we formed a plan to return to the burned Apple Tree House and retrieve the approximately ten pounds of buds we had hanging in the drying boxes, not to mention the twenty-one pounds of packaged buds we had stacked below them. All was just up the hill and around two bends in the road from the blackened site.

CHAPTER 24

"If you've got it, flaunt it!"

–Susie Reynolds

I WAS STILL NOT ABLE TO walk well enough to take on this rescue, so Susie went to Nepenthe and contacted Kade. She brought him back with her to the Big Sur Lodge where I was holed up, and we sat down in the living room.

"So, this is your hideout," Kade said. "How long you gonna milk this thing?"

"I still can't put much weight on my foot," I said. "Have you been up to our drying boxes?"

"No, not yet. But we have to get up there. That pot is way dry. I haven't seen the sheriff on the Ranch Road."

"I'll go with you," Susie said, looking at Kade. "I can package that pot."

Kade and I looked at each other. I shrugged. We needed some help and, though it was going to be sketchy, there was no reason why Susie couldn't do the work. We agreed that they would meet at Nepenthe and go up early the following morning. Later that day Susie recounted their story to me.

Susie and Kade put together fresh paint buckets, a couple of oranges, old bed sheets, a scale, and two pairs of dikes, and then began the approach to the burned-out cabin in Kade's old Volvo station wagon. The move was risky. There was no way of knowing if the sheriff was there or not, so they drove to the top of a neighboring hill along the Julian Fuego homestead road that looked down on the old cabin site and surveyed the scene. There was just the burn spot, but no parked vehicles. They then drove over and up to the old cabin site, hoping that no one had shown up in the interim.

Only a hundred yards beyond the burned cabin, around two bends in the road, they stopped and parked at the trail leading to the drying boxes. Kade removed the dead brush that obscured the trailhead, and they hauled the supplies down to the site. Both boxes were full of hanging buds, trimmed and dry, waiting for packaging. In addition, there were forty two buckets of already packaged sinsemilla stacked against the walls. They were spreading the sheets out on the ground as a workplace when the sound of a car engine came up from the canyon below. Kade stood and walked over to a vantage point where the canyon was visible. He saw the car moving swiftly in the canyon and said calmly, "Sheriffs."

Kade was not one to panic, and Susie had grown nerves of steel in the last couple of days. Concealed in the brush under the shade of the ceanothus, they held their ground and waited. There was now no means of escape by car, and the license plates on Kade's station wagon were a bust anyway. Kade walked quickly up and re-plugged the path to the boxes, then returned to where Susie sat, and they waited.

The sheriff's car pulled into the driveway of the burned cabin, and two uniformed deputies got out of the car and started milling around. Susie and Kade could hear their voices clearly and, after some conversation, learned that the sheriffs were waiting to meet a Forest Service investigator at the scene. They looked at each other, shrugged, and got to work packaging the pot. There they were, high-centered on two paint cans, calmly clipping buds into other cans, while only a hundred yards away, two sheriff's deputies were walking around pointing and kicking ash on the burned-out property.

Finally, after a couple of hours, the investigator arrived in a green Forest Service truck and the three officers walked around talking, trying to reconstruct what they could of the fire and subsequent bust. In the brush nearby, our heroes just kept trimming.

When the voices ceased, Kade listened for the sound of the vehicles starting, or driving away, but heard none. They waited and kept working. When all the buds had been packaged and the site cleaned up, they listened for an hour more. They were confused as to how they had heard the cars coming but not heard them leaving and were concerned that it might be a trap. The sheriff could be waiting for them, or someone else, just around a corner.

Still, it had been some time since any voice or noise had been heard, so they elected to take a dry run down the hill without the pot to see if anyone was around. They drove to the bottom of the canyon and, seeing no one, returned up the hill for the buckets. It was a very ballsy move. They hauled the sixty-two buckets of bud up the trail to the station wagon, leaving the boxes empty. They covered the buckets with sheets and packed up their supplies, then waited another half hour and went for it. Down the hill they drove, apprehensive around every corner, expecting to run into the sheriff, all the way to Kade's house. They were having a lucky day and made it without incident. Once there, they made the required trips to the hidden boxes and stashed everything away. Now all our pot was definitely, once again, in one basket.

When Susie returned to my hideout at the lodge and told me this story, I was amazed and more than impressed. I knew Kade was a cool customer—he and I had gone through some shit—but Susie had shown incredible steel and resolve in stepping up to handle the recent events. It was one of the gutsiest stories I had ever heard.

One week later, the fire chief drove up to my room at the lodge, this time in his role as the resident California Highway Patrol officer. My heart sank when I pulled back the curtains and saw the black-and-white cruiser outside my room. So much for my being on the lam—the local CHP seemed to know everything, including where I was hiding out.

He wasn't there to arrest me, he said, but I was being charged with possession of nine ounces of marijuana for sale and needed to contact the sheriff's department. I said I would. He asked about my foot and drove away. It felt funny to be hiding out in full sight of the CHP. Those guys knew everything that was going on, probably more than they wanted to know, and were still able to juggle the law and a sense of loyalty to the community. Most locals understood how fortunate we were as a community to have them.

It was odd being charged with possession of nine ounces because the buckets had been weighed and I knew each one contained eight ounces of pot and held between them exactly one pound. I found out later from friends who were there that the sheriff's deputy had stopped at Fernwood on his way back to town and showed off the buds to some locals in the parking lot, passing the open buckets around for all to see. Somehow, seven ounces of very good seeded marijuana never made it to the substation.

In the end, after an arraignment, there was the expected wheeling and dealing between the district attorney and my lawyer. My record was clean, so the sales charge was dropped, and I ended up pleading guilty to possession of nine ounces of excellent, albeit seeded, marijuana and sentenced to one year's probation.

I moved back into my old truck that had been my home in 1970, parking it on a switchback above the cabin site with sweeping ocean views near the drying boxes. I holed up there to heal and figure out where I was headed next.

CHAPTER 25

"New beginnings are often disguised as painful endings."

–Lao Tzu

BY MID-FEBRUARY 1978, MY FOOT was healed up pretty well, and I was thinking of moving onto my property on Simson Ridge. My grass-growing days along Juan Fuego Creek were over. I was a red pin on a map somewhere in the recently formed Sheriff Department's Marijuana Eradication Team's planning room. In addition, the garden I had shared with Kade was looming large in the mind of some coastal bud thief, and my cabin was just a black, sooty spot on the hillside.

I walked into Fernwood Resort one afternoon for a drink. On my way to the bar I noticed Luca sitting next to the restaurant fireplace with a newer friend I had just recently met named John Stalkinger. John had recently been hired at Nepenthe to work on the maintenance crew. I walked over and sat down next to them. At just that moment, a glass broke at the bar, and there was the unmistakable sound of someone being hit with a punch. Someone gave a short yell. We looked over just in time to see the bartender, Doc, come from behind the bar. Two guys were rolling on the floor.

"Hey!' his voice boomed through the room. "Not in my bar!" Doc was tall and strong, and he bent down and grabbed both guys by their shirt collars, hauling them up to their feet. "Now quit it! Any more of this and you're both eighty-sixed. Got it?" Doc glared at both of them.

Both men nodded their heads, and Doc pushed them away. He stood there and stared at the men until they sat back down at the bar. Doc returned to polishing glasses behind the bar. One of the men ordered another drink to replace the one that spilled. Doc made the drink, and the room returned to normal.

John gave a short laugh. "Just like the Old West. I like it!"

"What the hell was that about?" Luca reached for his drink.

I just shook my head and laughed. "Always something going on here." I looked over at John. "Hey, John, getting settled in at your new job?"

He wiped some beer from his beard. "Oh, hell, man, it's just steel, wood, nails, and wrenches. No big deal."

John was a big man, maybe six feet, one inch tall and 235 pounds, with shoulder-length hair and a beard. He had grown up on a farm in central Washington that bordered the Columbia River. In the short time he had been at Nepenthe, he had impressed everyone with his life experience. He was a mechanic, a welder, and a gunsmith, and he could ride the hell out of both his motorcycles, one a big Harley, the other a powerful Suzuki off-road bike. If a problem needed a solution or something needed fixing, John could do it. He was more of a MacGyver than MacGyver was.

Luca was looking at Doc, who was still polishing glasses with an eye on the two men at the bar. "What are you drinking, Wesley?"

"I'll get it," I said, standing. I walked up and stood beside one of the combatants at the bar. He shot me a look. He had a small cut above his right eye.

"Hi, Doc, tequila grapefruit juice," I called out. Doc made my drink, and I returned to the fireplace.

"John and I were just talking about the reasons people die," Luca said.

I looked at him. "Really? There's a lot of reasons, I imagine."

"Heart failure," John said. "It's always heart failure. There's no death without heart failure involved. Think about it. You've never heard of a person dying and their heart was still beating. If it's still beating, you're alive. It's plain and simple. Everyone dies of heart failure."

"He's got a point," Luca laughed.

"Yeah, I see what you're sayin," I said. "That makes it real simple."

John put his drink on the table. "Another thing, have you ever noticed when you listen to the news that in a lot of crimes arson is suspected?"

I laughed and almost spit out my swallow of tequila grapefruit.

"Think about it," John went on, "such and such happened and arson is suspected! I hear it all the time."

"And then there's foul play," Luca joined in. "I've heard 'the authorities suspect foul play' many times in news broadcasts."

"Not to mention 'mayhem'," I laughed. "Mayhem is often involved in these crimes."

John laughed. "Here you go, a man was found in an alley dead of mayhem. Arson and foul play are suspected!"

We all laughed.

"So, what's going on up at your place, Wesley?" Luca asked.

I took a drink from my glass. "I'm living out of my old panel truck and trying to figure out how to clean up the mess the fire left. I'm okay. There's the refrigerator, hot water heater, the old boiler, two sinks, a bathtub, and lots of metal pipe lying there in the ash. I need to get it to the dump."

Luca leaned forward, "I'll help you with that."

"Count me in too," John pitched in. "I don't know if arson or foul play are suspected, but I'll bring the Nepenthe dump truck up there, and we'll get all that mayhem to the dump in one load!"

We all laughed again. I was grateful for the offer of help. I raised my glass in a toast. "Fantastic!"

We made arrangements to meet at the cabin site two days later.

John and Luca arrived in Nepenthe's dump truck at the cabin site bright and early and for five hours we loaded the bent, charred metal pieces into the truck's bed. I soaked the ash with water from the hose, and we raked it into piles, shoveling most of it into the truck. By midafternoon the site was clear, with just the parallel lines of the rake's tines running across it. The walnut tree and the apple tree were both badly burned but still stood defiantly over the blackened building site. I followed John and Luca in my truck to the dump in Moss Landing north of Monterey where, with one pull of a lever in the dump truck, we left my whole history of the Apple Tree House lying on the ground, a dark twisted pile of rubbish in front of an auto crusher.

After the fire and while I was healing, Tom Rummsen surprised me by selling the 500-acre Juan Fuego Creek portion of his ranch where I lived to a young man with old money from the south. Included in the sale was the Julian Fuego homestead, one of the coast's most valued flat acreages. The young man's name was Bradford Berkshire, and he was my new landlord.

Bradford's family had connections throughout wealthy South Carolina, and he had married into the well-known and very respected Gottlieb clan from Georgia. His wife Laura was a beautiful free spirit who was immediately at home in Big Sur. Bradford, however, I was not so sure about.

I first met him on the ashes of the Apple Tree House. He drove up in a new Jeep with his wife, Laura. She opened her door and hopped out with a squeal. "Wow! This is beautiful!" she spun around in her country dress with her arms extended. "I love it!"

Bradford opened his door more slowly and stepped out wearing a polo outfit, complete with helmet and knee-high black boots as though he had just dismounted his horse after a chukka at the arena. He extended his hand. "Bradford Berkshire, and you are... Wesley, I presume?"

I shook his gloved hand. "Yes, Wesley Daggert."

He motioned toward his jeep. "Please, meet my wife, Laura."

She walked over with a smile and took my hand in a curtsey. "I'm Laura. A pleasure to meet you, I'm sure."

I bowed my head. "Laura..."

Bradford waved his arm in a grand gesture. "I own all this now, and I must say how disappointed I am at the loss of this cabin. It was intact when I was negotiating with Tom Rummsen on the purchase of this property."

"Yes, it was a big disappointment," I said. "Maybe it can be rebuilt."

"My thinking exactly. The building site is just too special not to have a cabin on it. I'd like to ask you to stay on."

He walked toward the ashes and spoke over his shoulder. "We can move a temporary trailer onto the property while my attorneys establish a building permit. This is a big ranch, and I will need someone to watch this side of it. I have taken up residence at the Julian Fuego house up on the hill and have extensive plans there." He turned back to me. "What do you say?"

Taken by surprise and not knowing what to say, I said, "Yes. I can stay on. What are the terms?"

"I will buy the trailer and place it just here," he said, pointing. "You will pay me $250 per month until rebuilding commences. At that time, we will renegotiate our terms."

"You may want to consider another site for the trailer," I said. "You'll need this spot for building materials."

"Yes, we'll give that some thought," he said.

"I'd like first refusal on the new cabin when it's available for rent," I said.

"Done!" he said, turning toward the Jeep. "Oh, and there's to be no growing of marijuana on my property. I've heard stories."

"Of course," I said. "I understand."

I was smiling as Bradford drove back down the road with Laura leaning back in her seat, waving at the sky. It was an interesting proposition. I wasn't really ready to move onto my own property. I still had a mountain of brush to clear up there for a building site and had not yet established a water source.

The thought of living in a newly built Apple Tree House was very intriguing. It would bring the tragic events of the fire back round-robin to some sort of closure. Complicating matters as well, at least logistically, I had several slabs of redwood and three dismantled redwood wine tanks stacked and stored in the cool canyon below. Moving them to a hot, sunny, unprotected Simson Ridge without a plan was not smart. The wood would check, warp, and split. In essence, I was buying some time. Having Bradford as a landlord would be interesting, but his heart seemed to be in the right place, and I had nothing to lose.

I had lost my job at Nepenthe, being unable to work during a time when they were gearing up for the holiday season. They had needed to replace me and now, in February, with people laid off, they weren't hiring. I was flush with cash and thinking of not going back anyway.

Jimmy and David Stafford had paid me a visit since the fire, and we had done some business out of the back of my truck. Both were shocked at the loss of the cabin but managed to joke about doing business that way.

"Reminds me of Haight-Ashbury in the late sixties," Stafford remarked. "I bought plenty of pot from the backs of vehicles in those days!"

Jimmy quipped, "Like a drive-up hamburger stand, roll your window down and place your order. You need a good looking carhop on roller skates!"

Between them they had purchased twelve pounds of sinsemilla, and I had deposited another $18,000 in my new safety deposit box at Wells Fargo. I thought about paying off my Simson Ridge property, but then thought it would look better if I paid it off over time.

Kade and I had divided our buckets up. It was a lengthy process resembling a divorce settlement, involving complete fairness of weight, quality, and like kind of product. After way too much of each other's company, we ended up happy with the split.

I was holding fifty-three pounds in 106 buckets scattered in hiding places around the cabin site and on my property on Simson Ridge. Eighty-five thousand dollars in unsold sinsemilla was not money in the bank, but it gave me swagger, especially in 1978.

Bradford Berkshire purchased a twenty-foot travel trailer, and we placed it above the cabin site on a small flat with an open ocean view. Richard Gable had stayed on as ranch foreman, working now for Bradford. Richard brought the backhoe up and dug a large hole for a temporary septic dump for the trailer. We covered the hole with wood planks and covered the planks with dirt. The propane company came and relocated their tank to a position close to the new trailer. I extended the water line up the hill and made the connections.

The trailer seemed spacious compared to my old truck/van, and I enjoyed the newness of it. It had a queen-size bed, a kitchenette, a dining area, and two comfortable chairs for lounging. I placed a table and folding chairs outside in front of the view and called it home.

Bradford had his attorneys working on a permit for a new cabin and was finding out how difficult the building process was along coastal Monterey County. His building proposal was lavish and complicated.

I told him if he did away with the turrets, ramparts, and maybe the drawbridge, and just proposed a simple cabin similar to what had been there, it might make things easier, but he was on a Knights of the Round Table trip and was seen occasionally around Big Sur sporting a chain mail shirt and a foppish cap with a long peacock feather sticking from it. I didn't think the permit would come anytime soon.

I hired two guys to start clearing brush on the Simson Ridge property to open up a couple of building sites I was considering. There were two slide areas below the access road to the building sites where the cut brush was being dumped. I had worked out a temporary water connection with one of my neighbors, running some black poly pipe overland to my property and establishing some random hose spigots.

One of my neighbors had a bulldozer, and he cut a road through the brush into a clearing surrounded by redwoods. I purchased a small travel trailer off a lot in Watsonville and placed it on wooden blocks in the clearing. Behind the clearing, farther back in the redwoods, a deep hole was dug and an outhouse built over the top of it. I called the propane company and had a tank dropped just off the road. A galvanized gas line ran from it to the trailer. I now had a comfortable place to stay on Simson Ridge when I wanted to be closer to Big Sur.

After the fire and in among all of this resettling and expansion toward Simson Ridge, Susie and I were seeing less of each other. She was busy in town and at her house, and I was busy in Big Sur. Then, to further complicate things, she somehow got back involved with her ex-boyfriend, and we called it quits. It was quite a blow. I wasn't sure how it had happened, but with everything going on, I had no choice but to get philosophical about it. Sometimes when you're forward-thinking, your life just doubles back and bites you on the butt, there's no getting around it. I was beginning to almost expect it in my life. She was apologetic but unabashed, and I thought he was a bit arrogant. I was feeling jealous and left behind. It was clear I needed to pull my head out of my ass.

In mid-March, on a crystal-clear morning, I was sitting outside the trailer above Fuego Creek. I heard Kade before I saw him. He burst around the corner in his station wagon and slid to a stop in front of my trailer, pushing a cloud of dust over my table. I hadn't seen him in a while. He climbed out of his car.

"Hey," he said, and pulled up a chair.

"What's goin' on, Kade?"

His eyes were taking in the scene. "Nice trailer. You growin'?"

"No. You know I can't grow here, and I don't want to start anything on Simson. There's too many people up there."

He leaned toward me. "Do you want to grow? I found a place just south of my property that looks good."

"Partners again?" I asked.

"Yeah, same as before, only things have to be different."

I raised my eyebrows at the loaded statement.

"With you being busted, you have a reputation now. Everyone knows you grow. If people see you and me together, they'll put two and two together, and I'll be fucked with Tom Rummsen."

"What do you propose?"

"You can't drive over to my property. Ever. I have to meet you somewhere else or drive over here and pick you up. You have to ride up with me. You'll have to lie down in the back of the truck or the station wagon, so nobody sees you. It's the only way."

I laughed and shook my head. "That's fucked, Kade. All summer long riding back and forth lying in the back of your car? Why wouldn't people think we were just friends? That I was just visiting?"

"Because we're not, and you'd be there too much. Everyone knows you grow grass, and if it gets back to Rummsen, I'll lose my property. That's the deal, take it or leave it."

"Shit, why do I feel like I'm going to regret this?" I said.

Kade grinned at me across the table, then reached across and slapped my shoulder. "You want to make some more money or not?"

"Yeah, I do. Maybe we can salvage those nets from our old garden."

Kade stood up. "Fuck those nets. I don't think they work. We don't need them anyway. Come on, I'll show you."

He opened the back door of the Volvo and folded the rear seat down. "Climb in," he said.

"Jesus," I said under my breath as I climbed in.

Kade got behind the wheel, started the car, and put it in reverse. "Lie down," he said.

I lay down and he started rumbling down the road like he was in a hurry. I was rolling back and forth and bouncing up and down. I called up to him. "Hey, man, can you slow down a bit? I'm rolling all over the place back here!"

"Yeah," he said, and then I could swear he sped up.

Five minutes later we bumped to a stop in front of his cabin, and he got out. I sat up, opened the side door, and climbed out. His wife was standing there looking at me, and then she turned and walked into the house.

"Let's go," Kade said.

We walked down to the phony outhouse and took the trail that led to his drying boxes. Kade stopped there and removed a large brush plug from a new trail. We walked south through the dense brush, then across a wide headland that sloped gently toward the cliff above the highway. The ocean beyond spread for as far as the eye could see. There were no houses or roads in sight.

The trail was narrow and the brush was shoulder-high, sometimes overhead. We walked for about a quarter mile, then zigzagged down into a steep ravine with a trickle of water running through. The bottom of the ravine was damp with a profusion of stinging nettles growing in it, and the trail went through them and up the other side in a series of crude steps cut into the sidehill. My hands were prickly and turning numb from the nettles as we reached a low-lying branch where the trail led underneath into a tunnel cut through the brush.

We were on our hands and knees for another hundred feet before we were able to stand up. I stood up under a beautiful canopy of tall ceanothus in full bloom, small blue starburst flowers hanging under a tent of green foliage. The area was large, maybe 200 feet long by half that wide. We were on the flat of a ridgeback that sloped gently toward the ocean before dropping off in a precipitous run to Highway 1.

"Wow!" I said.

Kade reached up and broke a branch from a tree. "Nice, huh?"

Just then a small plane flew by over the ocean at about eye level, visible in and out of the tree branches as it passed.

"They can't see us here. The leaves are the same color as the pot, so we'll be good," Kade said. He kicked the ground with the toe of his boot.

"The soil here is deep. These flowers have been falling and mulching for years. The place is perfect! We just need to get some water here."

I was impressed. "Where's the nearest water source?" I asked.

"Potter Creek, down this south side," he pointed. "We need to walk up from here and find a place to dip into the creek."

Potter Creek was a much larger creek than Fuego and had cut a much deeper canyon on its way to the Pacific. We were easily 400 feet above the creek at the point where we stood and looking at a very long eastern climb before we would intersect the creek and any flowing water.

Kade walked around breaking branches. "We can stage at my house, walk everything over here without being seen. This cover is perfect. No one's around here, no one will see us. We can set up a kids' pool, a big one this time, and just let the water flow through the whole garden. What do you think?"

"Let's find some water!" I said. "Then we'll know for sure."

CHAPTER 26

"From the tops of the ridges where the yellow grass falls off toward the sea, Highway One is just a series of road cuts connected by a thread, often covered by a blanket of white fog."

–Army Jack

WE SET OUT FROM THE new garden site and walked straight uphill to ensure some fall for the water line, then angled out to a path closer to the canyon edge, high above Potter Creek. From there we stayed under the cover of brush and walked slightly uphill toward the back of the canyon. Occasionally we emerged out of the brush into a bare spot and had to crawl on our bellies until we were under cover again. We walked for an hour, ever higher and nearer to the running water of Potter Creek.

Up ahead we saw a logistical problem looming—a house built on the steep slope above the canyon. From its south facing deck, the ground dropped off in a rocky fall to the creek. We sat under cover and surveyed the scene.

"We have to go right under that deck," Kade said.

I could see he was right, we were skirting a cliff above the creek and had no choice but to pass just underneath the deck.

"The good news is, they probably never go beneath the deck because it's just too steep," I said. "We could lay the water line in that brush line just above the cliff and throw some dirt over it. They'd never see it."

"Let's move up to that chunk of brush and get under the deck to the other side. I don't see anybody around."

We crawled silently through the chamise and sage until we were on the other side of the house. I fully expected someone to shout down and ask us what we were doing crawling around their property, but it never happened. We were soon under the cover of oak trees on the other side of the house and could see the water of the creek running below. We walked a slightly uphill course until we got to the creek bed.

Potter Creek was wide and flat at this spot, and the Rummsen Ranch road was visible where it crossed the creek a hundred yards above us. In the middle of the creek, with water running around it, was a knot of tree limbs and boulders. Just below it, on the downstream side, was a still pool of water.

"This is a good spot," I said. "Any higher and we're right next to the road. We can put the source beneath this pool and run our water line off from here."

Kade nodded. "This is it. Let's go back."

We paused again, hidden in the oak trees, and looked at the house that was in our way.

I nodded toward the house. "We'll have to plan this for a day that's foggy and drippy as hell, 'right in your face' kinda fog, right here, they won't be outside, and we'll have some cover. Let's get enough pipe to get us past this house and stash it here. We can build the catch basin and wait for the right time to lay the pipe."

We crawled back under the deck of the house and back to the garden site. The fall in elevation was consistent but not too steep. We walked back to Kade's place in good spirits and made a shopping list. The next day we drove to town in Kade's truck and bought twenty coils of three-quarter-inch black poly pipe with assorted connections and hose clamps and threw a tarp over it. At a salvage yard we bought a deep stainless steel sink with one drain. Our last stop was at a window fabrication shop where we bought a square yard of stainless steel screen.

Before sunrise the next morning, we drove up the Ranch road to a pullout just above Potter Creek where we planned to establish our water source. I rode in the cab tucked down on the passenger-side floorboards. We quickly off-loaded seven coils of pipe, screen, the sink, and some fittings. Kade turned the truck around while I hid everything under a fallen tree. We'd have to wait for the fog to roll in to set up the water system.

Three days later we had a sudden change in the weather, and a strong storm began forming off the coast. Kade and I made plans to work in the worst of it. We watched and waited. The storm hit late the next night with gusting winds and slashing rain. Kade was outside my trailer holding his hat down on his head at dawn the next morning.

It was a cold, wet morning with wind driving the rain slightly uphill. We drove over to his property, me hugging the floor of his truck. We dressed in drab green camouflage rain suits and, after gathering some hand tools, hiked the trail to the garden site. By the time we arrived we were sweaty and sopping wet. After a brief rest, we hiked up the water line trail toward our source, carrying a shovel and a pick. When we came to the house above our trail we paused to see if anyone was visible, but there was only the pelting rain and waving branches of the storm-blown trees. We crept below the house and into the cover of the oaks on the other side.

Walking out into the open of the creek bottom, we pulled the sink out from its hiding place and began working feverishly, digging in the pool of water below the confluence of the creek to set the sink down where it would be submerged. The water was up over our ankles. The falling rain and blowing tree limbs masked any sound we were making. We used the pick to cut a channel from the pool down toward a brushy outcrop at the creek's edge. Then we attached a roll of pipe to the sink drain and pushed the sink deep into the pool, rolling the coiled pipe down the trench we had dug. With some back filling, we buried the pipe under dirt and gravel. We cut a narrow trail through the brush, dropping downhill from our source until we were under the oak trees and looking at the house.

The rain was still falling heavily and the wind seemed to be picking up. We continued our pick work, burying the pipe completely from view as it left Potter Creek. We then went back to the source and attached the screen to the top of the sink with wire. We built a rock dam around the sink and topped it with some downed tree limbs. A deep pool formed around the sink and covered it completely.

Suddenly, over the sound of the storm, we heard a truck approaching. We flattened out on the wet creek bed. It was Bo Rummsen driving down the road. I could see him clearly as he looked straight ahead, not seeing us.

We did more work, directing the creek toward our sink and placing stones strategically to mask our pipe and catch basin. We then moved down to the oaks that grew below the house. The storm was still blowing strongly, and we were as confident as we could be that we were alone outside. With one eye on the deck, looking for anyone at all, we cut a trench underneath the deck from the tree line to the brush line west of the house. We unrolled the pipe into the ditch, me holding the pipe coil in my arms and backing along the edge of the steep fall to the creek. If anyone had walked out of the house to the edge of the deck, they would have seen two crazy men in rain gear laying a water line just below their house. I hadn't even considered what my answers might be to their questions.

Water was running through the pipe coil and spurting out the open end. Every time I rolled the coil around a complete turn, the water gushed over the top of me, but hell, you can only get so wet. Kade fed the pipe into the trench and covered it with dirt and rock as we moved along. Soon we were under the cover of brush again, and I dropped the spurting coil. We went back, smoothing over the trench line, throwing sticks and branches over it, and walked into the creek bed to inspect our work.

There was a pile of brush and rock in the center of the creek with a natural pond at its base. The creek seemed to flow toward the pond, but there was no sign of our sink or pipe. It was all submerged or buried beneath the shifting gravel of the flowing creek. There was no sign of our pipe leaving the creek bed or traveling below the house. And the heavy rain was rapidly covering our tracks.

We had used 600 feet of pipe to exit the creek bed and pass under the house deck. I shouldered the last unused coil of pipe, and we crawled back below the house, into the welcoming shelter of brush on the other side. The rain kept pouring.

Over the next couple of days, we ran the water line all the way to the garden site. We had to go back to town and buy more coils of pipe until, in the end, we'd connected 4,800 feet of pipe. The water line ran close to a mile, edged high over Potter Creek and closely below one unsuspecting house, all the way to our garden. Where it crossed even an animal trail, it was buried.

We were probably the only two guys on the coast who had an inventory of kiddie pools. We set up a twelve footer, eighteen inches deep, just above the garden. Covered in camo netting and set under the trees, it held close to 1,600 gallons of water and was the terminus of our water line. Kade had started 300 plants in small peat cups hidden deep under cover, and I had another 100 started from a bag of high-grade seeds Stafford had left for me. It was late March, and we were looking forward to the chicken-shit marches.

CHAPTER 27

"Hell hath no fury like a woman scorned."

–William Congreve

KADE BEGAN HAULING THE BAGS of chicken shit to his house on his own. He used his own truck and his own time to haul the loads. He wanted to limit how much he and I were seen together. He stacked them on wooden pallets off the turnaround in front of his house. Every two bags represented a trip to the garden. There were 100 bags.

Over the course of the next week, the stack of manure shifted slowly from Kade's place to the garden site, strapped two at a time to our packboards. The route wasn't that difficult except for the last 300 feet, where it got dicey dipping down into the mud at the stinging nettles crossing. The packs were heavy and the makeshift steps leading up from the hole were now just muddy skid marks. It was just our finger holds on tufts of grass and broken branches that enabled us to make it up the wet hillside. The last 100 feet through the brush tunnel, crawling on our hands and knees with sixty pounds on our backs, seemed completely ludicrous.

During one morning's trip, I saw what I thought was the hoof print of a cow on the trail. I bent over and examined it. There were no cows anywhere around, and I realized it had to be the track of a wild boar. The print was huge! I had never seen one as large, and I now had something else to think about on my hikes along the narrow trail. The local wild pigs were heavy, tough, close-to-the-ground animals. They had razor-sharp tusks and would defend their young aggressively. For their size and weight, they were surprisingly fast in a straight-ahead charge. Kade was also impressed with the print, saying he had heard Bo Rummsen talk once about a giant old boar that roamed the hills high above the ranch. It was seldom seen and very cagey, avoiding both hunters and traps. I found he was on my mind every time I crossed the moist dip through the nettles.

We carried the starts over to the garden and began digging holes beneath the perfect canopy of ceanothus. It was a large stand that covered most of the ridgeback and had grown in an open manner, leaving it easy to walk beneath while also providing cover from above. Where necessary, we trimmed branches to enhance our movement or to let more sunlight in. The soil was rich, deep, and loamy as we had hoped, the result of many undisturbed years of the blue flowers falling to the ground as mulch.

We planted 400 starts, snaking a drip system through the garden that delivered four gallons per hour to each plant. When we arrived at the garden, the drip system was turned on, and it ran until we left. The bean cans had been retrieved from the other gardens and more were collected from outside Nepenthe's lettuce cage. Every plant grew through a round metal barrier.

Rat poison was placed outside the garden area in bird-proof dispensers. Sow bug poison was sprinkled around the cans. We decided against a fence, knowing deer would easily jump a six-foot fence from a standing position. Instead, we just planted more plants to make up for future losses.

Kade and I had taken to wearing pistols on our trips to the garden, though for different reasons. He wore a western-style .45 revolver in a classic western rig around his waist. I carried a Smith & Wesson .44 magnum in a shoulder holster under my shirt. I carried mine in case I came face to face with the monster wild boar along the trail or in the garden. Kade said he carried his to shoot any deer he found in the garden.

One day while we were checking the drip system emitters for blockages, we talked about it.

"So if you come over here and see a deer, you're going to shoot it?" I asked.

He looked at me like he was surprised by the question. "Yeah, of course. Wouldn't you?"

"No. I've been down that road. I'm not supposed to shoot deer."

He threw me a look. "What? Did you have some divine realization?"

"Something like that," I said.

He laughed. "But you have no problem killing a boar? How very Zen of you!"

"Look, there's a larger issue here," I stepped toward him. "If we start shooting our guns around here, everyone inside a mile will know something's going on. Let's not worry about the deer."

"And the boar?" he leaned over and adjusted an emitter.

"Self-protection. Look, I'm not going to blast a boar just because I see one. But if I corner one by accident, I want some firepower."

I looked at him standing there like John Wayne with his .45 strapped to his leg. I pointed at his gun. "What are you going to do if you show up here one day and the cops are sitting here waiting for you? Have a shoot-out?"

"Maybe."

"Well, you'll be a dead hombre."

"Maybe. What are you gonna do?" He cocked his head to the side.

"It's not going to happen. But if it did, I'm sure as hell not going to get into a shoot-out with the police. If we're wearing these guns, they're just going to shoot us dead anyway. Ask questions later."

"So, stop carrying your gun," he said.

"After the old boar dies," I answered.

The garden schedule was easy for me this time without my job at Nepenthe to work around.

The garden schedule was not as easy for Kade. Because I couldn't drive to his house, he had to come and get me so that I could do my share of the work. On one such day when it was my turn to water the garden, he came over to pick me up in his station wagon.

He sounded agitated when he told me to get in. I got in and lay down in the back. Then he said from the front seat, "I'm busy today and need to get back to work."

We bumped and bounced over the road to his house where he finally slid to a stop. I sat up, opened the side door, and climbed out. Kade climbed in and raised the back seat in the car. Serene was walking intently toward us, holding the hands of her two kids.

"You know I have an appointment in town today, Kade. You just don't care about anything!" she said, pushing the kids into the back seat of the car.

"I had to get Wes," Kade said.

"Always Wes! Always the garden! I hate that garden!" she screamed, getting in behind the wheel.

I was standing behind the car when it started, and I could see Serene looking at me in the side mirror. She threw the transmission in reverse and stomped on the accelerator. Her eyes were still in the mirror as the car lurched backward, throwing gravel underneath. The rear bumper was inches from my leg when I jumped to the left in an arching dive that carried me off the road rolling in the dirt. I jumped up as she slammed on the brakes and slid to a stop.

Kade ran to the car and jerked open the driver side door, then backhanded Serene across her face. "You crazy bitch!" he yelled.

I could hear him slapping her and the kids crying in the back seat.

Kade slammed the car door shut and the tires spun again in reverse.

This time I was well out of the way.

Serene threw the car into drive and floored it down the driveway in a cloud of dust. Then, silence. Even the birds were quiet.

I looked at Kade as the dust settled in the oak trees.

"Sorry about that," he said.

I was shaking my head. "We got problems, man. You got problems. She's not a happy lady!"

"I'll deal with it," Kade said. "You need to water the plants."

I didn't see him for a week after that. Kade wasn't at work and wasn't coming over to pick me up for my shifts. I wasn't worried about the plants, I knew he would keep them watered, but I was a little concerned about his relationship with his wife.

I was sitting outside on Nepenthe's terrace one evening having dinner when he walked up on the terrace and sat down beside me. "Hey," he said. "Long time no see."

I put my fork down and turned to look at him. “Where you been?”

He grabbed a french fry off my plate and tossed it his mouth. “Mostly in town. I rented a house in Monterey for Serene and the kids. They moved into it yesterday.”

“So, is she pissed?” I asked. “What’s stopping her from turning you into the sheriff about the garden?”

“I’m covering all her expenses,” he said. “I told her I’d buy her a house at the end of this year. She likes that idea. Don’t worry about it.”

“I’ll try,” I said. “It’s a scary liability. She could blow our whole scene at any moment just to spite you.”

He nodded his head, looking somewhere down the coast. “She knows if that happened she would lose everything too. She likes not having to work. Let me worry about it.”

“How’s the garden? I missed a couple of days.”

“It’s good.” He stood up and looked around. “See you tomorrow morning. Your turn to water.”

CHAPTER 28

"Retribution has a balance, a symmetry, that is very satisfying."

–John Stalkinger

By mid-June the garden was thriving. The plants were overhead and declaring, and we had a pile of male plants already pulled and covered by black plastic. We were in the garden almost every day checking for males and ensuring the drip emitters were clear and working. There had been little rat or deer damage, and no shots had been fired. Kade said he had hit one deer in the ass with a thrown shovel.

There had been a couple of overflights by the sheriff's department above my trailer at Fuego Creek, a deputy circling to see if I was stubborn or stupid enough to grow there again. At the new garden south of Kade's, they flew by without circling and seemed to have no interest in our location. We'd been careful to not have anything shiny or reflective out in in the open. Shovels, saws, and loppers were all hidden under brush when we weren't using them. Even our hose clamps were all spray painted flat black.

Serene was living in town, and I didn't hear any more about her. Kade said very little about his personal life anyway, but now seemed even more private and withdrawn. This was okay with me since our relationship was entirely professional, and if we did talk about anything, it was usually in the form of an argument.

I tended to have the hot temper with the flash point, but, in my own defense, I was also the one who desired peace on earth. Kade, on the other hand, was hardly ever angry, but was constantly stirring shit and pushing buttons. It was a strange relationship—I didn't really like him, wouldn't seek him out for companionship, but I did trust him and knew I could count on him to do every bit of his share. How he felt about me I can only guess, but it was probably similar.

Bradford Berkshire was making little to no progress on getting the permits to rebuild the cabin. He had expected to walk in and lay out a plan for the next building of Camelot without encountering any opposition. I could imagine the County Planning Department felt his approach was at best condescending and theatrical.

Monterey County, quite accustomed to grandiose development proposals by eccentric characters, actually cared more about the spotted three-winged grasshopper, the blue-bellied salamander, and the late-blooming night iris than it did about human beings. I knew that if the county was able to postpone Bradford Berkshire's permit long enough, he would adopt the persona of some other character, perhaps a flashy pirate buccaneer, and apply for a permit to build a black three-masted schooner where the Apple Tree House had once stood.

It was thought there had been Esselen Indians living in the Fuego Creek drainage, and Monterey County required qualified archeologists and tribal representatives to review Bradford's permit as well. Lastly, Monterey County had concerns about the Devil's Quarry and wanted a geologist to sign off on the long-term stability of the building site.

Bradford tended to show up at these meetings with his lawyer, I'm sure subconsciously, dressed in period costumes from the late seventeenth century, and would contest every issue as though he was an arrogant barrister from old England. The county was not amused, or maybe they were, but the fact was the permit was going nowhere.

One afternoon I was parked in the redwood canyon next to my stacked redwood wine tanks, talking with Bradford's foreman, Richard Gable. We stood beside our trucks talking about how slow the permit process was going for the new cabin. I mentioned to him that I was getting discouraged and thinking of moving on to my own property on Simson Ridge. He thought it made sense. "Might as well get on with your life," he said. "Down here you're just one of the Knights of the Round Table."

I laughed, "Who are you, Sir Lancelot?"

He grunted, "More like Sure-Works-a-Lot." I laughed at his joke. We each took a swallow of brandy from his flask and parted ways.

About a week later, in the early evening, I was on my way home from a social stop at Nepenthe. I was driving up Fuego Canyon on the way to my trailer when I looked off to the side of the road where my wine tanks and slabs of wood were stacked. I noticed the black plastic covering the wood had been disturbed and was spread out on the ground. I figured it was maybe animals or maybe the wind that had ruffled things up and pulled my truck over and stopped. I got out to cover things back up.

I picked up a corner of the plastic tarp and noticed my largest slab of redwood, a prized piece that was three feet wide and fourteen feet long, was missing. There were scrape marks on the ground where it had been dragged and then lifted onto a truck. I had been robbed. I looked around for clues and figured it had to have been at least two guys with a truck, but beyond that I couldn't figure it out. Whoever had stolen it knew my gate combination and obviously wasn't afraid of being caught. I was perplexed.

I asked around for a few days. Had anybody seen anything? Was anybody talking about a nice new slab of wood they had come across? I was hoping for loose lips and such, but nothing was in the air, no rumor was turning in the mill, all was quiet, and no one had a clue.

Sitting at Nepenthe's bar late one night a week later, I was just about to head home when Richard Gable walked in and sat down. I rarely saw Richard off the ranch, and the bar was empty, so we sat and talked. I told him about someone stealing my slab, how I had no idea who would come through my gate and steal from me.

Richard leaned back, tossing down a tequila, slammed the shot glass on the bar, and wiped his mustache. "Bradford's got it," he said. "He took it as collateral to cover your last month's rent."

I was stunned. "Collateral?" I said. "I haven't even given him my notice! If he took it for collateral, why wouldn't he leave me a note? Why did I have to think all week that I had been robbed by someone who knew my gate combination?"

Richard just shrugged. "I don't know, man. The guy's all worried you're just going to split without paying. You know how he is. He thinks the slab probably belongs to him anyway."

"I just *might* split, but I wouldn't leave owing him money! What an asshole! Where's the slab?" I asked.

"It's behind his house, leaning against a tree."

I looked at Richard. "Did you help him steal the slab?"

"No, Wes. I just saw it behind his house and asked him about it. It's a nice piece of wood."

"Son of a bitch," I said. "I can't believe it."

I sat there stewing in a cloud for a few minutes. Bradford had stolen my slab. Taken it out of paranoia to serve as collateral for rent he thought I might owe. He had left me thinking for a week that I had been robbed by someone I knew on the coast who had my gate combination. I shook my head. My time living on Fuego Creek was over. It was high time I moved on to my own property.

"What are you going to do?" Richard asked.

"I think I'm going to cruise home," I said. "Thanks. Have a good night, Richard."

I slipped off the bar stool and walked to the back door of Nepenthe and out to the phone booth. I dialed Luca Renzo. Luca and I had developed a friendship where we were always available for the other and always exactly on time to any planned engagement. We both took pride in getting there five minutes early. Often, we both showed up at the same time, five minutes early. It was late as I rang his phone, but on the fourth ring he picked up.

"Yeah."

"Luca, it's Wes. I need some help."

"What'd you do this time?"

"Nothing. I found that stolen slab of redwood. My landlord's got it. It's at his place. I need to get it in the morning. Can you help me?"

"Yeah, sure. What time?"

"I'll meet you at the highway by your gate at five-thirty. I'll drop you back off when we're done."

"No problem. I'll be there. Should I bring anything?"

"No. I've got it covered," I said.

I hung up and called John Stalkinger. John had moved in with a waitress and mutual friend from Nepenthe named Sherry. Sherry had volunteered to fight the Buckeye Fire and now rented a cabin below the Nepenthe Restaurant parking lot. John picked up right away.

"John, it's Wes."

"Hey, man, what are you doing calling at this hour?" he asked.

I told him the story.

"Son of a bitch," he chuckled. "What an idiot."

"I need some help getting the slab in the morning."

"No problem, man. I could use a little entertainment! What time?"

"I'll be at your house at five AM."

"Cool," he said. "I'll have bells on."

I hung up and decided to spend the night on Simson Ridge. It was much closer to John and it was almost midnight.

After a sleepless night of planning and dozing, I was up at four AM putting a few tools in the Bad Ford. My plan was to hit Bradford at six AM sharp, maybe catch him still in bed, with just enough daylight for us to see what we were doing. I loaded up a length of rope, a spare padlock, a pair of wire cutters, and my 'universal key,' a three-foot-long bolt cutter, throwing them all into the back of the truck. I didn't figure Bradford would put up much of a fight—after all he was in the wrong and was no match for the shit storm coming his way. His costumes aside, I didn't think he owned a gun, and even if he did, I didn't think he'd use it. I headed down the hill in the dark to meet John.

The porch light was on when I pulled in front of Sherry's house at five AM. He walked out and to my surprise, Sherry walked out with him.

"She wants to go," he said.

It wasn't in the plan, but the clock was ticking with no time for last minute hiccups, so I said okay.

They climbed into the truck, and I drove south. Not much was said. Ten miles later we saw Luca standing alongside the road waiting for us. I pulled over. It was approaching five thirty. Luca squeezed into the cab of the truck, and we sat with the engine running as I filled everyone in on the plan. I didn't want any violence. In fact, I told everyone not to say anything at all to Bradford or his wife if they were there; we would retrieve the wood in total silence. I headed the truck back onto the highway and drove to the ranch road gate. Luca slipped out and opened the gate, and we drove up the dirt road. I was starting to get excited. I wondered if Bradford would be awake or not, or if his foreman, Richard Gable, might be up and around at that hour.

We approached an old abandoned road that veered off to the left from the main ranch road. It had not been used for years and was overgrown with brush. A crooked utility pole stood at the corner. It was a 'drop pole' from the main electric line going up the road. There was a wire looped to it, running down the pole, then off through the brush and stapled along an old fence line running up toward Bradford's place. It was the homestead telephone wire. I stopped the truck and got out, walked over, and, using the wire cutters, cut the telephone line. I heard Sherry say, "What's he doing?" with some concern in her voice. I got back in the truck and continued up the hill.

The gate to the Julian Fuego homestead where Bradford lived was just a quarter mile past Kade's driveway. I stopped the truck in front of it, shutting the motor off. It was closed and locked. I got out and grabbed the bolt cutters from the truck's bed, walked over to the gate, and cut the lock off the chain wrapped around the gatepost. I tossed the lock into the brush and opened the gate. I could hear Sherry say, "Oh, my God!"

Back in the truck, I floored it across the cattle guard and up the hill. The road laced through a sixty-acre meadow dotted with grazing cattle. On the hill above us sat the Julian Fuego homestead house, perched high on a knoll, overlooking the scene. We would be in plain sight for about a minute as we made our way up to the house. We were bouncing hard in the cab as the truck roared up the hill, everyone holding on tightly to whatever they could, four heads looking straight ahead and a rooster tail of dust spiraling behind us. We went up a steep grade, around a turn in the road, and saw the house looming ahead of us.

Unexpectedly, there was a wooden gate ahead, set in a fence line that surrounded the house. I could see a large turnaround on the other side of it. I didn't want to take the time to stop and get out, so I made a snap decision and floored it. The distance to the gate closed in a second, and everyone tensed as the Ford plowed through the wooden gate, exploding it in pieces that flew up and over the cab. I slid to a stop. In a cloud of dust, I turned the wheel sharply, accelerating in a sharp circle while scanning the property for the slab.

I heard someone yell, "Goddamnit!"

"There it is!" I saw the slab lying against a tree at the end of a short access road that ran right beside the house. I threw the truck into reverse. "No one say a word to this bastard," I said, backing up toward the house.

Moving slowly backward past the house along the narrow drive, I looked down through a bedroom window and saw Bradford, complete with a morning woody, slipping on a leopard-printed bathrobe. He looked up as we rolled by. When the truck reached the slab, I set the brake and jumped out, leaving the motor running. "Let's load it. Don't say a word," I said.

We all jumped out and went to the rear of the truck. I dropped the tailgate. Luca and John already had the slab in the air and were dragging it to the truck. We were pushing it in when Bradford came out and around the bed of the truck.

"Hold it! Stop!" he said.

Not one of us said a word. John and Luca were lashing the slab down with the rope.

"Stop! Wait!" Bradford cried.

I walked past him, staring at his face, and climbed into the truck. Sherry, John, and Luca climbed in the other side and slammed the door. I put the truck in gear just as Bradford stepped in front of it and put up his hand like a traffic cop.

"Stop!" he yelled. "Let's discuss this! Let's talk!"

I looked right at him and popped the clutch.

The truck lurched forward, and he dove sideways out of the way, rolling over on the grass beside the house. I floored it, shifting into third as we drove out over the smashed gate and down the road.

John burst out laughing. Sherry couldn't believe any of it and was shaking her head, muttering, "Oh, my God," over and over again. Luca was pissed. Riding shotgun with one hand on the dash, he was turned toward me, pointing a finger. "Goddamnit, Wesley! The next time you get me into this kind of shit, at least tell me to bring a gun! We're sitting ducks here. He's got the drop on us right now, and if he's any good, we're fucked!" He was struggling to see up to the house as the truck bounced down the road.

"He's not going to shoot us," I said.

"How the fuck do you know?" Luca yelled.

We flew along the road, past the grazing cows, until we approached the gate with its severed lock, and I slid to a stop, shutting off the truck.

"Now what the fuck are you going to do?" Luca asked.

I looked at him. "Lock him in."

I jumped out of the truck and found my padlock in the rear of the truck. I closed his gate and wrapped the chain around the post, inserted my lock, and slammed it closed.

Bradford Berkshire was now locked behind his own gate with no telephone. It would, I was sure, take him a while to figure it all out.

"Well, that should slow him down!" Luca said, calming down.

Sherry and John were laughing. There was no longer any reason to hurry, and we ambled down the road to the highway. I drove north and pulled off at Luca's driveway. I got out to check the rope securing the slab. Luca and I met at the rear of the truck. I looked at Luca. "Sorry, man. I didn't see it becoming a shoot-out."

He gave a short laugh. "Yeah, well, someone else with bigger balls might have taken a shot at us back there, and all I'm holding is my dick! Anyway, we made it. Another adventure under our belts!"

I thanked him with a handshake, and he headed home. I drove north to drop Sherry off at her cabin.

"You guys are crazy!" she laughed. "That was fun!"

John rode up to my property on Simson Ridge with me to help unload the slab. "I wonder if Bradford Berk-a-Shit is out-and-about yet?" he laughed.

"I doubt it," I said. "He's not having the best of days!"

John got a thoughtful look on his face. "Do you think Berk-a-shit will report the damaged gate as cancer of the gatepost, or just arson?"

"Mayhem," I said. "Definitely mayhem."

Driving John back home, I said, "I've got to get my wine tank wood off the ranch as soon as possible."

"Hey, no problem, man. We'll just round up some guys with lumber racks and make a couple of trips. I can borrow the Nepenthe dump truck again; it's got racks."

"Well, it had better be sooner than later. Bradford may try to lock me out," I said.

John gave a laugh. "Do you really think so? More fun!"

A week later the local CHP pulled into Fernwood while I was getting gas. Officer Krebs walked up to me, pushing his hat back on his head. He leaned in close at the gas pumps and looked at me. "Leave Bradford Berkshire alone, Mr. Daggert."

"He stole my wood, Eddie. I—"

"I know the story, and I don't give a shit. Just leave him alone. There was some damaged property up there, and as of now, there haven't been any charges filed. Let it be," Officer Krebs replied.

"Okay," I said. "It's over as far as I'm concerned."

"Good," Officer Krebs said, cracking a smile. "Pretty funny story, Daggert." He turned to walk away, then pointed back at me. "Lay off."

CHAPTER 29

"Hauling too much baggage around only serves to slow the safari."

–Wesley Daggert

I HAD TO MOVE OFF THE ranch. The time had come, and my escapade retrieving my slab had made it more than necessary. A group of close friends with lumber racks on their trucks joined me one afternoon to move my three wine tanks and remaining redwood slabs to my property on Simson Ridge.

It was a scene out of Steinbeck's *Grapes of Wrath*, loading all the staves onto the various pickups and transporting them up to my property. It was a big job with a lot of driving and not everyone knew what they were getting into. One friend's lumber racks slowly collapsed from the weight of his load. At the end of the day, we drank cold beer, and I paid everyone twenty dollars for their efforts.

Moving out of the trailer was much easier with just two duffle bags and my guns to get. I had prepped a new drying box on Simson to hide my packaged pot. Hidden deep in the undergrowth, it was near where my camper sat in the redwoods. I had a few more trips to make.

Late one night about a week after the slab incident at Bradford's, I was on my last trip up Juan Fuego Creek Road to get the last of the packaged buds. I preferred to travel with the buds late at night because local law enforcement, barring an incident, didn't patrol at night. I drove up Fuego Creek Road into the straightaway where the wine tank wood had been stacked and saw the largest boar I had ever seen walking in the middle of the road ahead. It was huge and nasty, with a gray-and-white hide that made it look ancient. It had to be the legendary boar Bo Rummsen had talked about and that had left the giant hoof prints I had seen on the trail!

It stopped in the road and looked into the headlights of my truck. I floored it. I accelerated toward the huge animal as he put his head down and began charging straight at me. We were on a collision course, in a game of chicken, and I fully intended to ram him. As we neared each other, his course never faltered. I suddenly realized that he was much taller than my bumper and was probably going to end up in my radiator. I slammed on my brakes just as he veered off to my right. His profile was that of a gray short-necked steer charging head down. He left the road and raced up the hillside, disappearing in the dark. He was as big as a Volkswagen. I sat there in my truck, illuminated by my dash lights, with my heart pounding. I had finally seen the old monster boar! I definitely didn't want to meet him on the trail without a much bigger gun.

I drove up and loaded the last of the pot buckets into the truck, then paused to make out a check payable to Bradford Berkshire for the last month's rent. I left it in the trailer under a glass before driving down the hill, watching for the boar, and leaving Fuego Creek for the final time.

Two days later Kade and I resumed an intensive work schedule at the garden. The plants had all declared and were looking fantastic. There were 220 very robust ladies growing tall.

We had to work out another way for me to get onto the ranch and to the garden, and we decided Kade would meet me at South Coast Center, an old motel that had been purchased by Esalen to use as staff housing. I could park my truck among the other cars parked there. Kade would pull up, and I would climb into the back of his station wagon and cover up with a blanket. The ride to his property from there was just a few miles, but very uncomfortable rolling back and forth as he took the corners.

One day as were driving down the highway with me lying in the back under a blanket, Kade inexplicably pulled over and picked up a hitchhiker. There I was, lying in the back covered with a blanket, probably looking like a corpse, and this asshole picks up a hitchhiker! The guy gets in, slams the door, and Kade takes off again. I didn't know what to do. I had no idea if the guy had seen me. I couldn't say anything. I couldn't acknowledge that I was okay, that I wasn't dead. I couldn't show my face to the guy—that would defeat the whole purpose of my being covered by a blanket—so I just lay there, rolling back and forth, listening to them talk.

Kade pulled the car over again and stopped. The guy thanked him and got out, and Kade pulled back out onto the highway.

"What the hell did you do that for?" I yelled up to the front.

"Do what? Pick up the hitchhiker? I know that guy," he said.

"I'm lying back here under a blanket, and you're picking up hitchhikers? What the fuck?" I was furious. "He's probably telling people right now that you're transporting dead people!"

"I don't think he noticed," Kade said.

"Don't do it again, Kade."

We jabbed each other back and forth the rest of the day about it. I made my point clear that if he did it again, I was going to sit up with the blanket over my head and join the conversation. It was a typical Kade move—he thought it was funny but said he would never do it again.

As we got into late September, we began to assemble a trimming crew. Sandra was coming back, and I was seeing Susie again on and off. From our conversations I could only surmise that Susie's old boyfriend turned out to still be the same old guy with the same stuff that wasn't working before, and she was over it. She said she could work a few days a week also. My friend Bob from Nepenthe was going to join us, and Kade had found a couple from Esalen, Beth and Bernie, two employees who needed some side money. We cleared a room at Kade's house, covered the floor with sheets, moved in a folding table and several folding chairs, and bought six pairs of scissors. We pushed the plants as far as we could until, during the second week of October, we began to harvest the garden.

The plants were impressive. Fat, tight, juicy colas, dripping in resin, heavy on the branch and in our hands. We each made three trips a day back and forth, cutting the buds, placing them in black plastic bags, and carrying them back to the cleaners. Kade had been meeting the trimmers at the highway near Esalen and bringing them up together in his car. He didn't want the traffic in and out of his property to arouse suspicion with any of the neighbors.

Our connection at the sheriff's department, Irene, had helped us a couple of times by notifying us of police activity. If she could, she would call Kade's house when the deputies were coming down the coast for a marijuana bust. She never knew exactly where they were going, that information was kept secret, but she did know when they were heading in our general direction. Upon receiving that information, we would cancel our cleaning session or reschedule it, and also place a call that would start a telephone tree we had with other growers up and down the coast.

One week into our harvest, Susie, Bob, Sandra, Beth, and Bernie were sitting in a circle on a spread of sheets with a large pile of buds in the center. Their heads were down, focused on the snip of their scissors. The conversation was sporadic and rambling, as it often was during this mundane work.

Kade walked up behind Sandra. "Not so close, Sandra. Leave some for the customer," he advised.

"Sorry, Boss! Just trying to be perfect," she replied.

And they were trying to be perfect. It was a precision job that left just enough leaf around the bud to not disturb the delicate hairs. During the drying process, the little remaining leaf would shrink back and leave the bud fully exposed. Any leaf close to the bud was covered in resin anyway. The art of trimming was leaving just enough leaf, while not taking too much.

The phone rang, and Kade moved to answer it. "Yeah!" … "Okay, thanks!" He hung up. "That was Irene. Pack it up," he said. "They're coming down the coast!"

Beth had a worried expression as she asked, "Are they coming here?"

Kade was placing manicured buds in a plastic bag. "Can't know for sure. Bob, put that pile of buds back in the bag. Let's get it cleaned up!"

Bernie was folding chairs, and I was balling up the sheet on the floor. Susie had grabbed a broom and was sweeping.

"I'm going to stash these buds," Kade said, heading out the door.

Right then the phone rang again.

Kade came back inside and answered, "Yeah?" … "Okay. No problem." He put the phone down. "False alarm! They're going up Palo Colorado Canyon. We're okay. Back to work!"

So the sheets were spread out again, and the chairs set around them, and another fresh bag of buds was dumped on the floor.

"Better safe than sorry!" Beth said.

I headed out for the walk to the garden for another couple of bags. It felt good to get out of the house and into the sunshine. With all the trips back and forth, the garden trail had widened to where the brush on either side barely touched my shoulders as I walked. For much of the walk, the brush was overhead, but occasionally would expose a beautiful view of the ocean.

The trail had been laid out in zigzags to help break it up visually to the pilot of a passing plane. In some places the trail dipped into a tunnel, to be lost from sight altogether for a distance. At one location, just above Nettles Crossing, there was a sweeping view of the Pacific Ocean. I stopped there to take in the scene. There was a soft puff of breeze, scented with chamise and sage, coming across the headland. The ocean was a deep blue with only a solitary white cumulous drifting north with its shadow. About a half mile out I could see a small column of smoke coming directly off the surface of the water. My eyes stopped there. Smoke off the water made no sense. I watched it carefully to be sure I was seeing smoke, but there could be no doubt. Brown and wispy, it rose about twenty feet from a fixed spot on the surface and then was bent north with the prevailing breeze. I was perplexed.

At that moment, a rattlesnake went off just at my feet. I instinctively jumped back on the trail as the snake struck, hitting my right boot hard on the side. I looked down at the snake now outstretched on the trail and drove my heel down hard on its head with a grinding motion. The snake's body twisted and turned next to my boot. I ground the head deep into the dirt, then stepped quickly back. The snake flipped over and turned, its head smashed. It would, I knew, continue to move for hours. I immediately unlaced my boot and jerked it off, then removed my sock and inspected my foot. The snake's fangs had not penetrated the leather. I put my sock and boot back on while the snake moved in a slow death curl just a foot away.

When I stood back up, I looked out to sea, and a black submarine now floated on the surface where the wisp of smoke had been. I stared transfixed at the apparition. There was smoke coming from a pipe on the vessel as it floated on the ocean swells. Was it in distress? I had no idea. I watched a bit longer and then continued on to the garden. Once there, I looked out through the cover of the ceanothus trees but could see nothing of the submarine. I climbed one of the bigger trees and scanned the ocean. The submarine was gone, and so was the smoke.

A bit later, I walked through the door of Kade's house to a quiet group of pickers and a pacing partner. I dropped the bags of harvested buds on the floor at the corner of the room.

"Where you been?" Kade asked.

"I had an encounter with a rattlesnake."

"Guess you won," Kade said.

Sandra looked at me. "Did you relocate the rattlesnake?"

"Yes," I said. "He's been relocated." Then I told them about the submarine.

Their eyes got wide, and the conversation got lively.

"No way! It just came up? What was it doing there?" Bernie asked.

"Looking for us," I said.

"Smoke on the water? I think *you* been smokin'!" Bob said.

"Maybe the cook burnt the toast and they had to surface!" Susie said.

"Maybe someone on board farted!" Bob joked.

Everyone burst out laughing.

"The smoke could have been exhaust," Sandra offered.

"On a nuclear submarine?" Bob countered. "What? They don't run those with Chevy V8s, you know!"

Kade spoke up. "Could have been the Peruvian Navy dropping off some smugglers. They have diesel submarines."

I left them there, sitting in a circle, much more animated now than when I had found them, and started the twenty-minute walk back to the garden for two more bags of fresh buds. I thought about how things are not always as they seem in Big Sur. There is a parallel reality always at play, much like an echo coming back to you from a mountain canyon is the sound of the reflection of the sound and not the original sound itself. The two are close, but not the same. This is probably true everywhere to some degree, but in Big Sur it's magnified because life here is intense, the result of the clash of many dramatic extremes.

CHAPTER 30

"Recollections are short vacations for the mind."

–Richard Gable

THE TWENTY-FOUR-SEVEN DRAMA OF THE surf beating against the foot of the mountains that hold the highway above the ocean is the most obvious of Big Sur's dramatic extremes. Obvious to the locals who are affected by the landslides and rockfalls, seeing the changes on a daily basis, yet largely overlooked by the casual traveler who sees the power of the relentless pounding of water against rock as a subtle force played out in geologic time, producing beautiful vistas.

In fact, the highway itself, built in the 1920s and 1930s, would not be built today. The project would be deemed too expensive, too dangerous, ecologically unsound, and unsustainable. The torrential rains and winds that assault the precipitous coast each winter had begun slowly taking the precarious highway shelf apart as quickly as it had been built. Couple this with the added difficulties of living thirty or forty miles from town, up dirt roads that become muddy rivers in winter, on the edges of unstable cliffs lashed by storms that are called hurricanes back east, and the intensities of life on the coast become more apparent.

Balancing all this is the staggering beauty, breathtaking vistas, and perfect weather that describes most every day. The vast majority of people who travel the coast only see the latter, and never have reason to consider the darker, brooding intensity of the seemingly pastoral, meditative Big Sur.

For me personally, there were many lessons to learn after I'd decided to make my home there. One such lesson was that regardless of what I heard or who had said it, it was important to remember that a story needed to be researched before being repeated or acted upon. There are notable examples of this.

A woman, let's call her Sally, reported she had been raped and held prisoner by a man we'll call Dan. Immediately after hearing this, a posse spilled out of a local bar in pursuit of Dan, who had heard of the accusations and gone into hiding. Some of the posse, if not all, had been drinking heavily. (In Big Sur, being "on the wagon" meant you were doing all your drinking at home.) Threats of retribution and the need to reestablish a lady's honor were thrown about. Someone mentioned a good ass-kicking, while someone else wanted to hang him. Dan was nowhere to be found. This was fortunate, because the very next day, Sally recanted her story of abuse and admitted that Dan had only told her he was breaking off their relationship to pursue another woman. Dan had what could easily be described as "a close call" with a drunken mob.

Less dramatic were people quitting their place of employment and taking new jobs elsewhere based on rumors of mass seasonal layoffs that never actually materialized. People limped back to reclaim their jobs only to find out they had been given to fresher, more positive souls.

A popular bar that I personally liked to frequent was boycotted because it was rumored to have raised its prices to discourage local clientele. I went in two weeks later only to find the prices were in fact the same as they had been. Expensive. A disgruntled bartender had spread the false information. Interestingly enough, not long after that, all the other bars in Big Sur raised their prices to be equal to the bar in question.

There are many other examples, some more obscure, such as 'Road Closed' signs blocking your way even though there was in fact no closure. The signs could be driven around, the problem negotiated, and you were on your way again. If this happened to you even once, you were ruined for 'Road Closed' signs, much like when you 'fixed' your TV set that time by smacking the side of it. From then on, you always smacked your TV when it faltered, just as you would always drive around the 'Road Closed' sign to make sure it was really closed.

Rules stop pertaining to you when there's no repercussions for breaking them. When living on the edge becomes more rewarding and exciting, you stop walking the easy, more well-traveled trails. When the outlaw life and its vagabond spirit start paying the bills and opening the doors, you don't look back. You fire a shot in the air and howl at the moon, spur your horse, and ride into the wind.

I thought back to a warm night in June of 1973. Nepenthe was hosting its monthly astrological sign party. The wind was blowing down off the mountains, causing the fallen leaves on the terrace to spin in mini-spirals across the floor, and the party was in full swing. The moon had been up a couple of hours, a great luminous sphere in the night sky, illuminating the ocean and the mountains to the south.

It was a crowded party, the music was loud, and the terrace was packed with people dancing under the colored lights. Shoulder to shoulder, back to chest, animated with raised arms and spinning torsos, the revelers were pushed and pulled by the music, whirling with the leaves, back and forth under the stars.

Inside, two half-round tables had been pushed together to make one large round table, and there, lit by a dozen cakes blazing in candlelight, sat the Geminis being celebrated with the Happy Birthday song. It was three deep at the bar. The four bartenders were buried, moving swiftly, pouring drinks and opening cash drawers, held captive in front of a throng of jostling, thirsty souls. The music was as loud inside as out, piped through speakers above the restaurant and terrace. David Essex's "Rock On" segued into Creedence Clearwater's "Proud Mary."

I wanted to dance, but I was also blasted on acid, an LSD trip I had started that afternoon in the tranquility of a shaded glen alongside the river. I moved out into the sea of thrusting dancers looking for a small square of space to bust some moves. I found it and was soon stepping on every beat and flowing with every riff. I saw many people I knew, their wide eyes, crazed smiles, and pursed lips...I banged off a few shoulders, then slowly eased out to the edge of the fray under the moonlight.

The moonlight was intense. I stood there looking up into its bright roundness. Turning back to the party, I suddenly wanted to get away. To my eyes, the dancers were all in slow motion now, slowly bobbing up and down in a steady rhythm. The music and laughter seemed far away, so I turned and walked up the ramp to the parking lot above. Parked at the top with a view of the terrace was a long black Cadillac with its engine running. As I approached, the rear driver side window slid down. Through the black opening, I heard a familiar voice.

"Wesley! It's Carmine! How are you?" Carmine was a well-connected member of the Italian Family in Monterey. He and I had been introduced through my friend Luca Renzo.

"Carmine! I'm fine, a little lit up."

"You think you're lit...here, take this." He handed me a little orange pill through the window. "Take it."

It was a hit of Orange Sunshine. I tossed it back and swallowed. "Are you going down to the party?" I asked.

"Are you kidding me?" Carmine said. "I can't even find my balls right now. Looks like a fun party. You take care, kid!" And the window slid back closed.

I walked down to the lower lot, toward my truck, and was once again enthralled by finding myself standing beneath the brilliant moon. I looked up and decided it would be incredible to see its full splendor from Pfeiffer Beach. I got into my truck and headed up the highway.

Luckily, there weren't many cars on the highway, and I just stayed focused on the center line. I dipped off the highway at the turn for Pfeiffer Beach and flowed down the narrow one-lane road for two miles to the beach parking lot. I parked and got out. The moon was blazing with an aura of purples and blues. In fact, everything it shined on was splashed with color. My eyes began to tingle and my chest began to get giddy, swimming with the first pulses of the Orange Sunshine. There wasn't another car in the parking lot.

I moved across the lot and started on the path through the cypress trees to the beach. I could hear the waves breaking ahead. The darkened outlines of the branches overhead threw shadows over the white sand under the moonlight. I walked along the path, through the thick sand, and came out from under the trees onto the beach. Looking straight ahead, something caught my peripheral vision, and I turned my head up to my right, where a tall white church stood, complete with cupola and wooden cross! I froze and took it in. It was there all right, where it had never been before, tall and stately, with a wooden staircase leading up to the large, arched wooden doors. I was mesmerized. I was also very stoned. I knew the church didn't belong there, but there it was. As I walked up the sand dune toward the church, it just got bigger, the moonlight reflecting off its whitewash. Reaching the base of its staircase, I climbed the stairs, slowly at first, careful of its construction, until I stood at the tall front doors. I pulled them back and entered.

The interior was cavernous, with dozens of pews facing a simple altar table with three large candles sitting on it. There were angels chasing each other under a wooden cross hung on the wall. I slowly walked between the pews until I was at the altar and turned around. There, out through the open doors, were the breaking waves illuminated by the moonlight, crashing in multicolored rainbow mist onto the beach. I was astounded. The church had to be real because it was solid.

I walked back to the open doors. There on the beach, between the church on whose porch I stood and the breaking surf, was an entire Indian village. There were at least ten teepees made of painted hides with stone circles for fires and spears and bows stacked Brigadoon-style, in preparation for sudden attack. I stood and stared. There was not another soul on the beach, and I walked down the stairs, across the sand, and into the village. Even the darkness had colored dots of light now as I walked through the scene. It was a working village down to every detail, and I was the only person there. The waves were crashing just forty feet away, and the night was all about the moonlight. I didn't touch a thing, just took it all in, and finally walked up the beach a quarter mile with my beaming eyes throwing psychedelic rainbows.

The return trip down the beach was surrealistic as I slowly approached the Indian village and the white church, so out of time, so out of place, and yet so historically accurate as to be the real here and now.

I drove back to my cabin at Three Acres, now facing into the headlights of party revelers leaving the sign party, heading for a Fernwood nightcap. Each passing car's headlights shined deep into my black irises that had been wide open for twelve hours. I parked my truck and walked up to the cabin, retiring to a sleepless night of Indians and priests.

The next day, after asking around, I learned that I had stumbled onto the set of a movie being filmed. Based on the novel by Lillian Bos Ross titled *The Stranger*, the movie was to be called *Zandy's Bride*. The cast and crew had been at Nepenthe's sign party while I was on the beach.

Two days later, I drove up Coast Ridge Road to a favorite picnic spot I liked to frequent, high above the gorge, where the Big Sur River flowed out from the mountains. I parked and carried a deli bag along an old side road toward the picnic site. Normally, I would head up a hill of grass and lupine to a natural amphitheater sitting in a bowl above a stand of redwoods, showcasing the heights of Mount Manuel rising beyond. However, this day, as I came over the rise to the grassy amphitheater, there sat a homestead cabin and barn, complete with an old canvas windmill, a buckboard, and split rail fences. I walked down to the cabin, finding no one around. Everything was there as though I had arrived by time machine—the tools, furniture, barrels, and even an anvil were set in their natural places. I was at Zandy's cabin in the late 1800s, deserted this day for me to find pristine and fresh.

I knew I was looking at a movie set this time and marveled at the detail, moving from the cabin to the barn and back again. Finally, after an appreciative assessment, I walked back up the hill to find a place to enjoy the view and my sandwich.

CHAPTER 31

"Here's to a lasting friendship, or at least to the end of this bottle."

–Anonymous toast

THE REST OF OUR HARVEST season in 1978 went smoothly. There were no more snakes or submarines. Late October, early November brought a fair amount of rain, but by mid-November, we had the garden in and manicured. We had been working every day, keeping the trimmers busy. The five trimmers seemed to get along well with each other, while Kade and I worked in the brush packaging the dried buds. The dampness of the early rains had forced us to buy more heaters and made it more difficult to gauge the drying time. Every box needed to be checked daily.

Compounding things somewhat, Kade had insisted that we start grading our buds by size. Up to three inches was a C bud, three to six inches was a B, and anything over six inches was an A bud. He suggested graduating the price as well with per pound prices of $1,600, $1,800, and $2,000, respectively. I anticipated some pushback from my buyers, but in the end, it would be me who set the price for my pot. It was impressive to open a bucket and see all big buds inside it, though, and since it didn't take any longer to high-grade while packaging it, I went along with his idea.

By early December we were all packaged and splitting up our pot. We had packaged 137 pounds of sinsemilla. I moved my cut of sixty-eight and a half pounds up to Simson Ridge over several night trips.

Jimmy and David Stafford had visited me on Simson Ridge during the summer and purchased a total of twenty pounds. With the new harvest in, I had about eighty pounds stashed in various places deep in the brush around my property. I needed another Jimmy or Stafford to walk into my life. but success had made me more reluctant to talk about my pot situation than ever. Asking around about buyers was out of the question. The good news was that the pot could be stored indefinitely in the paint buckets, and I was not in need of money.

In January of 1979, the California Coastal Commission granted me a building permit for a house and guest house on Simson Ridge. I had been pursuing my permit for two years, making monthly trips to Santa Cruz for Coastal Commission meetings. My project was opposed by the Sierra Club and by a local Big Sur man who I'll just call Dick. Dick was a local and a hypocrite who occupied a powerful seat on the Coastal Commission. He had his five acres and didn't want anyone else to have theirs. He voted NO on everything, even though he himself had cut down three full-grown redwood trees to allow overhead electric lines to be casually dropped through the forest to service his house.

I had finally prevailed. During the pre-vote hearing, I was at the microphone, in front of the Commission, discussing my plans to mitigate my building project. Dick said that my permit would lead to more cars driving up and down the highway, so he was going to vote NO.

"Ladies and gentleman," I began, "I moved to Big Sur in 1969 and was already living there for three years the first time you counted the cars driving up and down the highway in 1972. Now, ten years later, I'm asking for a permit to build a house. I drive one of the cars you've already counted. Please don't count my car twice!"

There was some chuckling among the board members and around the audience. When the vote was taken about twenty minutes later, in spite of Dick's NO vote, my permit was approved by a solid majority. I was ecstatic. I thanked the board and walked up the aisle toward the exit.

A man with long blond hair, wearing a sweater under his blazer, stood and reached out to stop me. He leaned over and said, "I represent the Sierra Club, and I will be appealing this decision."

The guy was trying to bust my balloon! I stared at him and said, "Mister, I've been chasing this permit for a house on a perfectly legal, qualified parcel of land for two years. I want to get on with my life. I would hope you have bigger fish to fry."

For all I know, they might have appealed, but I never heard any more from the Sierra Club or the Coastal Commission. My next phase would be dropping off building plans to the Monterey County Building Department.

A few days later, as it sometimes goes, I got some bad news. I was sitting on Nepenthe's terrace when Kade walked up from the parking lot and sat down beside me. He looked tired. "It's over," he said, looking back and forth. "We're done."

I looked at him and asked, "What happened?"

"I've been thrown off the ranch. Tom Rummsen sent a surveyor up to my property to find one of my property lines. I didn't know he was coming. The surveyor stumbled onto one of my drying boxes and looked inside. There was still some pot in there, which he reported to Rummsen. Rummsen called me in and tore up my purchase contract right in front of me. He gave me forty-five days to get off the property."

I shook my head. "A surveyor? Did they call the sheriff?"

"No," he said. "I moved everything out right away anyway."

"Where?"

"Doesn't matter. South Coast. I may have a lead on a piece of property down there, get farther away from the fucking sheriff and people like Rummsen."

"How about our garden? Maybe we can find another way to get there," I said.

"Where? There isn't any place to get in there now except up from the highway. People would see our trucks. The ranch foreman would see our trucks. People would figure it out. No, we're done, finished. A really good garden gone to waste."

"Damn," I said. "How about the house you built? Are you supposed to just walk away from it?"

"I'm talking with Rummsen about it. I don't know. He's being tough. I may get something for it." Kade elbowed my shoulder. "Hey…that's life. I should have been more careful. Good being partners with you." He forced a smile. "See you around."

We shook hands, and he walked away.

I looked down the coast. There was so much land down there, yet not really so much from a grower's point of view. A good garden site had specific requirements. First of all, you had to have a reason to be where you were growing and a reason to park where you were parking. You couldn't just all of a sudden start parking on the side of the road every day. People would notice. You had to have cover from airplanes and public places, natural cover preferably. You couldn't be too close to neighbors. You had to have gravity-fed water. There weren't that many places to grow. I had friends that were walking five miles into the wilderness to grow marijuana, but that didn't appeal to me. It was far too much work for a smaller amount of product. At some point, you were exposed in a public place, whether parking or hiking, and had to work at night during much of the year to avoid being seen.

I was still shaking my head. I was out of business. Just like that. I had no clue as to another place to grow. I didn't want to grow anywhere near my own property, and Simson Ridge was too populated anyway. I'd look around, but I already knew what was available around me. I wasn't hopeful.

I walked into the bar and picked up a wine list.

The bartender looked up from washing some glasses. "Hey, Wes. Saw you sittin' outside. Gonna have some wine?"

"Yeah, I think I will. Let's see...Give me a bottle of the 1973 Chateau Montelena Chardonnay. Please."

"Drinkin' the good stuff, I see," the bartender commented.

"Yeah, celebrating," I said, putting a twenty on the bar.

The bartender pulled the cork, and I carried the glass and bottle out to the far reaches of the terrace. I poured some wine into the glass and raised it to the view. "Here's to not lying down in the back of Kade's car anymore!" I said, then took a big swallow.

CHAPTER 32

"Building your house is the largest canvas you will ever paint on."

–Bo Rummsen

IN THE SPRING OF 1979, I was without a garden but not short on things to do. With my building permits in hand, I had started building my guest house and working on laying out the foundation of the main house. My building permit was based on my finding water by drilling a well, which I had, but I didn't want to develop the water system first thing. My neighbor had let me run water from his house via a long black poly pipe. I bought a generator/welder combination to supply power for building. My plan was to build the guest house out of the twenty-two-foot wine tank. I would build it before starting work on the house, as it was a less ambitious project and would sharpen my building skills.

I was excited about building the guest house. The plan called for erecting the twenty-two-foot wine barrel on a twenty-six-foot square deck that would cantilever out from the driveway. My friend John Stalkinger, an accomplished welder, had agreed to help me with the project. The wine tank was essentially a large barrel, like a glorified whiskey barrel, that had tapered staves held together by steel bands. It was in pieces that were sequentially numbered for reassembly.

Our first stage was cementing nine large poles into the ground to support the deck that was to be the barrel's foundation. We had the holes drilled by a large auger mounted on a bulldozer and mixed the concrete in a portable mixer. Eight-by-eight-inch beams were run across the tops of these poles as girders. For the floor joists, we used four-by-eight-inch beams and ran them perpendicularly across the tops of the girders. A twenty-six-foot square deck of four-by-fours was nailed down to that with sixty penny nails and a two-pound hammer.

The wine barrel was in pieces, called staves, that measured three-by-six-inches by twenty-feet long. I didn't want the guest house to be that high, so I cut them down to thirteen feet. A groove was cut along the edge of each stave, and they were sorted in their numerological order for assembly. The tank was held together by steel bands, one at the top and one at the bottom, and these had been manufactured at a steel fabrication shop in Monterey. We routed out a channel in the deck that was the circumference of the tank. Marine plywood that would seal between the staves was painted black and ripped into two-inch strips. We were ready to begin.

Stave number one was stood up in the routed channel, caulking applied to the groove on its side, a strip of plywood inserted into the groove, and stave number two was stood alongside it. They were hammered together. This was continued, stave by stave. Temporary two-by-four bracing held the wall in place as it went up. What made it interesting was the staves tapered from their base width of six inches to about four inches at the top. This made the staves "lean in" as they went together and tended to make them go out of plumb after ten or twelve staves had been stood up. It was challenging to keep them plumb and leaning at the correct angle, but after several attempts, the "sweet spot" was found and the tank went together rapidly.

As this project was progressing, I was also laying out the foundation for the main house that was going to stand on the hill above the barrel. John and I got along well and shared a similar sense of humor that helped pass the time as we worked. Raised on a farm in Washington state, he knew how to do almost everything and his resourcefulness was invaluable. When braces were needed, John welded them. All the steel-to-wood connections were custom made, thanks to John. He fashioned an anvil out of a piece of railroad track, mounting it on a large stump. Many a project got hammered out on that anvil. When the redwood staves were all up, John customized the two steel bands to fit around the tank and hold it together. He built a round steel ring that accepted all the roof rafters high in the center of the tank. Held high above the floor by compression of the roof joists, it also served as a skylight in the center. When we cut windows and doors into the tank, John forged steel straps that ran above the cuts, preventing the staves from slipping into the openings. We were having fun building an unconventional structure with only rudimentary drawings to go by.

The building inspector was also challenged by the project and doubted the integrity of the building, pulling out his tape and slide rule on every visit. The building had been engineered by a local civil engineer and was actually overbuilt, its supports and calculations being much more than what was required, but the intrepid inspector couldn't get his head around the vision and his doubtful frustration showed at every visit. He would leave me notes when he was in the neighborhood, even red-tagging me once to bring me into the office for a review. Eventually he was transferred to another part of the county, and I hoped the frustration he'd experienced on my project had something to do with it.

Susie and I were spending more time together, though I was wrestling with a lack of trust that stemmed from her trysts with her ex-boyfriend a few months before. Sometimes people get together easily, seamlessly, with little or no effort, while others have to work at it, bumping along, sorting through their special circumstances. It had been the latter for us, and I doubted our ability to weather any potential storms. She was spending most of her time at my place again, which was just a small travel trailer with a deck for sitting outside. Set back under the trees, it was cozy, and she had brightened the little space with her feminine touches.

One sunny afternoon, John and I were working on opposite sides of the barrel wall preparing to lay the roof boards down. "Ever grow any grass?" I called over the wall.

"No. But I've grown almost everything else," he replied.

I was trying to find a way to open the conversation. "I've been growing grass, but I lost my place to grow. I've been trying to figure out a new place."

"I may know a place up Palo Colorado Canyon," he said matter-of-factly. "Friend of mine named Gene Weaver had some property up there, and he just keeled over and died about six months ago. His wife, Molly, asked me if I would go in with her on a garden up there, split fifty-fifty, to give her some income. I told her I'd think about it. I don't know much about growing grass, but it seems like a lot of work for one person."

I was curious. "You know her? What do you know about her?"

"She's got quite a story, man. She used to be a madam in a whorehouse in Sparks, Nevada, somewhere. The 'Velvet Roadhouse,' I think it was called. The place was popular, lots goin' on, a lot of girls working there. But she got burnt out. So then she meets Gene, retires from the whorehouse, and moves to Big Sur with him."

"And lives happily ever after," I said.

"Well, for ten years or so, until Gene died," John said.

"How did Gene die?" I asked.

"Oh, man," John gave a little laugh. "That's another story. So, it happened during sex with Molly. Gene choked on a gumball while having an orgasm. Sucked it right down his throat. Molly wasn't able to revive him."

"What? You're kidding!" I said.

"No. Serious. Death by gumball, with considerations."

"Sucking on a gumball while having sex?"

"That's the story. They think the choking brought on a heart attack. Anyway, he died right there. It was pretty traumatic for Molly, as you can imagine."

"Jesus Christ!" I was shaking my head. "That's a terrible story! Damn." I thought about our tenuous hold on life for a moment and then called back to John, "Well, I'd be interested in partnering up with you. If you want, ask her if we can come up and look around. Maybe it's a good spot to grow, maybe it's not, but if it's good, a lot of money could be made. We could make it happen."

"I'll talk with her. She said she's heard of you. I'll let you know."

A week later John told me he had spoken with the woman, and she had agreed to our coming up and looking around. The property was eight miles up Palo Colorado Road and down an obscure private road that only she used. She was on ten acres that bordered the National Forest and thousands of acres of virgin land.

Located fifteen miles north of Big Sur and eleven miles south of

Carmel, Palo Colorado Canyon had a one-lane road that wound through a stately redwood canyon along Palo Colorado Creek. After three miles, the road left the towering redwoods and climbed up a steep grade called the Hoist, named after a large oxen powered hoist that had been used to pull wagonloads of tanbark up the hill earlier in the century.

We knocked off work early at my house on a Wednesday and drove the Bad Ford to Palo Colorado Canyon. After turning up the road and driving about eight miles, John pointed to a wooden gate. "There it is."

I pulled up to the gate, and John opened it. We closed it behind us and drove down the road. The road dropped off the ridge slowly and leveled out. It was dirt and deeply rutted, bouncing us around as we drove about a mile under large live oaks and bay laurels. Before too long, we came upon a large clearing with a cabin backed up to a hillside covered in oaks. The cabin was one story, built of redwood board and bat, with a long, covered front porch. Off to one end was an in-ground pool surrounded by a large tiled deck with five or six umbrella-covered tables on it. It was an inviting scene.

A tall, buxom woman with long brown hair tied in a ponytail walked out of the cabin as we jumped out of the truck.

"You didn't tell me she was good lookin'," I said under my breath.

John made the introductions. "Molly Weaver, this is Wesley Daggert. Wesley, Molly."

Molly and I shook hands.

"Good to meet you," I said.

She waved at the air. "Come inside, away from these flies."

We went inside, and she motioned for us to sit down at a table in the kitchen. The cabin was clean and colorful. We were in a large room that was both the kitchen and living room. There was a river-rock fireplace against the wall opposite the kitchen, and two large ferns hung from the ceiling on either side. A comfortable couch faced the fireplace, with two easy chairs on either end. Two doors led away from the living room, I thought probably to bedrooms. There was a large framed painting hanging between the doors of a scantily clad woman in pink chiffon, lying back on a red leather couch. She was holding a glass of champagne. Underneath it was the caption, 'Welcome to the Velvet Roadhouse.'

"Can I offer you gentlemen a cold beer?" Molly asked.

John pulled out a chair from the table. "I will definitely have a beer."

"Please," I smiled.

Molly pulled three beers out of the fridge and pulled the caps off, then set them on the table. "So, where do we start?" she asked, sitting down.

I spoke first. "Let me say first how sorry I am for the loss of your husband."

"Thank you. It's been hard. I miss him in more ways than one, but we have to keep on living, don't we?" It was more of a statement than a question.

"Yes, we do," I looked down at the table, then back to Molly. "John mentioned that you were interested in growing some pot back here."

"I need some income," she said. "I've got 240,000 acres right out there to do it on. I just don't know how to go about it. I got the wild idea to split a garden with someone, they do the work, I supply the place, or in this case the trail. I thought of John because he's capable"—she patted him on the shoulder—"and I trust him. I wasn't thinking of more than one partner, but John says you've got experience, and I've heard you're an honest man."

I smiled. "Word's out?"

She smiled. "Big Sur doesn't keep secrets, it just passes them around. I'm sure you know that, Wesley."

"Yeah," I swallowed some beer. "Here's the thing. It really takes two to make any money growing grass. There's a lot of work to do, a demanding schedule, and you're right, having a place to grow is the largest part of the equation, without a doubt. But first things first. We need to find a location out there with the right cover and water supply."

"What kind of split are you thinking?" she asked.

I shrugged and looked to John.

John shifted on his chair. "I don't know, man. Everybody gets a third, I guess."

"Sounds good to me, if you're up for it," I said to Molly. "A three-way split on the proceeds from the garden, with John and I doing the work and you supplying the access. We split the expenses evenly."

"Sounds okay," she said. "But I don't have much money since Gene passed. I don't know how much I can help with expenses."

"We'll keep a ledger and settle it out at the end. First, we have to find the garden site and the water. Do you have any close neighbors?" I asked.

"Over that way there's a couple, but they're old and don't get out much. East, out that way, is the National Forest and only the Boy Scout camp about three miles out to the south."

"They still use it?" John asked.

Molly took a swig of her beer. "Yeah, once in a while. I think the scouts stay close to the camp though."

"Can you show us around a bit?" I asked.

"Sure."

Molly walked us around her property, showing us her barn down a narrow driveway under the trees and pointing out her property corners to give us an idea of the lay of the land. We were in a shallow valley under oaks choked by intruding brush.

Behind the barn, she walked us to the fence line, "There's a trail that starts here and goes for miles. Or it used to. I haven't been on it for a long time. There's another over there, at that property corner." She pointed back toward the cabin.

We walked back to the cabin and stood on the porch. Looking around the property, I was impressed. I looked at Molly. "It's important that we not discuss this with anyone. As in *no* one."

"I understand that," Molly nodded. "People know too much already."

We finished our beers and agreed to meet back at Molly's on Friday morning. Everything I had seen and heard was encouraging. Molly walked us to the truck; we bid her goodbye and drove away.

On the way back to Big Sur, John and I talked about using Molly's property to access the National Forest. Every precaution had to be taken to disguise the trail so nothing led back to her property. The Boy Scout camp was a potential problem. How far from camp did the scouts explore? The thirty mile round trip from Big Sur to Palo Colorado Canyon was a hassle, and meant a lot of exposure on the highway, but we didn't have any other options. It was July and too late to grow, but that gave us plenty of time to find a good location and set up the water system, whatever that would end up looking like, for next season. We decided to go back up to Molly's the following Friday and begin our search for the right spot.

We rolled into Molly's at nine the next Friday morning. Molly was standing at the pool, barefoot, with a push broom. She gave us a wave and motioned us over. The morning was already warm with a buzzing of insects from the surrounding canyon as John and I walked up the stone stairs to the pool deck. Molly gave John a hug, and I extended my hand.

"Hi, Molly!"

"Hi, Wesley, please sit down."

We pulled back some chairs and sat at a table beneath an umbrella.

"So, what's on the agenda?" Molly smiled.

We talked a while about finding a growing space and a water source. When we were all on the same page, with Molly in agreement, John and I set off down the trail that started behind the barn. The trail was overgrown from lack of use, and we did our best not to break too many of the branches as we walked. We followed a contour line that descended gradually away from Molly's property until we crossed a small creek choked with brush on both sides of the trail.

"Soggy bottom!" John called out, the tops of his boots covered in mud.

"Our first water," I said. "But too close to home."

We continued on, passing through thickets of poison oak, manzanita, and chamise, the branches pulling at our clothes and scratching our skin, until after about a mile we dropped down to another small creek gurgling by. We were standing in an open area, a confluence of three hills, where every direction was up. The creek came in from the north where it had cut a narrow ravine into the hillside. We followed a deer trail, walking along above the creek for another quarter mile, hidden under a canopy of oak trees, until down below us, the ravine opened up into a sandy flat fed by two other seasonal creeks that were dry. We walked down to the flat and sat on some large boulders protruding from the sand. Four tall, oak-covered hills converged where we sat. The creek was under the sand at our feet but running openly above and below the flat. We kicked around a bit, following the creek uphill for another fifty yards, and returned to the sandy flat.

"Nice spot. It's hidden real nice, but too shady to grow," I said.

"Let's snoop around up these hills. Maybe there's more water up there." John stood and started uphill.

For the next three hours, we walked up and down the hills above Sandy Flat, as we now called it, finding several prime garden areas, but no water. The terrain and brush growth were the same on all the hills. At about 200 feet above the creek, the oaks gave way to bays, and the brush line squeezed in closer until it was just brush running up the hills. Under the oaks and bays, the soil was loamy, rich from years of fallen foliage. The sun was bright, and the tree lines provided shelter. In many ways, it reminded me of the first garden Kade and I had grown under the camouflage netting.

John and I sat down to rest in the shade under some oaks.

"Lots of good places to grow, but no water," I said.

John was off in thought. "Hey, why don't we just pump the water up here?" he said.

"Pump it?"

"Yeah! We build a piston pump and lift the water right up here. We could push water up any of the hills we climbed today!"

I was skeptical. "I don't know anything about building pumps, John. Anyway, people would hear the noise for miles back here!"

"No problem. I've built lots of pumps, it's just sprockets and chain, an engine, and a pump about the size of a cantaloupe. If we set it down at Sandy Flat, the noise would be muffled by the hills and trees. No one would hear it unless they were right on top of it. I think it would work."

"We would need a water tank at every garden site. How would we do that?" I was trying to keep up with his idea.

"I don't know about tanks. They're too heavy, but…hey! How about 55-gallon drums? They're light. We could haul two or three to every garden site and pump right to them!"

I was beginning to see how this might work. It was something I would have never considered on my own, but John was confident, and his idea was growing on me. I was now looking at the garden sites we had found through new eyes. They were perfect for camouflage netting, with tree lines that edged along the brush, so I told John about the nets.

"Sounds good!" he said. "I got real familiar with camo nets when

I was parking tanks under them for Uncle Sam while stationed in Germany."

We talked about ideas all the way back to Molly's place. We needed a route in for supplies that didn't create a highway to her property, and an escape route out the back way, maybe two. Growing on federal property was a serious offense; probably, I imagined, punishable by torture and endless incarceration. We couldn't afford to be caught out there.

We found Molly working in the garden and filled her in on what we had in mind.

"Sounds like quite an undertaking!" she said. "You two up for all that?"

"No problem," John said. "It'll be fun!"

"We've got plenty of time to put it together. Plants don't go in the ground until March," I added.

We were all in agreement and feeling pretty good about it. John and I drove back to Simson Ridge in an animated conversation fueled by a flood of new ideas.

Back home, I parked the truck, and John took off down the hill on his motorcycle. Susie was there sitting out in the sun under a straw hat, reading a magazine. I said "Hi," and continued on to the trailer for a beer. When I went back outside, Susie looked over at me and said, "Wesley, I need to talk with you." I suddenly felt apprehensive.

I grabbed an outside chair and sat it next to her. "What do we need to talk about?" I said, sitting down.

She looked at me intently. "I'm pregnant, Wesley. I'm going to have a baby."

An electrical jolt ran through my body, and I just stared at her. "I'm the father?"

"Don't even go there, Wesley. Of course you're the father. The doctor says I conceived last month. I'm due in March." She stared, searching my face.

I had always wanted to have kids, but like so many others, couldn't see how it would ever come about. An incredible feeling of commitment and resolve came over me. "Susie, we've had our ups and downs. I only want to do this if we're both committed to being lifelong partners. You need to take a hard look at us. I don't want there to be breakups and turmoil. I don't want my kid to have different fathers. Do you understand?"

"I feel the same way, Wesley. I want to raise a family. I feel good about this. I have a little munchkin in my belly, a new little soul that I'm nurturing, and it's your baby too. I can commit to a life with you."

I was overwhelmed. I gave her a big hug and placed my hand on her belly. "Hello in there," I said. "We love you!"

I was going to be a dad. I knew inside that my life was changed forever, that there would always be someone I cared more about than myself. I could feel a love blossoming inside that all other loves would be compared to, an unconditional love for a young soul that would need my encouragement and support from day one until forever.

"We have to get some champagne!" I said to Susie.

"No more drinking for me," she said. "Everything I eat and drink goes right into the baby. But you go ahead, have one for me!"

I looked at Susie, seeing that a change had come over her. She seemed to have a glow about her, an aura around her body, a vibrancy. For a woman who'd seemed like she never wanted kids, referring to them as rug rats and ankle biters, she had transformed into Mother Maternal, someone carrying precious cargo, and I could see in her eyes that a mighty love was growing inside her too.

CHAPTER 33

"Necessity is the mother of invention."

–English proverb

THE SUMMER WAS FLASHING BY. It felt liberating to not be tied to a watering schedule in a pot garden and to have so much extra time to work on my house project. September found us cutting window and door holes through the wine tank. The roof was on, and John had welded together a magnificent wood stove that stood on four legs, two feet off the ground, positioned inside the structure near the east wall. We had poured a concrete slab over the wooden floor and troweled it smooth. Cutting the windows and doors proved to be challenging as the tank was round and leaned in from bottom to top, but no problem seemed unsolvable, and both John and I enjoyed working out the various complexities the tank shape presented on its journey to becoming a house.

David Stafford and Jimmy had made a few visits over the summer, each purchasing several pounds per trip. Stafford and I had become good friends, and he often spent the night at my place when he was in town. Jimmy, on the other hand, the consummate professional, preferred to keep things strictly business. He was always cordial but kept his distance. I knew almost nothing about him, where he lived, whether he was married or not, or how he moved things around. He didn't offer, and I didn't ask. I liked that he never asked any questions of me, never wanted to know anything beyond the business at hand, and though he was a mystery to me, I trusted him. Things were slowing down for Stafford—he had lost a connection in southern California and wasn't moving as much pot. I still had about fifty-two pounds and wanted to move it out.

Work was also progressing at the garden site near Molly's. We had our trails in to the garden area and were establishing our escape routes. It was interesting watching John figure out the formula for the various components to build the water pump. It went something like this: The five-horse Briggs and Stratton motor turned at X RPMs at wide-open throttle. The piston pump, surprisingly small, needed to turn at Y RPMs for maximum output. John stood at the counter of a gear shop and computed what size sprocket wheels would enable the shaft turning at X to turn the pump shaft at Y. Sprocket chain was purchased, as was a length of inch-and-a-half angle iron steel. Back home, he welded it all together, complete with a chain guard. The pump was hard plumbed with an 18-inch three-quarter-inch pipe that also acted as a handle. We ran a water line to it and started the engine at the house to test it. A stream of water shot out thirty feet.

"We could pump water to the top of Mount Everest with this thing!" John said.

We found a supplier in Seaside for the 55-gallon drums we were going to use for water tanks. They were used but in good shape and had sealed ends that were plumbed and threaded for pipe. We purchased twelve and stashed them behind Molly's barn. Next to them was 1,500 feet of black poly pipe in 100-foot rolls for the water lines to the gardens.

We had found an army surplus outlet in Moss Landing that had a warehouse full of camouflage netting. I negotiated a price and bought fourteen large nets. They were the same nets I had used with Kade, and I still believed in them. In the brush, at any distance over 500 feet, they were invisible to the naked eye.

We had chosen four sites for garden areas, all several hundred feet above the Sandy Flat, in different directions up each of the converging hills. Each site was set back into the tree lines with good southern exposure. We cleared brush away from the tree lines and erected camouflage nets over the clearings.

"We've done a lot of work here, John. It'll be hysterical if the pump doesn't push the water up here." We were resting in the shade with our backs against a tree.

John tossed a pebble down the hill. "I wouldn't worry about that. The pump has plenty of lift. Besides, if for some reason it doesn't make it, we just have to have a second pump and a second lift. I'm not worried about it."

Early in October, we started building the water system. We wanted to wait until late in the year to see how much the water flow changed above Sandy Flat late in the season. While it did slow down, we still had water flowing, and created a catch basin using a five-gallon plastic bucket buried under a rock outcrop where the water ran over a small fall. The bucket was fitted with a pipe outlet, and we buried three-quarter-inch pipe from the bucket under the sand at Sandy Flat to a large shelf we had dug into the side of the hill. On the dirt shelf, we erected a kiddie pool that held 1,200 gallons of water. We plumbed the pool with a pipe outlet at the bottom to feed our pump. The pool was covered with a black tarp, and in a couple of days, it was full and overflowing.

We decided to test pump to the highest garden site, which we were calling garden four. We carried a coil of pipe to the top of the garden and unrolled it down the hill toward Sandy Flat. At its end, we attached another coil and unrolled it down. It turned out garden four was 450 feet above the flat. We hooked up the pump to draw water from the pool, attached the garden line to it, and started the motor. When the motor was running smoothly, we set it to full throttle and hiked up to the garden. When we arrived, water was flowing out in a strong stream about two feet long from the end of the pipe. We were in business! I slapped john on the shoulder. "You're a genius! Look at that water flow! We could go even higher!"

John looked like a proud papa. "Yeah, we could go another couple hundred feet higher easily!"

"That's fantastic!" I said to John. "Shit, this really opens up some possibilities!"

We ran back down the hill to turn off the pump.

"We should get some walkie-talkies so we don't both have to run up and down these hills," he said, out of breath. "One guy could pump, the other guy could radio when the water reached the garden!"

I was out of breath too. I nodded toward John. "That's a good idea.

Better for us to be in communication without yelling or running up and down these damn hills!"

We carried the coils of plastic pipe from Molly's barn to Sandy Flat, then up each of the remaining hills to the different garden sites. The hills were steep, and the climbing was difficult, often like climbing a ladder with the hillside two feet from your face. One day I was climbing with John behind me. I was carrying a coil of pipe, and I slipped sideways, falling into some sticks. I lay there panting and sweating. I noticed I had scraped my right forearm.

"Time for a break?" John said.

"It's fucking steep right here." I looked at my arm and saw it was turning black where I had scraped it. "Look at this shit!" I said, holding out my arm. "I scraped my arm, and now it's turning black!"

We watched as the scrape turned black and then formed a blister over it like a burn.

"What the…?"

"Maybe it's an alien plant species and you're going to die right after the new roots come out of your chest!" John said.

I looked around where I had fallen and saw some broken poison oak roots sticking up from the ground, fresh sap oozing from the tips. "I think I cut myself with a poison oak root," I said. "It must be the sap that's turning it black!"

John stood up. "It's just a flesh wound, Kitty. It's either gonna kill you or cause arson in your solar plexus."

"Well, bury me at Wounded Knee, or, maybe, Wounded Arm," I said, continuing up the hill.

We decided to haul three 55-gallon drums to garden four and finish setting up the system. The drums were manageable by one person on level ground, but two people sharing the load made it easier hiking uphill. At the top of garden four, we cleared enough brush to set the three drums level, side by side. The drums were plumbed in series across the tops, with the first drum receiving the pumped water and the last drum being plumbed at the bottom for release to the garden. A one-inch hole was drilled at the top of the last drum to allow the water to escape under pressure, to avoid rupturing any pipe or drums.

We bought two walkie-talkies from Radio Shack. When the lines were all connected from the pool to the garden, John hiked to garden four and checked in. "Big Turkey, Big Turkey, this is Alpha Zulu!"

I had to laugh. "Alpha Zulu, I never should have told you that story! Okay, ready?"

"Roger wilco, Big Turkey!" came his reply.

I started the pump and leaned it out, advancing the throttle to wide open, then looked at my watch and waited. I had my ear to the walkie-talkie when I heard John say, "That's it!" I shut off the pump and looked at my watch. It had taken twenty-two minutes, thirty-five seconds to fill all three tanks at garden four. I wrote it down on a piece of paper.

Over the next week, we hauled three 55-gallon drums to each garden site, plumbed them, and ran the water lines back to Sandy Flat. We test-pumped each one and timed how long it took to fill the tanks at each individual garden. We then walked each water line, burying it in a shallow trench. At Sandy Flat, the water lines ended at the bottom of their respective hills, and we covered those with leaves. A wooden storage box was buried under the sand to store the pump.

"Looks good," I said as we sat on a sidehill looking down at the flat. "I can't see the water lines at all."

"Yeah…it looks good, man! That pool's hard to hide. Once we're set up, we could bury it in brush. It doesn't look like anyone comes up here anyway," John said.

It was true, we hadn't seen sign or heard sound from another person since we had started working. We seemed to be isolated. We had covered the entry of our trail at the bottom confluence that we called Three Hills, but there didn't seem to be any security threat from the ground.

The water system was set. It was a forty-five-minute walk to Sandy Flat. Once there, one of us would uncover the pump, hook it to the pool, connect to each one of the garden supply lines, pump for the allotted times to each of the four gardens, then dismantle and hide everything again.

Including a visit to each garden to check the drip systems, the entire job would take about six hours per visit. Once the plants started to declare their sex, it would take a lot longer.

CHAPTER 34

"If it weren't for Kitty and Matt Dillon, the Long Branch would have been just another saloon and Dodge City just another cow town."

–John Stalkinger

WINTER SETTLED INTO THE CENTRAL California coast, which wasn't a bad thing with temperatures in the low fifties and cloudless days punctuated by an occasional severe rainstorm. If it wasn't storming, the weather was perfect, and I liked a good storm. John and I kept working on the wine tank house, having it fully enclosed by December of 1979.

We had started a rock wall that would retain the building site of the main house. It was a long circuitous affair that ran for more than 200 feet. I had started using river rock collected from the Big Sur River, driving the Bad Ford pickup down to the Fernwood Campground and showing a note from the owner saying it was all right to harvest rock. The owner was a good friend and welcomed the removal of the rocks. He felt it improved his 'beach-space' next to the river. John called it "Rock Rustling," backing the truck down to the river's edge and loading rock into the bed. We had learned from experience to choose only rocks that had two surfaces we could use, giving us more options when we placed them in the wall.

One day, while parked at the river's edge, we noticed we were running out of rock. We had picked it over pretty well. John walked out into the river, picked up a beautiful specimen from under the flowing water, and held it up. "Plenty more rocks out here!" he called.

I laughed. "Are you suggesting I drive the Ford into the river?"

"Why not, man? I doubt you'll get stuck and if you do, we can turn it into a boat!"

It didn't seem right, somehow, but what harm would it do? Any fish in the river would just swim out of the way. Crawdads might not be so lucky. I locked the hubs, put the truck in four-wheel drive, and drove out into the river to where John was standing. The river was about forty feet across at that point and was running about a foot deep, well under the running boards of the truck. I hopped out of the cab and stood calf deep in the running water. The campground wasn't very busy, but those who were there stopped and stared at us. I climbed back into the truck and set off. The water was flowing a translucent green over the rocks, and I couldn't really see what obstacles I was driving over. I drove for fifty feet, crunching and slipping slowly over the submerged rocks, and then set the brake, leaving the engine running. I jumped out into fourteen inches of water flowing under the truck. The engine and exhaust were high and dry.

John was standing beside the truck, wet to his knees. We began picking up rocks, selecting the good ones and tossing them into the truck bed. A couple of campers had gathered to watch the show from shore, while farther down the river, a fisherman gave us an over-the-shoulder raised-eyebrow stare. We filled the bed with rock and jumped back into the truck, both of us sopping wet. I put the truck in reverse and backed up slowly to where we could exit the river going forward. The truck climbed easily out of the riverbed. Back on shore, we got out and stood beside the truck, laughing.

"It's all over, folks. Nothing to see here!" John said in the direction of the campers, still laughing.

We had found a new source for rock. Over the next few weeks, we returned several times, unabashedly driving straight into the river without hesitation, once driving 100 feet downstream and almost getting stuck behind a big boulder that was sitting in a hole. Somehow the Bad Ford always found a grip and got us back to shore. We'd climb up the steep campground road to the highway, dripping water from the truck like we'd just left a car wash, our freshly rustled river rock glistening in the bed, and head for home where the rock pile was growing larger trip by trip.

The cement mixer was always turning with a now familiar hum, slide, and slosh rhythm. Sand and gravel were delivered by dump truck once a week, and stone by stone, the wall began to take shape. Once in a while a stone would turn up looking like a face or a mask, perfectly cut by the river, resembling a character from central casting, and we would place it in the wall in such a way as to break the plane by sticking out prominently from the rest of the stones. We started naming the stone caricatures and already had names like the Happy Drunk, Grandma, the Cheshire Cat, and the Ballroom Mask.

By February 1980, the wall was 250 feet long and rose to a height of seven feet. Ornamental stones purchased from landscaping shops were placed strategically in the wall to liven it up, including Arizona river rock, Oregon blue granite, and red lava. I said many times that no stone I drove by was safe from being hijacked and cemented into the wall.

Susie was a month from giving birth, busy building her nest and planting gardens. She had an English flower garden near our little trailer and a lush vegetable garden below the wine barrel. Wearing a broad straw hat and leaning back to balance her round belly, she worked long peaceful hours in the gardens. Lavender, assorted daisies, asters, and columbine thrived close to home, while African daisies and gazania, some spread by birds or the wind, were planted farther away to color our view.

Early in March, Susie and I were facing a problem. According to our obstetrician, our baby was engaged Frank breech, or butt first. We were planning on a home birth, but this position was too risky for our midwife to feel comfortable with the delivery. She was backing out. We were a week away from the due date with no plan B. Susie called doctors trying to arrange an appointment, but everyone was scheduled. It was looking like it might be an emergency room delivery.

We were stressed when, late one afternoon, John and Sherry called and invited us down to Nepenthe for a drink and dinner. Getting out and about seemed like a good idea after so much worrying about Susie's delivery, so we spruced up and went down to join them.

We arrived at Nepenthe just after dark and walked up on the terrace. The night was cool and the terrace empty, with all of the Saturday night diners sitting inside. We could see through the glass doors that the restaurant was packed and the bar, its horseshoe shape aglow with tall candles, was bustling with activity two patrons deep. We saw John and Sherry sitting in the middle of the bar and walked in to join them. John was holding a seat for Susie in keeping with the rest of the bar having only women sitting down and their men standing beside them. John slid off, and Susie climbed up on the bar stool and ordered an apple juice for herself and a tequila tonic for me. When our drinks arrived, we all touched glasses in a toast to a smooth delivery, even though it didn't seem likely.

I stood with John surveying the dining room. Every table was full, and the waiters were dashing about, carrying trays of food and drinks. A large fire burned in the fireplace. Two extra tables had been placed close to the bar, near the front doors, to accommodate extra guests. The hostess standing at the front door called out a name from the waiting list. "Rodgers! Party of four. Rodgers, your table is ready!"

Two women slid off their barstools and joined their dates at the front door while two more women took their seats at the bar.

I turned to John and spoke over the bustle. "The place is packed!"

"Yeah, I was thinking maybe we could get some food," John yelled. "But that doesn't look likely for a while!"

Just then a booming voice at the grill-end of the bar bellowed, "Women! My, my! Look at all these squaws!"

I turned and there stood Tom Dugan. At six foot four with a large barrel chest, Tom was an imposing fellow. Part French and part American Indian, Tom was known as a gentle giant, a man of poetry who lived high on a mountaintop in a ramshackle cabin. He had, some said, a harem of women living in tents in the canyon around him. Tom fancied himself to be a mountain man, the 'Jeremiah Johnson' of Big Sur, claiming he had hiked through the Rockies and wrestled trout from bears for his dinner. Tom was also known to be a bully and a loudmouth when he was drinking. Looking at Tom standing at the end of the bar, I could see he was very drunk.

"I'm Tom Dugan, down from the mountains!" he bellowed.

John and I looked at each other. "Oh, shit," John laughed. "Here's trouble!"

"Bartender!" Tom called. "Bring me a shot of brandy!"

"I think you've had enough, Tom," the bartender said.

"Bullshit!" Tom yelled. "I've only just begun!" And with that he wrapped his arms around the woman sitting at the first barstool and cupped her breasts in his big hands.

The woman cried out, and Tom reached out and grabbed her drink, downing it in one gulp. He then moved to the second woman sitting at the bar, reached around, and grabbed her breasts. Glancing at Susie, I could see it coming.

None of the men had made a move, maybe hoping he would just go away, so Tom moved to seat number three and grabbed that woman's breasts before downing her drink as well. Susie was sitting in seat five with a pregnant belly and swollen breasts, and I was not going to let Tom grope her. I knew Tom, knew he was strong as an ox, but also knew he was slow and lumbering and underestimated people because of his size. At five-eight, I was looking up at a huge man, but my legs and arms were hardened from four years of hauling chicken shit up steep mountains, and I was motivated. Tom grabbed the breasts of the woman in seat four. I transferred my drink to my right hand as the woman's date yelled, "Hey!"

Sometimes in life you cause trouble, and sometimes it just finds you. I stepped forward and pushed Tom's shoulder.

He turned toward me. "Back off, Tom! If you touch Susie, you and I are going to fight!" I said.

"Fight?" Tom bellowed and then slapped me hard across the face.

It stung. I took a step back and then threw my tequila tonic, glass and all, as hard as I could into his face. Someone screamed. The glass shattered and flew in small pieces twenty feet behind him. He stepped back and wiped some blood from his face and then came at me. I moved in quickly, grabbed his shirt, and pulled him over my planted right leg. When I felt him go off balance, I pushed him hard. Tom fell back out of control and landed in the center of a dinner table with four people sitting at it. The table flipped over, and the floor was immediately covered with all four dinners and a broken bottle of wine.

As Tom got to his feet he slipped on a piece of chicken, and I hit him hard on his nose. My foot slipped on the wet floor, and I moved away to dryer ground. Tom shook off my punch and came at me again, growling like an animal. I joined him halfway, grabbed his shirt again, stepped to his right, and pulled him over my leg. When I felt him go off balance, I pushed him again, this time breaking his grip on my shoulders with an upward jerk of my arms. Tom fell sideways into the edge of another table, capsizing it and sending four more dinners to the floor. The patrons jumped up, the women screaming, some moving to stand in the sills of the tall windows along the wall.

As Tom struggled to get off the floor, a waiter rushed me and threw his arms around me, yelling, “Stop it!”

John quickly grabbed the waiter and spun him around. “You stay out of this!” he said, pushing the waiter backward.

Tom came at me again, bleeding from a cut under his eye and from his nose. I hit him again on his chin, and his feet went out from under him, slipping on some spilled food. He fell backward between two tables and landed on his ass.

I could see my punches were having little to no effect on Tom. He was too big and too drunk, and mad as a proud bull. Tom reached up with each hand and grabbed a table on either side of him. As he stood up, both tables tipped inward, sending eight more dinners to the floor. People were standing screaming in a large circle around us, a littered mess of food, drink, and broken dishes at their feet.

Tom rushed me again, and I stepped in toward him, landing a solid punch to the cut below his eye. Blood spurted in a splash. John and three other guys rushed to restrain Tom, taking him to the floor where he continued to wrestle and thrash, finally crawling slowly out through the door to the terrace with John on his back, mimicking riding a bronco at the rodeo.

Except for Susie and Sherry, and Dirty Corner where the locals sat, the bar had cleared. The bartenders had stayed behind the bar and were busy serving drinks to the local characters in the corner, who were all enjoying the show. I looked around and spotted the hat I’d been wearing, upside down in a puddle of spilled wine. I picked it up and put it on. There were four overturned tables and sixteen dinners on the floor.

People were still focused on Tom outside, wrestling with John and two other guys trying to subdue him.

I turned to Susie. "Let's get out of here!"

Sherry told Susie to meet her at her cabin. We walked quickly through the restaurant with people staring at us and out the back door, just as there was a loud crash and another scream from the front of the restaurant. We walked down the dark supply road behind the restaurant to the parking lot, then down to Sherry's cabin.

"I didn't know you could fight like that, Wes," Susie said.

"He was drunk, and I was only defending your honor, Susie," I put on my best Dudley Do-Right smile. "But the facts be known, I couldn't hurt that bastard. He was too big and too crazy. My punches meant nothing to him. Luckily, he never got ahold of me!"

Susie put her hands to her belly. "Well, that woke somebody up! The baby's kicking all over the place!"

I put my hand on her belly. It felt like a fight was going on.

About fifteen minutes later, John and Sherry walked down the road to the cabin. John was laughing. "Well, that was fun! Reminded me of a Saturday night brawl at the Long Branch, in Dodge City! Where's Matt Dillon when you need him?"

"Did you guys get him calmed down?" I asked.

"Oh, hell no," John said. "He broke free of us on the terrace. He's still running around up there looking for you. 'Where's Wes? Where's Wes?' Back and forth through the restaurant with night security chasing right behind him. The only thing louder than him is all the people calling for their checks!"

We all laughed. The phone rang inside their cabin, and Sherry went in to answer it. A minute later, she stuck her head out. "Shirley's on the phone and wants to know if we'll come up to Partington to watch a movie with her."

Getting away from Nepenthe seemed like a good idea. We all agreed. Susie and I got into my truck and followed John and Sherry down the coast. Shirley was the daughter of a famous author and lived in his house on Partington Ridge, perched high above the ocean. She had one of the only VHS decks around, and we enjoyed watching movies there.

On the way down, we passed a brand new telephone pole lying along the highway next to a standing pole carrying power lines that was leaning heavily south. When we got up to Shirley's house, I asked John, "Did you see that pole lying down next to the highway?"

"Yeah. Brand new. Wanna rescue it?" he asked.

"Yeah," I said. "Let's rescue it. It could help support the house."

The movie was *Swept Away*, and John and I only watched for about a half hour. Finally, he gave me a look, and we begged off to the ladies.

"We have to go down the hill for a bit," I said. "We'll be back in an hour."

"Where are you going, Wesley?" Susie asked.

"To rescue a telephone pole," I said.

John and I climbed into the Ford and drove down the hill. After about two miles, we came upon the pristine telephone pole lying alongside the highway. I pulled off the road and backed up to it.

John bent down and picked up one end. "Ohhh, it's a ball breaker! But no problem, man!"

We scanned the highway for headlights, but there was only darkness and quiet. We got on opposite sides of the pole and picked it up to our waists, then dragged it to the truck, resting it on the tailgate. We both got under it and lifted it high into the air and set it on the edge of the lumber rack. We walked back to the middle and lifted it again, sliding it farther onto the lumber rack. Just then to the north, headlights swept around a corner, heading south toward us.

"Shit," I said.

The car was moving fast, so we ducked low behind the Ford and waited. The Monterey sheriff's car rolled quickly by. The interior lights were on, and we saw Tom Dugan sitting in the back. The sheriff was taking him home.

John started laughing. "They're taking the crazy fucker home! I thought they'd take him to jail!"

For us, it was bad luck. We'd been seen. My truck was well known, and they had passed it with a brand new telephone pole hanging from its racks. If the pole went missing, there would be little mystery as to who might have been involved. We pulled the pole back off the racks, dropping it on the ground, and drove back up to Shirley's to watch the end of the movie.

The next day, Susie went in to see the obstetrician for an examination. To everyone's surprise, the baby had disengaged from Frank breech, turned completely around, and reengaged, headfirst in the womb. The brawl at Nepenthe had been too much excitement for the baby, and it had kicked free. Happily, we were once again looking forward to a home delivery!

CHAPTER 35

"Four in the pool is better than two in the bush."

–Molly Weaver

On the Ides of March in 1980, on a ridge in the Skyline Forest above the city lights of the Monterey Peninsula, Susie gave birth to our daughter Savannah at our midwife's house, just a mile from the hospital. The house was darkened, with only candlelight surrounding a mattress on the floor. Susie was propped up against the wall, huffing and puffing, and after nineteen hours of labor, Savannah emerged with a warm rush into my waiting hands.

I looked at her little face, then placed her on her mommy's belly and, with the help of the midwife, cut her umbilical cord. The midwife wrapped Savannah in a soft coddling blanket and placed her into Susie's arms, where she snuggled, searching her mother's face with remarkably alert little eyes. I will never forget the look of love and serenity on Susie's face.

I stood in front of the floor-to-ceiling windows and looked down at the sparkling city lights. I had just witnessed a miracle. A young life gushing from her mother's womb, so vulnerable and exposed. I was braced by knowing that her life was now our responsibility. Her protection, her sustenance, her learning, her comfort, all depended on Susie and me. Of course, I was playing catch-up. Susie had known and felt this for nine months, but when I caught her little body in my hands and looked at her face, a bond formed that I knew would last forever.

We stayed at the midwife's house for two days, enjoying the support, ordering out, and allowing Susie the rest she needed from the birth ordeal. Some of Susie's lady friends from Big Sur were showing up to offer support and encouragement. I was handing out cigars that said, 'It's a Girl!' to anyone I met, while Susie was soaking up information on infant care from the women gathered close around her. On day three, we walked out into the sunshine carrying Savannah, thanked our hosts, and headed for home with our precious cargo.

Some of Susie's local friends set up a support system where, for a couple of weeks, someone brought dinner to our home every night and helped with small household chores. This was a godsend that enabled Susie time to get adjusted to the complexities of being a new mom and allowed me to get back to work.

It was late March. John and I had started carrying starts to the garden for planting. The chicken-shit marches had been brutal. Our hills were steep and the sixty pound packboards made every step a labor. We crawled as much as we walked up the hills to the four garden sites. We were digging our holes, mixing our soil, building our fences, and dialing in the watering system.

Garden four turned out to have a mostly hardpan base of quartzite covered by two inches of topsoil, but because we had put so much energy into the water system, we used it anyway. We hauled up a steel digging bar to help, but after twenty holes, we abandoned that approach and brought up large molded peat buckets to hold the plants.

By the third week of April, all the plants were in. We had run over 3,000 feet of drip line to water 1,926 holes. In areas where our soil was deep and rich, we planted two starts to a hole. Altogether, we had planted 2,000 marijuana starts from the very best seeds we could get our hands on.

Garden one and garden three were the largest and enjoyed the best soil. Both were set back under a tree line on their north edges. We had carried up a fourth 55-gallon drum to each one for an added water supply. Garden two had the best natural cover with tree lines on two sides and netting stretched between the trees. Garden four was the redheaded stepchild, with lousy soil and the highest altitude.

All the gardens were under camouflage netting tucked up under the trees and tied down to the brush line. Poles placed in strategic areas under the netting broke up the texture of the sight lines and gave the plants room to grow and us room to move about. As a final touch, we cut brush and threw it haphazardly up on the netting to further enhance the camouflage effect. We felt invisible.

Our pump worked flawlessly, and once we had it worked out, we knew exactly how long it took to fill the tanks at each garden. We would start the pump and time it, turning it off at just the right time. If we went over, the water would shoot up out of the last barrel like a geyser. Once the barrels were full, the water drained on its own through the drip systems. After pumping to all the gardens, we walked up the hills and inspected each plant. It ended up taking about six hours to water and check everything. With the hike and the drive, we were working just about an eight-hour day.

One day late in May, John and I were on our way up to the gardens. John wanted to take his motorcycle, the Suzuki 600, and I drove my truck. There was no way I could keep up with him; he was an accomplished rider with a calculated wildness. He liked to pass me like an arrow, speed far ahead, and then pull over to smoke a cigarette until I caught up. He was standing beside the bike smoking under the eucalyptus trees when I turned off the highway and headed up Palo Colorado Canyon Road. He gave me a nod as I drove by.

About three miles up the road, as I was climbing the steep hoist grade, I heard a roar. Here comes John, wide open throttle, pulling a wheelie past me up the grade! His front tire was two feet off the ground on a ten percent uphill grade, and John was leaning forward with a big smile on his face. He brought the front wheel down and disappeared over the crest of the hill.

He waited for me at Molly's gate, which had two pink balloons tied to the post.

"Is this for us?" I called through my open window.

John climbed back on the bike. "Don't know, man. Let's go see!"

I followed the bike's dust into Molly's place. John was parked next to a red Corvette and a newer black Mercedes sedan. Both cars had a light covering of dust over nice paint jobs. I parked and joined John, who was standing in the clearing between the parked cars and the cabin. We could see there was a group of people by the pool, some swimming, some standing, and all seemed to be wearing bikinis. Molly had some company. She waved from the pool, beckoning us over.

As we approached, John said, "Oh, my Gawd..."

I followed his gaze and saw four absolutely gorgeous women in skimpy bikinis waving at us from the pool.

"Hey, you guys!" Molly called. "Come meet my friends!"

We walked up to the pool area not believing our eyes. The women were even more amazing up close, manicured and buxom with gorgeous hair and makeup. "John, Wesley, meet Angel, Bunny, Cass, and Rose Marie. Girls, my friends, John and Wesley!"

I took the hand of the woman closest to me. "Pleasure, Rose Marie."

"Call me Rose," she purred.

John was shaking hands with Cass.

"Angel, Bunny, Cass, and Rose all worked with me at the Velvet Road House," Molly said. "They still work there, don't you, ladies?"

There was some laughter. "Still doin' the bump and grind," Angel said. "But it's not the same without you, Molly!"

Molly gave a big smile to John and me. "I invited the girls down for a pool party, you know, give 'em a couple days off, let 'em slow down a bit. Huh, girls?"

Everyone nodded, including John and me.

"We could sure use it, Molly!" Bunny said. "We've been busy with all the snow this year!"

"It's beautiful to be here," Angel said. "So quiet! I love this!"

"So, is the Velvet Road House closed down with all of you down here?" I asked, not knowing what else to say.

"Oh, no, honey, we never close. We just rotate in and out," Rose said with a smile.

Cass and Molly gave a short laugh.

"Well, I'll be damned," John said, mostly to himself.

"It's an absolute pleasure to meet you all," I said. "John and I have some work to do."

"Yeah, the boys have some business to take care of," Molly said.

"Well, come back for a swim," Bunny invited with a big smile.

"Will do!" John grinned, and we set off from the house.

On the trail, we were both animated.

"Damn!" John said. "I don't know which one was better lookin'!"

"Waste of time trying to figure that one out!" I said. "Interesting situation. Go figure. Four beautiful working girls and their madam swimming in a pool at our trailhead. Fringe benefits."

"Well, let's get this done," John said. "I wouldn't mind a dip myself!"

At Sandy Flat we uncovered the pump, made our connections, and started pumping up to the gardens. After pumping to all four, John walked up to check on gardens one and three, and I walked up to check on gardens two and four. I refilled two bait boxes with rat poison and cleared two clogged drip emitters below two very thirsty plants. Once back at Sandy Flat, we put everything away and walked out together to Molly's.

Coming up on the house, we saw that Cass and Rose Marie were still in their bikinis while Molly, Bunny, and Angel had changed into colorful sundresses. All were sitting under an umbrella at a table by the pool, laughing. They saw us walking up and started waving.

"Look, it's the boys!" someone called out.

We walked up on the pool patio grinning from ear to ear.

"How about a cold beer?" Molly asked.

"Hell, yes," John said.

Molly walked into the house, leaving John and me standing next to the pool.

Rose Marie stood up in her bikini and dragged two extra chairs from another table.

"Sit down, you two," she said, smiling.

Bunny was looking at our dirty clothes. "You boys should go for a swim!"

"The water's purrfect!" Angel cooed.

"I've got to get back home," I said. "But it does look refreshing. Maybe next time." I looked at John.

"Hey, man, I'm gonna stick around," John said.

"Okay. Don't blame you a bit." I smiled at the girls.

John sat down at the table next to where the girls were sitting and began to unlace his boots. I remained standing. Molly returned with two beers, handing them to John and me. We pulled the tabs. The cold beer washed all the dust from my throat.

"You boys gonna take a swim?" Molly asked.

"I have to get back home, Molly, but thanks!" I said.

"Aw, that's too bad," Molly said. "Maybe next time."

I said so long and walked to my truck. I backed the truck around and rolled down my window just as some screams came from the pool. I looked over just in time to see John's naked butt arcing into the water with a big splash. There was a squeal, and Cass and Rose Marie dove in right after him. My partner's afternoon was looking good. Was he just John in the swimming pool with hookers, or would he become a 'John' in the swimming pool with hookers? One view might be deemed illegal, possibly causing cancer in laboratory rats with local arson suspected. My buddy was already an outlaw, pushing the envelope at every corner and seam. This was superlative subterfuge in the hands of professional glitter, a sideways step that made the glove fit both hands perfectly. I laughed all the way home.

CHAPTER 36

"When in doubt, baffle them with bullshit."

–John Stalkinger

BY AUGUST, SUSIE, SAVANNAH, AND I had moved into the wine-barrel house. The extra space and newness was just what the doctor ordered for our mutual peace of mind. The windows provided sweeping ocean and canyon views, the distant hillsides sprinkled with other homestead endeavors visible by a driveway here and a chimney there, or the edge of a roof line jutting above a ridge toward the horizon. The setting sun was an every evening spectacle, dropping slowly into the ocean below spectacular fiery colors. We always paused and stared, hoping to see the Green Flash just as the sun blinked from view. I had seen it only once, while Susie hadn't seen it yet.

Savannah was having a difficult time sleeping. Falling asleep and waking up were dramatic events for her, both being thresholds that involved lots of tears. It was as if she feared sleep, its slide into unconsciousness, the dream world, and was then equally disturbed by awakening from it, having to leave behind the world she had traveled to. We found that driving her around in the car, up and down the dirt roads, helped lull her to sleep, and we put many miles on that dusty road doing just that. However, upon her waking, all we could do was try to comfort her and bring her back slowly, with reassurance, into our world that was home.

John's dive into the pool and subsequent stay over had resulted in a genuine connection with Molly that no one had seen coming. He had moved in with her lock, stock, and barrel, which for him was a suitcase, a truck, two motorcycles, and his tools. Sherry and he had been going through some relationship stuff until, one night after a disagreement, he told her he was going out for cigarettes and never came back.

Watching John and Molly together was like observing two friends who had lost and rediscovered each other unexpectedly. They were close and comfortable in their surroundings and seemed to understand each other effortlessly. Molly had needed a man around the house, to borrow an old cliché; her ten acres required a lot of upkeep to keep them running smoothly. John was raised on a farm and could do almost anything. What he couldn't do, he could figure out. It was a comfortable scene with something new happening all the time.

The pool parties at Molly's, where she hosted her friends from the Velvet Roadhouse, were growing in popularity with the working girls from Sparks, Nevada. Every couple of weeks, I showed up to tend the gardens and found myself in the midst of a colorful assemblage of beautiful women having fun around the pool. The women never brought guys—men were the last thing on their collective minds when they left Sparks. They were on vacation, loving the sun around the pool, the friendly gossip, and the warm, familiar hospitality provided by Molly. My partner had dived into a life bordering on fantasyland. I could swear he was developing new smile wrinkles.

John and I had discovered three new areas near our gardens that would be great for growing grass the following year. All could be reached by our pump. When we were done with a day's work of watering and checking our gardens, we were spending time working out a central watering system for the three new locations. We thought instead of establishing three separate water systems, we would bury twelve 55-gallon drums in a steep ravine above the three new sites and pump to just one location, routing individual garden lines from there.

One particular afternoon, we were in a salvage yard in Castroville, with my truck backed up to a stack of 55-gallon drums sitting on wooden pallets. We had gotten lucky and found these recently disposed of drums on a chance drive-by along a side street leading out of town. They were all painted green and had once held liquid fertilizer! We were stoked.

We paid for twelve barrels and loaded them into the bed of the truck, lashing them down with rope, and covered the load with a tarp. We drove slowly south down Highway 1, toward home. I was watching the tarp closely in the mirrors. When we got to the intersection of Rio Road and Highway 1, we turned into the Safeway parking lot, both of us hungry and thirsty and needing to take a leak. After relieving ourselves, we wandered around the store following our hunger up and down the aisles. I stopped at the meat counter and bought a slab of filet mignon. John grabbed some cheese, a baguette of artisan French bread, and a six pack of Michelob. We met at the check stand.

Back in the truck, we gassed up at the Chevron and hit the left turn lane at Rio Road. Waiting for the light to turn, I noticed a guy across the intersection wearing a green canvas hat and a backpack, trying to hitch a ride south.

"Let's give him a ride," I said.

"Okay by me," John replied.

I made the turn and pulled off the highway ahead of the guy. He started jogging toward the truck. No doubt John and I looked a bit rough. We were both dirty and scabbed over from our explorations into the brush surrounding our gardens. We had dirt under our eyes and caked around our noses, cuts and scrapes of dried blood on our hands and faces, clothes covered in mud and dust, and were driving a large green pickup with a tall load of something strange strapped down tight under a tarp.

John hopped out and held the door as the guy stepped up and looked inside. "Well, you want a ride or not?" he asked.

The guy looked up at John and then at me and nodded his head.

"Put your shit in the back and get in," John said.

The guy tossed his pack in the back and climbed up into the truck. "How far are you guys going?"

"I've been asking myself the same question for years," I said.

John slid in and slammed the door behind him, making himself comfortable as the guy moved a little toward me.

"No, I mean how far are you driving today?" the guy asked.

"How far are *you* going?" John asked.

"Big Sur."

"Well, we'll get you about half the way," I said.

We set out on the highway, winding through the Carmel Highlands and then out over the Mal Paso bridge, the hitchhiker squeezed tightly between John and me. Once over the bridge, John pulled the tab of a Michelob and passed it across the guy to me. I took a swallow and set the can between my legs.

"You want a beer?" John asked the guy.

"No, thanks," he said.

John pulled the tab on another and drank half of it in one pull, then reached out and took a clipboard from the dash. He turned it upside down across his knees and reached into the grocery bag for the filet mignon. Reaching into his pocket, he produced his Buck knife and opened it with a click. He sliced the plastic film over the bloody steak on the clipboard and started carving slices.

The hitchhiker's eyes were wide, darting from the raw steak to John and me. John stabbed a slice and offered it to our passenger. He shook his head 'no' in tight determined shakes. John passed it over to me, and I grabbed it off the knife and tossed it into my mouth.

"Damn, that's good! Needs some salt," I said.

John opened the glove box and brought out a saltshaker, shaking it over the meat. He stabbed another slice of beef and stuck the knife into his mouth. Blood from the beef was running down his lips. "You sure you don't want some of this shit?" he said to the guy. "You don't know what's good!"

The guy just shook his head no.

John continued to carve up the steak and pass me pieces. He pulled out the baguette with the cheese and put together some slices. Two more beers were opened. We were eating like kings.

As we drove over Rocky Creek Bridge, John was carving the last of the filet. "You sure you don't want some of this meat?" John asked our hitchhiker.

"No, I don't eat raw meat, but I think I will have one of those beers!" he said hopefully.

John handed him a Michelob as we passed the driveway of Rocky Creek Restaurant and headed toward the Palo Colorado Canyon turnoff.

We left him there alongside the road, his arms at his sides, holding a can of beer and his backpack. He looked lost but grateful.

I looked over at John. "What do you think he thought of his ride?"

"He's probably thinking, 'Fucking cannibals. I got a ride with fucking cannibals!'" We both laughed.

We delivered the metal drums to Molly's place and stashed them behind the barn. She came out of her cabin and walked over to John and me standing by my truck. "Hi, boys! How was your trip?"

"Successful," John answered. "We even managed to alarm a hitchhiker!" John told Molly the story of us devouring the raw steak with the guy sitting between us.

Molly laughed. "Oh, you two! That's just terrible! He must have been nervous as hell!"

"We were hungry as hell," I smiled back at her. "But it was comical!"

"Hey, Wes, I've got a question for you," Molly said. "You know Angel, my girlfriend from the Roadhouse?"

"Yeah!" I said.

"She asked me if I could get her a couple pounds of grass. She thinks she can move it pretty fast in Sparks. Can you help her?"

"I'd rather not have a business relationship with any of the girls," I said. "But I could bring you some pot, and you could handle the exchange."

"That works," Molly said. "How much for two pounds?"

"Thirty-six hundred."

"Okay, they're visiting next weekend. I'll let her know," Molly said.

"Sounds good. I'll drop it by."

I was pleased at the potentially good development because I desperately needed a new buyer. I said goodbye and drove home.

CHAPTER 37

"We're the law down here, Wesley, we can do any goddamn thing we want to."

–CHP Officer Eddie Krebs

TWO DAYS LATER I WAS driving up the coast on a clear, sunny morning, headed to Molly's place. I was carrying two pounds in four buckets under a tarp in the back of the truck. The ocean was a deep blue, sparkling under the sun, with an offshore wind peeling spindrift off the breaking waves.

I was on the flats by the lighthouse when I saw the CHP cruiser coming up fast behind me in my mirrors. He tailed me for about a quarter mile, then lit up his light bar and gave me a burst from his siren. I put on my blinker and pulled into a turnout off the highway. I was shitting razorblades.

I opened my door and dropped to the ground as Officer Krebs got out of his cruiser. "Mr. Daggert!" he said loudly. "Why do I think that you're in trouble?"

"Hi, Eddie. I have no idea."

Officer Krebs stood beside my truck. "You look nervous, Mr. Daggert." He reached into the truck bed and touched the tarp covering the buckets of pot. "Where you going to?"

"Town trip," I said.

Officer Krebs gave a short laugh. "Look, Wesley, the reason I pulled you over is I have a favor to ask of you. Your friend Bruce is doing a lot of drinking and driving, and I'm concerned about him. He's going to hurt himself or somebody else."

Bruce was a friend who lived not far from me on Simson Ridge and was a known drunk, especially after sundown. He was a proud man who became loud and belligerent after a few drinks and had known his share of vehicle accidents.

My heart started to calm down. "What can I say to Bruce, Eddie? He won't listen to me. He does what he wants to do. Why don't you talk to him?"

Officer Krebs looked down at his shiny black boots. "I've had a few words with him, but I don't want to put him in jail or have him lose his license. I like Bruce. I was hoping you would try to talk some sense into him."

I was anxious to get back on the road. I never felt sure where a conversation with Officer Eddie Krebs was going. "Okay, I'll talk with him. I'll do my best. Look, I need to go. I've got an appointment in town to get to."

"I'm sure you do, Mr. Daggert." He reached out and touched the tarp again. "You take care of yourself, Wes. I'd hate to see you get into trouble." He turned and started walking away, then stopped short and turned back toward me, smiling. "Say hi to John for me!"

I climbed back into the truck, totally rattled. It seemed to me that Eddie Krebs knew exactly what was going on with everyone on the coast. He knew there was something under the tarp but getting Bruce to sober up was more important to him. I pulled back onto the highway with Officer Krebs right behind me. He turned on his lights and siren and pulled up next to me. My heart leapt again, and I looked over to a smiling Officer Krebs. He waved and accelerated ahead around the bend. The guy enjoyed messing with me.

It was hot and still when I pulled into Molly's and parked. John was in shorts and barefoot, scrubbing the flagstone around the pool with a stiff broom and a garden hose. I grabbed the buckets and walked over to the cabin where Molly was standing on the porch.

"Hi, Molly."

"Hi, Wes. Is that what I think it is?"

"Two pounds," I said.

"I told Angel to bring the money. She'll be here Saturday. She doesn't know it's yours."

"Thanks, Molly." I handed her the buckets and walked over to John.

"Hey, man!" John said. "I'm putting a spit shine on the pool for the party this weekend."

"Another pool party with gorgeous women lounging all over the place. You're living a charmed life, Mr. Stalkinger!"

"Can't complain, man!" John said.

"I'm heading out to water the plants," I said.

John threw the hose in the pool. "Let me put some boots on. I'll come with you."

I walked over to a deck table and sat down to wait.

A half hour later we were walking along our trail, each carrying a 55-gallon drum across our shoulders. When we reached Sandy Flat, we dropped them on the ground and caught our breath.

"I've been thinking," I said. "It won't be long before we harvest. We need to clear everything having to do with this operation out of Molly's place."

"I've been thinking the same thing," John said. "We need to plug these trails better too."

"And really work out how we're going to get the hell out of here if we need to," I added. "We've got a good way out to the Boy Scout road, but what if the sheriff is on that road? We need another way out, in a different direction."

"I was walking around back here the other day and found a cave," John said. "It's really just a couple of huge granite boulders leaning against each other, but it goes way back. If we plugged the opening, we could hide in there. I'll show you; it's just up and over from Three Hills."

We each grabbed the end of a barrel and finished the climb to the new garden area we were planning for the next year. We stacked the barrel under a camouflage net beneath a tree. This was now the highest point in our garden system. Looking around, it was at the demarcation line of where the trees stopped growing and the brush took over. We were looking down on all of our garden sites, including the three new ones we hadn't yet built. None of the work we had done was visible.

We could see peeks of camo netting, but we knew what to look for and where. Nothing stood out.

I told John about my being pulled over by Eddie Krebs.

John laughed. "Eddie knows everything that's going on, man. He knew you were hauling pot. If he gave a shit, he would have arrested you. He once told me that he knew too much about the coast. That it bothered him."

The drone of an airplane interrupted our conversation. It was getting louder. Suddenly it emerged over the ridge and flew slowly over the hill to the south of us. It was a single engine Cessna. We jumped down under the trees and listened. The drone of the engine grew fainter and then changed pitch, growing louder again.

"He's coming back," I said.

We moved deeper into the tree line as the plane reappeared over the hill to the north of us, flying so slow it was a wonder what kept him in the air.

"He's looking for gardens," John said.

We could see him slowly dip his wings back and forth for a better view of the ground. He disappeared over the ridge, and the sound grew fainter. We stayed where we were for fifteen minutes, listening to the plane flying over places we couldn't see.

Finally, I said, "Let's water the gardens and get the fuck out of here."

Back at Molly's, we collected everything that had anything to do with our gardens. We worked fast and made five more trips back to Sandy Flat, carrying barrels, pipe, and netting. At the end of the day, Molly's property and barn were devoid of any incriminating paraphernalia. We worked until dark plugging the trailheads with brush. Exhausted after the day's work, we sat in Molly's kitchen and had a beer.

"Do you think they saw us?" Molly asked.

"We can't know for sure," I said. "I mean, he didn't circle us, but he did fly over us twice. Whether he was taking pictures or not, I don't know. We just have to be ready. I think I have to stop driving up here. I've got too much history. If they come here and find my truck parked, they're going to suspect something's going on."

"You could park at Rocky Creek Restaurant. I'll pick you up," John said. "You could lie in the back of my truck with a blanket over you while I speed up the hill!"

"You can shitcan that idea, buddy," I said laughing.

John chuckled. "No, really, we'll get you a helmet, and I'll pick you up at the restaurant with the motorcycle. No one will see our faces. I live here, so I've got my alibi, and no one knows I grow grass anyway."

"Sounds good," I swallowed some beer. "Meanwhile, we have to stash our shit around the gardens, wipe our fingerprints off the pipes, tanks, and pump, and figure out another escape plan. Other than that, it's just business as usual."

CHAPTER 38

THREE DAYS LATER IN A conference room off a back corridor of the sheriff's substation in King City, seven deputies sat around an oval table looking at photographs. Taken from a plane, the photographs showed the mountainous terrain of several portions of Monterey County. All of the eight-by-ten photos had areas circled by ballpoint pen. The pictures were being passed around the table with running commentary by Deputy Burt Pickett, who headed the newly formed Monterey County Marijuana Eradication Team.

Deputy Pickett, long incensed by the arrogance of the pot growers, had gotten his private pilot's license and, with local funding by private citizens, had been renting air time in a Cessna 172 to fly over rural Monterey County in search of active marijuana gardens. Flying with him, and seated at the table, was Deputy Brad Baker, an accomplished photographer who had taken all the photos being examined.

Deputy Pickett passed two photographs to his right. "These shots were taken over a ranch in eastern Prunedale," he said. "Notice the clearing surrounded on all sides by scrub brush. The even rows of marijuana are visible. The proximity of the ranch house to the garden area give little doubt as to who is doing the growing here. We will obtain a search warrant for the house and barn and cut the lock at the gate. The driveway is short, about 100 feet, so we'll come in fast to surprise them. We'll group up at the Salinas substation at 0600 Tuesday and drive straight there. Doug, Mike, and Jim will drive their pickups; the rest of you will ride with them. I'll be in the lead in a marked cruiser. If we make any arrests, I'll transfer the prisoners to Salinas. The rest of you will take the marijuana to King City to weigh and photograph it. After that, you'll take it to the dump, out in back there, and burn it. Don't forget your respirators. I don't want another repeat of last week!"

There were a few chuckles around the table. Two of the deputies who had burned the last load of confiscated marijuana had gotten so stoned they had called for help. They were now taking a ribbing around the substation.

Pickett stood up and walked to a large topography map pinned to a corkboard hanging from the green concrete block wall. The map was covered in colored pushpins. The pins were either black, red, or green. He picked a red pin from a small box and pushed it in on a spot just east of Highway 101 in Prunedale, then sat back down at the table and passed another set of photos to his right. "This next set of photos were taken just south of Cachaua, in Carmel Valley," he said. "You can see that there are plants in pots being grown just under the tree line. I suspect that a lot more are hidden by the trees. This grower is not so careful. He's left plants out all over the place. Notice in the far right-hand corner of photo B, there is a doghouse. This could be a problem. Could be a pit bull or a guard dog, so be smart. Photo C shows another garden that is just a quarter mile away from the first one. We'll hit that one at the same time."

Pickett stood and walked to the map. "We'll come in on Tassajara Road and stage here for garden one." He pointed to a spot on the map south of Cachaua. "Doug and Bob will take garden one in their pickups. Mike and Jim, you will continue on to just right here and stage. There's a small green structure at the side of the road visible in photo C. That's your staging area. The garden is due east of you there, about a hundred yards. I will be in the air on channel fourteen. I'll guide you in. We'll have a marked patrol car taking the lead at each site. We'll meet at the Monterey substation Thursday at 0600. Questions?"

Deputy Doug Barrister said, "I don't see any houses nearby. Are you going to be circling the area, waiting for us to get there?"

Pickett said, "I don't want to spook the growers before you arrive on scene. I'll be at five thousand feet west of Carmel Valley Village. I'll drop down into position when you reach your staging area. Be ready for fleeing suspects on your hike to the garden. I may flush them out." Pickett produced two more red pins from the little box and pushed them into the map just south of Cachaua, then returned to the table. "Last one for today," he said, passing photos to his right.

"These photos were taken over the National Forest just south of Botcher's Gap. You can see the terminus of Palo Canyon Road right here." Pickett pointed to a photo marked A. "You can see a couple of garden sites here and here at the base of these ridges, and one on the side of this ridge here. This is a very remote area with no obvious trails in. There is a Boy Scout camp visible in Photo C, two miles southwest of the garden sites. The camp is used by reservation, and not very often. The closest house to the garden sites is here," he said, pointing. "Note it has a driveway off Palo Colorado Road and a pool alongside it. This structure here is a barn. I think it's likely our growers are coming from this property. These gardens are large, and I'd like to take them a little closer to harvest time before we grab them, send a special message, so to speak. See this green pickup here?" Pickett pointed to a green pickup parked across from the pool. "I think I know this truck and the guy who drives it," he said. "I owe him one."

"I'll do another flight in two weeks and firm it up. The Forest Service will want to be involved with this one being it's on federal land. We'll take the lead with support from them. Any arrests will be federal. More on that later." Pickett got up and walked to the map, took a green pin from the box, and pushed it in just southwest of Botcher's Gap. "Gotcha!" he said under his breath.

The deputies all stood up from the table.

"Tuesday at 0600, Salinas Substation," Pickett said in a raised voice. "Let's put some more black pins on this board!"

CHAPTER 39

"Discretion is the better part of valor."

–William Shakespeare

ON SATURDAY MORNING I PULLED into the parking lot at Rocky Creek Restaurant and climbed out of the Bad Ford. The restaurant enjoyed a classic setting, built into the rocks above the surf line with wide views of the ocean. It was a spectacular cloudless day with an offshore wind peeling the water off the top of the waves in a fine spindrift mist. Rocky Creek Bridge, obscured in sea spray, could be seen arched over its creek a mile to the south.

Back in the day, the restaurant had been popular, a destination for both Carmel and Big Sur locals, featuring giant prawns, grass-fed beef, and garlic bread. The two owners—one the cook, the other the bartender—argued constantly, and somehow that was part of the charm. When the restaurant changed hands, the new owner made the classic mistake of trying to fix what didn't need fixing and fell out of favor with the locals. With a setting like this, it was a damn shame. I leaned against the Ford and waited for John.

Ten minutes later John rode into the parking lot on his 600 Suzuki and pulled up beside me. He set the kickstand and climbed off the bike. "Hey, how ya doin'?" he said, while working the helmet strapped to the rear of the bike loose. Handing it to me, he said, "Put this on. You'll be invisible!"

I pulled the helmet over my head as John climbed back onto the bike, then settled in behind him.

"Most of the girls showed up last night. Should be a good party!" John called over his shoulder. "Hang on!"

We roared up the driveway and then south onto the highway where John went through three quick gears. He downshifted, forcing us forward, then turned left into Palo Colorado Canyon, accelerating again. The road was a single lane with frequent pullouts that wound up through the redwoods. On its own, it was a nice cruise, but the locals made it dangerous. Almost all residents considered themselves the most talented race car driver on the coast. Men, women, new licensees alike, all careened around the canyon's corners in a tense, personal pushing of the proverbial envelope. Anticipation and hugging the right side were the keys to a successful trip.

John was moving aggressively into the turns, braking and accelerating hard, when suddenly a huge land-yacht of a car came around the corner on our side of the road. John braked hard, the rear tire coming off the ground and pushing me hard into his back. The large car swerved right, skidded on the moist pavement, and disappeared off the road into Palo Colorado Creek. The car was gone.

John shut off the bike, and we walked over to the edge of the road. The car was lying on its passenger side in the creek four feet down from the road's edge. The driver's door slowly opened up a crack and a head stuck out.

"Are you all right?" John called out.

"Yeah, we're okay," the guy said loudly. "Can you go call for help? We're going to need a tow truck!"

"Sure thing!" John yelled back.

We got back on the bike and drove the rest of the way to Molly's.

Standing next to the bike, I said to John, "We need to call a tow truck for that guy."

"Fuck that guy," John said. "Let him pickle in the creek for a while. He's forced me off the road several times. Serves him right!"

The parking lot around Molly's cabin was filled with high-end cars. Angel's red Corvette was there, alongside Cass's black Mercedes. Then there was a silver BMW and another blue Mercedes I didn't recognize.

A few of the girls were sitting by the pool, drinking coffee under a cloud of flying insects circling in a shaft of sunlight.

"It's going to be a hot one!" I said.

"Yeah, especially around the pool!" John laughed.

We walked up to the porch where Molly sat with two women I hadn't seen before. John walked into the cabin.

"Hi, Wesley!" Molly was smiling widely. "Come here and meet my friends. Wesley, this is Josie and Sunny. Girls, this is our friend, Wesley."

I shook hands with both girls, saying, "Hello."

Josie had jet-black hair and light cream-colored skin. She wore a pink and white sundress, while Sunny, a buxom blonde with blue eyes, wore a sarong over a bikini. Both girls looked to be in their late twenties.

"It's going to be a hot one, today," I said to no one in particular.

"Thank goodness for the pool," Josie said with a smile.

"I'm almost ready for a dip!" Sunny said.

"You'll have to join us later, Wes," Molly said.

"Thanks, Molly."

John pushed the screen door open and stepped out onto the porch. "Okay, I'm ready!" he announced to me. He had changed into long pants and a dark green T-shirt.

"Off we go," I said. We walked out behind the barn, crossed the fence, and unplugged our trail. "We better start plugging these trails behind us in case the sheriff shows up here while we're working."

"Why would they come in here? There's nothing going on," John said.

"I'm pretty sure Molly's is the closest house to our gardens. They might not be satisfied with just grabbing the pot. They might want to grab the 'growers' too," I said. "For that matter, we might want to put a few more plugs in on this trail. It leads directly to her place."

"Yeah, but it continues well past our gardens, and it's been here for years!" John pointed out.

Up to that point, except for a group of illegals growing deep in the back country, very few pot busts had resulted in actual arrests. The growers had the advantage of knowing the terrain and being able to hear the sheriff coming.

We hiked back to Sandy Flat and went through the watering sequence.

Three hours later, after putting everything away and covering our tracks, we hiked up to garden one.

Garden one was our second largest, and like all of them, it was under nets, lined by trees on three sides. The plants were amazing. They were six- to seven-feet tall, bushing out with buds everywhere. We pulled a few sun leaves to let more light into the interior of some plants.

"Our Money Trees." I was holding a large bud in my hand. "There's a lot of money here, just growing on the branch. I don't see buds, I see dollars."

John grinned. "Who said money doesn't grow on trees?"

"I wonder if it'll ever be legalized," I said.

John squeezed between two plants, looking for male branches. "Getting hard to move around in here," he laughed. "Thing is, if they legalize it, everyone will grow and the price will drop. I don't like that. I mean, that's bad news for us, but at some point, the government will get involved. They'll start taxing it, and the price will go back up, only they'll be getting the money!"

I saw some balls hanging at the crotch of a small branch of a large female plant. Damn hermaphrodite. I pulled my dikes and clipped the branch off. "What a mess that will be," I said. "I like it just fine the way it is. If the government's going to tax it, they're going to have to control it. There'll be more rules around growing grass than the IRS has for income tax."

"In the end, the price on the street will be the same. The money will just be going somewhere else," John said. "Education and potholes."

"Schools and roads—that would be ironic!" I laughed.

John gave a hoot. "More like merry junkets to tropical islands for the fat politicians. Flying stoned with a prostitute on each arm!"

"Easy, brother, that hits a bit close to home."

"Yeah!" John laughed. "I better keep my voice down!"

We walked to the other gardens, pruning and checking the water emitters, generally admiring our work. The gardens were all healthy and strong. We had another month of growing before we could think of harvesting. If we made it, it was going to be a hell of a year.

When we emerged from the brush six hours later, the pool party was on. Six professional girls from the Velvet Road House plus Molly splashed and laughed in the cool, blue water of the pool. Most were topless, having left their halters with their drinks on the table. A smoky mist lay over the pool, drifting from the barbecue. Cass and Rose Marie waved as John and I walked up on Molly's porch. Someone called a melodious "Hi, boys!"

We waved back, then headed inside to wash up—me in the kitchen sink, scrubbing my arms and face, running a wet hand through my hair; John in the shower doing a more thorough job.

John came out of the bedroom wearing a bathing suit. "Let's join 'em!" he said.

I nodded. "I'm good for one beer, then I need a ride back to my truck."

The afternoon was hot with the beginnings of a breeze that smelled of perfume, tri-tip smoke, and sagebrush. John and I walked along the pool's wet edge, got a couple of whoops from the girls, and took an empty table under an umbrella that was set back from the rest.

"What a scene!" I said, taking a swig from my beer.

It was truly an amazing sight. Six gorgeous women swimming in a beautiful pool punctuated by six small tables shaded by colored umbrellas. Aside from an occasional smile, they gave John and me little notice. This was their time for relaxation, and we were just the gardeners.

"My God, I'll say! Boy, howdy!" John slapped my arm. "I'll be right back."

He walked over and dove into the pool amid screams and laughter from the ladies. After doing the wounded dog-crawl from one end to the other, he pulled himself out and joined me back at the table. "That was fucking fantastic. You should go in, man!"

Despite the great view, I was thinking about the gardens. "Looks good, I'm in! Hey, give me a minute though. Let's kick some shit around first."

John leaned in. "Go for it, man."

I scooted my chair closer to John. "We know they've flown over our gardens, but we don't know if they've seen us or not," I said. "I think we have to assume they have. We're a month from harvest. We need to decide if we're going to harvest early or not, and where we're going to clean and dry it."

“Look, man,” John said waving his arm, “there’s nothing more we can do here. We’re clean. There’s nothing here to find. We’ve done all we can do at the gardens too. We’re done. We have to approach this like they’re not coming. If they get our shit, we’re done; if they don’t, we’re good. Business as usual.”

“Okay,” I said. “Well, let’s start building some drying boxes and go over our escape routes. If they’re coming, it’ll be soon. How about cleaning? Where can we set up for that?”

“Maybe here. We’ll know more in a couple of weeks. Maybe the barn. I’ll talk with Molly,” John said.

I stood up and stripped down to my tighty-blackies. “Into the unknown!” I said.

I dove into the pool, hearing a wolf’s call and then several splashes after me. The cool water felt great. I surfaced in a crowd of beautiful women.

A couple of hours later, John dropped me off at Rocky Creek Restaurant. As we cruised the Suzuki through the redwood canyon, we saw no sign of the car that had left the road trying to avoid us earlier in the day. I was trying to imagine the effort it took to raise the land yacht from the deep creek bed. There was nothing visible suggesting anything had happened, no skid marks on the damp road, no scrapes on the earthen shoulder, just a pristine road through a forest floor.

I thanked John and drove my truck south to Big Sur.

Coming through the Big Sur Valley, I was feeling parched and pulled off at Fernwood Resort, known among the locals as the Bat Cave. There were two men sitting at the bar, and I pulled out a stool. “Gentlemen…” I said.

Doc was tending bar. Tall with piercing eyes, he focused on a spot somewhere behind me. “Hi, Wesley.”

“Hi, Doc. Budweiser, please.”

Doc produced a Heineken and set it in front of me. It was then I noticed the other two men were also drinking Heineken. Whenever Doc had a buzz on, he would serve you Heineken regardless of what you ordered. You could order a rum and coke and still receive a Heineken.

Reordering would only get you another Heineken. There was no fighting it. I thanked him and took a long pull. My hair was still damp and felt cool against my neck. Just then Richard Gable, Bradford Berkshire's foreman, walked in and stood beside me at the bar.

"Hey, Wes!"

"Richard!" I said.

Richard looked me up and down. "Whatcha been doing?" he asked.

"Nothing." I turned my head toward him. "Been in town."

"Nothing?" He walked behind me and gave a short laugh, then clapped me hard on the back. His hand came off my back and slapped on the bar. Under it was a huge yellow marijuana sun leaf. "You picked up a hitchhiker!" he said, smiling. "So, you're advertising now?"

I couldn't believe it. The leaf had gotten involved with my flannel shirt like a Velcro tag and obviously been riding back there most of the day. How did everyone at Molly's miss it? I reached out and palmed it, rolling it into a ball in my fist. I glanced at Doc, but he was staring out the window. The other two men were involved in conversation.

"Damn," I said to Richard. "The shit's just falling from the skies!"

"Yeah," Richard laughed. "Glad I came by when I did!"

I started to laugh and raised my arm. "Doc! Another Bud and whatever this man's having!" I looked at Richard, shrugged, and cracked up. "Hey…don't ask me. I have no clue! A friend in need is a friend indeed!"

"Glad it was me and not Officer Krebs," he said with a grin.

Doc sat two Heinekens on the bar in front of us.

"I hope you like Heineken!" I laughed

"Long as they're wet." Richard reached for the beer.

We stood and talked a bit about the ranch and his job, until I looked at my watch.

"I've got to go, Richard, Susie's waiting for me at home, and I've been gone all day."

A little later I was sitting at home at the dinner table holding Savannah. Susie was at the stove making dinner. She was pissed, and I was in hot water.

"Put yourself in my shoes, Wesley," Susie was saying to the sauté pan.

"I come home and tell you that I've been swimming in my underwear in a pool full of male hookers! How would you like that?"

"Nothing happened, Susie."

"That's bullshit, Wesley. Something did happen. You stripped down to your skivvies and dove into a pool full of half-naked prostitutes—that's what happened. You wouldn't like it if I did that with a bunch of naked guys, and you know it!"

"I'm sorry, Susie. I used poor judgement. It was hot. It won't happen again."

I rocked Savannah back and forth in my arms as she looked up into my face. I had screwed up. I didn't blame Susie for being mad. As I had related the story of my day, I could hear my own words painting an uncomfortable picture for her. If I'd had a doghouse, I would have had to check in for the night. I kissed Savannah on her forehead and told Susie about the sun leaf on the back of my shirt in an attempt to lighten things up. She didn't find that amusing either. I was definitely in hot water.

CHAPTER 40

"We'll never catch the growers by chasing them through the woods, but we can wreck their gardens!"

–Deputy Burt Pickett

OVER THE NEXT TWO WEEKS, John and I built six drying boxes deep in the brush between Molly's property and our gardens. We chose three sites under trees and dense chaparral, erecting two four-by-eight-foot boxes at each location. The trails to the boxes were actually just tunnels, and everything had to be dragged in.

I was parking at Rocky Creek Restaurant, and we were driving John's truck to town for supplies. Things were tense—it had been two weeks since the overflights, and we figured we were either clear or about to be busted. We had heard about busts going down in Carmel Valley and other areas of Monterey County, and had been in contact with Irene at the sheriff's department. She said the main Marijuana Eradication Team had moved south to King City, and she was mostly out of the loop but would let us know if she heard anything.

John and I had dug back into the cave he'd found and plugged the opening with cut brush. The cave was above the trail and easy to walk by unless you knew it was there. In an emergency, we could slip by the brush plug and hide in the back of the cave.

We broadcast cayenne pepper up and down the escape trails and in front of the cave in an inspired effort to thwart search dogs. Whether it would work or not, we had no idea. We were used to clearing the shelves in a given store for things we needed but drew some comments while standing in line to pay for fifteen pounds of cayenne pepper.

"Grandpa's recipe..." I said to a woman in line.

Our two escape trails were established, both headed away from Molly's. One ran up from Three Hills, past the cave, and dumped out near the terminus of Palo Colorado Road. The other joined the main trail that led out toward the Boy Scout camp. After about a mile, it ended at the road that serviced the camp, and we plugged that end with cut brush. Anywhere the escape trails were visible from the air, we resorted to tunnels to keep brush over our heads.

We had always been conscious of what we wore to the gardens, avoiding whites and colors, but now wore army-issue camouflage shirts and pants as a rule. It was late September. This was crunch time. The plants were almost ready to harvest. They would get a little stickier, a little stonier, a subtle difference not lost on my buyers. They only wanted the best. I had a reputation to uphold, and even though the plants had great value at the moment, the next two or three weeks were crucial to setting them apart as the best.

John, Molly, and I had a sit-down to talk about the harvest and cleaning. It was going to take a while. We had 1,137 robust females that would average maybe ten to twelve packaged ounces each. We were looking at a minimum of 780 pounds of finished product. We were going to need some help.

Molly had serious reservations about using the barn for cleaning. She didn't want anyone to connect her property to the growing of marijuana and didn't trust the pickers to keep her secret. She was right, of course, and it left us in a dilemma that was getting compounded every day.

Then, suddenly, she and John had incredibly good news. The older couple who lived next door to Molly had decided to move to Carmel. The remote life of the upper canyon had grown to be too much for them. Instead of selling, they were hoping to find a caretaker to watch over their place. They had contacted their closest neighbor, who happened to be Molly, and asked her if she knew of anyone who might be interested. John applied for the position right away, and they hired him! The property was on a fifteen-acre parcel behind a locked gate. Among the scattered outbuildings was a large detached garage. The garage had an open, uncluttered floor with good lighting and could be locked up tight. After an inspection, we thought it would be perfect for cleaning the pot.

In order to avoid any surprise visits from the owners, we decided we would schedule our cleaning sessions for later in the afternoon. Also, if the sheriff did come for our plants, they would probably do it in the morning. Due to its close proximity, we would build a trail from Molly's to the Old Folks Home, as John and I were now calling it, to avoid driving any green pot on the canyon road. We would pay our pickers well and swear them to secrecy. We would only be in the garage in the late afternoon and into the evening and would clean up well after every session.

On Sunday, October fifth, John and I were out watering the plants high in garden four when the drone of an airplane sent us hiding under the line of bay laurels. The plane's engine grew louder as the single-engine Cessna flew over the hill to the south of us and climbed into a tight turn back toward our position. It crossed over above us and then banked toward the west where it went into another high turn. When it concluded its circle, it straightened out heading north, slowly fading away from sight and sound.

John was looking west. "Well, shit! I think it circled Molly's!"

"Yeah, it might have," I said. "It made a turn here too, although it was pretty high. Hard to say. One thing's for sure, this is the second time they've been here. They must have seen something."

We decided to cut some brush and plug the trail in a few more places. The plugs were easy enough to move out of the way, but they looked impenetrable and might convince someone to turn back. We emerged from the brush at the cabin, seeing a nervous Molly sitting on the front porch.

She looked up at us. "A plane just circled here."

"Yeah, we saw it. It circled the gardens too," John said.

Molly looked down at her hands. "I'm getting nervous."

I took a deep breath. I had a sense of foreboding too—it was hard not to. I wanted to calm her nerves. "You're okay here, Molly. We've covered the trail back to here in several places. It's an established trail to the Boy Scout camp anyway. Your property is cleaned up of anything that relates to growing grass. You're okay here."

"It's not just that," she said. "I really need the money. We're so close. I don't want to have to sell this place." She looked at John.

"Hey!" John said. "Let's not jump off the cliff just yet. Who knows what they've seen?"

"I know," Molly said. "It's just that I've never seen so much plane activity around here. By the way, Wes, Angel wants more pot. She sold all that I gave her and wants more. Four pounds more!"

"Wow!" I said. Angel was turning into that other buyer I had needed for so long. I could imagine a line of customers leaving the Velvet Road House happy *and* stoned. "Let's wait for a couple of days and see what rolls out."

"We've got the pool party this Saturday." Molly was looking up into the sky. "I'll tell Angel I need a little more time."

"Sounds good," I said. "I think we should start harvesting next week, say Monday. What do you think, John?"

"They're ready. Let's go for it!"

I stood up and put my hand on Molly's shoulder. "You're okay here. Try not to worry. John's right, we don't know what they've seen or not seen. It's going to be okay." I sounded much more confident than I felt.

"I hope so, Wes." Molly's eyes dropped to the porch floor.

CHAPTER 41

On Tuesday morning, October seventh, in the green cinder block room off the long rear corridor of the King City Sheriff's substation, the Monterey County Marijuana Eradication Team met. Deputy Burt Pickett and his team sat at the long oval table, joined by two officers from the United States Forest Service. Deputy Pickett passed four eight-by-ten photographs marked A through D to the deputy on his right.

"Gentlemen, these photos were taken two days ago, on Sunday." Pickett said. "Notice the circled suspected garden sites in pics A, B, and C. There are no obvious trails into this area, and even if there were, the hike would be too long and our support would be too thin." He motioned to the two seated Forest Service agents. "The Forest Service has agreed to provide us with a strike team and a helicopter."

Pickett stood and moved to the large wall map. "They will repel their team down to this knoll here, above this garden site, and clear a landing site for the helicopter. They will then pick up our team staged here at the Boy Scout camp. Once on site at the LZ, we will move into the garden areas here, here, and here, and clear the marijuana. We'll work in groups of two. Each group will carry light cargo nets. You will cut the marijuana to the ground and pile it on top of the nets. The helicopter will then hover above the nets and drop a cable. You will attach the net to the cable, and the chopper will deliver the package to the Boy Scout camp. We'll be working on channel 14. The chopper will be on yellow 16. When you've got your garden harvested, move back to the LZ. When everyone is assembled, you will be picked up and taken to the Boy Scout camp. Any questions?"

"Are we bringing anything else back besides marijuana, like pipe or fencing?" a deputy asked.

"No, not for this operation," Pickett said. "There's a lot of plants involved here, and we'll have our hands full. Wreck what you can, chop the water lines, knock the fences over, do as much damage as possible. Once we finish the operation, the Forest Service may decide they have to go back and clean up, but we'll cross that bridge when we get to it. Anyone else?"

Another deputy raised his hand. "If we flush out any suspects, how far do we chase them?"

Pickett nodded. "Our primary mission is to confiscate the marijuana. If you surprise someone, detain them for the Forest Service; we're on federal land. I don't want you guys splitting up and chasing coyotes through the woods all day. That helicopter is costing us a lot of money. Use your own judgment. Be smart."

Pickett sat back down at the table. "Photo D shows the closest residence to the gardens. It has a cabin, a barn, and a pool, here," he said pointing. "We've got a search warrant on probable cause that we'll serve here on Saturday. I want to catch these people home and unsuspecting. We have every reason to think this is the home of our growers. It will be nice to finally catch somebody red-handed. So that's it, people." Pickett's voice got louder as the deputies all stood. "Overtime on Saturday! We group-up at the Monterey Substation at 0400 tomorrow morning for the drive to the Boy Scout camp. Be on time! Operation starts at 0600 sharp. Let's use some of that training!"

CHAPTER 42

"The sun always rises, sometimes it's over a clear sky, sometimes over a dreary fog. The trick is in your perspective, realizing the sun is always there trying to find you."

–Molly Weaver

JOHN PICKED ME UP AT eight o'clock Wednesday morning at Rocky Creek Restaurant. We had decided to start a little earlier to beat the heat of afternoon. We rode up to Molly's on the back of the Suzuki. Molly was standing outside her cabin when we motored in and parked the bike. I climbed off the bike and removed my helmet.

"Happy Wednesday, Molly!" I called out.

"Hi, you guys," she said. She walked over to us and said softly, "There's something going on back there." Her eyes were looking east toward the National Forest.

"What?" John asked.

"I don't know. I've been hearing a helicopter every now and then. I haven't seen anything though."

I looked at John. The look on our faces said it all.

I looked at the sky to the east. "We better get out there and see what's going on."

Molly was kicking the dirt with her sandal. "God, I hope everything's okay."

"We'll let you know in a while," John said.

John and I walked to our trailhead hidden behind the barn.

"Let's move slowly and cover our trail as we go," I said.

John looked at me. "We don't have to go out there, you know."

"Where's your sense of adventure?" I grinned, not really feeling it.

"Hell, I'm game. I hid from helicopters in Germany."

We unplugged our trail and moved in, plugging it back up again. A hundred feet down the trail, we passed through another plug and rearranged it. We walked quietly without speaking for another half mile to Soggy Bottom, the first creek along our trail. We paused there and listened. It had been quiet since we started walking, just the occasional bird cry and snapping of twigs.

Another half mile in we heard a helicopter off to the south toward the Boy Scout camp, but it sounded faint and far away.

John paused on the trail. "If something happens, we should probably split up."

I nodded in agreement, and we continued on. We walked another half mile to Three Hills and stopped when I thought I heard someone talking. Then someone yelled, and the sound was much too close.

"Doug! Doug! Over here!"

John and I froze. Another voice farther away yelled, "Take it away!"

From over the hill we could hear the sudden wup-wup of the helicopter blades chopping the air as it emerged from the ridge top above us with a huge net filled with green marijuana hanging below it.

"Shit!" John yelled.

A deputy sheriff in uniform was leaning out of the open door of the helicopter, looking down. The sound was deafening, and the trees were blowing wildly in the down rush of air beneath the chopper. The helicopter moved slowly to our right, and we made eye contact with the deputy leaning out. He pointed at us and yelled something we couldn't hear. The chopper moved back over the hill, and we heard another voice yell, "We got coyotes! Down below us! Mike! Back me up!" We heard someone running down the hill through the brush and leaves.

I looked at John, and we each took off running, me toward the southeast along the trail we were on, John uphill toward our cave and Botcher's Gap. For a second I thought I was running right toward the sheriff, but I passed the narrow confluence he was running down and quickly put him behind me. I raced toward the escape route we had prepared, diving over the brush plug and landing in a dead run. I could still hear voices behind me and the helicopter off in the distance. The trees flashed by me, and I reached the first tunnel. I removed the brush plug and crawled in, dragging the plug in behind me. I was on all fours now, crawling like Baby Huey up a staircase. I thought of John and wished him well.

Suddenly I heard voices. There was a squawk from a handheld radio. “They’re chasing coyotes!” … “Roger that.”

I froze to get some bearing on the voice. I couldn’t tell how far it was from me, but it sounded above me and close. I heard some more talking from farther away, and then the returning helicopter. I kept crawling through the brush tunnel toward a stand of bay laurels I knew grew up ahead.

The helicopter grew louder and then moved over the hill above me, pushing a wash of air and dust below it. It moved slowly off to the west, and I crawled deeper into the brush. I rested there.

I couldn’t hear anyone behind me, just the helicopter moving slowly, maybe searching, off in the distance. They had found our gardens. I felt the angst of the loss beginning to rise up through the adrenalin rush of being chased. All that work for nothing. All the trips…all the blood, sweat, and hauling…gone…right at harvest time. So close, only to have it ripped from our hands. I wondered if they knew it was close to harvest time. Of course, they knew. They knew exactly what they were doing. Bastards. Maybe they wouldn’t get it all.

Just then the helicopter moved in close again, beating the air above me, whipping dust and trailing another large net of green marijuana lying limply in its death throes. Once lush and proud in the garden, it looked spent and wilted, just another weed crushed under its own weight in the net. I watched until it disappeared over the hill, then came out from hiding and crawled ahead to the stand of trees.

The bay trees grew close together and provided good shelter. I stood there and took inventory of myself. I had evidently cut my forehead on something based on the blood dripping into my eye. I had a long deep scrape on my right forearm that was scabbing over with dust. My knee was getting stiff from falling on a small stump somewhere back on the trail. Other than that, and a ripped shirt, I was fine.

Over the course of the next hour, I stayed under the bays and watched two more net loads of pot get hauled out. On the third trip, there was no net hanging from the chopper, just two deputies looking down from the open door at the hillsides below. This time they didn't see me.

I stayed put for another hour. I hadn't heard any voices since the radio chatter, and finally moved slowly out from my hiding place and east along the escape route. After about a half mile, I came to the final brush plug at the edge of the road to the Boy Scout camp. I was going to have to be very careful here, as this was the route the sheriff would take to get out.

I squeezed past the plug and walked out onto the road. I looked both ways and started walking north toward Botcher's Gap. I walked about a mile before I heard the grind of a transmission behind me and jumped off the road into a thicket of chamise. It was the sheriff's convoy—four private pickups with large covered loads drove by in a long cloud of dust. A few green marijuana branches protruded from under the tarps. The trucks passed in procession, and I watched them disappear up the hill with my pot.

I walked along the road eating their dust until I came to the gate at Botcher's Gap. There I waited off the road for a while, watching and listening. It seemed quiet, and I walked on toward Palo Colorado Road and Molly's gate.

I climbed over Molly's gate and walked down her driveway, still watching and listening. The sheriff could be waiting anywhere. I walked out of the trees into the open area of Molly's cabin and saw John and Molly sitting on the porch.

"Wesley!" Molly cried out.

"Hey, man, where you been?" John called. "I was beginning to worry about you!"

They both stood up and met me at the steps to the cabin. "Glad to see you made it!" I said to John.

"Those bastards couldn't catch a cold barefoot on a November night," John laughed.

"You look like hell, Wes," Molly said. "Come here and sit down."

She took my face in her hands and turned it. "You need some cleaning. I'll be right back." She disappeared into the cabin.

I looked at John. "Did they chase you?"

"Oh, for a minute or so," he said. "I ducked into the cave, and they walked right by me. Twice, as a matter of fact. I was so nervous I started fartin'!"

We both laughed.

John lifted his leg and cut a huge fart. "It's still happening!"

"I know the feeling well!" I laughed.

Molly came out from the cabin with a warm, damp wash rag and started dabbing at my face. "You two are pretty happy for a couple of guys who just lost their gardens," she said.

"Yeah, Gallows humor. Just letting off some stress," I said. "I'm just glad they didn't get us!"

"You're going to need a stitch here, Wes," Molly said. "Let me get a couple of beers and a closure bandage."

John told me about his escape, hiding out in the cave and then moving north along the trail from the cave to Botcher's Gap. While it had taken me five hours to get back to Molly's, he had gotten back within two hours after we had split up.

"How's Molly taking it?" I asked.

"Oh, she's philosophical, you know. I don't think it's sunk in just yet. What a fucking bummer, man."

Molly came back outside carrying three beers and a bottle of tequila. She set them down, reached out, and pinched the skin above my right eye, pushing the closure across my cut, then dabbed at it again. "There you go, good as new!"

We passed the tequila bottle around, each taking a good pull, then brought our beers together in a toast.

"We tried like hell," I offered.

"Got damn close," John said.

"Got to be a silver lining," Molly said, trying to smile.

We all sat down and drank our beers and listened to each other try to salvage some sense of acceptance from the bust.

"Well, we have a pool party on Saturday," Molly said, standing. "You should invite Susie, Wes. Bring Savannah. It'll be fun!"

"Thanks, I will. She's mentioned she'd like to finally meet you." I looked at my watch. "It's about that time. I better get going. I'll see you two on Saturday." I stood and gave Molly a quick hug. "Hang in there, kiddo."

"Thanks, Wes, I'll try..."

John gave me a ride on the motorcycle back to the restaurant.

"Beer?" I asked him.

"Maybe more than that," he answered.

We walked inside and took two stools at the bar. The waves were visible through the tinted windows, breaking over the sea rocks below. The bartender was talking to a waitress at the far corner of the bar. "Yeah," he was saying. "I saw the trucks coming out of the canyon when I came to work. Four of them! They were all piled high with cut marijuana sticking out from under the tarps. Must have been hundreds of pounds! The sheriff waved at me as they drove by. Somebody up there's feeling bad right about now."

I looked at John. We both looked like shit. Dirty and scabbed over, torn clothing, and me with a Rocky Balboa bandage on my forehead.

The bartender came over, looked us up and down, and asked our pleasure.

We each ordered a beer and a shot of tequila. I felt like shit. We had lost so much money just a few hours ago, it was hard to fathom. So much work was down the drain, and more importantly, we had lost our place to grow. The only peace came from not being chased anymore.

"Well, shit, Mr. Stalkinger, here's to a helluva effort!" I said.

We threw down the shots.

"You know, Wesley, I don't feel so bad. I mean, yeah, it's a big loss and all, but we can get it back. I actually had a good time growing all that shit!"

"I guess that's the only way to look at it," I said.

"Unless you want to get arson of the liver," John said raising his beer. "Cheers! It was a blast!"

"Cheers!" I said.

We agreed to meet at the restaurant in the morning. We were going to hike up to the gardens and see the extent of the damage. Who knew, maybe they had forgotten something.

CHAPTER 43

"The fragrance of these hills is intoxicating. A fine country bouquet."

–Wesley Daggert

THE NEXT MORNING I SAT drinking coffee with Susie and Savannah in the wine barrel house. The ocean was blue out through our window, contrasting sharply with the yellow grass on the sloping late autumn hillsides below the property. We were immersed in a quiet conversation.

"Well, Wesley, you worked all year with nothing to show for it. If you grow again next year, you'll work all year again before you know if you'll get paid or not."

"I know. You think I should quit?"

"I'm not going to tell you what to do. But let's face it, it's not getting easier to grow anymore. The sheriff is getting more sophisticated, you have a reputation as a pot grower, and we have Savannah to think about. Maybe we should come out of the bushes and join the community. Just sayin'."

I took a sip of coffee and looked out the window. Susie was right, of course. I would be starting from scratch again, and I was tired. The bust had taken away some of my spirit, some of the wind from my sails; there was so much work down the drain. I remembered my friend who owned Fernwood saying that he wondered how it would be if the pot growers really had to work for a living. I had been surprised by his remark. How could he think like that? Did he think we were just like Johnny Appleseed tossing marijuana seeds around and then reaping the harvest? He had no idea how much work was involved, but his interpretation wasn't my responsibility to correct. I would have admitted too much in the process. Stacking beer crates and managing food and liquor costs was definitely work, but we were talking apples and oranges.

I turned back to Susie. "I hear you. I'm feeling pretty much over it right now. Maybe I should go out and get a regular job. I'll ask around. Who knows what's out there? Oh, by the way, Molly invited you and me and Savannah up to a pool party this Saturday. She's having some of her friends over and said it would be fun to meet you."

Susie looked down into her coffee cup, and I braced myself for a sour response. She surprised me. "That sounds nice, Wesley. I've wanted to meet Molly for a while now too. You've spent so much time there, and the pool sounds nice. I'm up for it!"

"Great!" I said. "There's a barbecue too. It should be fun."

"I'll bring a salad," she said. "It'll be good to meet everybody."

I helped Susie with the morning dishes and set off to meet John.

An hour later I pulled into the Rocky Creek Restaurant parking lot. John was already there sitting cross-saddle, smoking a cigarette. "Hey, man!" he said. "Ready for the most disappointing hike of your shady career?"

"I guess," I said. "Let's get it over with."

We rode up to Molly's, where we found her on her knees pulling weeds around the pool.

"Morning, Molly," I said. "Susie and Savannah said they would like to join you for the pool party Saturday."

"Oh, good. It'll be nice to meet her."

"How are you holding up?" I asked.

"Oh, I'm depressed, you know, thinking about what to do now." She looked up at me. "It's a bummer, I was counting my chicks too soon."

I didn't know what to say. "Well, we'll see if they left us anything."

John and I walked to the corner of the property behind the barn and removed the brush plug from our trail. We started our hike up to the garden.

"I wonder if the bastards left somebody behind to capture our asses?" John said.

"I know, it seems like they would. I think when they ask for volunteers to stay the night in a ripped off pot patch, no one raises their hand."

We moved slowly along the trail, removing the brush plugs, stopping and listening every now and then. The woods seemed unusually quiet. Maybe it was the absence of the helicopter noise and yelling that had reverberated through the canyons the day before, or maybe the birds were still in shock from the exposure to the really big bird that had invaded their air space.

With heavy hearts, we arrived at Sandy Flat and immediately knew something was off. Things were not as they should have been.

"What the fuck?" John spoke for both of us.

There was no sign of anyone having been there. No footprints, no destruction. The pool was intact under its camouflage, and Sandy Flats was as pristine as we had left it.

"Holy shit, John…they didn't find this. Do you think…?"

John was already walking up hill. "I don't know, man. Let's find out!"

We walked as fast as we could up to garden one and there it was, fully intact, growing as rich and lush as we had left it! They hadn't seen it! The nets were intact, moving slightly in the breeze. We slapped each other on the back and ran to garden two. It was also undisturbed! We were ecstatic!

"They missed us!" John said. "Let's go check the others!" We went to garden three and four, and all were there just as we had left them.

"Who did they bust?" I said.

It's an interesting feeling when utter despair gets replaced by hope and then in turn, is suddenly displaced by pure joy. The dark veil is drawn back, the movement is upward and enlightening as the weight is removed from the spirit, and the soul is again set free. We just stood there and laughed. It was unbelievable. With all their flying and searching, they had flat out missed us. A creeping doubt started to come over me—*maybe they would come back*—but then I realized they would have already been back. They wouldn't wait, for fear of losing the edge. They had just missed us.

"Who the hell did they bust?" I repeated.

"I have no fucking clue," John said. "Let's go find out!"

We walked straight up from garden four to the top of the hill and stood in scrub brush and grass looking east to another hill that rose in front us. We hiked down to the bottom of the drainage and up the other side, to the top of the second hill, and looked over. There it was. We could see two sites where gardens had once been. Fences were down and black poly pipe was cut into segments. The ground looked like a herd of buffalo had run through. On a knoll to the southeast of the devastation was a cleared flat where they probably landed the helicopter.

"I'll be damned!" John laughed. "We had company back here and didn't even know it!"

"They must have been using the Boy Scout road. I mean there's nothing else out here," I said.

"Yeah or…maybe, just maybe, they were camped here, as in illegals!"

"Well, if that's the case, they're long gone!" I said. "Interesting they never heard our pump running."

"Yeah, well, I told ya. We're in a hole back there. Besides, if they were illegals, they wouldn't wanna do too much investigating."

I slapped John on his back. "Let's go back and water our plants! We're still in business!"

We were ecstatic. There was a flood of fresh energy in us and we ran up and down the hills as though on flat ground, tending to our lush crop that we'd had every reason to believe had been lost.

We were still energized with new life as we walked back to Molly's, carefully replugging our trails and walking a bit lighter, if not taller. We must have sounded upbeat, because I saw her look up. I plugged the entry to our trail at Molly's fence as John walked over to where she sat by the pool. Suddenly there was a scream and then a very loud, "I don't fucking believe it!" Her voice echoed throughout the canyon. Molly was back to life, and completely stoked.

On Friday, John and I returned to the gardens to water and check the plants. We were still expecting the sheriff to appear at any moment, so we kept quiet and listened to every distant sound. There were only bird sounds and warm rushes of wind through the trees. We still couldn't believe our gardens hadn't been seen by the marauding deputies. I thought of Kade and how he didn't trust the nets. I was sure that tossing cut brush up on top of the nets had helped tremendously.

All we could do was keep putting one foot in front of the other as we had since March. It was the life of a grower, the not knowing, the not counting your chicks until the eggs had hatched, the quiet worry, the angst, mixed with the exhilarating anticipation of making it through to harvest.

We were ready to harvest but decided to wait until after the weekend as we had previously planned. We had to assume if the sheriff was coming back, that it would be soon. We didn't want to be crossing Molly's property with bags of freshly cut buds as they showed up. There was also the pool party planned for the next day to think about. It was a no-brainer to wait for Monday.

On the way home through the canyon, I passed Cass's Mercedes and Angel's Corvette on their way to Molly's.

CHAPTER 44

"If just anyone could grow it, grass would be worthless."

—David Stafford

SATURDAY MORNING SUSIE AND I loaded up her VW with Savannah's gear, which now far outweighed our own. We were both smiling ear to ear that our gardens were still growing. It was an amazing change in attitude.

"So, Wesley, does this change your thoughts about growing next year?"

"I don't know, Susie. I know how you feel about it. Let's just get through this harvest and talk about it then. I'm so happy to still have a crop I can't think straight!"

We got Savannah's huge car seat strapped down in the rear of the car and set an iced cooler full of drinks and a Greek salad Susie had made beside it. We wanted to get to the party early to help out with the preparations. Savannah seemed calm and looking forward to the drive. We drove north to Palo Colorado Canyon and turned into Molly's at 10:30 AM. I parked under an oak tree between a blue BMW and a red Porsche.

"Damn," Susie said. "This parking lot looks like Pebble Beach!"

"Yeah, these girls do all right!" Then I looked at her and smiled. "Don't get any ideas about a new profession!"

"What? In Big Sur? I'd get paid with IOUs," she laughed.

The pool was already bustling with swimmers and conversation while John tended the fire at the barbecue. We unloaded the VW and walked to the cabin, Susie carrying Savannah and me carrying the cooler.

Molly met us on the porch. "This must be Susie! Oh, and this must be Savannah!" she exclaimed, giving them both a hug. "Welcome!"

After introductions, I left the girls talking and dropped the cooler off on the kitchen floor. In the living room, Rose Marie and Sunny sat talking. I said "Hi" and went back outside.

"Your girls are so cute, Wes!" Molly said.

"Yes, they are!" I said, "I feel very lucky!" Placing my hand at Susie's back, I walked her to the pool.

One of the women in the pool called out. "Look, it's a baby!"

"Oh, I wanna see!" another voice exclaimed.

"Wesley, look at all these women!" Susie said under her breath. "I can't believe it! This is scandalous! What have you been doing here?"

"Me? Nothing. Growing grass," I said defensively.

She just shook her head.

We found an empty table under an umbrella and sat down. I helped Susie and Savannah get settled, then excused myself and walked over to John at the grill.

"Hey, man!" John said. "Just getting the fire goin'. Tri-tip and prawns. Soaked some oak bark overnight, should be good. Is Susie here?"

"Yeah! She's over there." I turned and saw four girls standing around her in bikinis, one holding Savannah.

"Looks like she's doin' okay!" John laughed.

I was relieved. It could have gone a lot of ways, but Susie was talking, looking comfortable, and Savannah was loving it, smiling as she was handed from one woman to another.

"There's ten girls from the Road House here for the party," John laughed. "The word's caught on."

I looked around. It was a now familiar scene, gorgeous women in scant bikinis, some sitting, some swimming, laughing and talking, all under drifting smoke from the barbecue.

"The Velvet Road House is going to go broke!" I said.

John laughed and flipped a large tri-tip. "Least of my worries!"

I grabbed a cold beer from an ice bucket and walked back toward the table where Susie was sitting, now holding Savannah across her body, nursing her. A crowd of women, some sitting, some standing, were close around her, talking. Susie and Savannah were holding court!

Angel was smiling as I approached. "Wesley, your family is beautiful. Now I know why you always rush off at the end of the day!" I was grateful for that remark.

An hour later just about everyone was in the pool. A lot of the women were topless, including Susie. Savannah was asleep in her hooded travel bed, a soft baby blanket draped over it for protection from flies. I sat close by her, talking with John.

"Well, I'm almost afraid to say it out loud, but I think we made it!" I bounced my beer bottle off his.

"Don't jinx us, Wesley!" he said. "We got a ways to go. I can't believe they didn't see us though, man. Here's to the nets!" We joined beers again in a toast.

Then, over the laughter around the pool, we heard the sound of engines coming from the direction of Molly's gate and growing louder. John looked at me. I could hear more than one vehicle, and they were getting closer.

"Shit!" John said.

"More pool guests?"

"If so, they're in a big hurry!" John said, standing.

I could hear now that the engines were large and running hard. I stood up with John. Molly was also standing in the shallow end of the pool, she and several other girls looking in the direction of the driveway.

The police cruiser emerged from the tree line in a cloud of dust, followed closely by three unmarked pickups. They were pinched by the crowded parking lot and slid to a stop in front of the cabin. A tall, well-groomed deputy got out of the cruiser and raised his arms. "Monterey County Sheriff! Everyone stay right where you are!" He placed his hand on the butt of his gun as seven other deputies spilled from the trucks.

"Molly Weaver!" he bellowed. "Deputy Burt Pickett, Monterey County Sheriff!"

"Over here!" Molly's voice rang out from the pool as she walked topless toward the deputy.

The rest of us stood frozen and silent.

The other deputies were standing outside their trucks, looking at the pool.

"What are you doing here?" Molly shouted toward the deputy.

"Mrs. Weaver, I have a search warrant for your property, signed by a judge. Please put some clothes on!" Pickett ordered.

"I live here. I own this property. I don't have to put my clothes on!" Molly yelled. "Look away if you can't handle it!"

She walked up to Pickett, who was putting on his sunglasses, her breasts swaying inches from his uniform. None of the deputies looked away.

"I repeat, why are you here?" Molly's hands were on her hips.

"I have a warrant to look for marijuana, paraphernalia, and cultivation supplies," he said, handing over a folded packet of papers. "Please step back and let us do our job."

Molly accepted the papers. "You go right ahead, Mr. *Pr*ickett. You're barking up the wrong tree. Look all you want, and then, please, join us at the pool!"

Deputy Pickett turned and signaled his deputies to advance on the cabin. They started moving forward toward the cabin and barn, walking across the open space.

John and I hadn't moved an inch. I heard Sunny say, "Let's go, girls. Let's give Molly a hand. They're just a bunch of frustrated Johns!"

The girls from Sparks all left the pool topless and walked toward the sheriff deputies. It was an assault on all the sensory perceptions.

"Tell those girls to put some clothes on!" Pickett said to Molly.

"They don't have to, Mr. *Pr*ickett. They're my guests and now, so are you!" She turned. "Show them a good time, girls!"

Molly called over to John, "Go lock the gate, honey! We have guests!"

Pickett put his hand over his gun again, looking at John and me. "Hold it right there! Nobody move! We have a warrant!"

We stood still.

"How do you like this shit?" John said to me under his breath.

"We're clean. Just chill," I whispered back.

"Is that you, Mr. Daggert?" Pickett called out.

"How are you, Deputy Pickett? Nice you could make the party!" I replied.

"I knew you had something to do with this!" Pickett said loudly.

"I'm just a guest here, sir," I called out. "Did you bring your bathing suit?" I looked over at Susie standing in the pool, looking at me and shaking her head.

The girls from Sparks had surrounded the deputies. "Oh, my, there's something about a man in a uniform!" one of them said. They moved in closer, like closing the seine net around a school of sardines. "How big is your gun?" another girl asked.

The deputies were frozen, their eyes on the nearly naked women around them.

Cass and Angel came out of the cabin holding cameras and started pointing and taking photos of the scene. The deputies began to push through the gorgeous group of women. Two deputies walked into the cabin as two more, with two female escorts, walked to the barn. Cass turned around and followed the two into the cabin, snapping her camera while Angel walked to the barn with her camera.

John and I didn't move. We knew we were clean at Molly's. We stood and watched as a deputy walked the fence line. He looked at our trail plug for a second and moved on. I gave John a nudge. The girls were following the deputies like a rare perfume, with the hard men walking as though they were stoned and distracted.

I left John and moved over to check on Susie, who was now kneeling by Savannah. "Are you okay?"

"Oh, yeah, Wes, just hunky-dory. Maybe just a little too much excitement, don't you think?" She reached for her bikini halter and wrapped it around her back.

One by one the deputies returned and came together, surrounding Pickett at the cruiser. "Nothing here, Burt. House is clean, barn's clean, no trails out," a deputy said to Pickett. The other deputies were staring at the girls huddled a few yards away.

Molly, who had returned to the pool, called out, "Water's real nice, Deputy Prickett! You and your boys want to join us? My friends seem to like you!"

Pickett kicked the dirt. "Damn it!" he said. He pointed up toward the pool at me. "I'll be seeing you, Daggert!" With that he waved his men toward the trucks. "Get your eyeballs back in your skulls, let's go!"

"Bye, Officers!" one of the girls called out.

"Why can't they stay?" asked another.

"They were cute!" Sunny said.

"That was it?" Rose Marie said much too loudly. "I didn't even get to scream yet!"

Deputy Burt Pickett and his men climbed into their vehicles. The men were all looking at the scene around the pool. Lacking turnaround space, they were forced to back out the way they came in. Pickett was pointing out his window to direct traffic from behind. A cloud of dust churned by all the truck tires slowly settled over their caravan. We listened and then laughed at a honked horn as the sound of their motors grew fainter and faded away into the trees.

At the pool, John was greeting everyone with a garden hose, spraying the dust from their legs and feet. There was a lot of talking and laughter.

Susie leaned in and kissed me on the cheek. "This is a strange life we're living, Wesley."

I watched the dust settle under the trees, feeling my heartbeat return to reasonable.

John called out from the barbecue, "Food's almost ready!"

"I need a dip first," Cass said.

One by one, the girls jumped back into the pool, their laughter and squeals filling the air once again at Molly's mountain oasis.

CHAPTER 45

"The hardest part of growing is the trimming. I hate it."

—Kade Rudman

At four o'clock Monday afternoon our pickers met us at the Old Folks Home. We were ready with white sheets on the floor and a circle of folding chairs surrounding a large pile of freshly harvested buds. We had music playing and cold drinks on ice. There was a hotplate for making tea.

We greeted everyone and passed out scissors. Susie was there with Savannah. Sandra from Esalen and my friend Bob from Nepenthe had decided to join us again. We had hired three other people who had worked with Susie cleaning pot for her neighbor last year. Susie said they were incredibly fast and tight-lipped. Molly wanted nothing to do with the trimming, choosing to stay anonymous, and if anyone suspected anything, they were smart enough not to ask.

The trimmers were paid twenty dollars per hour and could keep the thumb hash scraped from their scissors. Payment in green buds was not permitted. We didn't want our pickers walking around with freshly harvested buds. Later, when we had packaged dry buds, we would give anyone who wanted one a bud to take home to smoke. I didn't want to get into selling to the trimmers and get involved with discounts or other arrangements. It was just cleaner and simpler to pay them in cash. We kept a running ledger of the money paid out for all our expenses, and the trimmers' wages were added to that. John, Molly, and I would sort it all out after our first sale.

The trimmers were a breed all their own, able to sit long hours bent over their work while still maintaining their mental acuity. It was a good paying job for them, and they treated it as such. They knew secrecy was important, as was punctuality. They reminded me a lot of Jimmy, who was still buying pot from me. They were serious about their work and stayed low-key. I had done plenty of trimming, and I couldn't stand it; in fact, I hated it. They all had my grateful respect.

After everyone was seated and working, John and I hiked back out to our gardens for another load of buds to keep the trimmers supplied and working. On the walk up from Three Hills toward Sandy Flat, I said, "It's hard to believe we're even doing this."

"Yeah! I thought we were done for!" John laughed.

"We just got lucky." I was shaking my head.

"Oh, I don't know. You know, man, once they saw that big garden over the hill, that's all they could see. They weren't looking anymore; they were too focused. I must say, though, Pickett was sure glad to see you at the pool party."

"Yeah. He'd like to put me in the slammer. Seems to be personal now," I said.

"Oh, hey!" John said. "Here's some shit: one of the girls, Josie, got a date with Pickett's right-hand deputy, the one who searched the cabin!"

"No shit?"

"I shit you not. He's going up to Sparks to see her. Could be we have another 'ear' in the sheriff's department."

"That's too funny!" I said. "When did that happen?"

"Out behind the barn, during the search, according to Angel. Anyway, they've got a date!"

Arriving at garden one, we started harvesting. We placed buds in large plastic trash bags, carefully, always aware of the added weight. We didn't want our cargo to become too heavy and smash the buds at the bottom.

We walked back down to Molly's and then up to the Old Folks Home, where we set the bags on the floor of the garage. The buds that had been cleaned were then tied into small bouquets with wire ties around the stems and again placed in plastic bags for the trip to the drying boxes. It was a cycle we would repeat more than 200 times over the coming weeks.

The buds were the best I had grown, heavy with resin, and for the most part, tightly packed. There was a compromise made for growing under shade—the buds tended to grow more loosely, but the shade granted more protection from the sheriff's overflights. In our favor, it was hot where we grew, some ten miles off the coastline, and our sites were like hothouses under the nets. The plants thrived.

We harvested into the last week of November with the best picking crew I had ever worked with. Our drying boxes were full, and we were packaging as it became ready. There were no more overflights in our area, though busts continued throughout the harvest season farther down the coast. John and I worked long hours trying to stay ahead of the harvest. By the first week of December, we had packaged 781 pounds of top-grade sinsemilla into 1,562 two-gallon paint buckets. We had paid our trimmers just over $42,000 in total, or $7,000 each, cash on the barrelhead. Our best estimate was that we were splitting $1,404,000 three ways. Though it was still unsold pot, it was a number that was fun to think about.

I took my buckets home late at night over the course of three weeks, driving the speed limit, sober as a judge, trying to avoid any encounters with Officer Eddie Krebs. I passed him once parked behind some bushes when I was fully loaded with buckets of grass, but he didn't pull me over. It's a good thing; I don't think I could have taken it. I would have pissed my pants.

John and Molly had 520 pounds of sinsemilla between them, totaling a potential $936,000. Angel was selling a lot of pot now in Sparks and Reno and visiting Molly on a regular basis for more.

My 260 pounds was home safe and stashed deep in the folds of the mountain along with the grass I had left over from Juan Fuego Creek. A quick estimate of my holdings was $594,000. David Stafford and Jimmy were both in high swing, visiting me at least twice a month. It was winter of 1981, and everything was coming up roses.

EPILOGUE

When the breeze touches your face, it carries a message from the places it's been, the ground it has blown across, the trees it has rustled through. It deposits a little of that in your hair and upon your skin. Just like when you walk through the forest, the breath you exhale lingers on the paths you've traversed. In similar ways, the memories of those days are forever a part of me. I remember every breath I took, every drop of sweat and blood that fell from my body to those dusty trails. We were like coyotes then, thin and hungry, with no direction too far or task too great. There was a camaraderie, an outlaw creed, a quiet trust between us, and a courage born of self-confidence that carried us through our labors.

When the days got shorter and thunderheads began to dominate the sky, the Indians would pull up their stakes and move south for the winter, following the flights of birds toward warmer climes. In much the same way, the helicopter was the sign winter was coming for the guerrilla pot farmers. It became more difficult to hide from the low-flying, hovering machines. The sheriff was motivated. We were pushed deeper into the forest, with our skinny trails becoming ever longer, leading to gardens that were growing smaller.

Deputy Burt Pickett was an honorable adversary. In 1983, he helped form the Campaign Against Marijuana Planting, or CAMP. Managed by the California Bureau of Narcotic Enforcement, it was composed of local, state, and federal agencies. Their stated purpose was to eradicate illegal cannabis cultivation and trafficking in the United States. With more than 110 agencies participating, CAMP was the largest law enforcement task force in the United States. Moreover, Deputy Pickett's colored pushpins on his wall map provided a yearly starting point for the local aerial searches. The sites they represented were sure to be revisited. This guaranteed that every bust or point of interest on his map was a dead zone for potential growers.

The available garden sites began to dwindle, leaving only the National Forest for large-money operations. Mexican cartels began dropping off crews deep in the forest to camp there for months on end, babysitting large, poorly thought-out growing sites. It had been one of these that had drawn attention near our garden at Botcher's Gap.

On the worldly scale of human endeavors and aspirations, everything must have an ending. It's just how it is in this life. Sometimes the end is a surprise, like a bug hitting a windshield, while other times, you just step from the train onto a quiet platform. If you're fortunate and paying attention, at some point in time, your inner voice and rational leanings can come together as an intuitive realization.

Susie and I were outside on our new deck below the skeletal framings of our future home. Savannah, one month from her first birthday, was being supported by Susie in her small inflatable pool while I sat in a folding chair nearby. It was February 1981.

"I think you should get a legitimate job, Wesley. How much longer do you think you'll get away with this?"

I had been thinking long and hard about my answer. I was feeling tired and chased. I wasn't feeling as positive and lucky as I once had. Everyone, including Deputy Burt Pickett and Officer Eddie Krebs, knew I was growing. I had lost the edge of anonymity and gained the red flag of notoriety.

"Okay," I said. "I'll go out and look for a job. I have no idea what I'll do, maybe something in the hospitality business, but I'll ask around. Promise!"

"Sounds good," she said.

Just then the phone rang, so I went inside the barrel house to answer it.

"Wesley! This is John! Can you hear me?"

"Loud and clear," I said. "Where are you?"

"Curaçao, just north of Venezuela!"

"What?"

"Yeah! Listen," John yelled into the phone, "I'm on the beach at a bar! I'm not sure I'm going to make it back to start working the garden. We've got some plans here."

"I'm glad you called, John. I think I'm done with growing. Susie and I have been talking, and the writing's on the wall. I think I'm done, man."

"Well, shit," John said. "I'm going to do *something* back there, maybe not as big as before. You can always join me later!"

"I'm done, man. I think I've pushed it as far as I can. We'll see. What are your plans in Curaçao?"

"A brothel! Molly put a down payment on an old hotel in Campo Alegre! The girls from Sparks all want to come down here. The place is amazing. Everything's legal here! You should get your ass down here."

"Of course!" I laughed. "A brothel! Molly is going to be a madam again."

"She wants to call it the Pirates Lair."

"Has a ring to it!" I said.

"I gotta go! There's a line here to use the phone. Talk with you when I get back."

I hung up the phone and gave a short laugh. It was so much like John to be off in some distant place starting a new adventure. Outside, I told Susie about the call. We were laughing.

"Well, Curaçao has no idea what's in store, that's for sure," she laughed. "That's hysterical…a John running a brothel!"

Susie raised her eyes, smiling. "Well I guess it's in the wind. Time to try something else!" She reached out and touched my arm. "What do you say, Wesley?"

I nodded my head. "I'm going to go down the hill and ask around."

Susie just smiled.

A couple of hours later I walked into Fernwood on my first official job search. I was standing at the bar drinking a tequila tonic, talking with friends, when the bar manager from Ventana, a guy named Dennis, came in drunk as a skunk. He was spraying saliva like Daffy Duck.

"I just got fired!" he said. "They don't want me anymore. All those years at Ventana and they don't want me anymore!" he proclaimed to everyone.

I took notice immediately and walked up to him. "What happened, Dennis?"

"When I got off work, I decided to sample everyone's drink I had made that was sitting on the bar. I just went down the bar and tasted them. You know, quality control...They fired me! Can you believe it? All those years...Hey!" he said to me. "Want a job? Go up to Ventana right now! It's a great job, man."

I looked at him for a moment before spinning on my heels and walking out to my truck.

Ten minutes later I walked through the front door of Ventana. The restaurant was empty. It was a beautiful afternoon, and everyone was eating outside. Classical guitar music wafted through the open terrace doors at the back of the dining room. The food and beverage director was sitting at the bar talking with the bartender. I had known him a long time and considered him a friend. I walked over to where he sat. He turned to look at me. "Well, hello, Wesley!" He stroked his prodigious mustache and extended his hand for a handshake.

I shook his hand. "I hear you're looking for a bartender."

He raised his eyebrows. "Yes, as a matter of fact I am. Are you interested?"

"Most definitely." I smiled.

His face broke out in a wide grin. "Your timing is impeccable, my friend. Have a seat, let's talk." He looked down the bar and waved the bartender over. "Thomas, pour this man a glass of wine..."

THE END

ACKNOWLEDGMENTS

Writing a book is much more involved than I originally thought and after finishing, I have a lot more respect for anyone who has written one. Few of our efforts are without the inspiration, assistance, or support of others, and so I would like to take a moment to acknowledge and thank a few people here.

I have been blessed with two beautiful daughters who have grown into strong, amazing young women. To my oldest, Jenny, your poise, balance, and heart-fulness are truly inspiring not only to me but to everyone around you. To my youngest, Natalie, your keen insight into human character and ability to stay positive through thick and thin are wonders to behold. Your own writing takes me to school with every read.

There is nothing so inclusive and complementary as friendship. I would like to thank my friend Denise Cagle for her support and encouragement through the writing of this book. She is herself a gifted writer, and I am grateful for her patient and seamless assurance throughout this project.

My heartfelt thanks to my friend Richard Russo. Yours is the bellwether of friendships and over the years has led to more adventures than I can count.

Many thanks to my friend John Huntzinger. Your creative ideas contributed greatly to the outcome of this book.

Thank you to Jan Tache´, manuscript reader extraordinaire, for helping flush out the more subtle oversights.

The importance of a professional edit cannot be overstated. The free association of ideas can lead a writer into a maelstrom of printed words. The editor somehow sorts all this out. My sincere thanks to my editor Debra L. Hartmann, who gently but firmly kept me and the story on track. You definitely made it a better book.

Thanks again to my mom who made sure I was getting a good education and never stopped encouraging me to write.

It's so important that we provide the best education possible for our children. Encourage them. They are our future.

ABOUT THE AUTHOR

Christian Van Allen called Big Sur, CA home for 45 years. He is the father of two beautiful daughters and presently lives in a small town in the Sierras with his cat Cocoa, sorting out ideas for his next book.

CPSIA information can be obtained
at www.ICGtesting.com
Printed in the USA
BVHW081155130819
555687BV00001B/73/P